Straw Man

by Lindsey Mellon

COPYRIGHT

This is a work of fiction, names, characters, places and incidents either are the product of the author's imagination or are used fictitiously. Any resemblance to actual persons living or dead, events or locales is entirely coincidental.

Copyright 2024 by Lindsey Mellon

All rights reserved. No part of this book may be reproduced or used in any manner without written permission of the copyright owner except for the use of quotations in a book review.

First Edition March 2024

Book designed by www.joi.agency

Paperback published by Northside House Limited.
www.northsidehouse.com

DEDICATION

For: Oliver

Straw Man

CHAPTER 1

12 October 1984. It should have been like
any other day in The Eternal City.

Haydon Talbot's phone rang in the early hours. A panicky voice from the Office informed him a bomb had exploded at the Grand Hotel in Brighton, where the Prime Minister and much of her Cabinet were staying during the Conservative Party Conference. The voice summoned him to London.

He rushed to get dressed and catch the early morning Alitalia flight. Heart pumping. At Rome's Fiumicino airport he watched the rolling TV coverage with horror, images of Mrs Thatcher being led out of the ruins of the Hotel by uniformed police, smoke billowing in the background amidst the sirens and flashing lights of emergency vehicles. Early reports were of multiple casualties amongst the distinguished guests. How on earth had the IRA smuggled a bomb past the extraordinarily strict security that surrounded the PM?

The plane was nearly empty. He pushed his seat back and tried to sleep, waking to the feel of cold saliva dripping down his cheek. He took out his handkerchief and wiped his face. *This was going to change everything.* His mind went back to his days as a soldier in Belfast: the same trepidation, that same niggle in the back of your neck. A premonition you were in some unseen crosshairs. You duck, then you wonder whether it had all been in your imagination.

Arriving at Heathrow, he dashed down the aircraft steps into driving rain, almost tripping as he fell into the waiting car. The journey to London

Straw Man

was slow, the wind gusting, rain splattering on the windscreen, the morning traffic clogged. Outside it was gloomy, the grey hues in stark contrast to the bright colours of autumn Rome.

He felt a throbbing in the pit of his stomach, it was all so depressing. They'd want to hear progress, but he had precious little to report. He'd give an update on his nascent recruitment of Lomax. It offered a plausible way into the top of the Libyan security establishment, but it was early days. They'd want more. Each grasping step you made up the pecking order brought with it greater demands to deliver results, an acrobat's job, walking a tightrope, and he was wobbling perilously. He rubbed his cheek with the palm of his hand.

It seemed an age before the car pulled into the underground garage below Century House, the modernist tower block HQ of SIS in Lambeth. As he entered the building and passed through the security checks, he sensed the solemn atmosphere, people scurrying around, heads down, oddly silent. He felt as if he were back in 1974, the three-day week, the sense that events were spiralling out of control, spiralling backwards into a new age of darkness. Back then it had been daily blackouts and violent riots between the police and the striking miners. Now it was terror.

Stepping out of the lift on the 20th floor, a tall, fair-haired girl greeted him and took his coat. She ushered him down a long, dark corridor, faulty strip lights flickering and giving it a surreal tone.

"Mr Glasson is expecting you, Sir. How was your flight?"

"On time. Thank you, Julia. How is it?" She was one of those cheery, well-brought up girls that gravitated to the Office, very much of a type. Attractive, bright, thoughtful. Never made it far up the ladder, the top rungs faced a stubbornly testosterone-dominated world.

Straw Man

"Everyone's in shock. News coming in every few minutes. Five reported deaths, including a Government Whip. The IRA has just released a communiqué, claiming responsibility. I've typed it up for Mark. Have a look."

He scanned the typewritten paper. "Listen to this."

'Mrs Thatcher will now realise that Britain cannot occupy our country and torture our prisoners and shoot our people in their own streets and get away with it. Today we were unlucky, but remember we only have to be lucky once. You will have to be lucky always. Give Ireland peace and there will be no more war.'

He read aloud. "They're damned right."

"Fates were kind." Julia opened a green leather-padded door and beckoned him to enter.

SIS's Director of Operations Mark Glasson was sitting behind his desk barking instructions into a red phone. He looked up as Haydon entered, nodded then turned away. He was short, the double-breasted grey flannel suit he was wearing amplified the squat, powerful build. Even with a dark blue knitted tie and well-ironed cream shirt, he looked badly tailored. Assiduous cultivation of connections in the corridors of power had smoothed his way up the ranks of SIS. Glasson was now one step away from the top spot and looking for every opportunity to bolster his chances. He and Haydon had joined the Service on the same day and remained close, their career paths criss-crossing as he tailed his friend's rapid ascent up the greasy beanstalk. Haydon noticed his fingers tapping away on his desk.

He walked over to the panoramic window and stood looking down over the river to the Palace of Westminster and Buckingham Palace, then

Straw Man

further on to Hyde Park. You could see all of central London. A perk of this irredeemable building. They were the supposed guardians of that peaceful-looking scene. He thought about Airey Neave's murder – a bomb in his car right outside Parliament buildings – the bombings in Hyde Park and Regent's Park, the bomb at Harrods. All within that small area he was looking at. Was the IRA winning? Right now it seemed like it. It was impossible to defend even that tiny patch of London, let alone the whole country.

Haydon thought of himself as a bright man, but not naturally genial. He found it an effort to laugh and suspected the result wasn't convincing. His army background had left him with an erect stance. He was tall, almost handsome, but with a slightly pock-marked face and a clumsy bearing. He was fluent in Arabic, Italian and Turkish. With the growing problem of Palestinian terrorism in the 1970s, he'd found his niche.

It was not Palestinian terrorism that was exercising the minds of the British security establishment, but the more parochial problems of Northern Ireland. The Provisional IRA had established links with Arab and Palestinian groups, the PLO and PFLP, who had supplied them with small-scale training and arms, and with connections to other terrorist groups active in mainland Europe.

When information trickled in that revolutionary Libya was intent on reopening the supply of arms to the IRA, No 10 tasked SIS with taking action to counter the threat. Haydon was the obvious choice to take charge of the operation. Tailor made for me, he'd thought. Libyan terror operations in Europe were known to be based out of their Rome Embassy, and he found himself posted back to his favourite city. A bit of luck and a following wind. His career was due for a prod upwards. *It had all looked so good, FELT so good. Now this.*

"Haydon, sit." Glasson put the telephone down and turned towards him. "Haven't much time. Meeting at Cabinet Office in thirty minutes, permanent session. Julia will brief you, get you up to speed. Julia!" Her face appeared around the open door. "Coffee? Oblige! Look after Haydon, will you."

She handed Glasson a sheaf of documents then left them, closing the door behind her.

"First indications it was gelignite, no trace of Semtex or C4. Worryingly they used an ultra-long-delay timer." Glasson rapped his knuckles hard on the desk. "First time they've used one. Frightening evolution. The PM was still working in her living room just before 3 a.m. The bomb went off right above her bathroom. Extraordinarily lucky. She was in the bathroom minutes before the explosion."

"What do you need me to do."

"Our political masters want assurances that Libyan Semtex can't end up in Provo hands any time soon. Long-delay timers plus Semtex is a recipe for catastrophe. Am I right in thinking Libya has taken delivery of seven hundred tons of the stuff? Is that even possible?"

"That's the best figure we have, solid intel out of Czecho. High reliability." Haydon grimaced. "The Libyans have been the biggest buyers of Semtex from Omnipol. If the IRA gets their paws on one ton, it will wreak havoc."

"I'll be busy with the response." Glasson looked over at Haydon with a gloomy expression. "I'll brief JIC about the threat from the rumoured shipments. Qaddafi pretty much confirmed his intentions in his radio broadcast last week."

Straw Man

"We'll get resources?"

"Considering how close we came to losing the PM and most of her Cabinet, we'll get everything we ask for. We need to make the twelfth of October 1984 the day we turned the tide of the war against the IRA." He wiped his forehead with a handkerchief. "You can't fail on this one; all eyes will be on you."

"Mark, our best chance is blanket coverage of the Libyan nest in Rome, follow them wherever they lead us. My priority is manpower, watchers, top people. Approval to follow them around Europe."

Glasson frowned, lines of worry showing on his forehead. He pushed his reading glasses up onto his forehead and leaned towards Haydon, hands flat on the desk.

"Look, this penetration agent you're developing, what's his name?"

"Charlie Lomax, code name DAEDALUS." Haydon stroked his chin, then leaned forward. "Look Mark it's got to be subtle. We're trying to launch this bird at two nasty stones in our shoe in one go. We get it right he damages Qaddafi's nuclear program whilst he builds himself up in their eyes, and we get a chance – only a chance mind you – to glimpse into their IRA connections. But it's got to be damned subtle."

"I want you to launch him."

"Not possible. Haven't closed the seduction. It's coming along, but I have to be careful. Can't be pushed–"

"–bugger him! Listen Haydon I don't give a shit." Haydon stared at Glasson. He could see sweat on his forehead, spittle on his chin. "We're at war. That means risks for everyone. Get him on board now and deploy him to Libya. That's an order."

Glasson looked at his watch and stood up. "Got to run, stay in touch via Julia."

"I'm not going to risk burning–" Haydon began, but Glasson had darted out of the door.

Christ, Haydon thought, that's what we're about. Brutal. Lomax is disposable. They'd toss him to the dogs. Untrained and vulnerable, no clue of the dangers waiting for him in Tripoli. He felt a twinge of sympathy. But his priority was clear. He had his orders.

Straw Man

CHAPTER 2

Seán Docherty sat outside at the Caffè degli Specchi nursing a tankard of beer. The Piazza Unità d'Italia, a pompous square in a pompous city where the Slavic and Latin worlds collided with a sigh. Trieste felt cut off, neutral, ironic even. He stared out over the piers towards the freighters moored in the bay, motionless on the water, the sea oily calm. A good choice for their meeting, the tables spaced well out into the piazza, unobstructed views in all directions. Not too many people. Just enough of a crowd.

Nasir el-Maghrebi was late. There was a chill autumn breeze pushing in from the sea. He shivered. Nasir was always bloody late; it defined the bugger. He would turn up. For sure he was running one of his 'dry cleaning' routines. Tradecraft, the fellow loved it; sure he adored being a bogey-man. Well, he might as well do the work for the both of them. Seán felt safe here. That made a change from Belfast. He sunk his mug of beer and ordered another. If the sod didn't turn up soon, he'd be pissed already.

He thought back to his first meeting with Nasir, five years before, at the Bin Ghashir training camp in the barren desert some way south of Tripoli. Nasir had seemed reserved at first; not unfriendly, just self-contained. They forged their friendship on long night marches over soft dunes, each heavy step forward sinking you backwards, engendering a sense of even time getting stuck. The others on the course were always complaining, but Seán and Nasir built a bond in sharing the discomfort. They seemed to share a greater capacity for suffering than the others.

They had little enough in common. A desert Bedouin from a small village in the wastes of the Libyan Sahara and an urban Catholic from the Falls

Straw Man

Road in West Belfast, a lapsed Catholic even. They both had rasping, hard to understand, English accents and a loathing of the British, particularly the tight-arsed British establishment.

"There's not even a drink in front of you." A slim, pallid-faced man with a mop of unkempt black hair slipped into the chair opposite Seán and smiled. "Are you sick?"

"I've a beer on its way, don't you worry." Seán scratched his head. "You took yer bleeding time then. Rotten sod, can't you ever be on time?"

"How are you, Seán?"

"You still teetotal? Or did you break out yet? What'll I get you?" Seán smiled back and leaned forward, touching the other man's sleeve. "Are we clean?"

"A coca-cola, and I'm hungry, I want something to eat." He picked up the large plastic menu and glanced down it. "Clean as Sahara sand. Three of my guys out there. It's easy, you see, this city is so small and quiet. I drove up from Dubrovnik. You?"

"Flew to Ljubljana. Train. No problems. Took me a few days, I was cautious getting out of Belfast. You never know when they're at you. Drove a winding route to Shannon, then Amsterdam, Vienna. Made me dizzy just to get here."

"That's good, you need to stay sharp, the way to stay alive."

"Speak for yerself."

"Remember, we're the ones handing out the goodies; we're your Father Christmas, you see. So it's for you to stroke me, make nice; listen to my clever talk."

They sat and ate and drank and talked. Two old friends. A little watchful. They didn't laugh a lot.

Straw Man

After dinner they strolled across the square, arm in arm, moving between snakes of tourists following their tour leaders, tiny white flags held high in strange processions, modern Pied Pipers. There was a bite in the air, but they were both wearing leather bomber jackets; like a uniform for spooks, he thought. They crossed the main road and walked out onto the pier. The sun had gone down and the last arched rays sprinkled a red sunset onto the sea.

A few old men sat leathery by the edge of the pier, holding long fishing rods. Silent, smoking, determined faces. Seán and Nasir walked to the end and faced out to sea. Not even one of those new parabolic mikes could catch a word out there; the nearest building was 200 yards away and behind them. They stood shoulder to shoulder and peered out over the flat Adriatic.

"You nearly scored the winning goal in Brighton. What went wrong?"

"Her guardian angel granted a reprieve. But we laid down a marker and scared the bejesus out of them."

"Cahill met the Leader last month, got along well. Brighton convinced him you can win the war with a little help." Nasir said. "The Embassy siege in London and the British reaction enraged him. Breaking off diplomatic relations, personal insults. The courage of your hunger strikers moved him. Bobby Sands' death was a big event."

"Ten of the lads died. They'll be avenged, so they will."

"He's ready to give you what you want. Even cash, which I didn't expect. Five million dollars. To assist with the set-up, buying vessels. You've seen the list of items that Cahill handed him?"

Seán nodded. "Sophisticated stuff, Joe told him we just need the basics. Semtex–" He enunciated the two syllables and laughed, "–that'll be the game-changer, and RPG's, heavy machine guns. The idea is we'll mount a Tet-style offensive. All over the province, all at once. It'll frighten the Brit buggers stiff and change the political landscape in London. But it can't kick off until all the arms are in and distributed. That'll take time. For security we need to split it into four or five shipments. We won't repeat the mistakes of the *Claudia* fiasco."

"Agreed. Nothing sensitive until the early shipments have got through. AK's, pistols, ammo, grenades, a few RPGs."

"Good. Fitzgerald told me to budget for 240 tons?" Seán turned to face Nasir. "We'll get two boats operating and plan to have the lot on the mainland next year."

A small boy holding his mother's hand staggered up to the end of the pier. He pulled away from her and threw a stone into the water, squealing as he saw the splash and the ripples. The mother struggled to hold him back as the boy peered down over the pier. Seán and Nasir remained silent as the child broke free and ran along the pier, shrieking with joy, pursued by his mother.

"Sure life was much easier back then, so it was. My Mam could never catch me at all, fast I was. And a holy terror."

"You still are, my friend. Worse!" Nasir chuckled. "Seán, about security. You've got to nail it down. Too many leaks."

"That's rich coming from you. Your Leader's forever gabbing. The Brits have more than an inkling about the meeting in Tripoli." He turned to face Nasir, a strained look on his face. "Look, the last place on this earth I want to end up is The Maze. After the lads and their Great Escape last year, once you've been shut in there, you're not coming out 'til your hair

Straw Man

is grey or it's gone altogether. The thought of it keeps me motivated; I'd rather go back to Bin Ghashir."

"Maybe your Yankee friends are tipping them off. NSA intercepts?"

"Maybe."

"I'm to deal with you, and in person. No phones, you see. Meet every couple of months, pre-agreed dates, fall-backs. All coded."

"OK." Seán lit a cigarette. "The Brit gobshites will be on full alert. We should expect they'll be dedicating serious resources to looking out for us. They'll be focussing on your ports."

"We'll use trawlers, disguise them as part of the fishing fleet. Mix it all up."

"I'm working to Fitzgerald on this. Cahill briefed him. We've someone out looking for vessels, got an eye on a tiddler for the first trips, we'll work on the bigger vessel to take 100 tons a go."

"When can you be sure of having the first one ready?" Nasir asked, looking over at Seán.

"Aiming for May. Get the lot done before winter weather sets in. We're talking to a skipper to run them."

"OK. We'll meet in spring to plan transhipment arrangements. Here again? Easy for both of us, you see. Same protocols, newspaper confirmations."

Seán nodded. They turned and sauntered back down the pier, passing the fishermen, still motionless, eyes fixed on their rods. At the main road, they turned and walked away in opposite directions.

Seán wandered back towards his Hotel. He was a little drunk. He felt elated. They had singled him out for this job. His quiet and reliable nature, the boss had said. And the Libyans trusted him. It was important for the

Straw Man

Movement, critical even, and it would get him away from the dismal daily struggles of conflict in Belfast.

He wouldn't hurry home. He'd spend an extra day or two in Trieste. Put it down to security, the need for vigilance, to ensure there was no surveillance. Here he felt at peace, away from the risk of sudden arrest. He didn't feel any need to be on alert, he'd been careful during his travels.

Fifty yards before his hotel, a red light flashed away at him– '*Bar Erotica*'. Its reflection shone back across his face from a shop window. *Why not?*

Straw Man

CHAPTER 3

Charlie Lomax's flat perched on top of the hill at the upper end of via Garibaldi, at the edge of Trastevere; it was small and poky, but the roof garden had views straight down into the Gianicolo gardens. He stood on the terrace and revelled in the beauty, the smells, the breeze. People didn't realise how much green lurked behind the walls of old Rome, always more secrets to uncover. His head filled with the noise of the Sunday church bells clanging from every direction. He shook his head, walked back into the bedroom and sat down on the bed.

"Let's have more rows, more making ups?"

Ines smiled up at him and reached up to touch his cheek. She had arrived back late the night before from Milan, where she'd been on a journalistic assignment, waking Charlie as she climbed into bed and nuzzling up to him.

"No more, too painful." He bounced on the bed, pushed her down and tickled her. "We English prefer to suffer in noisy silence."

"What time must we be there?" She pushed him away and stood up, going over to the dressing table and examining her face in the mirror, rubbing a small spot that had appeared on her chin.

"Need to get moving. They live on the Aventine, I have to chat with Haydon before lunch. Business."

"What sort?"

"Monkey sort."

"That's what you do for a living? Monkey business?"

"I'm what they call a *faccendiere*. A make-things-happen person."

"Sounds dubious."

"Living off my wits, yes."

Straw Man

"You make a living?" She screwed up her face. "Did you pay the rent?"

"Not quite. Soon! You don't have to worry." Charlie stood behind her and started stroking her hair. "I told Haydon on the phone about my meeting with the Arabs. Spiced it up. I'm going to sell him the idea of backing me financially to take my business into Libya."

"Why on earth would he want to do that?"

"Needs well-informed ears on the ground; there's a shortage of plugged-in Englishmen holidaying in Tripoli this year. His lot have budgets to pay for that kind of thing."

"Remember that Sicilian man and his missing toenails we read about. Would you suffer in silence while they pulled yours out?"

"Shhhhh. No dirty talk."

"Maybe I'd come and visit you in jail, bring you aspirin and stuff. Big story for me, a close up interview with a torture survivor–"

"–don't talk to journos, matter of principle. Only in bed."

"No bed in your dirty cell, no thank you. And I want photos. Missing toenails, missing toes even. Those sell newspapers."

"Won't happen."

"Tell me about the Talbots, how do you know them?" Ines started brushing her long hair, both arms above her head, eying him in the mirror.

"Haydon called me up out of the blue when he moved to Rome, sniffing out well-connected contacts to develop. That's me." Charlie bowed. "We go back to Cambridge days. College tennis. He was doing post-graduate stuff. Quite a few years older. Anyway it suited me to be sniffed out, Embassy connections are handy. We play tennis with the Ambassador. I drop his name with the best of them."

"Handsome?"

Straw Man

"Ugly bastard! Pretty much a bore. I used to get the foxy ones, he tried too hard."

"Unlikely. His wife?"

"Ros? Warm, reserved. Same year as me, read Modern Russian History at Pembroke. A few years later they turned up separately in Beirut, her first posting at the Embassy. Got married there."

She stood up and started dressing. "Do I have to be diplomatic?" She pulled a navy blue silk shirt over her head and shook her long hair free. His eyes followed her contours as she looked at herself in the mirror.

"Don't break a habit! They're friends, be as undiplomatic as you like. Isn't that the key to being a good journalist?"

"Unpredictability. That's the secret. Swish your sword up and down, sometimes diplomatic, sometimes not. Keep them dancing!"

Charlie allowed Ines to drive his scarlet Vespa. Her aggression surprised him. She scared him a few times with skidding moves through narrow gaps between the traffic, avoiding disaster at the last moment, the small tyres complaining. He wrapped his arms around her, hugging her. He could feel the beating of her heart through the silk of her shirt.

"Olé! Olé!" He shouted with each near miss.

"You can drive home." Ines said, pulling off her scarf and stepping off the scooter. She pulled it up onto its stand under an old orange tree; it looked peculiar, all the oranges lower down had been picked, it was as if the tree had grown a golden halo. Urban agriculture, he thought. Maybe it's the future.

"We see if you do it any quicker. I doubt!" He took her hand, and they ran up the steps together, giggling.

Straw Man

Ros Talbot poured two glasses of cold Vernaccia and handed one to Haydon. They stood side by side on the long veranda of their third-floor flat, looking down over the green of the Giardino degli Aranci and on over the Tiber towards Trastevere. She raised her glass and smiled at him from above heart-shaped dark glasses. He winked back. A statuesque woman in her late 20s, he thought she looked simultaneously severe and playful. Ceramic pots were overflowing with flowers, puddles of water leaking from their bases, providing a colourful fringe to the view. There was a low hum of bees and a strong smell of honeysuckle.

"You're tense, darling." She reached over and took his hand in hers. "What's it?"

"Blasted Libyans. Couldn't sleep. My career prospects slipping." He lifted her palm to his forehead, then lowered it and kissed it. "They're a danger. Their top bogey-man Ahmed Khalfari is in Rome, God knows what mischief he's planning."

"Worse than those flat-footed KGB clods?"

"Unpredictable, more dangerous." He squeezed her hand. It was no longer an abstract threat, like the faceless risks from IRA bombs in London, but something personal. The Libyans were capable of anything. "We need to stay alert. Keep our eyes peeled."

"That's worrying." She took a sip of her drink. "So, this lunch with Charlie–?"

"–all part of it. He met Khalfari on Friday. Bunfight at the Palazzo Vispoli. *Crème de la crème*. Terrorists and noblemen. Strange bedfellows. See why I can't sleep?"

"You're going to get that poor boy to do something he didn't ought to."

Straw Man

"Something like that." Haydon frowned. "He likes bad. He's a bit of a rake. Still, this girl seems to be lasting longer than usual."

"Tell."

"Ines. Bright. Serious journo."

"What's she doing with him?"

"You're asking me to explain female motives? As if–" he laughed. "You find out, you're the brilliant interrogator. You should be doing my job."

"SIS is doggedly misogynistic." She giggled. "You can be queer as an upside down coot, that's acceptable, traditional even, but to be a woman?"

"Maybe they know a thing or two–"

"–they seem to have forgotten the successes of Mata Hari, let alone SOE."

"Keep your seditious opinions to yourself." He put his arm around her waist and pulled her to him. "Look after her? I need him for a quiet chat before lunch."

They heard the screeching of complaining tyres and looked down: a red Vespa was swinging from side to side and racing up the hill.

"That's them? She's driving. Cute!" Ros waved her arms in welcome. "She'll run rings about him, I can tell already."

"I'm going to my study, send him along."

He strolled into the flat and down a long corridor to his study. Sitting down at his desk, he rubbed at his forehead. He felt a migraine coming on. Those nightmares. Attacks on diplomats and embassies were on the up. The recent bombings of the French and American Embassies in Beirut had been wake-up calls, and the Libyans were known to farm out 'wet' operations to radical Palestinian groups. He needed to watch his back at all times. Ros too. He had to get her to stay on her toes without scaring her.

Straw Man

He was going to be proactive. Insist The Office approve the watchers he'd requested. Keep a close eye on the Libyan nest in Rome. Charlie's face appeared round the door.

"Charlie, come in. Cigar?"

"No, thanks. Ugh."

Haydon started clipping the end off a long cigar, gesturing Charlie to sit. He looked over and grinned. He needed to play this right. Accelerate hooking of the fish. He coughed.

"So tell me, this party? I hear practically the entire government was at the Palazzo Vispoli, paying court to the nice Libyan gentlemen."

"The bearded goat, Ahmed Khalfari, was the guest of honour."

"Khalfari? The Americans won't be pleased. Their friends in the Italian Government cosying up to Qaddafi's No 2." Haydon ran the cigar back and forth under his nose, sniffing it. "What's Andrea Vispoli's interest in hosting a Libyan revolutionary with such fanfare?"

"Oil money flooding into Libya, Andrea wants a slice. He's got several construction projects on the go."

"A slice with no scruples?"

"Scruples are surplus to requirements in business."

"I'd like to meet him. Can you arrange it?"

"He's my mucker. From schooldays, St George's. You mustn't cause him trouble."

"As if!" Talbot chuckled. "And your role? Supping at the top table?"

"Complicated, Haydon." Charlie smiled and scratched his head. "Still trying to figure out the answer. I'm nicely positioned, that's for sure. But not sure for what exactly."

"What's he like, Khalfari? You meet him?"

Straw Man

"A charmer. Doesn't like the English, that's obvious. Odd dress sense."

"Qaddafi's chief spook. Bad guy."

"I met him again yesterday. In private. Andrea organised it. Together with his snake-eyed sidekick, Nasir something-or-other. Radical and ambitious. He's to be my contact. Sullen type, didn't seem to fall for my charms. But Khalfari invited me to Tripoli. Encouraging."

"You'll need to be careful around those guys."

"Wants to look at my wares. High-tech Swiss irrigation systems." Charlie continued. "I hinted I might help them with sensitive items. His interest was, one might say, piqued. God knows I need it. I can't go around forever with frayed shirts and holes in my shoes."

Haydon sat upright in his chair and stared at him, rubbing his neck with the back of his hand. Time to close in. Get the seduction done. He realised his feet were tapping up and down under the desk. A giveaway when he was being crooked? He made a conscious effort to stay still and took a long pull on his cigar, leaning back and blowing a cloud of smoke up at the ceiling. "Look, what I'm going to tell you is between us?"

Charlie nodded.

"We've been picking up intel about Libyan contacts with the IRA. After the disaster in Brighton alarm bells are clanging." He leaned forward, splaying his hands flat on the desk. He stared out of the window for a long while, then turned back to Charlie. "They're planning to restart arms deliveries. Maybe SAM-7's, surface to air missiles, and Russian anti-tank rockets. Imagine the repercussions of anti-tank missiles on the ground in Ulster. And the Army relies heavily on moving around Ulster with choppers, vulnerable to missiles."

"Why are you telling me?"

Straw Man

Haydon ignored him and continued. "Most worrying is the Libyans have been buying up large quantities of the explosive Semtex from Czechoslovakia. Disastrous if the Provos get hold of any. It's super powerful and easy to handle, odourless, sniffer dogs are no use. I'm tasked with interdicting these shipments."

"That's a big challenge. You winning?"

"I may have a way of working you into Khalfari's inner circle. After all, isn't this what you do for a living?" Haydon grinned. "You develop relations with useful people, massage them and arbitrage those contacts to obtain business for yourself?"

"No, I represent the interests of major international contractors and seek to obtain contracts for them."

"You're a natural spy." Haydon continued. "Made for it. Immoral and ambitious. Bit like me."

"Those Libyan guys would never talk to me—an Englishman—about that sort of stuff."

"We'd make it worth your while. Believe me, solve your money worries."

"They dislike the English and were humouring my friend Andrea Vispoli, he's close to both of them–"

"–aside from other mischief that Khalfari handles, he's tasked with developing channels for procurement for The Leader's secret nuclear programme. We've been working to create covert avenues to assist them. It's our speciality, we're good at it. False flag deception operations. We assist unsuitable state actors to get hold of dangerous items they desperately want."

"That makes no sense."

Straw Man

"The items supplied won't work properly. It's subtle, minimal risk of discovery." Haydon scratched his face and paused. He realised his feet were tapping again. He crossed his legs. *I can read your mind and you need the cash. I'm nearly there.* "You can help us. Steering Khalfari in the right direction, towards our friendly suppliers. Just another of your major international contractors–"

"–you don't know this guy–"

"–who are Swiss. Which fits like a silk glove with your legend. You could end up as the point man for Libyan government procurement; make a shit-load of money. Buy a yacht. Retire to Monte Carlo."

"Vulgar place full of overweight people. I prefer Rome." He looked up at the ceiling and rolled his eyes. "So alluring, Haydon. Not. Though I am, as you know, keen to serve Queen and Country."

"Here's your opportunity."

"There must come a day of reckoning when the – what did you call them? –*'dangerous items'* – have been ordered and paid for, the Libyans are verging on orgasm, and the *'items'* turn up but they don't work, they're duds, or worse still they go bang and emit a shower of nasty sparks?" Charlie gestured with his arms. "Someone would have to take the pain, and I don't wish to be someone. I value my neck and my balls."

"These operations need planning." Haydon made an arch with his hands and frowned. He felt a twinge of conscience. Had he become inured to seducing people into doing stuff that really wasn't in their interest? This guy was a virgin, too easy to lead by the nose. "The last thing I want is to lose an asset – in this case you – with the prospect you could report from inside the viper's nest. Think about it."

"So you'd be like my guardian angel?" Charlie pointed with his finger up at the ceiling and made flapping gestures. "The Archangel Haydon? I don't think so. Christ, you're bad enough as a tennis partner."

"The Swiss company we'd want you to introduce to your Libyan friends is a credible," Haydon swivelled from side to side in his chair, then took a long pull on his cigar. "niche player on the fringes of the nuclear industry. Technologically advanced, top reputation. Blue chip customers around the globe. Supply all the naughty items the Libyans want."

"Sounds like an appetising tale with a bad ending!" Charlie laughed. "I'll think about it. Not very hard though."

Haydon ignored him. *Time to get rough with this little shit.* "I'll cut to the chase. You want to continue as a smiling wannabe, showing off your old red banger that impresses no one? Kissing big boy's arses and hoping your charm will pay the bills."

"Easy Haydon. I thought we were friends?"

"I'm offering you a ticket to the top. Take it or leave it. Supply the tricky items they're dreaming of. They'll see you as a mercenary, you'll fit the mould they'll have cast you in. Another corrupt and greedy Westerner, like those rogue CIA guys – Terpil and Wilson, ready to sell their souls for enough bucks."

The door opened and Ros' head popped around the corner. "Which of you has sold your soul? I fear yours isn't worth much Haydon darling. Do you even have one? Tell us over lunch? Which is on the table, so if you don't want overcooked pasta. Ines and I are exhausted talking about you two and your bad habits."

"Thank you, dear. Two minutes." Her head disappeared.

Straw Man

"Well, thanks a lot. Corrupt and greedy westerner, you were saying. Should I take that as a compliment?" Charlie paused, then continued. "Look Haydon, your proposal would, I believe, be illegal? How will you cover me? I don't want to end up prosecuted for supplying Libya with banned nuclear material. Might end me in Wormwood Scrubs, uncomfortable place, worse than public school. Better than some ghastly dungeon in Tripoli, I suppose."

Got him. He'd just opened a negotiation. A sure sign he's in. He'd smelt the money and was going to take the bait. Glasson would slaver when he told him that DAEDALUS was ready to launch.

"Fair point." Haydon replied, smiling and standing up. "Don't worry, I'll get your assurances. Think it over. Let's talk after tennis next Saturday. Don't forget we're playing at the Residence. 4 o'clock."

"Drop it, Haydon, but thanks for thinking of me."

They were merry, they'd enjoyed an easy atmosphere over lunch. They sat side by side on the roof terrace of Charlie's flat, nursing glasses of white wine.

"I like Ros. She's warm. We're from such different backgrounds, but we clicked. Talked about everything. Even about you!" Ines tickled Charlie's chin with a sprig of jasmine. He shoved it away. She became feline when she'd drunk too much. "Whereas Haydon is so English. Tight-assed you say?"

"He's the opposite of an Italian. No arm-waving or tight shirts."

"He liked my idea. The–"

"–mine too. I can already smell the money rolling in." Charlie got up and started pacing up and down the veranda. "Lots of it. Like moist plum pudding–."

"He says Qaddafi loves to yabber, 'specially to foxy journos."

"You're a vamp. Be careful, he's a predator."

"Haydon says he's a flirt. Can you believe that? Surrounds himself with slinky bodyguards, they're known as the 'Revolutionary Nuns'. Blabs on, it's a shoo-in he'll provide stellar copy. Do you think your friend Andrea could take me down?"

"I'll ask him." Charlie replied, squinting against the low sun. "He'll do it if he feels like it. Stands to gain a lot from projects in Libya."

"Tell him I won't embarrass him? I'll be good."

"Haydon was naughty. He'd like to create a fog around the Italian initiative. Which the British don't like." He sat down again and reached over to take her hand. "The opportunity won't go away. If I was you, I'd wait a little."

"Why do I sense you're not keen for me to do a Libyan story?" She stared at Charlie, he could feel the coldness in the stare. "It would be a break."

"Go for it. I'm just saying–"

"–there you are, you're always talking as if these Libyans are nice, kind people. Read the papers, Kiko."

"I'm not saying–"

"–read The Colonel's speeches. Bad people, doing bad things. God knows what you're cooking up with Haydon? I read people Kiko, I detect hypocrisy." Ines stood up and walked to the door.

Straw Man

She knows I'm hiding something. No way I can tell her the truth. But that's the compromise I'm making, he thought. Everything has a price. He took a gulp of his wine.

"Hey, hold on, calm it. You do what you want. I'm just saying it's sensitive."

"You'll talk to Andrea?" She turned back to him.

"Of course. But what you want to do, what I want to do, it cuts into high politics. Maybe they're bad people, or simple people, but this is about trying to nudge them in a good direction. Come back here."

Ines disappeared into the flat.

Straw Man

CHAPTER 4

Haydon descended to the underground car park of the British Embassy in Porta Pia. A concrete, brutalist building designed by Sir Basil Spence. Bombproof, so they claimed. Israeli Irgun terrorists had blown up the previous building in 1946. He drove out and along the Corso d'Italia, enjoying the zest of competing in the wild traffic, some kind of male bullying competition at which he'd become adept. In the Via Sistina a van blocked the road. Honking his horn, he received a slew of insults from a workman in blue overalls.

He was late. Wiping his forehead, he gunned the engine. His tyres screeched on the cobblestones as he bullied the car up onto the pavement and raced along it, hooting his horn and scattering pedestrians. He parked in front of the Hotel Hassler, at the top of the Spanish Steps, jumped out, handed his keys to the uniformed doorman and headed for the lift.

He noticed the gaggle of burly men standing around the lobby, chatting and smoking. They didn't look like hotel guests. Bulging arms, badly fitting blue suits. Too tight. You never used to see bodyguards in Rome. A big change. And not for the good. A dark shadow was rubbing out the brilliance of the Dolce Vita. This city has taken over from Vienna as the *entrepot* of espionage and terror groups.

Admiral Carlo Pollitti was waiting at the table. He looked pensive, depressed even, gazing out of the panoramic windows over the roofs of Rome. Well into his 50s, bespectacled, the head of SISMI, the Italian external intelligence service, was grey-haired and urbane. He got to his feet, and they shook hands. The older man clasped Talbot's right hand in both of his and scanned his friend's face.

Straw Man

"You haven't changed, Haydon. Done a dirty deal with Beelzebub, have you? Sit. When did you get here?"

"Last month. In time for the Brighton bomb and to run back to London and get enmeshed in all the mayhem." Haydon tried out his smile. "Good to see you, Carlo." They talked whilst they waited for the waiter to come and take their order.

"The IRA got pretty close."

"Too close. I'm on a tightrope."

"Worse for me. The Red Brigades killed Aldo Moro. The most important politician in Italy." Pollitti sighed. "Nowadays they aim to decapitate democratic governments."

"Terrorists are getting more ambitious. And succeeding."

"Congratulations on your promotion, Haydon. Station Chief. I imagined you'd have become disillusioned by now. You seemed such an innocent schoolboy back then."

"Fifteen years since I left. My first overseas posting."

"We were youthful idealists, bursting with enthusiasm for the noble cause. Easy times." Pollitti said. "Do what you're told, no need to think. All so clear cut. Good guys, bad guys. Follow the Russkies, the Bulgarians around. They were all hopeless, boneheaded and obvious. We ran rings about them. Ha!"

"And had fun doing it."

He's slower, Haydon thought, more awkward. *Maybe we both are.* He wondered if Pollitti's mind was still as sharp. He'd never miss the smallest thing with those knife-like eyes. He needed to keep him close. Difficult when their masters were pulling in opposite directions.

Straw Man

"It's changed for both of us. For me, the massacre in Bologna – a huge bomb in the crowded railway station. Turned my world upside down. Mad fascists joining the loony lefties, Arabs and Israelis: we even have to keep a look out for far left Japanese suicide bombers, it's a challenge even to recognise them. They all look the same."

"I noticed the bodyguards in the lobby." Haydon drummed his fingers on the table. "People seem nervy."

"With our hair greying fast, our grown-up world has lost its lustre." Pollitti frowned and continued. "It may look like the same city you knew back then, sun-drenched and vibrant. But it's not. Rome has become a hornet's nest of terrorist groups."

"And I was looking forward to getting away from the bombs in London." Haydon ran his hand through his hair. "People walking the streets with their heads down, waiting for the next big bang."

"So we're bedevilled by the same adversaries."

"Except Carlo, our masters' interests are no longer aligned. Who'd have thought it? You promote moderation—in Lebanon, in Syria, Algeria, Egypt, Libya, above all in Palestine. You strive to lower the temperature between our friends in Tel Aviv and their Palestinian cousins."

"Whilst Her Majesty's Government," Pollitti replied, "remains in alignment with Washington's less generous point of view."

"We see several of those states as intractable, irredeemable even." Haydon frowned. "Moderation doesn't exist in their make-up."

"Somehow Italy survived the economic blitz caused by the 1973 oil price rise." Pollitti lifted his wineglass to Haydon, then raised it to his lips and drained it. "You can relax in an armchair with your God-given North Sea oil. Lucky you. We don't have that luxury. We have to work at it to ensure stability in the oil markets. That means placating OPEC, calming the Arab world."

"I need your help, Carlo. Qaddafi has promised the IRA boys large shipments of weapons. Semtex. Countering that risk is my priority."

"My friend, we need to be alert to our divergent interests. You and I aren't on the same side. Not always. I'm tasked with developing useful links with moderate elements of Qaddafi's inner circle."

"Yes, but we're allies. Surely what allies do is help one another."

Pollitti pushed his chair back and lit a cigarette. He remained silent for a while, eyes closed, smoke rising from his ashtray. The waiter brought their coffee and two glasses of grappa. Haydon looked over at his friend. The older man looked tired. The toll of being at the top, he supposed. Pollitti finally broke the silence.

"I like you Haydon, we go back a long way." Pollitti took a sip of his grappa. "But that counts for nothing. In this new world, it's all about relative value. We trade our secrets, there's a membership fee for the Old Boy network."

"That hurts."

"Get used to it." Pollitti leaned forward and touched Haydon's arm. "I'm going to tell you something I oughtn't, to keep under your bowler hat. You will repay me with a jewel of comparable value. Agreed? That's how it's going to work."

He nodded. *I can trade him info on the Red Brigades guys hiding out in Paris. Carlo will drool. But what's he got for me?* He rubbed the back of his neck. He could feel he was sweating, his shirt felt uncomfortable.

"The head of the Carabinieri in Trieste reported on a recent covert meeting. We got lucky. Smart cookies, those arse-pinching northerners.

Flagged it up, sent us snaps." He reached into his inner pocket of his jacket and took out two grainy postcard sized black and white photos, which he slid across the table.

"This one's easy." Pollitti tapped his forefinger on one of them.

"Nasir el-Maghrebi, an *'Undeclared'* at the People's Bureau. A cultural Attaché who's never been to an art gallery in his life. Heads up Qaddafi's security operation, the Mukhabarat, out of Rome. He used to be at their Bureau in London. We booted him out after the murder of PC Fletcher. And this one?"

"This one you're going to owe me for."

Haydon turned the photo around and stared down at it. A studious, bespectacled faced looked up at the camera. Youthful, maybe 30. Anglo-Saxon?

"Recognise him?"

"No clue." Haydon screwed up his nose.

"Seán Docherty. Low-level Provisional IRA operative. Belfast based. We know little about him; not our area of interest. One of our agents clocked him 5 years ago at a PLO training camp south of Tripoli. That's why we had his name and face on file. There was a brief period when the IRA was sending their guys for training there."

Haydon felt a surge of excitement. A name. The Ulster boys could get to work. He twirled spaghetti around his fork. *Lady Luck*. For all the pretence that it was painstaking legwork that made the difference, it was so often luck that awarded you success or damned you to abject failure. He sipped his wine and glanced around the room. Every table seemed to be occupied by unsmiling grey-haired men. He lived his life surrounded by grey-haired conspiracies. Maybe the young should rule the world.

Straw Man

"That's a big help, Carlo. The Libyans are running this op out of Rome. As we suspected."

"My Minister is not pleased. He instructed me to give Nasir a ticking off. Naughty meetings on Italian soil. Crosses a red line."

"You're dealing with the devil?"

"Yes, it's our job description. You know that." Pollitti pointed with his fork at a nearby table. "Dealing with angels is for those queer fellows in purple cassocks."

"Whatever happened to Good and Evil?"

"Manichaeism went out of fashion with The Reformation. Only Reagan believes in it nowadays." He leaned back and stared at Haydon. "Don't forget you owe me."

"We're developing avenues in Paris."

" The *Superclandestine?*"

"Yes. The Hyperion school." Haydon said quietly, Pollitti leaned forward and turned his head. "We're aware your French friends are not being helpful. We can fill in gaps."

"I'll be waiting." Haydon watched as Pollitti took out a cigar and tapped it on the table. The sudden lines on his forehead told a story. He likes it, Haydon thought, he's hooked. One mention of Hyperion and he was eager to trade.

"Let's take our pleasures while avoiding the indecipherable doctrines that divide us." Pollitti lit a match and started sucking away on his cigar. He closed his eyes and leaned back, beaming with evident delight.

"I'll drink to that."

Straw Man

Returning to the Embassy, Haydon put a call through on his secure phone to Glasson. He reported on his lunch with the SISMI chief.

"Good news. Pollitti gave me names."

"Which are?"

"Seán Docherty and Nasir el-Maghrebi. Covert meeting in Trieste." He paused. "Can you get me gen on Docherty?"

"I'm on it. You say DAEDALUS is in touch with this Libyan. Maghrebi?"

"Due to meet him again shortly."

"He's on board?"

"He'll play. Short of brass, but nervous. Wants legal indemnities." Haydon said. "He's not stupid, figured out he has to be far away before delivery time, I could see his brain calculating how much he could stash before he has to pull the ripcord – without ending up upside down hanging from a lamppost."

"Put him on a retainer and offer to pay his costs. I'll get clearance." Glasson's voice was oily, Haydon recognised the warning signals. "Play on his greed. Stress he'll make a big turn and be out long before the nasty stuff hits the roof ornaments. Everything verbal, mind you."

"Got it."

"I like the way this op is shaped. Two for the price of one. We're sniffing out any trace of the Libya IRA connection and stinging the Libyan madman's nuclear ambitions while we do. Move the bastard on."

"Mustn't rush–"

"–If we get what we want from your lad, the slightest chance to interdict a shipment to the Provos, that's the imperative. Our job is to save lives. He'll take his chances. It's a rough world. Don't get sentimental on me, we're too old."

Straw Man

"I want to bring in a team of eyes from your end. Check his back is clean, follow the Libyans. Put a watch out for the Irish connection."

"I'll sound out the powers that be. In the meantime, use local resources; you've got off books assets? Get it done."

"Mark, this could be our way in."

"Treasury won't wear it. Big cost item, there's competition for watchers. You need to demonstrate an imminent national danger."

"After Brighton, what is more imminent?"

"Haydon, I want your plan for confronting the Libyan threat. Draw up a paper, bring it to London, make your case to the top floor. Gotta go." Glasson hung up.

From the open windows of the Ambassador's office on the first floor, the clacking of wooden mallet on wooden ball provided a counterpoint to the hum of traffic noise and the blaring horns which assaulted the ears from the other side of the compound. A haven of sanity, Haydon thought, an incongruous corner of England in a foreign land. Splayed out in the shade of giant umbrella pines and the tall wall that marked the rear of the British Embassy in Porta Pia, the perfectly mown and unreasonably green croquet lawn seemed splendidly out of place.

A small wooden shack stood to one side of the lawn. He chuckled to himself as his eyes focussed on the word '*Pimms*' emblazoned in bright red on the painted roof. How on earth had it got there, an inappropriate piece of advertising outside an important Embassy? When he had looked inside, it had surprised him to find it well-stocked with cases of Pimms. He sat uncomfortably in an upright leather chair in front of the wooden

Straw Man

partners' desk, looking up at the Ambassador's broad back as he stared motionless out of the window.

"You intend to take provocative actions against the Libyan People's Bureau in Rome, if I understand you correctly?" He didn't turn around, but settled on the lintel and leaned further out, hanging on to the window handle. "Don't like it. Don't like it at all."

Haydon was aware of the Ambassador's aversion to what he called 'that other organisation' that operated out of *his* Embassy. He'd made clear he didn't like the waves they caused, and he didn't like Haydon Talbot in particular. The feeling was mutual.

"Always trouble from you chaps." He continued, brushing his hand through his silvery hair. "You never stop. Bunch of overgrown schoolboys."

"Ambassador. It's a national priority that we obtain intelligence on these IRA arms shipments. The dangers are extreme and self-evident." It was disconcerting to talk to the dark frame of the elder man's back. He supposed it was the art of diplomacy, learning to put your adversary at a disadvantage by small, subliminal stratagems. "We don't know the timing. What we know is the op's being run out of the People's Bureau here, controlled from Tripoli by Ahmed Khalfari – who runs the Libyan Mukhabarat. We've evidence of covert meetings with IRA operatives in Italy to plan the shipments."

Haydon watched a tall, gangling figure stooping over a yellow ball. The man swung his mallet wildly and missed his target by some margin, letting out a loud oath. He stamped his foot and cursed. His opponent doubled up in laughter.

Straw Man

"Masters, I'd thank you to curb your language. You'll upset the locals." The two men turned their heads to look up at the stern figure leaning out of the long window. The Ambassador coughed then turned to face Haydon.

"I intend to make my position known to London."

"My orders come down from the Joint Intelligence Committee."

"JIC can be made to change its mind." The Ambassador paced the room, conducting circles with his arms. "We're working to get the Italians onside for the European Council meeting."

"Ambassador, I'll take every precaution–"

"–Italy takes over the Presidency next month and we need the Minister on board to stand up to the bloody French." Haydon felt a flash of rage. It was like the man hadn't noticed how close the bomb had come to bringing down the government. He turned his face away. "The PM has been charming him, seeking to enlist his support. You won't want to find yourself on her bad-boy list; you'll end up in Port Stanley or that other place. Yes, South Georgia, populated by sheep and reportedly extremely unwelcoming."

"You have my word the op will be deniable."

"I still don't like it." He walked over to his desk, sat down, picked up the phone and started dialling. "Now listen, we'll play croquet. Do you know how to make Pimms? Good. Make a jug or two, plenty of ice, see. I'll be down in fifteen minutes. Tell Masters and whoever he's with they're playing with us now. You can partner Masters, he looks hopeless."

The Ambassador dismissed Haydon with a wave of the arm.

CHAPTER 5

Haydon got back to his office late. The croquet match had lasted almost two hours. The Ambassador had been bad-tempered, missing shots and demanding to replay them, claiming one of his opponents moved as he was about to play his stroke. He knew it would have been in his best interest to lose. He needed the Old Man onside, but he couldn't bring himself to. *Idiot!* High-level flak from London was about to burst over him. And he couldn't rely on Glasson to support him. He'd shove him off the cliff at the first sign of trouble.

He summoned Peter Etherington to his office. His deputy looked like a schoolboy, he thought, should be in short trousers, but perhaps underneath that innocent guise he posessed the needful – a twisted and dirty mind.

"Sit. Look, the Old Man's going to kick up a fuss about our watch on the People's Bureau."

"Our orders were Priority 1, direct from Chairman JIC."

"That's Whitehall for you. The ground moves under your feet whilst the mandarins are eating lunch. We need to shift up a gear, get a watch set up right now. Place Mister Nasir el-Maghrebi in our sights before the boom comes down." Haydon arched his hands and sat motionless. "I'm afraid it'll involve taking a few risks."

"Such as?"

"Get hold of that guy you used for the wet job last month. Albanian?"

"I know where to find him."

"Say you want his best boys. His lot know how to keep their mouths shut. False flag it, but delicately. Get him to drop hints to his lads, subtle, they're working for the Israelis. You know how to do it."

Straw Man

"He won't like that."

"Pay him extra. Two teams. Bureau and home. Details of foreign contacts, photos. We'll use the Nono fund. It's what it's there for." Haydon stroked his neck, then leaned forward. "He can pay his boys over the odds."

"Mossad never pay over the odds. Better–"

"–I don't care. Do it. And pray we luck out with Docherty, pick up a thread."

"We need to rush? The shipments won't happen tomorrow."

"We don't know when the shipments will happen. That's the point. Things happen quickly when you're not paying attention. Then you find you're screwed to the wall. We lucked out with Nasir and Docherty's names; we're not going to lose this trace because H.E doesn't like a few ripples."

"If our Israeli friends clock us?"

"Make bloody sure they don't." He took out his handkerchief and wiped his forehead. "It would even things up. They're always using fake British passports for their black ops."

The next week, Haydon flew to London. Glasson chaired the meeting. Ten senior members of the British security establishment sat around the long oak table in the main conference room. Haydon stood at a whiteboard holding a wooden pointer.

"Immediate requirements." He spoke in a clear voice, brushing his hair back with his free hand. "A radical uptick in GCHQ COMINT coverage on the Libyan Security Services and the People's Bureaus around Europe, particular focus on Rome. Yes?" A bald, bespectacled man raised his hand.

Straw Man

"Willetts, Special Ops, GCHQ. I'm authorised to switch resources. Won't be a problem. Can we meet after this to go over specifics?"

"Thank you." He nodded, then continued. "Regular photo-reconnaissance flights out of RAF Akrotiri in Cyprus, sweeps back and forth along the entire Libyan coastline: that's 1,100 miles. Emphasis on ports."

He tapped with his pointer on the board. "And dedicated analysts scouring the product for signs of outbound military stores shipments."

"I'll handle that as an inter-service request via the Cabinet Office." Glasson said.

"Approval to accelerate Operation TUMBREL, intended to insert a penetration agent – code name DAEDALUS – into top levels of the Libyan security establishment. The agent will dangle access to restricted items for their nuclear programme, via a credible European company with close relations to the Pakistani A.Q. Khan organisation. Goes without saying any items delivered will be of no genuine value in advancing their programme."

"Deployment to Rome," he tapped the board with his pointer again, "of a team of reconnaissance operatives. Round-the-clock surveillance of Nasir el-Maghrebi and his people at the People's Bureau. This is our best chance of identifying and intercepting the IRA link team."

"May I suggest you recruit them from the Province?" A tall man in army uniform with the red collar flashes of a staff officer chipped in. "You'll need them to be familiar with Provo faces and voices."

"Good suggestion." Glasson peered over his reading glasses, then scribbled on a notepad. "I'll make a request to the JIC for a squadron from The Det out of RAF Aldergrove. They're the cream, unparalleled knowledge of IRA faces. They'll argue they're over-committed in Ulster, but I'll get them for you."

Straw Man

"We need intel out of Ulster." Haydon paused. "Who is the prime contact with Libya? We know Qaddafi likes to deal with Joe Cahill, and we judge he's in overall command, but current intel places him in the USA. The Provo Chief of Staff – McKenna – will be briefed in but not directly involved. It'll be a small stand-alone cell and we need to know who is running it. So far all we have is a low-level soldier – Seán Docherty, who's been spotted with Maghrebi, but we doubt he's in charge. We need a list of likely candidates, senior IRA operatives who've dropped out of sight for any length of time."

"I'll see what I can do." Glasson stood up. "The Ulster security establishment is full of snakes and jealousies. I'll speak to the Security Coordinator."

"I need my Ambassador brought onside. He's making loud noises."

"Forget about your Ambassador." Glasson rapped hard on the table. "The PM is breathing fire, as you would imagine. I'm seeing the Chairman of the JIC with the Chief this afternoon. You'll have your answer tomorrow. Anything else?" He looked around the room.

"OK Gentlemen, get to work. I'll get back to you, Haydon."

He flew back to Rome the next day. Staring out of the aircraft window, he looked down at Lake Trasimeno, the site of one of Hannibal's bloodiest victories over Rome. Livy had written that the lake had stayed red for weeks, bloody from the 15,000 Roman soldiers killed on the lake's shore. Now they faced another incursion from North Africa. He hoped it wouldn't produce similar rivers of blood.

Straw Man

Glasson had rung him early that morning to say the Joint Intelligence Committee had signed off on his proposals. They'd approved everything on his wish list. A full team of watchers from The Det, being briefed now in London and on their way to him in a week. Then they'd scour the Libyan's underwear and garbage until they found that IRA link.

"Oh, the Chairman said, I'm quoting him here–*'Mark, we're giving Haydon a free rein. He has to make this thing work, no buts. He'll get the support he needs, material, political and diplomatic, but we can't have a ton of Semtex landing on Irish shores. The resultant bloodshed would be unimaginable.'"*

He was being lined up as the sacrificial lamb. Fascinating to watch Glasson positioning himself close enough to claim parentage, to bask in the operation's brilliant success, but far enough away if they came looking for someone to blame for a failure. Haydon had watched him throughout his career. *Why can't I get to grips with this manoeuvre?* Perhaps I'm just not subtle enough, he thought. I'm too blunt an instrument for high office?

There was no one to whom he could pass the parcel. At least there was no chance of him ending up in some wretched Libyan dungeon, or with a bullet in the back. No, it was his career that would go bang. Charlie would be the one exposed to physical danger. His life was about to explode, go in crazy directions he'd never imagined. Because Glasson was in a hurry. Charlie was a guy who thrived on risk, so he'd have to fend for himself. He stood to make a great deal of money, so it was right he should live with the risks. They'd have to be lucky to get payback from TUMBREL before it all went haywire.

With a squeak of tyres, the DC9 touched down at Fiumicino.

Straw Man

CHAPTER 6

The little jet climbed fast, bumping its way up through the fluffy summer cumulus that fringed the jagged Italian coast. Nasir peered through the round window and watched the green and brown humps of Sicily come into view, then a far off pinprick that was Malta, a brown blemish in the carpet of dark blue far below. Ahead he could make out a thick wall of dust that heralded the Libyan coast.

Two universes. The contrast between the lush, productive green of Europe and the barren orange of his desert homeland. The Leader had his vision of turning the Sahara into a giant green farm, back to what he said it had been in the days of ancient Carthage – the breadbasket of the Roman Empire. They said the aquifer system under the desert had sufficient water to turn the country green again. Nice idea, but would it ever happen? To achieve development, they needed to avoid conflict, but with the quixotic nature of the Leader that seemed improbable.

Out of the corner of his eye, he watched his boss. The elder man appeared preoccupied, leaning back, his eyes narrowly open, the tip of his tongue sticking slightly out of his mouth. His hook nose combined with his unsmiling demeanour to give him a disapproving air. He hailed from the Magarha tribe from the south of Libya, a tough, nomadic people. He had been at school at Sebha with Colonel Qaddafi, and later they were classmates at the Military Academy in Benghazi. He was one of the few who could claim the Leader as a friend.

As Qaddafi's intelligence supremo, he wielded absolute power over Nasir's career. He needed to be on constant alert, watch his words. But he didn't feel cowed. He could see through the bluff to his weaknesses.

Straw Man

Khalfari was too open to flattery. He liked to play the Big Man a little too much, which laid him open to manipulation. And he was lazy, leaving stuff for Nasir to do which allowed him space to play his own games.

"Drink, Excellency?" A lithe flight attendant walked up the aisle and bowed. Khalfari looked up. One of those toughies, Nasir thought, as arid as her desert origins. A slim figure wearing the distinctive green uniform of the 'Revolutionary Nuns'. Qaddafi chose them for their looks as well as their fighting qualities.

"Bring me an orange juice. You?" He gestured to Nasir, who nodded. "Bring two. How long is our flight?"

"Two hours, Excellency. We land at 18.30."

Khalfari waved her away, then leaned forward to fix Nasir with a chilling glare.

"Pollitti took me to one side at the airport. He knew all about your supposedly covert meeting in Trieste, he even knew Docherty's name. His name! He gave me a not so veiled warning. Fuck you, Nasir!" He stamped his foot. "Don't you understand what's at stake? Our European network depends on there being a benign eye in Rome."

He thumped the coffee table so hard water spilled from his glass onto his trouser leg. He rubbed at the stain with his handkerchief. "I chose you because I thought you'd get on with it and do nothing to put my important operations at risk. Let me be clear. No dark meetings in Italy! None, never, ever!"

Nasir flinched as he felt spittle on his face. Khalfari's face had gone puce and screwed up. "You understand?"

"Yes Sir, but–"

Straw Man

"–no buts. No buts! From now on, use false papers, false names. It's the Leader's project, needs to go without humps. You have the resources you asked for, so get the job done, and quietly." He fell silent and stared fixedly at him, his lower lip vibrating.

Nasir sat stiffly upright in the plush white leather chair, facing his boss. He could feel the dark cloud over his head, the hawk's eyes boring into him. He was on probation; for sure they'd keep a watch on him for a while. He'd tough it out, be careful. Have to be harder on Seán. That was where the security lapse must be. He shut his eyes.

Khalfari reached over and poked his arm. Nasir flinched.

"Check out Vispoli's friend Lomax. Issue him a visa, find out everything you can. Have him tailed. Meet up with him, shove him around a bit." Nasir's eyes followed the rapid movements of Khalfari's hands, which were winding a set of wooden worry beads around his fingers. "Get his office and his home wired. Ask around. Get Vispoli to give you background. If he's another greedy mercenary, maybe you turn him. He might be a useful back-channel to MI6. Scratch his story. Scratch it hard. Understand?"

"I'll get my guys onto him; they'll count the fleas on his body." He gestured with his fingers. "I won't rely on Vispoli. Naïve–sees the best in everybody."

"Do it as soon as you get back to Rome this weekend. No delay. I want a report on my desk by the end of the month." He stroked his chin and peered out of the window. "I want you to work up a plan for surveilling the British in Rome, their spook guys at the Embassy. Find out if they're watching us. If Pollitti briefed them about Trieste, I'd be surprised if they weren't, so we need to get ahead of them."

"Do we want them to know we're watching? Send a signal?"

Straw Man

"Maybe we make them worry for their safety, get them off-guard, cause them a little pain. Accidents, warnings, car crashes, small things. Send me ideas."

The aircraft's nose dipped, and they began their descent towards Tripoli.

Nasir watched them as they emerged from the front door hand in hand. The man walked over and opened the garage door, then waited for the girl to drive out in a scarlet Alfa-Romeo Spider. Great car. She paused and revved the engine while he closed the garage door, then climbed in. If that beauty was mine, he thought, I'd never let a girl touch it. He found himself daydreaming about wiring it up and watching it explode into a thousand fragments. Maybe he would, if he found out the smooth Englishman wasn't as innocent as he claimed. He shook his head. *Focus.* He watched them from over his newspaper. He could hear high-pitched laughter before they sped off noisily up the hill, tyres screeching on the cobblestones. He noted the time –13.11– on his pocket notepad. His assumption was they were going for lunch.

He remained seated at a table at the pavement cafe opposite, smoking and sipping coffee, steam rising in the nippy air. He pulled the cap down over his eyes and wound the thick scarf around his neck. He looked up at the windows of the apartment building. No movement. He felt a rush of excitement. Kicking off on a black job always gave him a burst of energy. This was one he'd wanted to do himself. He'd take the rap if it went wrong. You don't want a foul up, do it yourself.

He'd stationed Vito to work lookout at the bottom of via Garibaldi. One way up the hill, plenty of warning. Vito would radio in, he'd be alert

Straw Man

and ready to crash out if he got a signal. He wouldn't need over twenty minutes to complete the setup. He turned his head, slowly scanning both ways. The street was empty, quiet during the Roman lunch hour.

Standing up, he dropped a pile of coins on the table, put on a pair of thin leather gloves and crossed the street to the front door. He leant forward as if he was peering for a name on the Entryphone. It took him a few seconds to open the simple latch on the front door, using a stiff plastic card. The guy hadn't even double-locked. What fools people were, might as well leave the thing wide open.

He pulled the door closed behind him and started up the stairs, sprinting noiselessly in a practiced crouch. Target was the top-floor flat. No one on the stairs. It took him 3 minutes to open the deadlock on the flat door using a set of standard skeleton keys. Simple. There'd been a grey-haired *schlosser* on the course in Germany, a pro. Made them practice over and over again. He could work a standard deadlock with his eyes closed.

He made a stealthy walkthrough of each room, watchful for oddities. It was a small flat: bedroom, study, living room, kitchen, bathroom, wide veranda. He could smell the woman's scent, it permeated through stale cigarette smoke. He was careful to touch nothing, move nothing. He stood motionless in the living room for a minute and let his eyes take in the scene.

Tracing the wires from the phone to the main junction box in the living room, he followed the extension lead that ran off to the study and the bedroom. He unscrewed the cover of the phone and inserted a small device, carefully attaching it to the wires and pushing it well back into the wiring. The tiny transmitter would work on the phone and the extensions; it would act like a microphone.

Straw Man

He walked over to the desk by the window and carefully leafed through the papers. Nothing interesting, bills and circulars. No filing cabinet, the guy must keep his stuff at his office. Letting himself out and re-locking the deadlock, he descended the stairs slowly and let himself out of the front door, bending down and cautiously scanning the street. He checked his watch. 13.29. 18 minutes. Perfect.

He'd done the outer installation work earlier that morning, fixing a recording device disguised as an electricity meter onto the wall of the next-door building. Low enough for easy access. Dressed in the overalls of STET, the national telephone company, Vito held the ladder whilst he did the job. Easy money for the Neapolitan, a petty crook, a drug dealer, but useful. Four hours' work. Cash in hand. He'd use him again when he did the setup on the guy's office. He'd meet the guy there, sniff out the angles, look for alarms on the windows. Then go back and do the plant on a weekend.

He jogged down via Garibaldi, humming softly. He'd get to know this sleek character better than he knew himself. Never trust an Englishman: they concealed themselves so well behind distantly friendly faces.

Straw Man

CHAPTER 7

A staff car drove Sergeant Babs Stoner through the heavy morning traffic to Lambeth and deposited her on the pavement outside Century House. Her first impression was of a dilapidated 1960s tower block, not what she'd expected. She was wearing civilian clothes – anorak, dark jump suit, hair tied up – but a trained watcher would have noted her military gait. She'd spent her childhood on Army bases in Germany, Cyprus and Singapore, both her parents had served in the Second World War. Dark-haired and dark-eyed, she had an oddly long face. She attempted to dampen down her femininity but wasn't sure it worked. Her peers thought her attractive rather than beautiful.

She was one of the few left from the original intake when The Det, or more formally 14 Intelligence Company, was formed in 1972. With the specific purpose of conducting covert surveillance against suspected IRA operatives and their arms caches in Ulster, it sought to avoid firefights and publicity, operating quietly in the shadows. The unit was unusual in that it ran on strictly meritocratic lines, its strength measured in roughly equal numbers between the sexes. They recruited from the ranks of elite Army front-line units and they trained with the SAS. At 33, Babs was wiry and fit. She had gained a reputation for mental toughness and for operating well in extreme discomfort – important qualities in reconnaissance work.

A bored-looking receptionist directed her to a cramped waiting room furnished, if you could call it that, with orange plastic chairs set around the walls and wire-caged strip-lighting flickering above. Smelling strongly of detergent. The walls were an institutional green and crying out for repainting. Perhaps there was some psychological reason why they wanted their visitors to feel depressed?

A tall, well-dressed girl wearing a Hermes scarf wound round her neck approached her, smiled and held out her hand.

"Sergeant Stoner? Julia Brooks." They shook hands and eyed each other. "Sorry to keep you waiting. This way."

"No worries, Julia. Just got here. Babs, they all call me Babs."

"We're tearing our hair out, less than a week since the bomb and we're operating in a pressure cooker."

"Your hair looks well-coiffed to me!"

"Nobody notices, it's pretty male around here. I don't have to try hard."

"Tell me about it." Babs smiled. "That's why I'm togged up like a grungy bloke. Makes life so much easier."

"I'm too attached to my makeup. Couldn't give it up."

They took the lift to the 18th floor, Julia led the way to a small meeting room. Babs walked over to the window and stared out. It was a clear day, just a few cumulus clouds breaking up the arc of blue sky. She thought she could see Hampstead in the distance. Below her the major landmarks of London were splayed out.

"Coffee? Tea?"

"Let's get to it. What have you got?"

Julia unrolled some large-scale maps and laid them on the table.

"You've received your general orders. Deploy with a detachment of 12 watchers to Rome, seconded to our command for the duration of the watch."

"Overall boss?"

Straw Man

"Haydon Talbot. Head of Rome Station." Julia ran her fingers through her blonde hair. "Professional, ex-military, para. You'll find him easy."

"James Bond or George Smiley?"

"Neither. Happily married. He's all right. You'll get along. He's a little stiff, but sharp and trustworthy. Under pressure to perform on this one." She screwed up her nose. Babs noticed the freckles. "Your estimate is two weeks to be operational on the ground in Rome?"

"I'm working to shorten that. Hand over current assignments. Details?"

"Round-the-clock watch on the Libyan People's Bureau – that's what they call their Embassies. There–" she took a black marker and drew a circle on a plastic map of Rome, close to Vatican City, "and the apartment of their top bogey-man Nasir el-Maghrebi – here. We're looking for linkages to a cell of IRA arms smugglers, number unknown. The only traces we have are these two blurry faces."

She placed two blown up black and white A4 photos on the table. Babs pulled them towards her and stared at them. She tapped one photo with her forefinger.

"This one's easy. Seán Docherty, low-level soldier. Belfast Brigade. Second Battalion. Falls Road. Usual form. Pulled in more than once. Nothing stuck. Orphan. Drinker. Done nothing high profile, just a front line guy. Bang bang. He won't be running this, there's got to be a higher-up somewhere."

"Impressive, and?"

"This one, nothing." Babs cocked her head sideways, then pushed the photo back across the table. "Arab, obviously. Sullen face. I'm assuming he's our primary target, Nasir el-Maghrebi?"

"You assume right. Unpleasant, clever and dangerous. Here's his form." Julia smiled and passed her a file. "You'll be cleared to go anywhere

Straw Man

the trail leads–except for Libya, and behind the Iron Curtain. Out of bounds. How do you feel about deploying away from the Province for an indeterminate period?"

"Eyetie boys in tight shirts pinching my bum!" They both laughed. "I'm looking forward to sunshine, pasta, to getting away from the sodden grit of the Shankill Road. The lads will see it that way. No problems."

"Language?"

"I bought a guidebook." Babs smiled. "One of my lads speaks passable Italian, but we'll rely on local liaison to help us out."

"One of your first tasks will be to obtain sound at the primary targets, video if it's feasible."

"How will host country relations be handled? Italian Services onboard?" Babs asked. "It's cleaner if they handle intercepts."

"Babs," Julia smiled wanly and reached behind her neck to adjust her hair clip, "this op is way off books. Cleared from the top, but black as soot. The Eyeties don't share our concerns about Libya and the IRA, they can't be looped in. We think they've done a deal to leave the Libyans alone, so long as they don't do naughties on Italian soil. Our PM will talk to their PM when they meet at the European Council in December. Which might change their position. Or not. So don't rely on collaboration."

"Makes it tougher. You've local off-books dark assets?"

"On tap." Julia nodded. "Dark as you like."

"Good. But operating solo will up our requirements." She paused, drumming her fingers on the table. "We need full-time translators. Two. And techies, local signals guys, with an in to the phone company. We'll assume the Italians are keeping their own watch on the Libyans, so we'll need to scope them out and create work-arounds."

Straw Man

"We think it's unlikely the Libyans will meet their IRA contacts in Italy again, the Italians warned them off after they flagged the meet between Maghrebi and Docherty in Trieste." Julia frowned. "Our best guess for future meets are Malta, Cyprus, Yugoslavia, Greece and Lebanon, maybe Switzerland. You need to be ready to follow at short notice and operate surveillance on arrival."

"That's a helluvan ask." Babs said. "I'll study potential venues and draw up contingency plans for crash deployments in each case."

"I'll set you up with a room." Julia continued. "Draw up a list of everything you need – logistics, equipment, access to maps, satellite imagery and so on. In the current political climate, we'll get pretty much whatever we ask for."

Straw Man

CHAPTER 8

Nasir el-Maghrebi was rigorous as usual. Walking, walking. All over the city. He didn't need to go to a gym, that was for sure. He deployed four men with a car and two motorbikes as part of the dry-cleaning process, two days scurrying around Athens performing intricate patterns before concluding there were no watchers. His side was clean.

They had drummed the necessity for discipline into them at the Friedrich Engels Military Academy in East Berlin. The Stasi were tough on their students. They laid great stress on the consequences of lax tradecraft.

"Mossad is *völlig unversöhnlich*—unremitting!" Major Mölke would repeat. "You won't get second chances. Ever. These Hebrews are shit hot. No shortcuts. Make sure you're clean, then do what you can to ensure your counterpart is clean. They'll be your weak link. Take as much time as necessary. It's your life on the line, take care of your precious hides."

He sent Seán a coded message delaying their meeting by 24 hours, then ordered his team to set about tracking the Irishman and flushing out any ticks he might have picked up. As the reports came in, Nasir reflected that either Seán was a fantastic operator, or, more likely, he wasn't paying any attention. His demeanour seemed blithely unconcerned; his gait was lazy.

Watching for watchers without getting spotted required sharp skills. Nasir prided himself on blending right in and keeping his team far back whilst retaining command of the target. Seán made it easy. He strolled around, stopping often to look in shop windows. He spent most of the evening hours drinking alone in a bar close to his hotel, leaving plenty of room to observe. By the time Seán staggered back to his hotel a little before midnight, Nasir was certain he was also dark.

Straw Man

Nasir never drank alcohol, believing it a weakness which led to failure and suffering. He liked Seán and felt comfortable in his company, even when the Belfast man was at his bottles. He never got difficult, or even much changed. But he couldn't get over the feeling that a weak link was contained in the glasses of beer he consumed so voraciously. He'd been over in his mind the circumstances leading up to their meeting in Trieste. What was it that alerted the Italian secret police? He was certain his side had been clean, he'd been rigorous. He concluded that Seán or one of his associates must have been indiscreet on the phone. It was the drink that worried him. It made people sloppy. And he'd seen Seán slide away out of the safety zone.

They set the meet for Hadrian's Arch, a tall Greco-Roman marble structure standing beneath the Acropolis Hill, surrounded by a small, wooded park. For late autumn it was a scorching day, the park offering welcome coolness amongst the trees dotted around the gardens. The air was tinder dry, making it tolerable, even pleasant. It reminded Nasir of home. He sat, motionless, on a shaded wooden bench and looked around him, his eyes roaming back and forth, automatically seeking subliminal anomalies.

There were a few tourists milling around, picking their way down from the Parthenon. It looked like a fairy-tale castle, he thought, as he stared up at it, perched high in the sky. He spotted Seán sauntering into the park and wandering around the Arch, gazing at it with a curious intensity, to all the world another tourist. He was wearing a grey anorak. In this weather? What was it with the Irish? They wore the oddest things.

Straw Man

Both men were carrying a folded copy of the Herald Tribune in their left hand. No Trib: abort and go home. Trib in right hand: walk on, start a counter-surveillance routine and aim for a fall-back meeting set for twenty hours later at a different location. Nasir stood up and sidled over to Seán.

"Greetings friend, let's go for a cultural stroll." They fell into step, wandering together away from the Arch. "Sweating a lot? Not well? What's with the heavy clothing? Expecting rain?"

"Nasir, bloody hot this place." Seán said. "The coat keeps the sun away off my skin. You Arab fellows should know that? It's not as hot as that trip to Leptis Magna. Remember? We poured sweat over ancient marble objects. I'd rather have been stuck in the classroom with my hands trembling, trying to wire together dodgy Russian detonators."

"Cooler here than that awful trip. Didn't get many outings, everything was so serious. Training, eighteen hours a day. Not much humour. How are you, friend?"

"I've a passionate thirst," Seán gestured with his hand, as if raising a mug to his lips, "cold beer is what I need." There was something almost pleading in his voice.

"You're unfit, Seán. Getting old." Nasir chuckled. "Come home with me. I put you back in the camp with one of our hard instructors. Jassim, maybe. Remember Jassim? Violent guy, pock-marked, one-eyed, with a bald head and a nasty temper. He'd spruce you up!"

"Get away with you; I'm out of my element in this heat. You should come to Belfast, Nasir. That would fix you properly. Grey, dark, rains all the time, cold as hell. You wouldn't like it, for sure. It's what I'm used to. Will we go to a cool bar and relax ourselves?"

Straw Man

"We'll talk first. Safer in the open. By those columns–that's the Temple of Zeus. A view of everything around us. Zeus will look after us." Nasir punched Seán's arm. "When we've done our work, I'll buy you cold beers. OK? I'll even pay for them if it makes you smile again!"

They sat on the marble steps in the shade from the massive columns. Seán had taken off his anorak but was still sweating, which amused Nasir.

"Your top guys still in hiding after Brighton?"

"It's calming. The Brits got the message right enough." Seán leaned in towards him. "What we need now is some kilos of Semtex, then we'll finish the job."

"My people want to meet your bomb-maker. Using long-delay fuses was impressive."

"I'll talk to McKenna, maybe we send him down to you?"

"Seán, you do that. Now we've got a problem." Nasir's voice was sharp.

"Just the one? We're doing well then."

"SISMI, the Italian spook boys, they clocked our last meeting. I got flak from my boss; the Italians gave him a hard time. Rapped my fingers. You use the phone in Trieste, on your way there maybe?"

"No way. It's religious with me. No phones. Never." He shook his head and waved a finger at the other man. "Will you ever consider it might be your side? The Colonel is forever making wild broadcasts telling the world how he'll support us against the wicked colonialists. Hadn't they maybe followed you from Rome? I'm certain on my side. I was black."

"I've been meticulous, Seán, been over it minute by minute in my mind. Send any faxes? Could they have bugged you when you briefed your people in Belfast?"

Straw Man

"No. My reporting is in person to Fitzgerald. He talks to Cahill, who's in charge of the operation. I meet the man at one of his safe houses dotted around Dundalk, near the border in the Republic. I don't even know where I am or where I've bloody been. They stick my head in a sodding canvas hood and drive me round in circles, changing vans, shoving me around so I'm so jumbled as if I'm in a washing machine. They're all paranoid." Seán scratched his head as if in pain. "The Chief of Staff, McKenna, he's aware, but he doesn't know details. We learned the hard way. It wasn't our side."

"OK. We redouble disciplines. I'm forbidden to meet you on Italian soil. We'll meet here, Malta, Dubrovnik, Vienna, Larnaca. Never travel directly. Strict dry-cleaning before any contact. Existential. I'm keen to keep my head attached to my body."

"I'm with you there. Although our heavies don't chop our heads off. We're civilised people, you know!"

"Yes?"

"We get a nice, quiet bullet in the back of the neck." Seán chuckled and leaned down to retie his shoelaces. He murmured. "Nasir, have you thought of running CI on the Brit bogey-men in Rome? You must know who they are? Watch them, see where they lead you. You might have a mole there?"

Nasir fixed the Irishman with a penetrating stare. *Good thinking, Seán. Reading my mind, are you?* "I'd need approval. Might be difficult with the sensitive diplomacy we've got going on."

"Don't just wait for the Brits to hit you. Push them off balance. That's the way we think back home. Never let them get a free shot at you. They got to know to watch their own backs. Can't relax even when they're having a nice barbeque in their back gardens. Maybe you should do them some actual harm."

Straw Man

"I'll think about it."

An old man shuffled into view, limping and leaning on a walking stick. He was dressed in rags and mumbling to himself. The two men sat watching until he disappeared off into the park.

"That's us in just a few years. I'm already past 30."

"How are you getting on with ships and crew?" Nasir asked.

"Buying a trawler out of Kerry, solid vessel. It'll take time to get the registration done. Takes up to 20 tons. Needs a little work. Got a skipper signed up. A pro. Drug runner. Not a believer, mercenary. Solid guy, tight-lipped." Seán smiled. "Your end?"

"10 tons for the first shipment. AK47's and ammo, pistols, grenades, RPG-7's and DShK12.7mm heavy machine guns – game changers. No Semtex 'til the first two shipments get through." Nasir reached into his pocket and passed a sheet of paper to Seán. "A list of what we'll have. You can't keep it, memorise it."

Seán took out a notebook and scrawled some notes, then handed the paper back to Nasir.

"Will you ever imagine how those Brit gobshites will scream when we hit a few of their convoys." He beamed. "They're so smug behind their armour. Safe as houses, they think they are."

"I'll need to meet your skipper. I'll bring one of our naval people and they can work out transhipment stuff." Nasir paused, taking out a small diary and riffling through it. "Oh, one more thing. Good news, which will please your bosses, you see. We'll make a first payment. A million bucks. I need written instructions from your leadership. Cash, somewhere in Switzerland. I'll send you details for the meet."

Straw Man

"That won't be a problem." Seán laughed. "I'll have the instructions all right. Payday, cash! Jesus! That'll make the bosses happy. The Movement is always short. We have to rob poor bloody post offices."

"Don't forget to bring a big enough suitcase!" Nasir slapped Seán on the back.

"Don't you worry! We'll communicate the usual way. Well, that's all agreed. Now will we get my beers, I'm parched."

The Irishman stood up and grimaced at the bright sunlight. The two men meandered arm in arm out of the park.

Seán got back to his hotel room feeling wobbly. He lay on the bed with his hands behind his head and stared up at the cheap plastic ceiling fan clanking and sending down a slight breeze. Even that little zephyr was welcome. He was sweating and feeling sick. He shut his eyes.

Nasir was right, he was unfit. These sweats. He needed to sort himself out. He was a soldier. It defined him, but he didn't feel soldierly at all. God knows he'd needed that cool draught, it wasn't just the parching heat. Every day now he needed that first drink to take away the edge and give him back a sense of being in control. But that initial slug led to another until he staggered to his bed fluthered. Not good. Too frequent.

It had been easier when he'd been a foot soldier, waiting for orders. Which were straightforward to carry out. No responsibility, just wait and get told what to do. This job was the opposite. Maximum security meant maximum responsibility, maximum loneliness. No one to tell him how to carry out his tasks, to share the load. And he reported to a dangerous, unpredictable man. How it was going, what he'd been doing.

Straw Man

He had to make all the decisions, and if it went wrong, it was down to him alone. Jesus!

If they had a whiff of suspicion! Over the years he'd met some lads from the 'Nutting Squad'. They operated on their own, terrible guys, you needed to stay away from them. The Unknowns, they called them. He'd once met Jon Joe McGee, the guy who ran it, a bleeding, vicious psychopath. No, he had to keep this one together, mustn't be a muppet.

The news about the Italians' rumbling their Trieste meeting hadn't surprised him. Not at all. The Libyans were naïve. Nasir's self-belief was typical. His friend thought he operated on the same level as Mossad or MI6, that his six months training in East Germany had honed him into a top-level professional. Laughable! Nice guy, but simple; and simple translated to dangerous.

The question was, how could he mitigate his friend's overconfidence? If the shipments didn't get through, it would be down to him alone, his failure. No excuses. The Brits were pros, he couldn't guarantee anything. They'd got the Claudia in '73, and that was Cahill's gig. It wasn't even the Libyans' fault. The German crew had drawn attention to the ship, going into Tripoli harbour when they were supposed to rendezvous on the high seas. A Brit submarine had followed them as they motored out of Tripoli harbour.

Seán had listened to Qaddafi's inflammatory speech earlier that year, in which he'd announced to the world he intended to provide the IRA with quantities of arms.

"The People's Committees will form an alliance with the secret IRA because it champions the cause of liberating Ireland and liberating the Irish nation from the tyranny of British colonialism."

Straw Man

Noble words! Seán couldn't have put it better. How did the Libyans expect the Brits to respond? MI6 would dedicate all its resources to thwarting any shipments. Those new satellite things, comms intercepts, reconnaissance planes. Above all manpower, teams of watchers to follow every known senior Libyan Intelligence and IRA member that might be involved; until they fixed their sights on the people in the cell. Him and Nasir. They'd send the SAS boys to take them both out. The Brits must know Nasir ran Qaddafi's European dark operations out of Rome. He needed to keep prodding Nasir to play these MI6 guys back hard, maybe flip an RPG through a bedroom window at night, just let the buggers know they were in the cross-hairs.

Cross-hairs. You could be plumb in the bastards night sights and you wouldn't even know it. You'd never feel the bullet. His mind wandered back to Belfast. He was in the Felon's Club in the Falls Road; the band was playing. They were all singing. Fenian songs. His songs. Drunken faces. Thick smoke, wild fiddles screeching away, bottles clinking, the music swirling around his head. Arms around each other, man to man, the girls gaggled together across the room, smiling across coyly. The falsity of jovial solidarity, fake friendships, he didn't believe any of them anymore.

He thought about the cash. A million dollars. In cash. How big was it, he wondered? A wad like that? In Switzerland. Enough to see him right in some far part of the world? Australia, Argentina perhaps. A new name, a clean passport and stay right down low.

But they'd look for him. The Nutting Squad. Killers. Sleeveens, the lot of them. Keep the fantasies away, boyo. His head kept spinning. He shut his eyes.

CHAPTER 9

Haydon's nostrils quivered at the hint of musty moss. The Villa Wolkonsky in autumn. Months without rain in the centre of the arid city, but still the gardens were filled with colours and smells. He strolled down the ancient, cobbled path alongside the aqueduct, built 2,000 years ago to bring fresh water to Rome. Pausing, he glanced up at the imposing house, covered in creepers. It had served as the HQ of the Gestapo during the war. He shivered. One of the better war reparations Britain got at the end of the Second World War.

He was feeling put upon. It had been so much easier in the Army; life without any need for compromise. Clarity of purpose and no mirrors required to remind you who you were, or weren't. Omnipresent superiors barking orders, telling you what to think. No need to consider other people's feelings, not even his own. Now he felt like some kind of damned shrink, figuring out how to get what you wanted from people, without issuing orders. He'd got DAEDALUS doing his bidding, he'd send him down the rat hole fast enough. Now it was time to smooth the guy's feathers.

Passing the swimming pool, tucked away from the main house in a shaded dell, he stood still, struck by the embracing noise of cicadas rising to an almost deafening crescendo. Abruptly the cacophony stopped, as if a conductor's baton had swept down. He turned and saw Charlie Lomax jogging up the track behind him, dressed in tennis whites and carrying a sports bag. He looked spindly in baggy shorts, running with loping strides.

"Morning, Charlie. Deep in meditation or thinking about girls?"

"It's a jungle here."

Straw Man

"Know the history?" Haydon pointed at the house. "When the Zionists blew up our Embassy in 1946, the Villa Wolkonsky served as our Embassy until the new one opened in 1971. Since then it's been the Ambassador's residence."

"My father's last post was Ambassador to the Holy See. We used to come here for tea."

"I forgot your diplomatic heritage."

"Still, every time I come I discover a new hidden gem – a rose garden, ancient pots, ponds, fountains, grottoes."

"If you want to keep being invited," Haydon swung his tennis racket in a practice stroke, "don't whack the ball directly at HE like you did last time. He's not the quickest of beasts."

"His ample belly will have protected him." Charlie frowned.

"What's bothering you?"

"Thinking about your indecent proposal."

"Talk after tennis. Sit and chat."

Giant umbrella pines shaded the tennis court from the chill wind. The Ambassador and a pink-faced man were knocking up when Haydon and Charlie strode onto the court. The Ambassador was a shortish, pugnacious man in his mid-fifties, fit for his age. He walked over to greet them. Haydon sensed his dislike. Which didn't seem to extend to Charlie.

"Morning Haydon, Charlie." The Ambassador's voice boomed. "Prepared for a run-around from your elders and betters, eh?"

"We'll see, Sir." Charlie smiled.

"You know Peter Etherington, our new second secretary? Haydon's latest protégé. Peter, meet Charlie Lomax, don't ask him what he does, he's a poor player." He guffawed. "Peter's a Tennis Blue, down from Oxford.

Straw Man

As he works for me, at least nominally, he'll be my partner. Hope you don't mind?"

"Haydon reminded me to apologise for hitting the ball into your midriff during our last game."

"Poppycock, obvious attempt to intimidate. Failed miserably." The Ambassador laughed. "Let's play. I'll serve."

Haydon waited while he bounced the ball up and down and prepared to serve.

They sat side by side on a stone bench in a grotto built into a bay of the aqueduct. The evening sun arched down between the pines, the shadows giving way to a shaft of sunlight which caught the mass of dog roses and burst them into colour. Haydon was panting; the match had been tough and even, he'd played badly and they'd lost. It annoyed him that it even bothered him. He took out a small cheroot and ran it under his nose. "Want one?"

"Filthy things." Charlie screwed up his nose and waved his hand in front of his face. "Remind me of my father. I went to see him yesterday. Depressing. Ageing is shite."

"Happen to you soon enough." Haydon leaned forward and lit the cheroot. "Better get used to the idea."

"Alzheimer's? Let's hope it bloody doesn't." Charlie grimaced. "Hard to recognise him, no longer a diplomat that's for sure – rude and aggressive. Except with his Eritrean nurse. She handles him like a naughty child."

"Enjoy life while you can."

Straw Man

"Look Haydon, I'm meeting Nasir el-Maghrebi this afternoon, straight from here. I'm nervous. He insisted on coming to my office. Wants to talk irrigation projects. He's going to suss me out, sniff my office."

"Let him sniff. Play the coy virgin."

"That's unnatural!"

"You can revert to your role of old tart later." He looks so young, Haydon thought, he's not ready for this sophisticated stuff. And he's already spooked. Still, at least it meant he's on board, he's already crossed the line in his mind. "You need him believing you're an innocent. Let him figure out how to corrupt you."

"Hint I might supply forbidden fruits?"

"Stick to irrigation, bang on. Bore him. Let him make the moves." Haydon leaned back and exhaled a cloud of smoke. "How was the weekend?"

"Grown up." Charlie chuckled. Haydon knew he and Ines had spent the weekend at the Vispoli's villa in Portofino. "Impressive guest list."

"Who?"

"The PM's bagman – Maximilian Ruff, ratty bloke. The Fiat guy, he's close to the Minister – elegant, smooth. The Christian Democrats have brought the Socialists on board for their policy of encouraging the so-called reformers in Libya. Other big wigs. Plenty of self-congratulation about juicy trade opportunities to seal the rapprochement – ENI, Fiat, Montedison and so on."

"Your friend Andrea is plumb in the centre of the power elite."

"They love him. He's charismatic. Always has been." Charlie gestured with an erect finger in front of his mouth. "I've a gobbet for you. A narrow circle, to treat with caution."

Straw Man

"What I do for a living," Haydon smiled and leaned forward, "listen to people's secrets, keep them under my first eleven cap. Think of me as a secular Confessor."

"No thanks," Charlie said. "The Libyans are making secret donations to political parties in the governing coalition. Andrea acts as a signatory for covert accounts in Switzerland belonging to the Libyan hierarchy. He let drop he made two payments. One at The Minister's behest."

"No surprise. He's known for being too close to big business." Haydon frowned. "And the other."

"Socialists. Ruff managed the transfer."

"Here's an unhinged Dictator arming himself to the teeth, determined to get his hands on an atom bomb. If he gets just one, just the other side of the Med. Well, surely–"

"–they get it, but they think they can steer the Libyans away from destructive behaviour, push them towards economic prosperity." Charlie said. "Might seem naïve, but you can't accuse the Minister of naivety. He's the Cardinal of Realpolitik."

"So the Libyans are paying the Italians for the privilege of being seduced by them. What an irony. And we have to worry about arms shipments to the IRA." Haydon turned to him. "My proposal. Ready to do the right thing?"

"Saving civilisation?"

"You'll earn a pile of cash." Haydon grinned. "Look Charlie, I've got approval to pay your Libya costs and a monthly retainer. Happy?"

"And my Get-out-of-Jail-Free card, so I can sleep nicely?"

"Wording being crafted. Not carte blanche, dirty minds think you might be tempted to abuse it. They're not trusting."

"And I am?"

Straw Man

"We want you comfortable." He reached over and touched his arm. "I'll make an initial payment. Good faith."

"I'm not–"

"–We need to kick this off now. Hook you up with these Swiss guys. Then you can make your decision, properly informed and reassured. No pressure. Meet in Zurich next week?"

"Next week?"

"From now on behave as if you're being surveilled, wiser to err on the safe side." He tossed the butt of his cheroot to the ground and stamped on it. "Peter Etherington will meet you on Monday. Report on your meeting with Nasir. And no phones, OK?"

"Got it. I could get to enjoy this Bond stuff. It's a little like infidelity, the honeyed frisson of deceit and forbidden pleasures, but–" he leaned back and laughed, "–with a *laissez-passer* in my wallet."

"Better to focus on an image of a violent husband coming home early carrying a large baseball bat–"

"–I'd be out the window in a flash."

Straw Man

CHAPTER 10

It had taken Charlie an hour to get to his office. Weaving in and out of motionless traffic, slicing through gaps between hooting cars and arm-waving and insult-shouting drivers. The wild Roman auto-polka cleared his head, zig-zagging between images of his angry father in his wheelchair and thoughts of the fruits of his forthcoming success. Things were nicely poised.

His office was in Parioli, in an anonymous block of flats in a mid-market residential area, inconveniently far from everything. Its principal virtue was low rent. It hinted at his real, rather humble, position in the pecking order of things, rather than the affluent one he sought to portray to his friends and business contacts – and carried off rather well, he thought. He was careful who he invited there. He would have preferred to meet Nasir on neutral ground, but maybe it was cleverer to let him glimpse financial frailty?

He tried to work through the paperwork on his desk, but voices in his head kept dragging him back to Haydon's proposal. If he played it right, he'd be at the top table when the big deals were being done. Italy-Libya trade was about to see a big uptick, he had the perfect in: with the companies, the Italians, the Libyans, and the dark arts of Haydon's department at his disposal. Subsidising his costs. But could he trust Haydon? There was something serpentine about him. No, he needed to fend for himself. If he stuffed it up, it would be worse than lost opportunities. But it would be a couple of years before they would deliver any 'items', maybe more. He might be able to engineer delays. He couldn't have dreamed it up, this one big chance. Not to be blown. Make a big enough return fast enough, get well away before things got rough.

Straw Man

The doorbell rang. He started. Springing up, he walked through the entrance hall towards the door. Pausing, he looked at himself in the mirror. Pasting a friendly smile onto his face, he smoothed his hair, winked at his reflection and opened the door.

The Libyan was taller than Charlie remembered, the mop of curly black hair giving him a wild look. He was dressed in a fawn safari suit, pockets all over the place. At first he thought the man was grinning, but his mouth was skewed and his eyes darted about, looking past Charlie and taking in the surroundings. Charlie ushered him into his inner office. They sat at a low coffee table facing long French windows, sipping coffee and looking out at the view over the lush green of the Villa Glori and the silver ribbon of the Tiber running north into the distance.

"Thanks for coming." Charlie smiled. "I'm grateful for the opportunity to tell you what my people can do."

"Mister Charlie, our relations with British are not good." Nasir looked at his fingernails, then scratched his face, avoiding Charlie' eyes, again looking past him over his shoulder. It was disconcerting. "We are alert to the danger of foreign agents. You see–"

"–hah, I'm honoured." He laughed, a deep-throated sound. "My friends all tell me I can't keep my mouth shut!"

Nasir rapped his finger on the table. He paused and glared at Charlie. "You stay in touch with people at the British Embassy?"

"Yes, naturally. I know the Ambassador, play tennis with him."

"Mr Khalfari asked me to find out the real reason you wish to come to Libya. Not many English are queuing up to visit."

Straw Man

"Opportunism. I'm a salesman." Charlie sipped his coffee. He could feel dislike permeating from Nasir, he could almost smell it. "The question is, what can I sell you? I'm what you might call catholic in my approach."

"You studied languages, Andrea tells me? What do you know about agriculture?"

"Not enough to feed myself. But my Swedish and Swiss firms know a great deal." He leaned forward and pressed his hands together, frowning. "Look, Mr Nasir, if you'd rather not deal with me, I understand. My people can come down and explain to you directly how they can help fulfil your Leader's plans."

"You misunderstand me. I wish to understand your motives?"

"Andrea Vispoli is a good friend. His party was a perfect opportunity to meet Mr. Khalfari. He's an important man." Charlie smiled. "You need high-tech agriculture, improved versions of the centre-pivot irrigation systems you're using at Kufra. I can supply brilliant solutions."

"You might help us with items we're having difficulty sourcing?"

"I'm well connected in many areas. What did you have in mind?"

"We're building a civil nuclear reactor at Tajura. Research purposes only. Our Russian friends are constructing it. We need certain items, mainly to do with enrichment."

"Tough sector. People and companies want to operate with a certain deniability, but I could probably help, yes."

"We don't care about deniability; we're interested in reliability and discretion."

"You provide a list, I'll respond."

Charlie' eyes followed Nasir as he abruptly stood up and walked over to the window, leaning out and staring down at the piazza below. He stayed

Straw Man

like that for a while, shading his eyes with one hand and scratching his neck with the other. Finally he turned back to Charlie, donning a pair of thick dark glasses.

"Are you for real?" he looked at Charlie, eyes hidden behind the heavy shades, his mouth pinched as if to sneer. "You see, I keep wondering."

"Yes, I often wonder that myself–"

"–bring your people to Rome. They can make a presentation to me at my office. I'll fax you a list of items we're looking for. Then I'll decide whether we want you to come to Tripoli."

Nasir lounged in a deep armchair in Andrea Vispoli's study, nursing a coffee, a cigarette burning down in a crystal glass ashtray on a side table. Bookshelves lined the walls on three sides, the fourth was dominated by an open French window through which evening light streamed into the room. His eyes followed the snakes of late autumn leaves blowing around the garden like ghostly creatures. He shivered. He missed the vital heat of home; he was a desert nomad to his bones.

He glanced over at Andrea. His friend was sitting behind his desk, staring out of the window and talking into the phone, waving his arms about, the handset tucked under his chin. He didn't look like a business tycoon, more like the hippy he'd met all those years ago.

Nasir had come to Rome as a language student, part of an Italian Government aid initiative. Italian was then the second language of Libya, and Rome the natural destination for further education for Libyan students showing promise. Andrea was the first Italian friend he made, maybe the only one. His friendly demeanour surprised him. Living an impecunious

Straw Man

student life, sharing a small, cheap flat on the outskirts of Rome with four other Libyan students, he had little opportunity to meet people. Andrea had taken him under his wing.

When he'd returned to Tripoli, they lost touch. A decade later, when Nasir's star had risen in Qaddafi's revolutionary Libya and he'd been appointed to an important role at the Libyan People's Bureau in London, he'd contacted Andrea. They'd met on a glorious spring day at the rooftop bar of the Hotel Raphael, sitting at a corner table overlooking the rooftops of Rome.

It was his first recruitment operation. His new boss, Ahmed Khalfari, had a reputation for intolerance of failure. He'd told him this would be a test of his ability to work in overseas operations. His orders were to identify and recruit a confidential agent who would manage covert bank accounts with no obvious connection to Libya. He'd been nervous, but the meeting with Andrea had gone well. His old friend had expressed concern about the possibility of any links to Palestinian groups, but Nasir had been able to reassure him.

He'd introduced Andrea to Khalfari, and they'd come to an agreement. Andrea opened the accounts, and during the intervening years they'd grown in number and size.

He watched his friend laughing into the phone, cigarette ash dropping onto his lap. Nasir had increasingly come to rely on him as the relationship between Italy and Libya burgeoned. When Andrea's elder brother Marco died two years before, crashing his Ferrari into a bridge, Andrea had taken over running the family construction business. But he'd continued to manage the accounts. He knew that Andrea suspected everything wasn't perfectly clean, but access to these funds provided a distinct advantage in

Straw Man

building up the family construction business, and the associated political influence gave him an advantage over his peers.

Nasir stood up and walked over to the window. An elderly gardener was bent over, raking leaves into a large pile. A sudden gust of wind blew the pile off into a long dust devil. The gardener looked up at the sky.

He was walking a wobbly tightrope, sending out moderate signals, playing Khalfari's reasonable tune, at the same time maintaining covert relations with radical Palestinian groups, the IRA, ETA. Sometimes receiving direct, often contradictory, orders from the Leader. Andrea wasn't aware of this, so he couldn't turn to him for advice. At last Andrea put down the phone and looked up at Nasir.

"All done, payment's gone to Ruff's nominated account. Getting the Socialist Party on board is a big step forward. You'll be able to complete the arrangements for Khalfari's official visit."

"And the other–?"

"–already done. A million dollars."

"Was that his little joke, the account name?"

"Probably, The Minister's known for his wit."

"Dressing up an inducement as charitable giving?"

"Nasir, don't you get it?" Andrea rubbed his chin and smiled. "We Italians revere hypocrisy. It's why we admire the English so much."

"This Charlie guy." Nasir inhaled on a cigarette, blowing a smoke ring towards the ceiling. "I went to see him. I don't know, there's something doesn't figure. You see, Andrea, we trust you, but Khalfari doesn't like Englishmen."

"Oh, he's hardly English! Spent most of his life in Italy. We're the oldest of friends, since we were eight. I know him through and through. He's like me, Nasir, he likes a good time, to enjoy life, to sail, make big money. He sees an opportunity in Libya. If I had a criticism, it's he doesn't take life seriously. He'll do things he shouldn't to make big bucks."

"Can we trust him?"

"He's connected with important companies around Europe. With access to advanced technologies." Andrea leaned forward and continued in a confidential tone. "Your requirements for a peaceful nuclear research programme, it's controversial, you know that. I can't be seen to help you, the Americans will be out to hinder you. Where's the risk? Try him out and see what he comes up with. He'll be confidential, I'll stress the need for discretion."

"You say." Nasir thought for a moment. "Maybe you bring him to Tripoli. I need a little time, you see, do more digging, work out the angles, I need to cover my ass."

CHAPTER 11

From the back of the Zum Storchen Hotel, from the cheaper rooms that is, Haydon could almost reach out and touch the Paradeplatz, home to the largest Swiss banks and their infamous numbered accounts. He thought about those banks and their dark secrets. What was their purpose other than to promulgate and perpetuate malign power? Entrepôts of illicit human activity: Nazi gold, revolutionary accounts, drug dealers, bank robbers and black funds from half the world's intelligence services, plain and simple tax dodgers: every conceivable form of pond life. Still, he'd like one if he could afford it. *Dream on.* His was a profession where they peeked down on the stage from behind a thick curtain, they were never part of the action on view.

He stood leaning over the balustrade on the veranda of his room, staring down onto the small square and the hotel café, colourful with large umbrellas and tablecloths, a hive of activity. He could see Charlie sitting quietly at a corner table, smoking a cigarette and scanning a newspaper. He saw that Charlie had finished his coffee and was waving at the waiter for his bill. Leaving his room, Haydon pulled a cap down over his eyes and strolled down the back stairs, standing motionless near the main entrance until he saw the tall figure wandering past.

The guy needed training, he'd ensure he got it: it could be a life and death thing. Following him was a breeze. Charlie meandered aimlessly through the maze of narrow streets that make up the old town, lingering in front of shop windows. He watched him jog across the busy tram lanes in the Paradeplatz, then paused to look into the darkened windows of UBS and SBC. Was he looking at his own reflection, vain bastard; or drooling

Straw Man

at the displays of unrestrained wealth? Haydon didn't make much effort to hide himself, he was curious to see if Charlie would spot him. Almost certainly not.

He followed him across the square, then darted into a tram shelter from where he had an unobstructed view. The younger man walked into the Sprüngli Café on the corner and past its long window displays festooned with multi-coloured macaroons. He walked on into the café at the back, where he found a corner table and sat down.

Haydon waited for five minutes before following him into the café.

Walking up to Charlie's table he said. "What's so amusing? You look like you've just eaten a slice of lemon. Is it the prices?"

Charlie started as Haydon patted him on the shoulder.

"Just because I've agreed to fund your business doesn't mean you can afford to drink coffee in Zurich."

"No, have a read of this." Charlie handed him the menu card and pointed at the potted history on the back–

"The Sprüngli café on Paradeplatz is a traditional meeting-place of the elderly ladies of Zürich's upper class. Local folklore has it that young men who attend the café alone may signal their availability to these well-to-do women by turning over their coffee spoons in their cups."

"Tailor made for a handsome guy like me." He laughed. "Safer than what you're proposing. Wouldn't work for you, not with your thinning hair and those awful Hush Puppies."

Haydon's eyes scanned the room, and he noticed several attractive middle-aged ladies, complete with fur stoles, sitting alone at banquette tables, smoking and looking well-to-do. Maybe he'd try it sometime.

Straw Man

"Don't knock my Hush Puppies. They've been padding silently behind you, keeping an eye out for your back–"

"–you've been following me?"

"You resembled a starry-eyed suburban window-shopper, dreaming and scratching your arse. You need to be alert."

"I haven't said yes. Maybe I won't."

"You will. You like the darkness of it, I sense it."

"How was London? The atmosphere?"

"Like May 1940. Fear. As if the world was shaken to its core. Shock that the IRA could get so close to decapitating the government." Haydon frowned. "Then came Mrs T's speech. Churchillian, the hairs stuck up on the back of my neck. The IRA had failed. This time."

"How did they get the bomb into her bathroom with all that security: dogs, searchers?" Charlie asked. "Should have been impossible."

"The Provos installed it six months ago. Checked themselves into the suite and worked away undisturbed. It sat there ticking ever since. The police are sifting through previous occupants day by day. Long process."

"Terrifying. The idea that bombs can be planted so far in advance."

"They used gelignite, wrapped it in multiple layers of plastic sheeting, sealed it in an impermeable container. Sniffer dogs useless. The Provos are upping their game."

"You've been dealt dodgy cards, Haydon."

That's the truth, he thought. They're closing in on us and we have our hands tied. His mind went back to the miserable streets of Strabane, patrolling on foot, seeing the soldier standing beside him shot in the neck. He'd never even heard the shot, just watched the guy crumple beside him.

Then watching the hate in the eyes of the crowd that gathered. He lit a cigarette and leaned back in his chair.

"Your meeting with Nasir? You were nervous."

"Came to my office. Sniffed me out, doggy fashion." Charlie leaned forward and lowered his voice. "Quizzed me about my contacts with HMG. I told him I had good relations with people at the Embassy, bragged a bit. Went over my contacts with suppliers around Europe."

"Friendly?"

"Made me queasy." Charlie replied. "But he's going to send me a list of items to quote for. For their nuclear power programme is what he said. Got my rod twitching."

"Good." Haydon patted Charlie's shoulder. "Time to bait the line."

"Who do I meet?"

"The company is Zantech SA. Offices at 16 Gottardstrasse, 6th floor. Ten minutes walk. Ask for Armin Fürrer, the CEO and owner." Haydon said. "He'll sign you up as their agent for Libya, subject to an exploratory visit in the country to assure himself of your contacts. Normal stuff. You just proceed as you would in any similar relationship. He knows me as John Sadler. Always use that name."

"John Sadler? OK. Suits you. Debrief?"

"Room 48 at 16.30, down the corridor from you. Stay alert for Chrissakes."

Straw Man

CHAPTER 12

Dr Armin Fürrer cut a Falstaffian figure, a fat man with a fat-belly-laugh and a crooked smile. Wearing a loud tweed jacket, trousers of a salmon pinkish colour favoured by a certain sort of Englishman in summer, and a yellow bow tie. As they shook hands, Charlie felt as if his right hand had disappeared into a massive piece of moist velvet cloth.

"Yes, yes, Herr Lomax come in, come in, yes please sit. I've been looking forward to meeting. Our friend John Sadler said nice things. You are a perfect English gentleman, he says. Coffee? Yes?" He emitted a grunt and his body quivered with laughter. "There is such a thing? A perfect English gentleman? I doubt."

They sat at a long conference table presided over by a panoramic window with views over Lake Zurich and the snow-capped mountains behind. The furniture was Vitra, masculine chrome and black leather. Furious black and white abstract paintings covered the walls. Fürrer emitted another shaking noise and began a monologue about Englishmen he had known. Then he clapped his hands.

"To business. About my company. I founded twenty years ago in 1964. Myself alone, with my two sons. Our motto describes what I set out to do." Fürrer rubbed his hands together and laughed. "*'We find hard-to-get objects for customers all over the world'*. This has brought success ever since."

"What sort of objects?" Charlie asked.

"High-tech, high-quality engineering. Machinery, parts and know-how. Our clients are second or third world, they don't have the scientific depths to source the complex items they require. We help them, we advise them. We

Straw Man

make them happy." Fürrer vibrated with mirth, his chair seeming to bounce up and down with his shaking. "And we make a great deal of money."

"Good recipe."

"Appetising, yes, yes. Offices or partners around the world including Zurich, Chicago, Malmo, Karachi and Djakarta. We assemble machinery in plants in Turkey and Singapore."

"Sadler told you I'm working with senior people in the Libyan Government." Charlie lit a cigarette and leaned back. "They're embarking on an investment plan funded by increased oil revenues–irrigation, agriculture, power generation and other sectors. I'm looking for a partner to help me supply their procurement programme."

"We have seen lists circulating in the trade," he smiled at Charlie, "so we understand what they're looking for, much of which seems—at least at first glance—to be for their civil nuclear power research centre."

"Which would not be restricted?" Charlie asked.

"The lists I've seen include items that could be considered 'dual-use', but there are ways of navigating around these constraints. For example," Fürrer leaned back in his chair and adjusted his bow tie, "instead of ordering a complete assembly which might be restricted, a customer could place orders for its component parts, materials and precision machine tools, which we can supply."

"Legally?"

"Oh yes. But we increase prices as if it's illegal."

"No come back?"

"We'll have supplied unrestricted sub-components. Kosher as a Dover sole, you say?" He beamed and laid his pudgy hands flat on the table. "If the customer contracts in Asia or elsewhere to reassemble the pieces into a complete, and therefore a restricted item, that would be no affair of ours."

"Seems absurd."

"Yes, absurd. And we have advantage that your Mister John Sadler has our backsides covered."

"A soothing thought."

"Made simpler," Fürrer went on, "by Eisenhower's 'Atoms for Peace' initiative, which encouraged countries to build peaceful nuclear reactors. Did you know the US built reactors for Iran, Israel, and Pakistan under this plan?" Fürrer burst into another fit of laughter. "All of which have subsequently built nuclear weapons programme."

"Crazy."

"So you see, things are confused."

Charlie sensed that Dr Fürrer's jocular exterior disguised a sharp wit and intelligence. Greedy, that was obvious. Could he be trusted? Certainly not, the overpowering aroma of avarice was too strong. Travelling to Libya with him would be entertaining. He wondered what the humourless Libyans would make of him.

"So, next step." Charlie got out his diary and lay it on the table. "Meeting with Nasir el Maghrebi in Rome? I introduce you, we go over their list of items; tell them what we can and can't supply?"

"Now listen. All meetings are covert. All meetings. No names. Never. No introductions. They'll expect it that way. We shake hands and smile. We talk. That's the way it's done in this business. You need to remember, it's your–" He emphasised the word, his face had changed from roguish to somehow menacing, "–branding on the box. Your name, your face.

Straw Man

That's how you'll earn your money. You've nothing else to contribute. Never mention the names Zantech or Fürrer or Sadler."

"But they'll find out?"

"Never spoken, so they can't be picked up by recording devices or phones. Understand? You are our *uomo di paglia* - our Straw Man."

"Meaning?"

"Meaning you'll get paid a lot for placing your handsome mug in the middle of the frame. While the rest of us stay well concealed in the undergrowth."

"Straw Man, I've been called worse!"

They agreed on dates for Charlie to organise a meeting with Nasir.

"Goodbye Charlie, if I may call you that. I look forward to a deal of fun and mountains of profit."

"Armin, a pleasure. I'll be in touch."

Haydon watched Charlie pull the cork out of a bottle of Blauburgunder and reach over to fill their glasses. They had their overcoats pulled tight and scarves wound around their necks. Seated on the veranda of Haydon's room, they looked down over the river. The November sun had brought out the crowds, people were strolling along the riverside.

"Not bad, considering the rotten climate around Zurich. Drinkable."

Haydon rolled the wine around in his glass, peered into it, sniffing it. Nothing like Her Majesty's expense account to improve a vintage. He looked over at Charlie. Our man in Havana and he's my vacuum cleaner salesman? Maybe that was too cynical. Perhaps he actually would provide the keys into the IRA connection. Or maybe he wouldn't.

Straw Man

"Did you like him?"

"Fürrer? Rotund rogue, questionable whether he's on the side of the good guys?" Charlie laughed and sipped his wine. "With the existential threat from nuclear proliferation, is it all as terrifyingly simple as he makes out?"

"'Fraid so, we western intelligence agencies act as gamekeepers, but illicit supply networks keep popping up all over the place. Atomic whack-a-mole." Haydon grimaced. "South Africa, India and Pakistan, Egypt, China, Iran, Brazil, North Korea, Israel, Iraq, Argentina and others, they're all trying. A long list. Swapping technologies with each other; drawings for rocket motors from one in return for centrifuge ranges from another. Some of them helped by France, others by China."

"Your wheeze of inserting faulty parts into these supply chains works?"

"Great success. We are the masters of deception, remember. What's elegant is, building a nuclear weapon is so complex, the science so difficult, that when the process goes wrong–as the result of our defective parts," he paused, flicking his cigarette out towards the river, "the recipient usually believes they didn't get the process right."

"But the IRA." Charlie stubbed his cigarette out, grinding it into the ashtray. "There's no way I can bring that subject up, they'd smell a skunk straight away."

"Trust me. I wouldn't be paying your costs if I didn't think I'd get value for money."

"But the Libyans will never–"

"–they may not, but you'll pick up what may seem to you to be little things. You won't understand them, but I will." He reached into his pocket and took out a thick envelope, handing it to Charlie. "First of many, I hope."

Straw Man

"Many what?"

"Cash. Three thousand. Kick start your Libyan enterprise." He beamed. "Your retainer will start next month. You're officially operational."

"Happy days!" Charlie put the envelope into his jacket pocket, refilled his glass and raised it. "May this trickle grow into a gushing waterfall."

Haydon watched Charlie lean back and close his eyes, a look of contentment on his face. Innocent lamb to the slaughter. He stared down at the tourists ambling along the river, throwing lumps of bread to the swans, taking photographs. The wine was doing its job. He felt a surge of pleasure. Lomax had reached out and taken the King's shilling and now belonged. To him. The afternoon sun warmed his cheeks. He listened to the sounds of glasses clinking at the waterside bar, the hubbub of raised voices. He needed to nurture him, give him the best chance of establishing himself in the Libyan nest.

"A word of caution." Charlie opened his eyes; Haydon reached behind his neck and started massaging it. "You're not trained, not in the arts of deception. So you'll be on my conscience. I want you always to play it safe, don't take risks, don't get overconfident. Err on the side of caution."

"My strong point Haydon."

"Just let it come to you, no need for you to stir the pot. Please."

"Got to go." Charlie stood up and started packing papers into his briefcase. "Airport."

Haydon stood and walked him to the door, looking Charlie in the eyes.

"Now we're going live I'm running counter-surveillance around you, checking your back, I'll sweep your office and flat for bugs." He reached out and touched Charlie's arm. "Get used to the idea you're being followed, watched. We need to know if the Libyans trust you. Most likely they don't."

Straw Man

"My Protector! I am reassured my back is covered. Don't worry about me, Haydon. I'm a born survivor." Charlie waved. "See you on the tennis court."

Next morning Haydon was leaving his hotel room for the airport when the phone rang. He dashed back and picked up the receiver.
"Talbot."
"Sergeant Stoner here." A woman's voice with a slight Ulster intonation. "Peter Etherington asked me to update you."

Julia had briefed him about this woman Troop Leader, describing her as impressive and efficient. Modern times. Back in his day, a female commanding a section of elite front-line troops would have been unthinkable. It wasn't what he expected, or wanted, for a sensitive op. She'd be a dragon, he thought. You'd need to be a dragon to keep a bunch of hard men in line. And The Det had the reputation for extreme toughness. The troop had assembled in Rome that week, and he'd deployed them immediately to watch Charlie's back.

"Go ahead."
"Your target got himself a tail. We were lucky. Sergeant Cooper and I were parked up on the kerb as he drove out of the airport car park. His red Alfa's easy to eyeball. I was about to pull out and follow when I clocked a taxi pulling in a little too close behind him. Just didn't look right. We held back, followed them like a procession to via Garibaldi. Target parked his car in his garage. Taxi drove on. That's it."
"You get eyes into the taxi?"
"Negative. Driver, one in the back."

Straw Man

"Roger that. Stay on him. Come to see me at the Embassy tomorrow please."

Christ! They were on to Charlie. That was a worry. They couldn't have been around them in Zurich? No, he'd been alert. Maybe they'd followed him from his flat on his way out, staked out his car. But that demanded dedication. He wouldn't have thought the Libyans so capable. He'd need to redouble vigilance. He grabbed his case and dashed for the door.

Straw Man

CHAPTER 13

There's something almost sacred, Charlie thought, about the bonds with one's oldest childhood friend. Your journeys through life diverge, your interests change, the circles in which you move, your love life, but your oldest friend remains your oldest friend. Nothing gets in the way; you don't have to try. Still, he was aware of the disparity in wealth and power between them. They didn't live life on even terms. Andrea never said anything, but it niggled.

He was riding his Vespa, wobbling from side to side in frustration as he made slow progress through the throngs that crowded the narrow streets zig-zagging parallel to the Via del Corso. Ines was riding pillion, dark hair flowing behind her, singing and beating time on his shoulder. He'd got back from Zurich, dropped his bag, lifted her up and danced her around the small flat.

"I did it! I'm on the up elevator! Come on, we're going out to celebrate. Meeting Andrea at *Jackie O*. Get changed!"

He thought back to his first encounter with Andrea. He'd been scrapping in the schoolyard at St George's with a tall boy from the year above. Charlie's nose was bloody, but he had got the other boy on the ground in a half-Nelson and was about to win the fight, or so he thought, when this grown-up looking face with an unnaturally large nose peered down over them. He'd beamed a wide smile and reached down to pull them up, put an arm around each of them and walked them towards their class. "Come to my house after school? We're going to eat a giant sea lobster tonight."

He had gone to supper, and so had begun their friendship.

Straw Man

He emerged from the city centre gridlock and sped up the Via Veneto, tyres squealing as he turned into via Boncompagni, pulling up in front of the entrance to the *Jackie O* and hauling the scooter up onto its stand. The uniformed doorman waved them past the waiting queue, palming a banknote as Charlie brushed past him.

They walked up the garish mirrored staircase hand in hand, smiling confidently at the multiple images of themselves, on past the dance floor to the VIP area. A scantily dressed cigarette girl pouted as she raised the tasselled cord to let them pass. The club was buzzing. Although it was only just after midnight, the floor was packed with gyrating figures. Strobe lights flashed out a black and white tableau below them, dancers frozen, arms raised high, heads bent back. A young waiter dressed in white led them to a leather padded booth, then removed the 'Reserved' sign from the table.

"Champagne, Enzo. A bottle of Perrier-Jouet."

"Good God, Kiko, what's come over you?" Andrea's face appeared and leaned over him. He put an arm around Charlie's neck and pulled him up, leaned over and kissed Ines. "Pick someone's pocket? Or just filthy drunk?"

"He's made a little money and wants us to know it." Ines said, ruffling Charlie' hair. "Hope he remembers to pay the electricity bill."

"Bloody rude! Not just to know it." He grimaced. "But to help me spend it. Big difference. To my ever-increasing success!" The three of them drained their glasses.

"Another bottle, go on. No need to skimp, Kiko."

"Gotta thank you for the introductions to Khalfari and Nasir." He smiled at Andrea. "It's kicking off, looks like I'll be supplying a lot of gear."

"Legally?"

"Kiko doesn't give a shit about legally." Ines laughed. "It's the cash he's after!"

"Your friend Nasir doesn't like me much. He's a suspicious type."

"Came to see me. Digging for dirt." Andrea was sitting between the two of them, an arm around each.

"That's encouraging." He grimaced. He was feeling a buzz from the champagne. "Shows he's interested."

"Naturally I told him what an arrant shit you are."

"So nothing personal?"

"Icy relations with the British ever since the Embassy shooting. I wouldn't read much into it. I think he's a bit shy."

"A shy bogey-man." Charlie laughed. "Oxymoronic."

"You two will never grow up." Ines stroked his cheek. "It's another of your games."

"We're the bent jokers surrounded by upright hypocrites."

"How do you work that one out?" Ines said.

"This afternoon I had to transfer a million dollars for the Libyans. For the Minister. To the Vatican Bank. The account name is wonderful–*'for the widows and orphans of the poor and miserable'*. Charitable donation."

"That's a novel description." Ines chuckled. "A scoop for me?"

"It would be your last one." Andrea poked her with his finger.

"Only joking!" She giggled.

"I like it, it's imaginative." Charlie ran his hands down Ines' back.

"You guys, it's not a game." Ines leaned forward and poked her finger at Charlie. "These Libyans support terrorists, not just Palestinian groups but others–Red Army Faction, IRA, ETA. You can't just brush–"

Straw Man

"–Ines, I know these people." Andrea turned to her and smiled. "Yes, they keep tabs on those groups. Just bargaining chips in their pockets, they toss them on the table when they negotiate with the West."

"Take me with you to Tripoli." Ines pouted and blew a kiss to Andrea. "I want to meet these guys, to interview Qaddafi."

"And you say it's not a game?" Andrea threw his arms open in a gesture of openness. "I'm drunk. Let's get on the dance floor."

CHAPTER 14

The two men hunched side by side at the window of a 3rd floor room at the Hilton Hotel, perched on a hill facing down towards Vatican City. Peering through rubber eyepieces, Haydon could see over the small terrace and into the living room. The glass doors were wide open and Nasir el-Maghrebi was slouched on a sofa watching TV, drinking from a glass.

It felt good to be on the front foot. And working with Army people. It cheered him up and reminded him of the camaraderie that was sorely missing amongst his SIS colleagues. Banter which kept your spirits up when wheels were at risk of coming off. The long binoculars, mounted on a heavy metal tripod, were angled downwards, pointing directly towards the lights of a residential apartment building set back from the via Trionfale some 200 yards down the steep hill below them. He carefully traversed the heavy instrument upwards. He could easily make out the alarm panel in the corridor behind.

"Cooper, have a gander." They changed places. The brawny man leaned into the eyepiece. "The alarm pad. What do you think?"

"It's doable. This Generation 2 gear is sharp. If we're lucky, it'll be four digits." Cooper reached forward and adjusted a screw, moving the crosshairs one click to the left. "We should be able to make out the pattern of his finger movements, save us a world of grief. Guy looks like a right creep."

"Libyan bogey-man. Not to be underestimated."

"My Enfield Enforcer would put a big one right through the middle of his forehead. Bastard wouldn't know a thing. Bang!" Cooper made as if to pull a trigger. "Save us from all this buggering about."

"Nice idea, wouldn't help us find the Irish boyos. They're the ones you need to drop. And we're unarmed."

"Unarmed?"

"Orders. This op is way past black." Haydon turned and gave him a hard look. "You lot are not here. You are optical illusions."

"My aching butt tells me I'm not an illusion. My arse hurts, therefore I am." Cooper's face wrinkled. "I'll feel naked, running a black op bare-assed?"

"Do your jobs properly you don't need to be tooled up."

"Let's hope he heads out soon." Cooper yawned and leaned back. "Might be a long wait."

"Relief team will be here in an hour. I'm getting too old for this malarkey."

"Come back to the Province. We'll sort you out."

"I've done my time there. No bullet holes. I prefer the sunshine now."

Haydon looked into the eyepiece. Nasir appeared relaxed, unaware. Maybe he was really good? They were dangerous ones; the ones that knew how to act to deceive you. Operating on full alert with their peripheral vision, while you thought they were drinking beer and watching TV.

"Will it be midnight creeping?"

"Probably not. He does long hours at the Embassy, plenty of daytime opportunity. You'll be phone engineers."

"Plant audio and video?"

"Pillage documents while you're at it." He gestured to the eyepiece. "See that filing cabinet in the corner of the living room?"

Cooper moved over and peered into the eyepiece. "Got it."

"You'll fillet it. Take photos."

"How long we surveil before we act?"

"Need to be sure of his patterns. A couple of weeks maybe. January."
"Who'll go in?"
"Plan for four, lightweight. Lock man - your best *schlosser* to manage the alarm. Three for muscle, look out and search."

Haydon stood up and started pacing the room. Staying alert was the draining bit, those endless, uncomfortable hours of monotony. He remembered lying up in the roof trusses of a house in Newry, leg jammed against a wobbly timber frame, rifle jammed into his shoulder, watching for a sniper to poke his head out of the old tyre factory. Which he never did. Let your guard down for a few seconds and risk missing the thing that would keep you safe. Could be months. And sometimes the months led you nowhere, and you had to start all over again. No, he preferred his comfy office chair.

The internal phone on Haydon's desk was ringing as he walked in.
"Job done. Someone's been busy. I've got the team here."
"Bring them in Peter." He replaced the receiver.

Haydon watched Babs Stoner enter with Skelton, a tall, almost bald, stooping man with a mournful face. She was wearing a trouser suit and her hair was tied back. She had an Israeli look to her, he thought, stern and unsmiling. Behind them came Peter, carrying a thick folder. Haydon motioned them to sit.

"I gather you worked this one together?"
"This is Skelton." Babs gestured. "My techo. He'll report on the sweep."
"Result?"

Straw Man

"His car was clean, which is something I suppose. A pretty little red Alpha Spider. Devices at his flat and his office." Skelton talked in a ponderous tone, long pauses between each phrase, as if he were speaking in Morse code. "Simple audio transmitters, up to date, US manufacture, professional grade, wired into the telephone system. Turns the phone instruments into voice activated microphones – frequency flooding we call it. Transmits audio to nearby receiver-recorders. Mounted outside in disguised junction boxes–"

"–which need to be serviced?"

"Every week I should think. Replace the cassettes. Cumbersome, but works well enough. We left them that way, of course."

"So we watch the Libyan watchers, see who they've got managing them, maybe place CCTV to monitor the boxes?" Haydon asked, swivelling his chair back and forth. "No chance the devices picked up evidence of your sweep?"

"None." Skelton replied sharply. "We made cleaning-lady noises, turned on the vacuum cleaner, the radio, the kettle. Masked all sound whilst we disassembled the phones."

"Good. We use the bugs as a helpful back conduit." He turned to Peter. "Peter, brief Lomax before he leaves on his Christmas trip. Warn him about the devices and tell him we're leaving them operational. He's to act as if there are bugs everywhere, even his car. He's an excellent actor. That's it."

"As Peter instructed, I've had a loose watch on you two." Babs said. "So far no signs of hostiles."

"Reassuring but keep the watch running. We're not going to underestimate these guys. They're rough monkeys."

Straw Man

Haydon sat at a long table in the ops room at the Embassy in front of a bank of phones and radios. His foot was tap-tapping on the floor. Babs sat next to him, headphones covering her dark hair, murmuring into a mouthpiece. He was about to find out how good this Det lot really were. So far, so promising. The teams' walkie-talkie traffic was being relayed live from Frankfurt via phone link. Every few minutes the silence was broken by tinny, distorted voices squawking from a large speaker on the wall. The room was airless and windowless, a low hum of air conditioning dampening the voices.

A GCHQ intercept of an unguarded phone call to Tripoli from the People's Bureau in Rome had tipped them off that Nasir would travel on the Monday. No destination mentioned. Skelton had hacked the IATA system in Rome and traced a booking in his name on an Alitalia flight from Fiumicino to Frankfurt at 09.00. It had been tight, but a team had deployed to Frankfurt airport ahead of the target's inbound flight.

They pinpointed Nasir straight out of arrivals. He danced them around the city centre for several hours, obviously trying to scrub his back, using what was clearly a well-rehearsed routine. Train to the centre. In and out of two large department stores with sudden reversals and pauses. On and off the U-Bahn and city busses, a staccato sequence through an underpass followed by a dash through an empty park. On and off a tram at a half-run between stops and into a busy pedestrian shopping area in the Romerberg district.

Babs's team kept command of the target throughout, one pincer hurrying ahead, the team operating wide, switching back and forth in well-practiced moves. Haydon marvelled at the disciplined radio traffic. It was like

Straw Man

observing a game of 3D chess. Brief exchanges he couldn't decipher. But in a narrow one-way street by the town hall it had all broken down.

"*12.43 watcher five target jumped taxi marktplatz we're stuck in traffic lost him repeat lost him OVER*"

"*blue team leader all units call in sightings target query OVER*"

"*red team leader negative.*"

Babs thumped the table. She looked over at him. She was touching her neck with her right hand, her eyes seemed to be focussed inwards, her posture alert. She stayed stock still. He wondered if she'd frozen. Then she leaned forward and pressed the transmit button.

"*12.47 mainstay red team deploy immediate to airport blue team deploy immediate to main railway station all units watch international departures priority acknowledge OVER.*"

They'd lost him. Needle in a haystack stuff. Not enough manpower, too thin. So that was that, start all over again time. And wait for how many weeks, months? Shit. That was the thing about watching, it was long haul stuff. And you needed luck. He got up and wandered over to the coffee machine.

"Want one?"

"Pour me a strong cup of cyanide."

"I'll make a pot."

They sat quietly sipping their coffees. People dashed about, frantically checking flight and train schedules and reading them out on the HF radio. Haydon felt a familiar buzz. The metallic shiver of an op in midstream. Somewhere between boredom, despair, and exultation. Anything could happen. He looked down and saw his foot tapping up and down again. He laughed.

Straw Man

"Something funny?" Babs squinted at him.

"It's my feet. They're tapping away. On their own. It's a good augur, believe me."

"I didn't have you down as the superstitious type."

The relay speaker crackled–

"*15.33 watcher seven target boarded Geneva direct train repeat target boarded Geneva direct train watcher two following OUT*".

"Cooper, bless that ugly papist bastard and his eagle eyes." She pumped the air, turned to Haydon. "He'll go out of range. I'm ordering my teams to Geneva. Gut tells me we should be there."

"My head agrees. Let's go."

CHAPTER 15

Like a bloody American tourist's whistle-stop tour of Europe, Seán thought. It's Thursday, so that bleeding great waterspout in the middle of the lake proves I'm in Geneva. It had taken him five days to travel from Belfast, but he revelled in the feeling of being lost in time, away from the bitterness of the dark city.

He'd spent two nights in Brussels, during which he switched hotel and identity. He'd left his city centre hotel at dawn that morning and padded the empty streets, following a planned route designed to flush out watchers. There weren't many cars about at that hour, just a few pedestrians, heads down against the rain, scurrying to early jobs.

Three hours later he was at the main railway station from where he boarded a direct train to Amsterdam, paying cash for his ticket onboard. He ran another circuitous routine around the narrow streets of the old town, pausing on bridges over canals and doubling back, sitting on benches by the water and jumping on and off trams until the hairs on the back of his neck signalled there was no inkling of surveillance. He was black. They should make it an Olympic sport, he thought. Spooks hide-and-seek. Good for fitness levels and enjoyable to boot, but he reminded himself there was a deadly cost for failure. He took a taxi to the airport, caught a flight to Geneva.

The Hotel de la Cigogne was tucked away in a little square, away from the bustle of Geneva's city centre. The reception area was a deep burgundy colour and felt warm and cosy as Seán came in from the blustery street late in the evening on a wild winter's day. He handed the receptionist a dog-eared Irish passport in the name of Peter Hennessy. The Receptionist

Straw Man

was an elderly, stooped man with a boxer's nose. What kind of man ended up as a night receptionist, such a solitary job? Like his. The man handed him back his passport together with a red tasselled room key. "Room 58, Monsieur. Second floor. Lift is over there," he gestured then said unctuously. "Let me know if there's anything I can do to make your stay at the Cigogne more pleasant."

"Sure I will." Seán turned and walked to the lift. The guy's a midnight pimp, but his stay wouldn't be more pleasant if he said yes. No, he'd wake with a dreadful hangover and an empty wallet.

His room was large and comfortable, affording a view up to the lights of the Old Town. He double-locked the door and made a slow examination of the bedroom and bathroom, checking the cupboards and drawers and glancing under the bed, peering behind pictures. Behind the double-bed hung a portrait of an elderly, severe-looking man in military regalia, a row of medals decorating his bottle-green coat. He seemed to glare down at Seán with a disapproving stare. He placed his overnight bag on the bed, unlocked it, and clicked open the catches.

Taking a small penknife from his pocket he carefully slit the stitching along the inner lining, removed an envelope and two passports which he placed in the wall safe together with his Hennessy passport. He locked the safe, pocketing the key. The third passport was the one no one knew about. No one. A sweet blue British passport in the name of Robert James Albert Norton. A just-in-case secret he'd treasured and stashed for that blessed rainy day. Which was now. One advantage of contacts with the Belfast underworld. The Jewish guy who'd done him the passport had left Belfast and returned to his native Ukraine. Sweet of him. So no one knew.

Straw Man

He turned his attention to the minibar. All that running about had been exhausting. He deserved it, sure he did. He took out a beer, snapped off the cap, raised it in mock salute to the soldier in the portrait and took a long swig. *Disapprove all you like, you tight faced old bugger, I'll enjoy a couple!* Taking another swig, he drained the bottle, opened the minibar and took out another.

He sat down on the plush sofa and leaned back, closing his eyes, breathing slowly, massaging his neck with his hands. That was better. He'd stumbled into a once-in-a-lifetime opportunity to end his monotonous, rain-swept life in Belfast. To metamorphose into another human being, one of his own invention. In a new country, with a history he'd write for himself. He'd never have another chance like this. He got up and grabbed another beer from the bar.

Seán willed himself to stop these fantasies rolling around his head, conducting somersaults and jigs. *Chrissakes will you ever shut your bloody droning,* he told his jerky and disordered mind. The more he tried to quieten them with lectures about the morality of theft and the risks of betraying the Movement, the more the thoughts popped back into his mind. He tried to focus on the raw bleeding dangers of it, a bullet through the head maybe, or worse, you never knew with those butchers. Instead, he saw revolving visions of filling a suitcase with thick stacks of cash.

Tomorrow. A brand new case. A brand new life. That would be the moment of truth. He wouldn't come back to the hotel. Instead of taking the train to Lausanne and depositing the money in the bank as they'd ordered him, he'd walk to the lake, get on a boat and disappear. Stay calm, Seán. This was the time for focus. Make the jump and run.

Straw Man

The offices of Mathies & Rougemont Cie stood on their own in a narrow cul-de-sac in the centre of Geneva, set discretely back from the ranks of private banks that dominated both sides of the Rue du Rhône. As Seán approached the gleaming mahogany doors, they swung silently open and a tall, uniformed doorman gestured him towards a gilded reception desk.

"Mr Hennessy for Mister Rougemont, please."

The receptionist nodded and motioned towards the lift, where a uniformed attendant held the door open for him. Seán entered the wood-panelled lift, smelling overwhelmingly of polish. The lift ascended noiselessly. Stepping out into a thickly carpeted hall, another attendant ushered him down a corridor and into a meeting room lined with leather-bound law books. He motioned to Seán and left, closing the door behind him.

It's so unnaturally quiet, Seán thought. He could just about hear his own heart thumping; it was like being in a sodding anechoic chamber. The display of restraint shouted discretion, or was it just secrecy? Same difference? Stinks of money, everything so well-oiled. A blessed rarefied atmosphere, with a heavy hint of power. Heavens! An IRA foot soldier and a middling Libyan spook don't belong in this kind of place.

He sat down at the long cherry-wood conference table. He felt a little faint; he hadn't slept well. Those rotten, alluring thoughts and frightening images of discovery had kept circulating about his head. Even now he couldn't be sure he'd go through with it. He kept trying to block out the thoughts. He needed a drink. He felt his hands were trembling; sweat trickling down the back of his neck. *Must calm down.* The door opened and Nasir entered with a gaunt, elegant, man, both of them wearing dark suits and conservative ties. Seán stood up.

Straw Man

Nasir embraced him. "Welcome, friend. My lawyer Maître Rougemont." He motioned to the other man, stooped, grey-haired and with a blankly charming face. "How are you, friend? You look tired. Pleasant trip?"

"Lack of sleep is all. Long journey. Took forever. How the devil are you?" Seán smiled. They shook hands and sat down, the lawyer at the head of the table. "Mr Hennessy, may I please have your passport," he asked, "We require a photocopy for our records."

He took the Hennessey passport from his pocket and passed it across the table. Nasir picked it up and examined it.

"The letter of authorisation, please?"

He reached into his inner pocket and handed over an envelope. Nasir picked up a paper knife from the table, slit it open and read it. He passed it and the passport to the lawyer.

"I'll leave you gentlemen to conduct your business. Ring if you require anything." Rougemont motioned to a bronze bell button on the desk, took the passport and left the room.

"You received separate confirmation?" Seán said. Nasir nodded.

"This authorises me to make the payment in cash to you. Half a million dollars. Count it and sign the receipt here." Nasir passed a briefcase across the desk and chuckled. "Don't spend it all at once."

"Half a million?" Seán realised his voice sounded a little high. He attempted to calm himself. "A million Nasir? You told me a million at our Athens meeting? That's the amount I told my people expect."

"My instructions, Seán. They informed your people. Next payment will be a million, when the trial shipment has got through. Help you with the purchase of the larger vessel. We'll discuss it this evening."

Straw Man

It wasn't enough. Half a million won't buy me a new life. I'll need to wait. More waiting. *Jesus!* He breathed in deeply as he counted the thick bundles of notes, held together with rubber bands. He knew he was sweating; he needed to quieten himself. After two attempts at tallying the notes before losing count and starting again, he gave up and raised his head.

"That's fine then, all correct. Five hundred thousand dollars." He reached over and signed the receipt, handed it back to Nasir, avoiding his eyes. "We'll meet this evening then. Now I have to take this case on a little trip. Make my bosses happy. Well, so long as they don't think I've kept back half a million for myself!"

Seán left the lawyer's offices and walked up the cul-de-sac towards the Rue du Rhône. He flinched at a sudden movement by his ear and looked up. A pigeon raced out of a plane tree, flapping furiously, then darted up the road. As he followed it with his eyes, a face in the background seemed to stare at him. It turned away, a little too quickly maybe, and the man hurried off. Something about the demeanour, the setup, it seemed wrong. It niggled. Had he been made? Seemed unlikely. He quickened his step.

He took a taxi to the railway station, watching the traffic behind him, then jumped on a fast train to Lausanne. No one had rushed up onto the train behind him; nothing seemed out of place. He was certain he was black. Still, that face gnawed at him. Had he seen it before? Impossible.

The weather had changed. It was a glorious, warm autumn day. The sun massaged his face as he stared out of the train window over the shores of Lake Geneva towards the snow-capped peaks to the south. He tucked the suitcase under his seat. What a relief! It was like he'd had a let off. So

Straw Man

he wouldn't be starting a new life today. There was no crazy rush to stay ahead of unknown pursuers. The lake went hurrying by. His eyes followed two old-fashioned ferries making courtly progress across the water.

That roundish face. A farmer's face. He needed to stay alert. To steal from the Movement. Jesus, the thought. He'd build up his rainy day plan. Just in case. For another day, no fear today. His brain churned round and round. The lake shore disappeared from view as the train rushed into a dark tunnel with a snap that hurt his eardrums.

His mind went back to Belfast. Lord, how he hated it. The city of his wretched birth. Where he'd been made an orphan. A drunken Prod had run into his parents' car head-on when he was seven. Then the oscillation between greedy foster carers and vicious Boys' homes. And always the drink-sodden priests. Cruelty that made him strong. Turned him into a survivor. Gave him the anger that was somewhere there, the stored hatred from those punishments. And so he served the Movement. Which had become his family, given him the opportunity to get even with life.

Nothing positive ever seemed to permeate from odious Belfast, not even the glorious unreachable dream of a grand united Ireland. He no longer felt any spark of joy from drunken singing of rebel songs in crowded, smoky bars. About putting one in the eye of the vicious colonial power. That was the motivation, never about some golden age of Ireland that would follow an IRA victory. Just hatred of the occupying Brits and their arrogant, fearful, pink-faced soldiers. How much better to have something positive to work towards. A life that aimed for bright and optimistic things.

The train drew into Lausanne. He left the station and walked a few minutes to the address he'd memorised. The bank was small, unimpressive and anonymous. What a contrast with the lawyer's office. He'd been told

Straw Man

to ask for a Mr Ritter. He was ushered into a small, sparsely furnished, meeting room where he sat for a few minutes before a short, middle-aged man appeared. He noticed the spattering of dandruff on the man's collar.

Seán handed over the Peter Hennessy passport as identification, opened the case and deposited the fifty wads of dollar bills onto the table. The banker didn't seem surprised by the stack of cash. He brought out a small banknote counting machine from a cupboard, pulled off the rubber bands from the wads, and began stuffing them into the contraption. It made a satisfying whiffling sound as it counted.

"Five hundred thousand US dollars, Mr Hennessy. If you'd wait here, I'll draw up your receipt and take a copy of your passport."

Ritter lifted the wads of money onto a plastic tray and left the room. Through the glass partition, Seán watched him carrying it into the banking hall and handing it to a cashier. His eyes followed the man as he crossed the room, sat down at a desk, lifted the telephone and dialled. So they're monitoring me each step of the way. Makes sense, Seán thought, I'll need to plan a careful workaround, shorten the time I'll have before the hounds come baying. Reckon on getting maybe four or five hours' lead before the flares go up. If I've worked it all out, that'll be enough.

Ritter returned with a signed and stamped receipt which he handed to Seán, together with his passport.

Leaving the bank, he strolled over to the Metro station and took the steep funicular railway down to the lake shore. The whole thing had been easy. Large sums of cash didn't raise any eyebrows here. He would stash the money away and get out of Switzerland. Find a bank in Chiasso: that would be best. Right on the border with Italy. A short bus ride to

Straw Man

Milan. Only busses and trains until he was well away, several countries away, no records. Yes, that would work.

As he strolled from the crowded Metro station at Ouchy towards the lake, he turned the details of his future life over in his head. Out of the corner of his eye he spotted a tough-looking man sitting on a bench, reading a newspaper, a small carrier bag next to him. He was wearing a flat cloth cap pulled low over his face and had a distinctive birthmark on the left-hand side of his face. If Seán hadn't been alert, he might not have recognised him as the same man who he'd noticed wearing a raincoat and trilby when he boarded the train at Geneva that morning.

I know that face, his mind whirred. I've seen it in Belfast, somewhere on the street? Christ, they've suspicious minds, a babysitter even. He walked out onto the quay and bought a ticket for the next ferry to Geneva. Staying alert, ears and eyes pricked up at all times; survival, that was the target, survival until he'd got far, far away. He'd have lunch on board and snooze, maybe a couple of beers, relax a little before his meeting with Nasir that evening.

CHAPTER 16

Haydon was sitting alongside Babs on an overstuffed faux-velvet sofa in his hotel suite, watching a red sun coming up over the lake. He saw there'd been a dump of new snow on the Salève. It was going to be a brilliant winter's day; he'd woken before dawn in a blur of excitement. He stretched his arms up and yawned. He'd ordered Babs to deploy her full squadron to Geneva.

"Today's the day, it's in my bones. We're going to follow this Arab turd down any badger hole he runs to, and he's going to lead us right to his IRA contact."

Two burly comms operators were setting up military grade radio gear on the table, khaki canvas suitcases strewn on the floor. Haydon puffed at a cigarette and exhaled towards the ceiling.

"God, do I want one. More than a year now, the addiction doesn't let you alone." Babs's face was flushed, he noticed her lipstick was smudged. "Big day, and I've got a hangover. Your fault."

The evening before, they'd raced to catch a late flight from Rome. Cooper had picked them up at Geneva airport and briefed them on the drive into town.

"Nasir's train got in at 21.30. Guy walked straight out and got in a taxi."

"Aware?"

"No, didn't look about him. After all that dancing around in Frankfurt, I'm not surprised."

"Quite a pro. Ran you ragged?"

"Like advanced training, but with a bigger price to pay for failure."

"And?"

Straw Man

"Two of my guys trailed him to the Noga-Hilton, on the lake shore."

"Registered as?"

"Yousuf el-Badr. Room 3204."

Haydon raised his eyebrows.

"Silver changed hands. Portuguese Night Porter smiling."

"Well done, Cooper."

"I was getting jumpy yesterday." Babs wiped her face with a silk handkerchief. "I needed that break. Owe you one, Coop."

"Shitting hailstones I was. Jumped the train as it was moving off. *Polizei* shouting after me, I dropped my accessory bag on the platform. Whoever picks it up will be perplexed. I was sure he'd make me."

"You're wonderfully forgettable!" Babs punched his shoulder.

"Let's hope he hasn't come to Geneva just to squirm around with some ritzy mistress." Haydon smiled.

"Frankfurt proves he's up to something he doesn't want observed." The tyres squealed as Cooper braked suddenly and pulled into the kerb, looking all the while in his rear-view mirror. He let them out at the hotel and drove off.

Haydon and Babs had gone for a drink in the hotel bar, which turned into several. She didn't flirt or play on her femininity, neither did she seek to compensate by playing a laddish role. Like Modesty Blaise, he thought, maybe that was her role model. He was curious to find out how she'd made it to the top of this tough unit, but she'd deflected his probing and stuck to discussing the op and the options. He'd nearly made a pass, one more drink and he would have. He felt sure she'd wanted him to.

Straw Man

Shit. He needed to stay on topic. Looking up, he watched as the comms guys noisily tested the radios. He tried to concentrate on work papers but couldn't focus. He stubbed out his cigarette and drained his coffee.

"Babs. Today's deployments?"

"Six watchers on foot, positioned to operate a switching-box routine around the target as he leaves the hotel. One guy in the lobby, two cars on standby on the lakeside. Three watchers standing by in reserve."

He watched her curling her hair, twisting it round her forefinger. He'd seen her do that before. She was nervous, he realised. The loudspeaker crackled. He jumped up.

"*09.11 watcher one target solo on the move heading south on lakeshore OVER*"

"*Mainstay roger stay on target OVER*"

"*09.14 watcher one target turned left heading south on pont du mont blanc OVER*"

"*09.22 watcher four target turned right into cul-de-sac negative follow pulling back watching entrance address one zero two rue du rhône OVER*"

"*Mainstay one zero two rue du rhône checking location will revert OVER*"

"Peters, find out what's at that address." She turned to one of the Comms guys. "Chop-chop."

"Haydon, my watchers will interchange every few minutes. Altering items of clothing and accessories between each pass. Two men, two women. Concealed cameras. Snap every face coming out of the cul-de-sac."

"Sergeant, the building is a firm of lawyers. Mathies & Rougemont." The Comms guy struggled to pronounce the name. Haydon chain-smoked and fidgeted whilst they waited. Babs kept sniffing at the smoke, screwing up her face. How long before she gave in?

Straw Man

"*10.04 watcher three Seán Docherty repeat Seán Docherty exited cul-de-sac heading north direction lake confirm have photos green trousers beige anorak no headgear request instructions OVER*"

"*Mainstay to watcher three query did target two make you query OVER*"

"*Watcher 3 possible unsure OVER*"

Haydon watched as Babs turned her head up and scratched her scalp. She inhaled deeply. He could see her heart was thumping under her smock top. He could sense her mind whirring. Risk alerting the guy? Or losing him? She pressed the mike key–

"*Mainstay to all watchers stay in position on target one repeat stay on target one watcher three return base confirm OVER*"

Babs stood up and started pacing the room. "Can't afford to risk spooking him."

"Goddamit, we can't risk losing–"

"–no, can't. If he made my guy, he'll be on alert."

"And if he disappears? Total loss. Crazy!" Haydon flushed.

"Look, Haydon, Docherty was in those offices for less than half an hour." She reached over and took a cigarette out of Haydon's pack and lit it, inhaling deeply. "Likely they'll meet again. This evening or tomorrow. We'll stick on Nasir like limpets. We'll get a proper fix at the next meet."

"You'd better. Or we'll all be immersed in a carnival of manure."

It was pouring. Rome was so dramatically monochrome when it rained, all colour bleached out of the normally vibrant city leaving it seemingly a drab grey. Haydon leaned forward on his elbows and gazed out of his office window. A ghostly face reflected in the glass stared back at him with

Straw Man

a haggard look. He scowled back. He was wearing a double-breasted blue blazer, looking at his image, he straightened his regimental tie, then combed his hair.

He'd had an urgent summons back to Rome to nursemaid a visiting Ministerial delegation and caught the last flight from Geneva. He hadn't slept well. When he got home, Ros had been distant. She'd rolled away from him, pretending to be asleep. He wondered if he was emanating some kind of guilty pheromone. Even though he wasn't guilty of anything. Except the thoughts. He spent the next day waiting for updates and feeling dull, a sense of let-down after the excitement of the chase.

There was a knock on the door. He brushed ash off his blazer sleeve and stubbed his cigarette into a pewter ash tray.

"Come!" he barked.

Peter Etherington entered with Babs and Corporal Rathbone. Haydon stood up and shook their hands, gripping Rathbone's arm in a friendly gesture, feeling the hardness of the man's muscles. A stocky, flat-faced man, not tall, but jovial. A priest's face, he thought. And a toughie, you could tell. A loner.

"Well done. They told me you guys were good. They were right."

"Luck shined down." Rathbone spoke with a pronounced Ulster accent.

"Give me lucky Generals!" Haydon laughed.

"Lucky NCO's more like it." Babs couldn't disguise her femininity, he thought, even in a grey sweatshirt, baggy pants and trainers. She was absent-mindedly stroking her hair. "I was sweating. One day you make the calls and they work, another day it all goes wormy."

"Now we've got the IRA link nailed, we move into predator mode."

"I doubt Docherty is running this. There'll be a higher-up around."

Straw Man

"Follow the trail and we'll sniff him out." Haydon frowned, picked up a tennis ball and squeezed it. "Corporal Rathbone, it was you who clocked him?"

"His face flashed straight up, bells clanged in my head." Rathbone replied. "Guy wasn't wearing a hat. Clicked my camera, turned away and walked off sharpish."

"The evening meet." Haydon said, "Your team got close in?"

"We had eyes on Nasir from his hotel." Babs was doing that thing again, twirling a lock of her hair round her forefinger. "He ran a little routine, nothing challenging, doubling back, speeding up, looking in shop windows. Just before nine he circled back and entered a Chinese Restaurant on the lake shore close to his hotel–the Hung Wan. Ten minutes later, Docherty arrived in a taxi. They were there just under two hours."

"How did they seem?" Peter asked.

"Sat next to each other at the back of the nearly empty restaurant. Too risky to enter. I detailed a watcher to park across the street. Maggie. Got a few shots, here and here–" Rathbone laid a sheaf of photographs on the desk. "You can see, heads down, cosy, relaxed demeanour."

"Yeah, body language is warm."

"Maggie had one of these new parabolic mikes, you can focus them, range up to 15, 20 yards max, position was sub-optimal. As they parted on the street outside the restaurant, she picked up fragments. You can hear, not clear 'tho, listen–"

Rathbone switched on a small tape recorder. It emitted scratchy and indistinct noises. He played it back several times.

"We'll have it enhanced in the lab back in Belfast, but the gist is they agreed to meet again in Geneva in January."

"Can't make out a thing, just crackle."

"Nasir walked back along the lake to his hotel." Rathbone continued. "Next morning went to the lawyer's office, stayed two hours, took a taxi to the airport. Direct flight to Tripoli, using his own name."

"Docherty?" Peter asked.

Rathbone replied. "Cooper and I followed him to a small hotel below the old town." He checked his notebook. "Hotel de la Cigogne. Registered under the name of Peter Hennessy. In the morning he checked out at 09.00, took a cab to the train station and boarded an express to Strasbourg."

"Get on to your people in Belfast." Haydon scratched his head and turned to Babs. "Add the Hennessy name to every watch list. Let's see how long he takes to reappear on the street. Get him surveilled, top priority. Who is running him? I'll get the word to drop from on high. Obviously, he mustn't know we're on to him."

"Done." Babs nodded.

"Draw up a snatch plan. We'll aim towards this January meet. We can't touch him in Belfast without exposing ourselves. We grab him on his way home from Geneva. We'll need a safe house there. Funding no object."

"On to it." Babs said, writing in a notebook.

"Then we turn him. The hard way."

"I'll have something on your desk within two days." There was something in her tone that jarred. Haydon looked up at her. She turned away.

"Got a problem?"

"The snatch, no problem." Rathbone said, the harsh Ulster tone coming through. "We're watchers, we handle black bag jobs–"

"–my unit doesn't do 'hard'." Babs interjected. "You'll bring people in? Coercive methods specialists?"

Straw Man

"I hadn't figured you for a softie." He stared at her, scratching his scalp.

"Need to be clear about the limits of our work scope." She stared evenly back at him. "We're a Recce unit. It's what we do."

"You do the planning. I'll figure out the who does what."

That's the problem with women soldiers, he thought, there'll always be a drip of sympathy, humanise the bad guy. They feel revulsion in the dirty, real world of spooks and terrorists. Here we have bombs tearing at the heart of government, democracy under threat, and she's worried about a little rough stuff. Safer to paint the bad guys black and keep them that way. No room for squeamishness.

"Meanwhile, keep a good look out for Libyan eyes." He drummed on the table with his fingertips. "Mustn't be caught napping.

"Better to err on the side of paranoid." Babs said "We'll keep running Charlie Sierra on you both, and we've a regular watch on DAEDALUS' back."

CHAPTER 17

One thousand kilometres away from the British Embassy in Porta Pia, on the second floor of an anonymous three-story villa on the outskirts of Tripoli, Nasir el-Maghrebi was making his trip report to his boss.

He sat on a low metal chair, talking in a monotone, having to raise his voice to compete with the bass hum of the air conditioning. He was wearing shirt sleeves. The room seemed icy cold. It was large and sparsely furnished, dominated by a partner's desk surrounded by tall, metal filing cabinets. Like the owner, he thought, sparse and humourless. A dusty Turkish carpet covered the floor. Khalfari was lounging on a sofa, leafing carefully through a file of papers on his lap. Nasir knew his ears would be perfectly attuned to the intonation of his voice. The pudgy face was impassive, but his boss had an instinct for picking up a lie, boast or slip of the tongue.

"Docherty assures me they'll have the vessel and crew ready for the first shipment in April. I plan to take our naval liaison officer – Captain Hassan Ali – to meet their skipper in January or February, complete the planning of transhipment protocols. We plan this for offshore Malta, you see, well outside any national waters."

"Good. Nothing to point to us. Clear?"

"Understood." Nasir paused. "I made the payment to Docherty. Cash. They'll use the funds for a down payment on a vessel they've identified. I told him I'd pay the second tranche at our next meeting, after they've demonstrated readiness of the vessel."

"Go ahead."

Straw Man

"He reconfirmed the Army Council plan that Cahill discussed with the Leader. They'll cache the first shipments of arms and won't distribute to their Active Service Units until they've landed the entire 240 tons in Ireland. Then they'll parcel them out and begin the main offensive."

"Hostile surveillance?"

"None. I ran routines in Frankfurt and Geneva but remained clean throughout."

"Certain?" Khalfari looked up from his file, eyes darting.

"Yes, Sir. I was careful."

"Your watch on the MI6 people at the Rome Embassy?"

"My teams are ready to go, subject to your approval. I plan to kick it off with this Etherington, I've met the guy. Doesn't seem impressive."

"You may proceed. See who he leads you to." Khalfari looked at him with piercing brown eyes. "I want details – home addresses, car registrations, routes to work and back, family status, phone numbers. We'll prepare to smack them at the right time. Blood on the streets. Pay them back for what they did to us in London. We'll use covert assets. Nothing to do with us. We can't be seen hitting the English ourselves. Off limits."

"The Italian reaction, Sir? Pollitti may be sensitive."

"This will be kept far away from us. We'll contract it out to Abu Nidal, Belgrade based, no connection to us. The Italians will see it as Palestinian payback." Khalfari ran his hands through his hair and sat silently for a while. "Passive surveillance right now, but act as if you're on a war footing. If you see a way to harm them with no blowback, do it. And watch your own back while you're after theirs."

"I'll have a team ferreting around me. I'm adding numbers, recruiting locals. Criminals."

Straw Man

"Do it." Khalfari frowned and waved the subject away with a gesture of his hand. "You've been digging into this Lomax?"

"Wired his flat and office. Recent transcripts, Sir, our meeting at his office is at the back." Nasir handed him a sheaf of documents. Khalfari held up his hand to quieten him and shuffled through the sheets. Nasir looked out of the window. Endless orange brown sand hanging in the air, obscuring the vague outlines of nearby buildings. Arab fog, he thought. Everything disguised. That defines my life now, a hidden existence amongst murky views.

"This record of your meeting: he sounds cocky, keen to please. I think you were too harsh; you need to be encouraging. Chat him up, make friends now." Khalfari handed back the papers. "Your impression?"

"His office is simple, it's obvious he's desperate to make money, sees the opportunities here as a big tick upwards." Nasir wiped a drip of sweat off his cheek and shivered. "He didn't flinch when I mentioned nuclear requirements. I think he'd sell us anything to make a buck."

"Anything else?"

"Heterosexual. Girlfriend's a journalist."

"Pity."

"Nothing to indicate he isn't what he's supposed to be."

"We need to be certain. Keep at him, take him to lunch, hint we may use him for big purchases. Press him to see if he's ready to be dirty. Give me your impressions. Two weeks, maybe three. OK?" He waved his hand in dismissal.

Straw Man

CHAPTER 18

Haydon and Glasson had been members of The Travellers Club in Pall Mall from early in their careers, its masculine ambiance reassuringly like a continuation of public school by other means. They sat in the Smoking Room with a wooden chessboard between them, puffing on long Cuban cigars, nursing balloon glasses of Delamain 'Très Vénérable' cognac.

At the far end of the room, under the fairy lights of a tall, elegant Christmas tree which twinkled on and off, a group of white-haired members conversed in loud voices. It's coming my way soon enough, Haydon thought; they're so deaf they have to shout, and all that shooting in his Army days wouldn't have helped. He frowned and reached down to move a pawn on the chessboard.

"Can you turn him in such a short space of time?" Glasson asked. "If you do the snatch in Geneva on his way home, you'll have a week at the outside before sirens scream all over Belfast."

"Can do. Sure of it." Haydon rapped the table with his knuckles. "Your move."

"You'd need to get him back in play within 72 hours. Bit of a stretch?"

"Full on hardball. Drug the bastard, set up a tableau with a roomful of our guys, all decked out in SAS uniform, clickety-click. Maybe add a few rent boys for colour." Haydon took a sip of his cognac. "Record audio for the techies to frig with, splice it into compromising phrases."

"Can they do that?"

"You bet. His own mother won't suspect it's not him." He laughed and raised his glass. "Once the techies get going, he'll be laughing away arm in arm with the hated enemy, pint in hand."

Straw Man

"How do you close?"

"Screen him a show-reel, all smiley. Then drop the bombshell we'll get it into McGee's hands before he's even made it home to Belfast. Your move." Haydon pointed to the chessboard. "He'll understand the horror of The Nutting Squad getting their hands on him after seeing our kompromat. Wouldn't be pretty. No choice, one-way ticket."

"Go ahead. But deniable. Clear?" Glasson's voice was hard. He stared at the board and then slowly reached down to move his queen. "We can't be seen to be yanking people off the street in peaceable Gnomeland."

"These Det people are good." Haydon moved his bishop. "Check. They'll snatch him as he leaves his hotel on his way home, fake taxi probably. He won't be missed, he'll plan to take a slow laundry run back to Belfast. We'll have ample time."

They fell silent while a waiter refilled their glasses. There was a burst of rowdy laughter from the white-haired group. He'd got the go ahead, bingo! He'd worried that Glasson might feel the risk profile was too high. He puffed on his cigar.

"The product?" Glasson stroked his cheek. "What'll you expect?"

"Cargoes, ships, names, dates - the works. No Semtex for the IRA. Job done."

"How long could you run him?"

"Maybe we let a couple of shipments through before we hit them? Might be the smart move."

"You're joking?" Glasson looked up, eying him sharply.

"We mark the arms with radio transmitters, follow them to the Province, sabotage them in their remote dumps." Haydon smiled and picked up a pawn from the chessboard. "Give the boyos a shock when their lovely new gear blows up in their faces."

"And Docherty?"

"Pull him out before we seize a ship." Haydon paused. "Quickly, before they fillet him."

"I'm not in the mood." Glasson reached down and knocked over his King. He swirled the amber liquid around in his glass and sniffed at it. "My masters keep upping the pressure to interdict these shipments. Get it right and both our careers get a boost. Get it wrong–"

"–our interests are entwined."

"What about the Libyans?"

"My team is getting ready to go into the People's Bureau and el-Maghrebi's flat to plant devices."

"With a false flag, I hope?"

"Yes, but–" Haydon stubbed out his cigar. "–might it be better to send them a message? Or wait and hurt them later on, after the seizure. Make it all very public?"

"Needs thought. They'd want payback. Do we want war on the streets of Rome? Maybe you wouldn't be safe?" Glasson leaned back and drained his glass, then stood up and looked down at Haydon.

"One more thing. We keep Operation TUMBREL going, whatever happens. I want your guy DAEDALUS in play to counter the Libyan nuclear programme."

"I'm in process of launching him. It's developing well." Haydon started replacing the chess pieces on the board, positioning them neatly in their squares. Pressure off, he thought. *That's a relief.* He could feed Charlie into Libya slowly, safely. No more pressure to rush down and poke his nose into where it shouldn't be.

"Run it as a separate op. Extract it from the IRA file. Make sure it pays."

After a brief bow and handshake with the Ambassador, Haydon and Ros made it out of the long reception line that wound along to the front gate of the Swedish Residence in Rome. They walked up the steps to the crowded ballroom, dominated by a Christmas tree reaching to the high ceiling, brilliantly decorated in sparkling silver and red. In front of the tree, a dozen girls in long white dresses and scarlet sashes with silver crowns on their heads were lighting white candles. The clamour of conversation drowned out a small orchestra playing on a dais. They took proffered tall glasses from a tray and clinked them.

He looked down at her cleavage. Super foxy, he thought. Her black satin cocktail dress verged on the edge of indecent. Not tarty, just alluring. He took her hand in his.

"What is this firewater, anyway?" Ros screwed up her face. "My legs are wobbly just sipping it."

"*Glögg*, Swedish version of mulled wine, brandy added." He gave her hand a squeeze. "I like it when you're wobbly."

"Isn't it a bit early for Christmas festivities?"

"Sankta Lucia celebrations are a big deal for Swedes. More important than Christmas itself."

Through the crowd he glimpsed Carlo Pollitti standing on his own, staring up at vast, colourful tapestries depicting gory battle scenes which seemed to cover all the walls. He guided her towards him.

Straw Man

"Carlo, Hi." The two men embraced. "Feast for the eyes."

"Wait 'til the singing starts," Carlo held up a welcoming arm, "spine-chilling stuff."

"Ros, this is Carlo Pollitti; an old friend from my first posting in Rome."

"Enchanted." Pollitti bowed and raised her hand to his lips, looking into her eyes, then turning to Haydon. "How did you capture this beauty–"

"–what's the big deal about Sankta Lucia?" Ros smiled, holding his stare.

Pollitti let her hand drop. "A celebration of light. Maidens singing away the long winter darkness. Sankta Lucia, this Swedish heroine, was actually an Italian martyr from Sicily, where the winters aren't as long and dark, but myth–"

"Look, they're starting." She pointed. The lights dimmed, flickering candles illuminated the large room. Orange shadows from the gothic fireplace danced off the walls and up the vaunted ceilings, adding to a medieval feel. Conversation died as the girls paraded slowly around the room in silence, candles held out in front of them. From behind the Christmas tree Sankta Lucia appeared, a crown of candles on her head, her companions following in pairs as they sang–

"Night walks with a heavy step, Round yard and hearth, As the sun departs from earth, Shadows are brooding. There in our dark house, Walking with lit candles, Sankta Lucia, Sankta Lucia!"

A burst of flame from the fire illuminated a hawkish face in the background, giving Haydon a jolt. Nasir el-Maghrebi, he recognised him from photos. He seemed to stare at him but turned away. A little too quickly? *Damn.* This could be uncomfortable if he came over to talk to Carlo. He needed to compose himself. The girls sang on, a series of haunting chants, precessing slowly around the room. He felt Ros shiver and pulled her close. The lights came on and the gathering burst into applause. Ros wandered off towards the singers. Haydon watched Nasir pushing his way towards them through the crowd.

"Admiral." He reached out his hand to Pollitti.

"Mr. El-Maghrebi, good to see you." Pollitti raised his arms in welcome. "May I present Haydon Talbot from the British Embassy, Nasir el-Maghrebi from the Libyan People's Bureau. Delighted to introduce you two on the peaceable soil of the Swedish Embassy."

Nasir nodded and turned to Haydon. Haydon reluctantly reached out to shake the Libyan's hand. The Libyan's hand felt hot and clammy. Haydon felt as if he had an entire slice of lemon in his mouth.

"Mind you, I'm not sure how peaceable." Pollitti pointed up at the tapestries. "Have a look at those."

"The ancient warlike tradition of Sweden, from the Vikings to Charles 12th." Haydon took a swig from his glass. The *glögg* was having an effect. He felt light-headed. This was going to be OK. He smiled at Nasir, who looked away. "Their neutrality only dates from getting themselves stuck in the middle of the Napoleonic wars."

"Whilst you English maintained an unbroken habit of aggression?" Nasir said.

"True, we stand up for freedom and democracy, and oppose dictatorships." Haydon's voice was strained. "The second world–"

"–many recently independent nations would disagree."

"Look at us Italians! Worst of all worlds, always unwilling belligerents. Inevitably choosing the wrong side." Pollitti beamed. "Nowadays we're cast as mediators, a more natural position."

Straw Man

"You are forgetting, Admiral, that as one of your ex-colonies, we see it differently."

Haydon watched Nasir's face flushing, his posture stiffening. A zealot, he thought, even takes cocktail party banter seriously. Unimpressive. *You just wait, you nasty little Arab shit, I'm going to fix you big time.* Better in a way they'd looked into each other's eyes. He realised he was staring fixedly at the Libyan. He turned to Pollitti.

"Look, we're here to celebrate the coming of the Light."

"Haydon, didn't your Mr. Churchill say *'better to jaw-jaw than to war-war'*?" Pollitti said loudly. "I'd be pleased to facilitate that."

"I'll drink to that!" They raised their glasses. Haydon noticed an ironic scowl on Nasir's face as he raised his glass.

"To the Light!"

CHAPTER 19

It was dark when the taxi dropped Charlie and Ines outside his flat, cold January rain splattering down as they ran together for the front door. He lugged the suitcases up the steep stairway, fumbling around trying to get the key in the lock in the dark corridor, rainwater pouring off his raincoat. They giggled. He leaned over and kissed her.

She threw her small bag on the bed, took a shower and grabbed her bag and raincoat.

"Wish me luck! Got to charm my editor, get his approval."

"You don't need luck, you've got him wrapped around your little decolletage."

"Not so little! See you." She ran out of the front door.

They'd been so cut off. Six of them aboard Pippo Lansa's classic sailing boat – the *Borealis* – cruising slowly around the remote Dahlak islands in the Red Sea. Harmony. The weeks had rolled by, time slowed to a standstill, the prospects and dangers of the Libyan business had melted away. Before they left, Haydon had warned him his flat and office were wired and he was being followed. Leaving him feeling self-conscious. Especially in the bedroom.

He sat at his desk and looked gloomily around the room. Back with a bang. Leaning down, he collected up the pile of mail scattered around by the front door, then gathered in the lengths of shiny fax paper crumpled out over the floor of his study. The price of a wonderful month away. Pressure. He'd got used to life with no pressure. He disregarded the beeping and flashing answering machine. That could wait. He thought about the bugs. It was eerie to know that everything they said and did was being listened to.

Straw Man

Their departure from the *Borealis* had been abrupt, a golden aura seeming to snap as soon as they stepped off the boat at Massawa. On the last evening, Andrea had invited Ines to fly down with him to Tripoli the next week. There was the possibility of an interview with Colonel Qaddafi.

He didn't want her involved; he didn't want her going anywhere near Libya. And particularly not with Andrea. A grimy blob of jealousy stabbed at his chest. He tried to suppress it and jerked his head from side to side as if to shake it off. His instincts screeched NO. Andrea and he had played the jealousy game before, butting horns in an ancient rutting ritual. Not that Andrea had real designs on other women. He was happily married to Gianna, though no one ever seemed to see her or the children. She lived at the vineyard at Tuscany and seemed content to let him live his crazy life away from there.

On a trip in Tanzania, they'd watched young bull elephants in musth, driven insane by the aphrodisiac smells emanating from the cows. Trumpeting, secreting from their eyes and their ears and their cocks, the bull elephants had shaken their heads to escape from the all-conquering power of their sex drive, ready to fight anything that stood between them and their cow. A frightening state. The cow played a dignified and submissive role. Whilst directing the whole play, pulling the puppet strings to guarantee her own satisfaction. Olfactory elements floating invisibly in the air are so powerful, so subliminal. They drive us every single day in ways we never even know.

No, Andrea might try to sleep with Ines, but somehow it would have no meaning, none. Just another form of edge, like flying under a low bridge, or playing chicken on his Ducati 900SS.

Straw Man

On the boat, his inner jury kept popping up and pointing an accusing finger. What he was doing for Haydon was a betrayal of Andrea, who had introduced him to Nasir as a kind favour. All right, a betrayal on behalf of his country. To save unknown lives from death, from mutilation. A higher interest. From the orchestra of inner voices, a quiet one dripped poison. *But the money?* He put it out of his mind and focussed on sorting through the piles of mail, slitting open envelopes, glancing through the contents and sorting them into piles. The voices grew louder. He needed a drink to shut them up.

Going to the kitchen, he poured himself two fingers of scotch, adding a splash of water. Glugging it down, he poured himself another, then took the bottle and a jug of water back to his desk. He went back to work. He felt better already. Those judgmental voices were easily tamed.

The church bells had chimed midnight by the time Ines let herself into the flat. It was still raining heavily, and her hair was dripping. She dropped her drenched raincoat on the floor and walked into Charlie's study, where he was still sitting at his desk reading letters. She leaned over and kissed him on the back of the head.

"*Amore*, you stink of cigarettes and booze." She said, smiling and waving her hand in front of her face. "Trip's on. I can go. I told them the interview with Qaddafi isn't confirmed, but they agreed if I don't get it, I can do a general interest piece about life in Tripoli, the cultural legacy of Italian rule. You may congratulate me!" She put her arm around his neck and stroked his cheek.

Straw Man

"Not really." He pulled away, sounding petulant. Something about her simple joy raised his hackles. *All about her. Her ambition.*

"Not really?" She pinched his face and smiled. "Not really what?"

"You'll write an irresponsible article which will mess things up."

"Andrea doesn't think so, or he wouldn't have asked me to come."

"Admit it." He turned away from her, picked up a letter and started to read. "You'll do an Oriana Fallaci and damn the consequences for the rest of us."

"I'm going, get used to it."

"Listen to yourself."

"Meaning?"

"You sound like a brat!"

A look of hurt came over her face. As if he'd slapped her. She moved away from him and slumped onto the sofa facing his desk, water dripping from her hair like tears.

"Are you drunked? Isn't like you. Unkind. My career is less important than your business interests?" Her voice was trembling, her knees shaking like a little girl. "Why are you being like this? We had a wonderful trip, such a happy time. Now you're trying to spoil it?"

"I'm not trying to spoil anything. I just wish you wouldn't go to Libya. You're the one who is spoiling everything, doing the one thing you know I don't want."

"Are you jealous of Andrea? Is that it? You know–"

"–I am not."

He lit a cigarette and leaned back, taking a gulp of his drink and refilling the glass. The silence between them was painful. It was true. He was jealous.

Straw Man

He felt burning anger rising in his chest. A five-year-old's rage. He turned away, staring out of the window, breathing deeply.

"You've pushed and pushed him to take you down with him." He talked calmly. Just needed to calm this down, he thought, think of something nice. "Ever since I introduced you at Portofino."

"He's old enough to make up his own–"

"–it looks as if you're leeching on him. That's so embarrassing."

Her face flushed red. She stood up, quivering, and moved towards him, fists clenched. He flinched.

"Embarrassing? You mean I might embarrass YOU by finding what dirty things YOU are doing!" She was shouting, her face puce, her hands shaking, her eyes glazed over. "It is you who are embarrassing! I thought you might have principles beneath your greedy exterior. But no. Selling material for their nuclear programme. You can't get lower."

"You've not the faintest idea what I'm doing."

"You think I don't know?"

"You know nothing, and–"

"–you think I don't hear–"

"–you listen at keyholes and make up stories, I suppose that's what journos are famous for?"

"You think I'm deaf and blind?"

"There you go. Embarrassing yourself again."

"So maybe you don't want me to write about you helping a Dictator who supports terrorists to get an atom bomb. *Jesu!*" She pointed her finger at him and shouted, "Who the fuck are you?"

Straw Man

Picking up a cut glass ashtray from the table, she hurled it at the wall, shards of glass sprayed out over his desk and the floor. "Embarrassing? You prick!"

Charlie swung round in his chair. He felt an ogre's mist welling from his stomach. He wanted to grab her, to hit her. He breathed in deeply, looked down and casually brushed pieces of glass off his trousers. *He must not react. He must not react.*

"Santa Ines, is it? Holding your nose?" He shouted, an angled sneer contorting his face. "You can't see your own selfish ambition? Fluttering your cunt at Andrea like some kind of *troia* - Slut! Hypocrite! If you have such a low opinion of me, what are you doing in my life, in my bed?"

Ines turned towards him. He could see she was about to cry. Her eyes were half closed, as if they were bruised. He had to stop this somehow; he knew he had to stop it. He made to stand up and move towards her, he half raised his arms as if to embrace her. She flinched and turned away, yelling over her shoulder.

"Which is a good question. You are right, I don't want to be in your life. Thank you for showing me who you are. Emotionally absent, morally absent, a handsome sack of emptiness. A nothing bastard!" She shouted, holding back tears, knocking a lamp off the table as she spun away from him and rushed towards the door. "And I don't discuss with a nasty drunk."

The lamp crashed to the floor. He stood, head down, motionless, holding himself in, pain stabbing in his chest.

She picked up her coat from the floor and ran out of the flat, slamming the door behind her. Charlie heard her footsteps clattering down the stairs. He didn't move; he felt rooted. His eyes focussed on the puddle where her coat had been. What a terrible exchange! How could they, no how

Straw Man

could he, have destroyed everything so fast? Impossible. Five minutes. And the Libyans listening in. Oh Christ! At least he hadn't hit her. That was one salvation.

Pouring himself another scotch, he gulped it down. He walked over to his cassette player and fumbled around in a drawer for a cassette. He knew what he wanted to play, that would amplify the pain and hurt and loss and pierce him to hurt more, as if the hammer of pain might cure something bigger and incurable.

He inserted the cassette, depressed the play button and cranked the volume up. He took another gulp of whisky as he waited for the painful first chords. *"We've already said... "* He felt the tears welling, then he started singing, almost shouting–*"... goodbye. Since you gotta go, oh you'd better go now, go now, go now, before you see me cry..."* He put the song on repeat, continued singing, shouting, drinking, crying.

CHAPTER 20

Charlie felt dreadful. He had an awful hangover. A mist of black dread engulfed him. His head, his stomach, his chest was heavy with painful balls of fear and shame. His tongue and mouth were dirty. He felt guilty and humiliated and hoped he could make it through the day's meetings. He had gone to his office early to wait for Fürrer, who was flying in. Later they were to meet Nasir. The veins in his forehead throbbed.

He opened the door to Fürrer and, as they passed into his inner office, he signalled with his arms in a circular motion around the room and then pointed to his ears. Fürrer gave him a thumbs up and a wink to show he understood the room was not secure.

He tried to put on a welcoming smile. "Armin, good to see you. How's gnome winter-land?" Shaking the man's hand, he felt the dank sweat on his own.

"I've been travelling during the holidays, so I'm not up to date with fairies." Fürrer laughed. "Charlie, you don't look well, still seasick?"

They chatted for a few minutes, then Charlie opened a file and pulled out some papers. "We'll go for lunch in a while. Can we go through the list?"

"Nothing difficult, we can source it all in Europe. A few items–look here's a good example, these P-1 centrifuge components, motors and frequency converters. They could be dual use, so we can't quote for them. But they split them into vacuum tubes, valve equipment and so forth there'll be no problem. Can you get the client to rewrite his requirements as per this list–" he handed over a folder containing several typed sheets of paper and pointed with his finger, "reduces the difficult items to their sub-components."

"What's the order of magnitude?" Charlie asked.

Straw Man

"Not huge, I've shaved the price right down to be competitive: just on $4 million." Fürrer gestured towards the ceiling and smiled. "Starter order. I read it to be a test to see how we perform, and we'll fill it no problem."

Caminetto, in viale Parioli, had the advantage of being a buzzy Neapolitan restaurant with excellent food. They could talk freely with a high noise level guaranteed to thwart listeners. Charlie swigged a strong Bloody Mary and immediately felt better.

"Bugs at my flat and office, our client is checking on me." Charlie leaned in towards Fürrer. "Useful forum to address them."

"Give them a foretaste of our price." Fürrer smiled. "Well padded. If we perform well, they'll come back asking for real naughties. There's the big money."

"Are you involved with Sadler's other operations?" Charlie asked, tilting back his glass and finishing the dregs of his Bloody Mary. He summoned the waiter and ordered another. "Extra strong please, and *piccantissimo*."

"Meaning?"

"Enabling the supply of restricted material to rogue regimes whilst ensuring the items disrupt their progress?" Charlie laughed.

"Only you twisted English could come up with such a distorted idea." Charlie noticed he hadn't answered the question. "Cheaper than military intervention, which is unpredictable and comes with dangerous consequences."

"So where are the risks?" Charlie asked, lifting his glass again. He felt the vodka burning down his windpipe, calming his nerves.

Straw Man

"If the client works it out, damage to them is limited and the lucrative business ends. Risks of retribution. Bad for one's health."

"So how can they work it out?"

"There are a few competent foreign scientists contracted into these programmes – South Africans, Indians, Dutch, Swiss, German, even British. Mercenaries. The best known is A.Q. Khan, a Pakistani who manages a network of people and companies supplying technology, personnel and equipment. These guys understand the detail of the processes and will be on the lookout for dud stuff."

"They must know Western agencies are watching them?"

"Yes, and the trade in nuclear components is narrow. There are maybe ten, maximum fifteen buyers, maybe the same number of brokers." Fürrer took a sip of his wine. "We all know each other."

"These operations get rumbled?"

"Now and then." Fürrer replied. "Two years ago there was a gigantic blowout in a Siberian pipeline, similar in scale to a nuclear detonation. Visible from space. The Americans spotted it and thought it might be a Soviet missile launch. It turned out to result from a CIA sting operation to sucker the Sovs into stealing booby-trapped software, which caused terrific over-pressure and eventually the pipeline exploded with a big bang."

"No bangs, please! I rely on you to keep us in good health for years to come. Look, the clients are coming to the office at 2.30, we'd better head back."

"Charlie, please don't forget," Fürrer frowned, reached over and touched his arm, "no names. If there is any need to refer to me, call me Mr Smith. They'll understand. The only name we want in the room is yours."

Straw Man

Back at the office, Charlie excused himself and went into his private office. He felt more human after his lunchtime drinking. A wave of love rolled through him. He needed to see her, to make it better. He picked up the receiver and dialled a number. Sandra Lansa was Ines's closest friend, Ines would have gone to stay with her.

"*Pronto*. Sandra, it's Kiko. How have you been?" He tried to sound upbeat but knew he wasn't succeeding.

"Kiko?" Her voice was cold, he thought, so unlike her. *She knows*.

"Look, Sandra. Ines and I had a row last night. She stormed out. I don't know where she is and I have to speak to her." He dabbed sweat off his forehead with a handkerchief.

"I don't think so."

"I don't know what came over me. I was drunk. I said horrid, untrue things. I'm feeling awful. Have you heard from her?"

"She doesn't want to speak to you." Sandra snapped. "Leave her alone."

"Will you tell her I'm sorry–"

"–I'll tell her you called. I warned you, Kiko, I warned you not to hurt her." She put the receiver down.

"Tell her I love her and don't want to lose her. That I'm ashamed and lonely and sad." Charlie said, before he realised he was talking to nobody.

"Shit, shit, shit!"

They sat around the small conference table in Charlie's office, drinking coffee and smoking cigarettes. Charlie thought it was going well, Fürrer's optimism seemed infectious, and he was careful to sidestep questions about legalities. Nasir managed the occasional smile.

Straw Man

"Our company motto is '*We find hard-to-get objects for customers all over the world.*' We exist to serve the buyer's needs. Your needs." Fürrer's chins shook with infectious laughter as he pointed a fat finger at Nasir. "If we can't get it, nobody can. If items are complicated, we advise on mitigating strategies–even if it means losing that business. Naturally we comply with every applicable law."

"You see, I will oversee this procurement. I'm an electrical engineer, so I have understanding of the issues." Nasir was wearing his thick dark glasses and a safari suit, some kind of uniform, Charlie thought. "If we go further, I need you to come to Tripoli to meet my superior, Ahmed Khalfari, and discuss details with our technical people."

"No problem with your list, although Mr Lomax has suggestions regarding the text."

"If you could amend your RFQ and use the revised wording please." Charlie handed an envelope to Nasir.

"We would like to have your quotation as soon as possible."

"You'll have it by fax within a week."

After Fürrer had left the office to return to Zurich, Charlie explained. "Mr Smith is a careful man, stickler for legality. He wanted me to explain that if you rewrite your list using this wording, he foresees no problems with supplying the required items."

"A clever man." Nasir replied, "My people will study the details of these subcomponents and assemblies and come back to you."

It was late afternoon by the time Nasir left. Perhaps the Libyan had been a little friendlier this time. Anyway, he'd got through it without betraying his dark state of mind. He sat at his desk, head in his hands, and thought about Ines and what he should do. He felt so ill.

Straw Man

He considered writing a letter and delivering it to Sandra, but he was feeling so bad he went home and put his head under the pillow and slept. It would be better to write the next day when his head was clearer.

Straw Man

CHAPTER 21

They had parked the white Transit van before daybreak in a far corner of the almost empty car park of the Hilton Hotel. The Roman dawn was invisible, hidden somewhere behind pounding grey rain, the leading edge of a cold front racing in. Peering forward from the back, Babs could see nothing but the rapid splattering of raindrops on the windscreen. The weather report had warned of the possibility of snow, a rare event in the Eternal City.

In the closed off back of the van, the breach team was rechecking equipment. Skelton was sorting heavy electronic gear into a canvas backpack. Next to him, Rathbone was leaning down, a head-torch illuminating a small canvas case of skeleton keys, carefully ordering them. Babs was sitting motionless, eyes closed, as if in meditation. No one spoke. She checked her watch. Still two hours to kick off.

She thought about Geneva. They'd got a little too tipsy that first evening, she'd been waiting for him to hit on her. He hadn't. What would she have done? And then regretted. She'd been horny, living under the pressure of working in an unfamiliar environment, a big responsibility. She didn't approve of sleeping with married men. But what did morality have to do with subliminal needs? The subconscious had much more power than the puny conscience.

She felt at ease with her mute Det colleagues. She hated long waits with operatives who felt some primal urge to chatter. Maybe noise reassured them, calmed their nerves. Watchers placed high value on silence, she was convinced chatter impeded focus and operational concentration; which were not the same things, she'd learned in training. Focus closes your mind to

Straw Man

everything but one small and narrowing area, each of your senses reaching out to home in on a tiny gap in 4D space, which was where your target was. Concentration was the here and now, waiting for an op to kick off, nothing at all to focus on, the detailed preparations done. You were blind, your mind empty, in readiness to react to sudden and changing events.

She rechecked her watch. Still only 07.45. Christ, another hour before they expected the target to move off. Four weeks they'd been following Nasir, watching his flat and office, observing him from every practical angle and at every time of day and night. They'd shot hundreds of reels of covert 8mm film, stacks of still photographs which they'd studied and magnified in a search for details that even he wouldn't know. They knew his wardrobe and his gait and his habits, the vehicles he used, his assistants, his few friends. More importantly, they'd got to know Enrica: the blonde, big-breasted, Neapolitan hooker he called up every Saturday night.

She thought about Haydon. There was something there, but what? She sensed a warming down there, just thinking about him. Yet he was so strait-laced, so rigid. Not her type at all. She didn't go for officers. What was it then? No obvious sense of humour. He was fit, handsome in a plodding sort of way, and married. And those were the plusses. Maybe it was his palpable crookedness? Spooks kept everything hidden, it was their credo. They led you down tortuous paths. So far his seduction technique had been obvious, although devious. She preferred things straight. Or did she? Christ, what was she going to be like at 40 if she was already so cynical? She closed her eyes and started a meditation routine. Focus on the moment.

Cooper's voice broke into her reverie.

"Boney, your moniker got changed? Now they're calling you The Ever-Ready Boner."

Straw Man

Had she been dozing? She checked her watch. 08.30. Cooper was slouched in the driving seat; the window cracked open to let out smoke from the cigarette hanging from his mouth. Rain splashed in and wet the shoulder of his blue coveralls. "Compliment, you see."

Rathbone replied. "Fuck off and do your job. They call you The Poop Scooper! You follow us round and pick up our shit. Not a compliment."

"Have you done her then?" He blew smoke out through the small crack. The window steamed up. "On expenses?"

"Look, I don't like cheap champagne." Rathbone stretched his arms. "Or big knockers."

"Which is why I chose him and not you," Babs pointed her finger at Cooper, "I could rely on him to keep his eyes open and his flies closed, not the other way round. You–"

"–she's earned her money several times over." Rathbone said in his mournful voice, "the alarm code, which alone makes it worth the brown envelopes."

"And if she got the code wrong?"

"That's when this bag of electronic tricks comes in." Skelton lifted the backpack. "No need for you to worry."

"You won't need them." Rathbone said. He'd been tasked with suborning Enrica. He'd followed her to the nightclub where she worked, spent two long evenings buying her drinks, charming her with his friendly, reserved personality. She'd agreed to collaborate with surprising alacrity. "Fiver says so."

"Done." Skelton laughed. "Pay me now if you like. You think a tart can remember a four-digit number?"

"She liked me, you see. Said she preferred English gentlemen."

Straw Man

"That would rule you out."

Every Monday afternoon he'd gone to her small flat off the via Cassia and handed her an envelope, in return for which she provided helpful details to fill gaps in their knowledge. Not just as to the quirks of his manhood, but the layout of his flat and the building and its doors and locks and all sorts of bits they couldn't easily observe from their lookout post 200 yards away in the Hilton.

"We know him better than he knows himself." Babs said. "We're going to know him a lot better once these cameras are up and running."

"Seems like baby stuff with these ragheads." Cooper flicked his cigarette out of the window and wound it closed. "With Paddies you gotta be right on edge, never know when you're in their sights. They're sharp and vicious, you gotta stay in the zone 24/7. Or you're very dead. Bang! Through the head. These guys, they strut around in thick dark glasses–"

"never underestimate an enemy." Babs tapped him on the back. "If you think there's a mug around then it's–"

"*08.44 watcher two target on the move OVER*" A Walkie-Talkie hanging from the roof by a canvas strap had squawked into life. Babs reached up and pulled it down.

"*Blue team leader watcher two copy advise target vehicle exiting garage OVER*"

"*Blue team leader mobile one and two stand by to follow OVER*"

They were on. She checked her watch and pressed the stopwatch button.

"Lads, I want this over and done inside 60 minutes, max." She checked her watch. "Standby."

"*08.53 watcher two target exiting garage usual Blue Beamer one on board*"

Straw Man

"Blue team leader mobile one and two follow and report OUT"
"Let's move. Heads down."

Cooper started the engine. The van crept off, following the winding Via Trionfale for a mile down the steep hill, before turning off into a small housing estate made up of several small apartment buildings. Pulling up in front of one of them, he reached down and pulled up a large plastic sign 'RIPARAZIONI IN CORSO' which he placed on the dashboard. Then he went around to the back of the van and opened the door.

Rain splattered on them as they ran, heads down, for the main entrance to the building. They were wearing blue peaked caps and coveralls with the logo of STET, the national telephone company, and carrying metal toolboxes. They saw no one as they waited outside the front entrance for Rathbone to work his magic. Babs left Cooper in the van, covering the approaches, engine ticking over in case the entry had to be aborted. This was a danger moment, a resident coming out might well smell a large rodent, the op could be over before it began. She felt her knees knocking together as the tall man hunched over and worked his key tools with both hands, like a surgeon performing a delicate operation. It seemed to take an age, but in less than a minute they were in.

They took the fire stairs to the second floor, springing upward silently on rubber soles. Pulling a cotton mask over her face, Babs breathed deeply. She felt that special calm that enfolds you when an op kicks off. Rathbone worked the front door locks, then beckoned to Skelton, who pushed past, holding a small metal box with wires and crocodile clips. As he shoved the front door open, an alarm warning whined. 30 seconds. Standing by the alarm box, Skelton punched in the four numbers Enrica had provided. The whine stopped.

"Best fiver I ever lost." Skelton smiled. "Move!"

Babs and the others raced past him into the living room, pulling on rubber gloves. Closing the door, Rathbone turned and went down on his knees, opening his toolbox and extracting and carefully threading a thick cable through the letterbox. He attached a small, cubed gadget which burst into life, showing a bright black-and-white image of the corridor outside.

"Camera's on, all clear."

Babs raised her Walkie-Talkie and pressed the transmit button.

"09.10 blue team leader we're in OVER"

"Mobile three all quiet OVER" Cooper's voice barked over the radio.

"Mobile one target approaching office OVER"

"53 minutes. Let's go." Babs entered the living room, pulling a Polaroid camera out of a bag. She started snapping at surfaces, laying the developed photos out on the glass desk. When she'd covered the room, she called out. "OK, done here! Work this room. Whatever you move, put it back where it was, check it against the Polaroids. I'll do the bedroom now."

Rathbone walked over to the tall metal filing cabinet by the desk. Holding a big bunch of keys, he started working his way through them, trying each.

"In!" He pulled open the top drawer. Reaching down, he started leafing through hanging files. "Harvest!"

Babs came back into the living room. She checked her watch.

"47 minutes. Take your time."

She joined Skelton by the desk and the two of them sorted through the files one by one. Those that looked interesting they placed on the desk, methodically holding open and snapping pages with a Minox camera

Straw Man

she'd taken from a pocket. This was looking good. They'd be out long before the deadline.

Skelton had laid out his equipment on a white sheet on the floor. Lengths of cable. Battery operated drills and screwdrivers. Fittings. Perspex boxes containing miniaturized cameras and microphones. He stood up and walked over to the mantelpiece, leaning down and feeling with his fingers under the ledge.

"Babs, I'm thinking right here, the lens will give good coverage of the desk and the seating area. OK?" She looked over at him and nodded. "I'll run a copper antenna the length of the ledge, cover it with putty. Colours are neutral."

"Do it. 41 minutes. Plenty of time." She announced, turning back to the thick file she was holding. Rifling through it, she stopped at a grainy photo of a man in a street, taken from the side and above. She raised it to the light and stared at it. Peter Etherington. No doubt about it. A classic surveillance shot. So they'd been watching him. For how long? She laid the file back on the desk and turned the pages, her eye was caught by an address. Christ, they'd even got his home pinpointed. Could he have led them to her team? She kept snapping with the Minox. A throb of anxiety ran through her. She felt a niggle in her gut. Something was wrong. She could feel it. This was not good.

She looked over at Skelton. He was kneeling on the floor, assembling the items he needed for the micro-camera installation. She watched as he measured out and cut a thin filament of copper wire. He turned to look up at the mantelpiece, reaching with his hands to estimate the depth of the ledge, then turned his eyes up to the photograph of Colonel Qaddafi in military uniform hanging just above. It was crooked. He was one of those men that instinctively noticed those things. She saw him flinch and leap up.

"Fuck!" He knocked over his neat pile of equipment. "Babs quick!"

"What the hell–" She read the alarm in the other man's face, moving towards him. He pointed up to a small black box clipped to the top of the picture, a little red eye blinking rhythmically. "Motion detector. Camera. It's either another hostile–no, no I don't think so, too obvious, not concealed. Light's blinking, Jesus it's recording us right now–"

"–or?"

"Shit!"

Babs stood stock still. Her mind went icy. A set-up? Made sense. Shit, could they have missed all the signs they were not the predators at all, but the prey?

Snatching up the Walkie-Talkie, she pressed transmit.

"Blue team leader mobile three query status crash urgent STOP prepare abort Code 3 departure confirm OVER"

No answer. She waited for ten long seconds, then pressed the button again.

"Blue team leader mobile three query your status immediate OVER"

Nothing.

"Abort! Abort!" She shouted. "Gotta get out of here. Fast."

Skelton started packing up his gear, laying it neatly into the canvas holdall.

"Leave your stuff. Now! If Cooper's been rumbled, we've no time and we're unarmed. Code 4! Repeat Code 4! Staircase. Rear exit. Over the wall. Yomp uphill into the woods. Go NOW!" Babs yanked the blinking camera from the wall as she dashed for the front door. Rathbone was already there, crouched down, peering at the little fuzzy screen.

Straw Man

"Corridor's clear!" he called. They rushed out. Above the thumping sound of their rubber-soled feet pounding down the stairs, Babs could hear police sirens.

They burst out of the fire door into pelting rain, the sound of sirens louder. Thank God for this rain, Babs thought. They might just have time to get away unseen. Then it'll cover us and our tracks for long enough to make it to the tree line.

The four of them ran fast, lungs bursting, sloshing their way through soggy flowerbeds towards the wall at the rear of the complex. She tripped and fell face down into thick mud. For a moment she couldn't see anything and felt panic rushing at her. She scrambled crazily onto her knees, hands flailing the sticky mud. The sound of sirens was deafening. She felt arms lifting her up, pulling her along. Her legs pumped away, boots squelching, into the driving sleet. Through the brown cloud of mud on her face she could make out blue lights reflected against the wall ahead. This was going to be close.

Straw Man

CHAPTER 22

Haydon was leafing through pages from a thick file, occasionally reaching down with his pencil to make an annotation. A red telephone handset was plugged into a silver metal loudspeaker stand on his desk. Every now and then he'd look at it, as if willing it into life. He was in his office at the Embassy, feet crossed and resting on the desk, a cigarette burning in an overflowing ashtray. Rain spattered onto the windows, rattling the panes, muffling traffic noise. The room was smoky and close.

He couldn't concentrate, his mind was on the op. He put the file down and stared up at the ceiling. He felt the blood pumping in his temples. This could be the biggest day in his career. They'd have both ends of the conspiracy pinned down, Nasir's flat on tap and his files filleted, crosshairs on Docherty's forehead and a plan to turn him. If The Det team managed to wire the People's Bureau, then they could take their time to roll the whole thing up.

He thought about Babs. Sharp as a whistle. Her whole team emanated self-confidence and independence. Tough but relaxed, no sense of bravado. He'd organise a dinner for them to show his appreciation. Maybe take them to *Galeassi* in Trastevere. He had this pulsing sense that he was in her sights. Maybe she had a thing for older men? Or maybe that was an old man's wishful thinking?

"Barker will open the net as soon as the target leaves his flat for the People's Bureau." A voice broke into his train of thought. Peter Etherington was sitting on the sofa opposite, a yellow notepad balanced on his lap, sipping coffee.

Straw Man

"His range of vision?" Haydon's spoke sharply. He was in operational mode. He felt his heart thumping. "Weather's shite."

"From the O.P–the room at the Hilton–he has an unobstructed view into the living room of the target flat. Viz will be degraded by the rain."

"Comms?"

"Barker's monitoring the VHF spectrum."

"Time estimate?"

"Job time 60 minutes max. Target leaves every day at around 09.00, clockwork. Doesn't seem to watch his back much unless he's up to something naughty. A CI scrubber team sometimes follows him from the office. Doesn't return for lunch. Cleaning lady comes on Fridays."

"Dogs? Children?"

"No dogs, no wife, no babies. Maybe in Libya, we don't know. Hooker comes on Saturday."

"Debrief?"

"If Babs emerges clean, should be here by midday."

"Let's hope the filing cabinet yields the contact routines with the Paddies." Haydon carefully moved his legs off the desk and sat upright.

"Bugs at his office and home, a matter of time before we nail the bastard."

"Then I'll be able to sleep."

The red phone rang. Etherington reached across and flicked a switch. *"Go ahead Barker, you're live and secure."*

"Target departed, mobile 1 following." A tinny voice floated out of the speaker.

Haydon stubbed out his cigarette and picked up his pen, tapping it on his teeth. Every few minutes the speaker would squawk a progress report.

"Mobile 3 entering the complex, he's going out of my view behind the building. It's raining heavily, I have poor visibility."

"The line is open. I want real time updates."

"Blue Leader confirms team's entered the building."

"I have eyes on the team now, I see them moving around in the flat."

Haydon lit another cigarette. He wished he was there at the sharp end. He remembered that buzz in your guts as they'd pull out of the fortified base in their Saracens, a few rocks clanging off the armour as they drove off into the hot zone. Now he sat and listened to a tinny voice on a box. The price of age.

"Mobile 3 is driving out of the complex."

Etherington stood up and walked over to the loudspeaker. He pressed the transmit button. "Barker, repeat."

"Mobile 3 has driven out of the complex. Heading north up the via Trionfale."

"That's a helluva quick in and out?" Haydon put down his file, looked at his watch, smiled, and turned to face Etherington. "Champagne time, is it?"

"Too quick." He pressed the button. "*Confirm Team exited target flat?*"

"Negative. Team remains in the flat. Bad viz, but I see movement."

"Makes no sense. Why is he driving off? *Barker anything from him on the radio?*"

"Negative, no VHF traffic."

"Might have got moved on by a nosy resident." Etherington said. "He'll turn round and go back in."

"This is not feeling right."

"I'm hearing sirens, more than one. Can't see them, don't know where they're headed."

Straw Man

"*Barker, Request an urgent update.*" Haydon was standing now, pacing the room. There was urgency in his voice. "*Ask why Mobile 3 has moved out.*"

"*Stand by, I have incoming.*"

"*Blue Team Leader is querying Mobile 3. No response.*"

"*Two Police cars moving fast down via Trionfale towards the apartment complex. Lights and sirens on.*"

"*Signal the Team to crash abort. Repeat Crash Abort. Immediate. Advise them police are entering the complex.*"

"*Standby.*" They heard him calling on the VHF.

"*Roger that, I think I see them exiting the flat now. The cop cars are turning into the access road. They're going to run right into them as they exit the building.*"

Haydon ran his hands through his hair and scratched. Christ, this was going to be a disaster. The Ambassador would go crazy. He didn't want to think of the call he'd have to make to The Office.

"*Barker, exfiltrate the O.P right now. Consider it blown. Clean it and get out. Report in from a call box. Out.*" He reached down and flicked the switch. The call ended.

"There's nothing we can do for them. They're on their own. We have to pray they're not reeled in."

Haydon picked up a tennis ball and squeezed it repeatedly. How to frame this? Before the Press got hold of it. Before the phones rang red hot. Or had the Libyans already tipped them off? *We've been played, we didn't glance at the other side of the chess board.* He turned to Etherington.

"We are going to deny everything. Internally and externally. Put your best mask on and keep it fixed. No wobbles. Eat tranquilizers if you have to. We know nothing. There was no op, no team, nothing. Just a quiet day at the office. Even to The Ambassador."

"Is that credible?"

"Do it. Where the fuck did that Cooper guy go? Makes no sense. I'd better go see Polliti before that side of Hades explodes on my head. Like going to see the headmaster but worse. We're dogged, the bloody fates have got it in for us."

CHAPTER 23

They scaled the wall at the back of the compound, rain lashing down on them; it was no higher than the obstacle course at the base on RAF Aldergrove where they trained. Dropping down into thick mud on the other side the four figures trudged clumsily upwards through sloshing waste ground towards a wooded copse which ran up to and along a steep granite bluff.

Babs could make out the outline of the Hilton complex perched above the cliffs. She gestured the others on. They climbed fast for twenty minutes until they were well into the thick cover of the woods. The rain was letting up now; the skies to the West were brightening. Stopping on a grassy mound surrounded by old oak trees, they turned and looked back. Blue flashing lights winked at them from the walls of the apartment blocks. Babs took out a pair of compact Zeiss binoculars and scanned the area.

"Two cop cars. For a minor diplomatic break in. I bet the bastards called in the Press too." She frowned and passed the binos to Rathbone. "They won't search for us up here; we're in the clear. For now. But we're on our own, completely deniable. Can't contact the Embassy directly. Emergency comms. Let's hope the flat isn't blown."

"Cooper?"

"God knows, pray for him. What a debacle!"

"Anything we left behind that could link to us?" Babs looked around at their faces. "Think carefully. Damage control. There'll be a diplomatic shitstorm."

Skelton shook his head. "We checked each other this morning. Nothing changed."

"Go through it again in your mind." They were silent for a while, then one by one they shook their heads.

"That's something. Now let's get out of here." She was soaked through and covered in mud. They all were.

"Plan?"

"I'll call for extraction from the Hilton grounds; from round the back entrance, down the bottom by the Hertz office." Babs said, pulling the Walkie-Talkie out of a zipped pocket.

"Use the O.P at the hotel, get cleaned up there?" Rathbone asked. He was scraping mud off his coveralls with a long knife.

"No, we head to the flat and plan our exit, out of Italy by car. We're blown. We'll be on police watch lists. They'll probably have footage from that damned camera."

"God knows if the radio is secure, better presume it isn't." She paused, looking around at her colleagues, her mind racing. "They've been listening in. How else could they have known our timings? I'm going to have to use it now to call in our mobiles and order the guys out of the hotel. Then we bury it and run."

She held it to her ear and pressed the transmit button several times, then shook it. "Dead. Must have got wet or taken a knock." She switched it on and off, then took out and replaced the batteries. "No go. OK, so we can't risk the hotel. We'll head south along the edge of the woods. Before the main road we ditch our coveralls."

"Thank God the rain's stopped." Skelton said. "At least we won't look like sodding frogmen walking down the street in shirt sleeves."

"Down the hill to Piazza Mazzini, maybe a mile." Babs continued, "Pick up two taxis. OK?"

Straw Man

They set off through the woods in single file, skirting the back of built-up areas, walking fast. They've been watching us for ages, she thought. Underrating an opponent, beginner's stuff. Shit! She hoped the guys at the Hilton had got out; they would have seen the cop cars and should have read the runes? But Cooper? Had they grabbed him, maybe a hostage? Nightmare. What did the Libyans want?

Who would have thought Libyans could work something so sophisticated? They'd been patient, waiting for us to make our move. *To send us a clear message.* A professional setup. We walked right in, so pleased with ourselves, with Enrica's neatly available alarm code to ease our access. She'd done a number on Rathbone. Christ! And if Skelton hadn't spotted the camera when he did, we'd be bang in the centre of a diplomatic hiatus, hung out to dry on live TV, the works. She'd never experienced failure at this level before. A total wipe out.

Babs peered through the peephole in the front door before unlatching and opening it. Peter Etherington stepped in and shook himself on the doormat, stamping his feet, snowflakes falling from the shoulders of his overcoat like giant dandruff. He shivered, rubbed his hands together, removed his hat, thick woollen scarf and blue double-breasted overcoat and handed them to her.

"Never seen snow in Rome before." He plumped himself down on a long sofa, legs splayed. "Come to think of it, never seen a fiasco like this one before either. The caca is flying higher than a nuclear-powered Swiss muck spreader. You win the prize for setting off fireworks. The Libyans

Straw Man

have issued a démarche with the Farnesina, blaming us for the break in and demanding Haydon's expulsion."

"Where's he?"

"Head in his hands when I last looked. Waiting to face serious incoming from London." His cheeks were ruddy from the cold, almost scarlet. He reminded her of a cocksure school prefect. Trying to look stern and assertive, not quite making the grade. "At least the *Polizia* didn't bag you in the act. That's something. Still, our job at the Embassy has been straightforward–issuing repeated indignant denials."

"Cooper?" Babs sat down on a chair opposite him. The rented flat was dark and furnished with heavy wooden furniture. Depressing, with the brilliant light of Rome, to be holed up in this dingy hole. Several of the team sat around a dining room table, set apart from the seating area, beer cans and glasses strewn about. At the mention of Cooper, their faces looked over at Etherington.

"In hospital with severe concussion and two broken legs. He may have a fractured spine. Doctors say it's 50/50 he'll pull through. Police found him late this morning at the wheel of the van, turned upside down in a ditch. Near the refinery at Ponte Galeria. That's Fiumicino way. An empty bottle of vodka on his lap. No ID, thank God. We got a quiet heads-up from Pollitti. The Consul's going to visit this afternoon at the Policlinico."

Babs touched her throat and leaned forward; her face lined with worry. Poor bastard, in the hands of those Arabs. God knows what they'd done to him. She looked out of the window; snowflakes were blowing past, almost horizontally. "Signs he was mistreated?"

"Luckily too little time." Peter was picking at his fingernails, avoiding her eyes. "They must have driven him there directly from the grab. Drugged him, shoved the van off the road. He can't have been alert, they hijacked him pretty easily."

"Cooper's a pro. They must have surprised him; it was raining heavily, maybe he couldn't hear." She wondered how he'd let them get that close. "Can you extract him? Or will he face charges?"

"Drink driving for sure. We'll slip him out somehow, if he lives. First step is to get him moved to a private clinic. The Italians have a good idea of how this went down, we'll have to come clean." Etherington leaned back and lit a cigarette, his face a mask.

"Can't you get him out, to a hospital back home?"

"Right now our priority is to get you lot out of here and off Italian soil." He raised his voice and turned towards the men sitting at the table. "Orders are you're to leave immediately. Pack up, quick as you can, get on the road and drive through the night. South of France, Nine hours drive, maybe ten. This snow will clear, won't affect the autostrada. You have room reservations at the Nice Airport Hotel. You'll be met there and given further instructions."

"Copy that." Babs said. Several of the men got up and walked out of the living room.

"Debriefing in London on arrival. Lessons learned." He put his hands together in a tall arch, bent his head forward and frowned. "The counter-intelligence boys want to run through the op start to finish. They want a written report. Expedited."

She caught an aggressive tone in his voice. He looked so chubby-faced and innocent, but he'd caught on fast. So they were already figuring out who was going to take the blame for the mess. *And I'm perfectly located.*

"I'll get it done."

Straw Man

"Haydon would like your verbal reflections; how could you have let this happen?" He pointed his finger at her. "You were looking in the wrong direction?"

"A lot we haven't figured out ourselves. Were they listening to us?" She raised her arms to the ceiling. "If so, which of us and how and when? You need to get sweeps done everywhere to answer those questions. Were they monitoring our radio frequencies? Do they even have the gear for it? They certainly knew our timings, that's clear. And worrying."

"Maybe you weren't careful enough?" Etherington stared at her.

Babs reached into her jacket pocket and took out the Minox camera and several small film cartridges, which she laid on the coffee table.

"Peter, please get these off to London with Queen's Messenger? CI will want to develop them before our debrief."

"What's this?" Etherington picked up the Minox, turning the tiny camera over in his hands.

"Rathbone and I were going through Nasir's files, snapping the ones that seemed promising. Mainly in Arabic. We got maybe a third of the way through when the balloon went up. We came across a thick file on you, several blown-up surveillance photos. My first thought, you can tell Haydon, is–" She stared at him, her eyes suddenly cold. "–did they follow you people back to us? Have you been careful enough covering your backs?"

"I'll get them off with tomorrow's Messenger." He stood up, pink cheeks reddening. He avoided her eyes as he pulled on his overcoat, winding his scarf around his neck.

"Good trip! I'll tell your contact to expect you by soon after midnight."

Straw Man

CHAPTER 24

Haydon and Glasson stood side by side, rigid and erect. Two ex-military men, hands clasped behind their backs, staring silently out of the long window in Glasson's office on the 20th floor of Century House. Their expressions were sombre as they looked down at the dirty Thames splayed out below and the Houses of Parliament beyond. The river was busy for a winter's day; cold, grey water, turbulent with bow waves from stubby work boats, buoys bobbing and straining against the flood tide.

They'd concluded a mammoth session in the main conference room, all the key players in attendance. Examination of the minutiae of a failed operation. Costs, damage, risks. No mention of blame, at least not in the open. Not yet. Just dishonest crocodile smiles. Haydon felt he'd displayed a calm demeanour, transmitting with a plastered expression towards his colleagues. It had not been easy, heated arguments going nowhere.

Inside he was seething. Glasson had positioned him in the centre of the cross hairs. Nothing much he could do about that. There was an obvious need for a sacrificial goat. And plenty of wolves were baying. He'd watched the greedy eyes around the table sizing up his chances of survival, wishing for his demise, salivating at a vacancy that would speed up their own careers. He was wounded. He needed to survive long enough to get the operation back on the rails. Slim chance.

Nasir el-Maghrebi's recall to Tripoli had signalled the Libyans would no longer run the IRA operation out of Rome. The Det Team had been ordered back to their base in Ulster, chastened after one of the few failures in the Unit's history. Haydon felt a niggle of guilt, he'd sought to divert some of the blame towards the unit for a 'failure of planning'. Wasn't fair on Babs, he wasn't proud of that bit of necessary politics.

Focus had switched to intensifying intelligence gathering in the province. The most urgent task being to find out who in the Provo High Command was running Docherty, and where the next meetings with the Libyans would be. They needed to pick up the scent by any means. GCHQ was monitoring the phones of Mathies & Rougemont. Geneva Station had been tasked with establishing a suitable safe house in readiness for any future meeting with Docherty being flagged up.

Glasson pivoted and walked back to his desk. He sat down and swivelled the chair back and forth, leaning back in a thoughtful pose. He motioned Haydon to sit.

"We got off lightly." He picked up a paper knife and started opening envelopes.

"If the police had caught them *in flagrante–*"

"You would have been flayed. Denials wouldn't have been credible; the Press would have crucified us." Glasson opened a file and started leafing through a long document, then looked up. "Why haven't the Libyans used the camera footage against us?"

"Maybe they expected our guys to be rolled up by the cops? Would have been more dramatic coming from the Italians." Haydon stroked his face in a pensive gesture. He felt stubble; he hadn't shaved that morning, he realised. "Better TV."

"Better count our blessings I suppose." He returned to reading the file. "We've been humiliated and lost the trail, but at least the entire world didn't observe us squatting by the side of a public road having a shit. The Libyans will up their security; it'll be hard to regain the initiative."

Straw Man

Haydon waited. At least he had DAEDALUS in play. Nasir had rung Charlie before leaving for Tripoli and confirmed he'd continue to be his contact for procurement; invited him to come down to Tripoli. That thin line remained, dangling tenuously in the water. Here we go again, Haydon thought, it's down to Charlie and his untrained sleuthing. I'll send him over the top and see what happens. *I don't have anything else.* Still, early retirement wouldn't be a disaster. Sometimes he dreamed of breaking free from the bonds of The Office. No Knighthood, perhaps a Board seat with a security company and an escape from the financial straits of a government salary.

"When are you back to Rome?"

"Tomorrow. I'm going to have to meet Admiral Pollitti and calm the waters." He was going to have to show unpractised reserves of humility. A gloomy prospect. "He won't be in a friendly mood."

"Suck his dick if you have to." Glasson's face reddened. "After all, they're the ones enabling Libyan terrorism."

"He'd offered some of his guys to watch our backs. Which at the time I judged wouldn't be helpful, so I fobbed him off." Haydon frowned. "Now he knows I just wanted the freedom to run a black op on his turf."

"Fuck him." His voice turned hard. "Look Haydon, TUMBREL is your priority now. Get it moving."

"DAEDALUS is ready to go."

"Get the bugger down there." He rapped hard on the desk and leaned forward. "Into the rat's nest, has to earn his pay."

"They're trying him out with this first list. It's not prudent to hit the 'go' button too hard."

"Fuck prudent! Sprinkle chickenfeed, give the Libyans a hard-on."

"We could speed up delivery dates, might help?"

"Nothing dangerous on the list. Be imaginative."

"We need the stuff to work. Prepared for that?"

"The slightest chance of picking up a trace of these shipments and we take it. I've got pressure clattering around above my head."

"Understood."

"Haydon, we need eyes in Tripoli." Glasson laid his hands flat on the desk and fixed Haydon with a steely gaze. "Take your guy as deep down as you like."

"You're saying DAEDALUS is expendable?"

"Put bluntly, old friend, Operation TUMBREL might save your career. A gamble, but you've nothing else." He dropped the file into his briefcase and leaned back, his hands behind his neck. "Over to you."

Straw Man

CHAPTER 25

Haydon walked from the Embassy, he wanted to clear his head before he faced Pollitti's wrath. He felt stuck in a cloud of negativity permeating from the London office. His flight back to Rome had been delayed, he'd got home at two in the morning and hadn't slept well. On the plus side, at least he hadn't been summoned to Pollitti's office for an official dressing down, which was encouraging.

Still, he felt as though he were on his way to the headmaster's study to own up to some childish idiocy. In his schooldays there had at least been pleasurable notoriety to gain from such occasions. Keeping your head high, ready to face the music, smiling heroically. If there was to be future collaboration, he'd have to admit the lot. Conducting a large-scale black op on a friendly service's turf, it couldn't get much worse. He would extract his price, but how big? They'd have to pay up whatever it was. As far as he knew, Pollitti hadn't shared details with his political bosses. At least nothing had bounced back from London and landed on Haydon's head.

He lingered in the park, savouring the warm February sun on his face. He sat on a bench for a while, inhaling wafts of the scent of early mimosa, watching dark-haired mothers pushing prams, dogs dashing about, squeals of small children. The air was brisk and clear. Looking eastwards, he could see the distant Apennines capped with new snow. He stood up and wandered down the hill.

Pollitti was sitting at an outdoor table at the *Casina Valadier* in the centre of the leafy spread of the Villa Borghese. Tall palm trees sheltered the table, which faced down the hill towards the Piazza del Popolo. He was leaning back, his eyes closed, the sun illuminating his cheeks.

Straw Man

"You're looking grey." He opened his eyes and stared up. Haydon sat down opposite him. "You should get out more."

"My life is grey, I'm reflecting that." Haydon replied, looking over at Pollitti, whose face was expressionless. Even more so than usual, he thought. He'd make a dangerous adversary at the poker table. "Since the Brighton bomb it's been endless crises, back and forth to London."

"We've had our own bomb, as you know, on the Florence to Rome train. Many more casualties than yours." He scratched his scalp vigorously, then unfolded his napkin and tucked it into his shirt. "And our threats come from both left and right: you only have to worry about the Irish."

"On call through the holidays?"

"I managed a week in Tuscany over Christmas, reading and walking. Cleared the head. Just me and Martha."

They chatted until the waiter came with their food.

"OK, Haydon. Spit out the poison." He took a sip of wine and smiled. "Tell your father confessor what you did that you didn't oughtn't to have done?"

"Underestimated the Libyans." Haydon twirled spaghetti around on his fork. "Never thought them capable of sophistication, let alone patient sophistication."

"Nasir came to see me before he left for Tripoli. Lodged an official complaint about what he termed your 'terrorist' actions. Told me his government expected us to demand your recall."

"Our terrorist actions? His guys broke my guy's legs, nearly killed him, he's still in intensive care."

"And you were doing what exactly? Aside from breaching the Vienna Convention in his diplomatic lodgings? Libyan soil even."

Straw Man

"Planting audio and video, filleting his files." Haydon brushed a fly off his plate. "Looking for traces to his IRA connection."

"I've had the pleasure of watching the thrilling footage of your people rushing round his flat. None of them masked, except for the Amazonian warrior." He laughed "Who on earth is she?"

"A senior sergeant in our elite Ulster reconnaissance unit. We're an equal opportunity employer."

"We like the haul of stuff your people kindly left behind." Pollitti dabbed his mouth with his napkin. "We want some of those miniature-cameras, thank you. Ours are too bulky. Also, that live cable-camera gadget you stuck through the letterbox, a few of those."

"You'll have them." Haydon nodded his head. "We'd eyeballed Nasir meeting Docherty in Geneva recently. Concluded they're getting close to restarting the arms shipments. London is shitting itself."

"Their digestive problems would have been worse if that footage appeared on the evening news, together with a report on your expulsion." Pollitti put his fork down and leaned back in his chair, fixing Haydon with a glare. "You messed up, Haydon. You got caught. A mortal sin. Nasir's gone off patch, which won't help you, although he did tell me he'll continue to liaise with my office."

"He played it well. We played it badly."

"You British love rules. Forever banging on about your precious 'rules-based system'. But you need to stick to them, you can't just go off patch and expect it to be painless." He jabbed his finger towards Haydon. "If our friendship is to mean anything, we have to be open."

"Agreed. My team has left the country."

Straw Man

"We know. We'd spotted them, clocked their overcrowded flat. Quite a fire hazard!" He chuckled and took a sip of wine. "We'd even observed Nasir's guys watching you. If we'd been collaborating, as we specifically agreed we would, well–"

"–you offered, thank you Carlo. I messed up." Haydon felt a stab of anger. Carlo should have warned him. That's what friends were for? "What do you have in mind?"

"A divine balance." He laughed and refilled their wineglasses. "While you lose sleep about Semtex ending up in IRA hands–"

"–you suffer nightmares about bombs on trains."

"You need to understand the Red Brigades are as dangerous to my government as the IRA is to yours." Pollitti took a cigar out of his pocket and rolled it around under his nose. "They kill another Minister or American General on Italian soil and my government falls."

"I got it. We both need to avoid bird shit on our heads."

"In Italy, that's a sign of good luck."

"So I'll wear a hat and pray?"

Where was this going? Pollitti was toying with him. He stared at his glass absent-mindedly, then took a sip. "What can we do for you?"

"More top Red Brigade leaders have fled to Paris, running things from there. Collaborating with ETA, Red Army Faction, others. Our French friends are still not cooperating. Those *Brigate* thugs have been meeting with hard-line Palestinian groups in Paris, we think they're planning arms shipments from Lebanon. Exact same problem you have." He struck a match and puffed away to get his cigar going. "We want more intercepts. Targeted. Your GCHQ has the capabilities."

"Specifics?"

Straw Man

"I'll provide you with a list of names and numbers."

"And?"

"You bring me convincing product." Pollitti chortled. "Then we put clothes pegs on our noses, look the other way. Maybe give you a wink now and then. Such as when you're being followed."

"May I come back to you?"

"Take your time. Your bosses will see sense."

"Carlo, our guy with the broken legs. Cooper."

"What about him?"

"He faces charges of drink driving. They splashed him with vodka before shoving his van into a culvert."

"And?"

"We need him out of Italy. He's seriously injured."

"By the time I hear from you, I'll have looked into it."

A look of contentment came over the older man. He leaned back in his chair and puffed on the long cigar. They sat silently for a while, the low hum of conversation from nearby tables washing over them. A small breeze rustled the palm fronds. Done, Haydon thought, we're in the clear. That was easier than expected. Glasson would get the approval for GCHQ to be tasked. *Bloody French*. And he could expect intel about Libyan intentions.

"Thank you Carlo, I appreciate your understanding."

"What are friendships for?"

"Anything on your wires from Libya? I hear you've had senior delegations?"

"Nothing helpful to you, but my Minister's policy is bearing a little fruit." Pollitti gestured with his hands. "Contacts with our Israeli friends to discuss improvements for the Palestinians. The Libyans pressuring their radical PLO allies to reduce actions on European soil. Working together to counter the spate of airline hijackings."

"We've picked up whispers of Libyan cash donations to your political parties." Haydon carefully folded up his napkin and rolled it up. "Anything in it?"

"My political parties? Mine?" He frowned and stared hard at Haydon. "Not my area of competency, domestic politics. Not at all. Take my advice, Haydon, shouldn't be yours."

His face reddened, Haydon made to speak, but he held up his hand in warning.

"Do you take a special interest in political party funding in Westminster, Haydon? Saudi contracts, that sort of thing?" He leaned forward, face a mask, and whispered. "What's wrong with you Haydon, can't you learn to take yes for an answer?"

"You're right, Carlo." Haydon grinned wanly. "Not my area of interest."

"And this was shaping up to be such a friendly lunch." He leaned back and puffed at his cigar. "Brandy?"

After three sets of tennis, the two men were sweating profusely. Haydon and Charlie were evenly matched and fiercely competitive. They sat in the shade of the wooden pavilion by the swimming pool at the Villa Wolkonsky, sipping cold lemonade. The air was still, the scent of mimosa was intoxicating. Roman spring was about to burst out. The noise of the downtown traffic seemed far away and muffled, the cooing of doves providing a calming background.

Straw Man

As they looked over towards the ancient Roman aqueduct, the vivid pink of blossom caught Haydon's eye, a sheet of colour hanging down. Like a Rothko painting, he thought, almost blinding. He pointed.

"*Cercis siliquastrum*. Such a special colour, almost violet."

"What is it?" Charlie asked. "It's a sort of jacaranda hue."

"Legend has it Judas hanged himself from one such tree. Unconfirmed." Haydon replied. "Which is why it's called the Judas tree."

"Perhaps that's why it feels poignant."

"Unfaithful? Again."

"Worse, broke up with Ines. Badly. Tears and drink." He looked down at his shoes. "She's been seeing Andrea Vispoli, so everyone is pleased to tell me."

"Painful. Sorry."

"I'm not used to it. Jealousy." Charlie pulled the sweatband off his head and slumped forward. "We argued. About Libya. She thinks I'm a vile shit, flogging atom bombs to ragheads in silly uniforms and dark glasses. She overheard you and I talking. The trouble with journos, they hear everything, even from long distances."

"That's women for you, not just journos."

"Thus, the poignancy. I'd been lying to her, and to Andrea. I'm Judas. Part of me believes I deserve the pain – lying to my oldest friend and the first girl I've ever really loved. Retribution."

"You need to can that line of thinking." Haydon reached out and touched his arm, smiling. Charlie flinched. "Crazy path going nowhere."

He could often appear so vapid, Haydon thought, but something touchingly vulnerable lurked beneath the smooth exterior. Does he have the resilience and endurance to play the role of double agent? We throw

Straw Man

him into a web of die-hard terrorists, so quickly. With no training, no backup? Glasson couldn't give a shit. Burned agents didn't necessarily result in burned operations. There was a random element that sometimes paid off. Antithetical, but spying was like that. Haydon realised with a jolt he cared about Charlie. Perhaps not enough to put his own career on the line? He felt a twinge of guilt.

"What you're doing is gutsy, Charlie. You're suffering because of good intent."

"Doesn't feel it." Charlie hung a towel around his neck. "I go to bed at night dreaming about the lolly rolling in, how I'm going to spend it."

"So what. Revel in it, for God's sake! That's human." Haydon got up and started packing his stuff into a tennis bag. "I would."

"I went to a ghastly whore last night. Got drunk and stoned." Charlie stood up and stretched his arms upwards. "Thought I might feel better. Didn't work, I just feel wasted. No wonder you beat me!"

"Charlie, you're not a complicated guy, just keep it simple." He slung the bag over his shoulder. "Look at it as I do: you're doing this for your country, we're in a dangerous underground war against two, that's two, lots of seriously bad terrorists."

"Maybe you're right. Just another of life's glorious adventures." Charlie picked up his bag. The two men jogged off down the path.

"I admire what you're doing. Throw yourself into it. Get yourself down to Tripoli and move this thing forward. Get away from here. Forget about Ines for a while. All that camel shit and sand will clear your head out, or else fuzz up your brain. Either is better than wallowing in your pain."

Straw Man

CHAPTER 26

Charlie woke from his siesta heavy and disconsolate. In Tripoli the dusk seemed to sew such a melancholy seed. Orange and dusty, it hung its hot, low shadows over the darkening town, the haze of gloom seeming to seep right into his soul. He'd been dreaming about Ines. Again. About the morning he'd first seen her at the club. The dream had been shockingly vivid. He woke just as she was hissing and spitting at him like a cat. He felt the spatter of her saliva on his face, which turned out to be hot beads of sweat running down his cheeks. His mind returned to that first coy smile, that freeze-frame instant he'd instinctively known was going to herald a change in his life. How had he driven her away? What a jerk! What a piss-arsed motherfucking jerk!

Curiosity. The false-gold allure of closed doors had driven so much of his life. He had this sense that because a door was shut to him, its varnished facade must contain something fascinating, brilliant, and he would set off to charm or connive his way in. Usually he succeeded. Then he would inevitably be confronted by Fool's Gold. But with Ines, the door had sprung open easily and what lay behind it really was captivating, valuable. And he'd treated it just like all the others.

The gloom never lasted. After a witching hour people woke from their siestas and stretched, drank a coffee, yawned. Then the evening began, a little cool descended, people came out to work and play, rested after hiding away in their beds from the dusk's malaise. He got out of bed and padded down the marble stairs to the kitchen. Filling the percolator, he made himself a strong espresso, daydreaming of Ines as the machine burbled

Straw Man

and hissed, leaning down to inhale the heavy aroma before pouring it and sipping. He sat at the kitchen table and closed his eyes.

It had been a tough two weeks of interminable waiting since he had stepped off the Alitalia DC9 into the baking heat of Tripoli's international airport. And it was only April, he couldn't imagine what the summer heat could be like. He learned quickly that patience was the bedrock to business success in Libya. He had spent hours in air-conditioned waiting rooms around Tripoli, reading old copies of well-thumbed agricultural magazines, seeking to overcome his irritation as other visitors came in and were ushered through while he sat twiddling his thumbs. His favourite reading, which seemed present in every anteroom, was Korea Today, the official magazine of the North Korean Communist Party. Filled with unlikely stories about record-breaking milking cows and harvests of biblical proportions, it provided better entertainment than the other dog-eared dross left behind by official delegations passim.

Another challenge was to avoid lapsing into a deep sleep in the sticky plastic armchairs that festooned important men's waiting rooms. To risk being unexpectedly caught off balance, saliva running down your face and your white shirt, as you were woken and summoned at speed into a Minister's inner sanctum. Charlie had heard of a French tractor salesman who had fallen asleep in one such office, only to awake after midnight, locked in until morning, desperately needing a bathroom and with few options available.

He had plunged with gusto into the local custom of long afternoon siestas. Offices closed at two. He would hurry back to the Canova guest house on the northern edge of Tripoli, eat a quick lunch and head for his air-conditioned bedroom.

Straw Man

He heard leaden footsteps clonking down the stairs. Armin Fürrer had arrived from Zurich that morning. The two of them were the sole occupants of the guest house.

"Charlie! Yes please." The deep singsong voice preceded Fürrer's large body through the door. "My sensitive nose tells me you're considering my wellbeing."

"Mister Smith. You're wrong, what you can smell are my selfish needs. I woke up feeling grouchy, but a sip of *Lavazza* and the energy poured right back into my veins."

"So kind." He reached his hand out. Charlie poured coffee into a small cup, handing it to Fürrer. It was hard to mope with the cheery figure of Fürrer around.

"Let's hope we put this order to bed, and I can head home tomorrow." Charlie plumped himself down on the sofa. "Bit unfair I've done the hard work and you roll up to collect the prize."

"As it should be. You young chaps should wait your turn."

Fürrer's shoulders shook as he took a sip of his coffee. He was wearing a pair of bright green trousers and a clashing pink linen shirt. He looked as if he were dressed for carnival in Rio. Perhaps the Libyans would mistake it as the height of European style?

"Nasir assured me the Minister will sign today and give the order for the down payment. Mind you, there's never anything definite in the Arab world. Except for waiting. That's definite. No, there's only *Inshallah*. They've only kept me hanging around for two weeks; perhaps a record for speed and efficiency."

"Worth the wait, Charlie." Fürrer emitted a grunt. "Your trouser pockets will soon fill with treasure."

Straw Man

"They're sending a car for us at eight." Charlie turned and headed up the stairs. "I've got to shower. See you down here in half an hour."

The official car arrived an hour later than promised. An old, dented Mercedes with broken shock absorbers and a young, white-uniformed driver. They bounced raggedly along the empty streets of Tripoli for half an hour, then turned into a dusty military compound. A barrier swung up as the car approached, jolting uncomfortably over potholes in the unprepared road. They passed what Charlie thought was a parade ground and pulled up in front of a three-story villa. Their driver led them up a stone stairway, then ushered them along a musty corridor into a large, air-conditioned office. Ahmed Khalfari and Nasir el-Maghrebi stood up as they entered. Nasir's greeting seemed genuinely warm. That's a change, Charlie thought. Step by step.

"Welcome brothers, welcome. Come in. Sit down." Khalfari beamed and plumped himself down behind the long desk. "I gather we've concluded our first business. Nasir informs me the Minister has signed the contract."

"Signed this afternoon." Nasir took a folder from his briefcase and handed it to Fürrer. "Your copy. I'm told you may speed up deliveries?"

"The orders will go to our suppliers immediately we receive the down payment." Fürrer read through the contract, then passed it to Charlie.

"The shipment will be ready within eight weeks." Fürrer beamed. "We want you to be a happy customer!"

"Brother, we'll be a happy customer for so long as you carry out your promises to the letter." Khalfari laid his hands palms down on the table and

Straw Man

frowned, as if in concentration. "Now we'd like your advice on another list. We worry some items are complex."

Nasir handed a sheaf of typed papers to Fürrer, who fumbled for his reading glasses, perched them on his ruddy nose and leafed through the contents. They sat in silence for some minutes.

"These high-frequency inverters," Fürrer ran his finger down the list and pointed, "You'd need to break them down and place an order for the parts. Fluoride resistant valves and vacuum tubes, no problem. I can't see anything difficult. Charlie will provide you with drafts of required changes to your text. We'll quote once we have the revised list."

"We're going to build good business with you brothers, not just in this area." Khalfari said, smiling warmly, opening his arms with a welcoming gesture. "We'll line you up with preferential bids for the Leader's Great-Man-Made-River Project."

That would be a leap forward, Charlie thought. Better, it would even be legal! Not even sanctions to worry about. The Leader's giant irrigation project was Pharaonic in scale and never ending.

"One last thing, Mr Smith." Khalfari's voice seemed to turn a little harsher. He stroked his thin beard and stared at his pudgy fingers. "We wish to acquire drawings and calculations for a gas-centrifuge facility."

The Swiss man closed his eyes, took off his glasses, leaned back, then remained still and silent for some time before responding.

"Difficult." He raised his arms as if in benediction and grinned. "It's common knowledge that centrifuge cascades can be re-plumbed to produce highly enriched uranium for nuclear weapons. My company couldn't supply drawings. Not even for a civil plant."

Straw Man

"But you have a way around it?" Khalfari frowned and drummed his fingers on the table.

The Libyan must have known the answer would be a firm No. This is the hurdle, Charlie thought, he's trying it on, seeing how far we'll cross the line into forbidden territory. To ensure we're properly compromised. Exactly as Haydon had told him they would. He glanced over at Fürrer; who looked like a Buddha, peaceful and unmoving. This was the critical moment.

"It's of the highest importance." Khalfari's expression had turned sulky. "If you are not prepared to help us, we have to re-evaluate if you are suitable partners."

Fürrer remained silent. He ran his fingers through his hair and leaned back. His face seemed to reflect the gaiety of his pink shirt.

Charlie turned to Khalfari. "Ahmed, I may have a solution."

"Drawings?"

"No. Better."

"Better?"

"We might be able to introduce you to a team of highly qualified scientists and engineers. With all the necessary know-how." This was Haydon's trump card, primed to ensure they cantered across the finishing line. Charlie turned to Nasir. "They could draw up detailed designs for you, to your own specification. They might be prepared to supervise construction."

"Mister Smith?" Khalfari raised one eyebrow.

"The contract would need to stipulate civil purposes."

"What nationality?"

"A team from South Africa. Brilliant people." Charlie said. "Their own programme is winding down, so we might induce them to do the work for you – at the right price. They won't come cheap."

Straw Man

"I'll discuss with my people and get back to you."

"Let us know. We can send preliminary details."

Khalfari stood up and gestured that the meeting was over. He and Fürrer stood up and shook hands.

"You understand the importance of this?" Nasir walked with them to the car and waved them off. Charlie nodded. *Well done, Haydon, just as you predicted.* He could feel Nasir's excitement. He nodded.

"I'll arrange a car to take you to the airport in the morning."

"Dollar bills were flashing in their eyes like fireflies!" Ahmed Khalfari leant forward and clapped his hands. "They stank of greed."

"They're ready to break the law. If we pay them enough."

"We'll get everything we need. Look how quickly they came up with a solution for centrifuge ranges! The Leader will be pleased."

"Once they've crossed those red lines, they're ours." Khalfari grinned. "Did you see their faces when I hinted I might cancel?"

"The Englishman looked like he'd eaten a spider."

"Get hold of the scientists. I want them to go over these first deliveries with magnifying glasses." Khalfari's plump face puckered. He picked up a packet of cigarettes and lit one. "Get the down payment off, let's see how quickly they perform."

"Shall I ask them for the details of the South Africans?"

"Do it. But no hurry." He paused, leaned back, intertwining his hands behind his neck. "Find out all you can about South Africa's nuclear programme. Bring me a report. I know they collaborate with Israel, but also with Pakistan. We'll check the names out with our Pakistani friends."

Straw Man

"I'll sound out the ISI guy at the Embassy."

"You see, there may be a larger opportunity here." Khalfari stood up and started pacing the room, gesticulating with his hands. Nasir sensed his elation. "After our success in making goats out of MI6 in Rome, we should press home our advantage. While they're off balance. Go in hard, double up, strike a blow that really hurts them."

"You want me back there?"

"You stay here, come and go as necessary. They'll be looking for a chance to get back at us; so maybe we offer them a way."

Khalfari looked down at the floor, then carried on pacing the room. He stopped and pulled on his cigarette. Nasir waited for him to continue.

"This Mister Charlie. Andrea Vispoli told me he's wired in at the British Embassy. We hook the guy deep enough, fill his bank account with dirty money. Then we use him to play a little game. Start with offers of quiet talks."

"You want me to act as a double? Play the part of someone keen to thaw relations?"

"Yes. They love moderates." Khalfari brushed ash off his sleeve. "But the Leader himself would need to approve any direct contact with MI6."

"I see where you're going. Play Lomax back and dangle bait. Offer an information exchange?"

"Yes, you hand them some delicate stuff – they dream of getting inside gen on our Palestinian brothers. But money. We offer to buy information for cash. For sure they start off handing us useless chicken feed, maybe even disinformation, that's OK. Then we wait and see if we can tempt one of those badly paid MI6 people over the line, just as we did with the CIA guys."

Straw Man

"That would be a first, turning an MI6 operative."

"We only need one hungry guy, you see. Work up a plan for me to take upstairs."

Nasir scribbled notes on a pad and looked back at Khalfari. His boss was too greedy and ambitious to sustain a long game. He'd never let the operation take the necessary time. He'd rush it. These stings needed patience to mature. You couldn't push them. He'd need to guide it carefully. The Trieste fiasco was forgotten, but he needed to be cautious. This could rocket him way up the ladder if he got it right. Was it possible to recruit an MI6 spy? Whoever was the handler would be a national hero.

Khalfari sat down again and tapped the table. "Now the other thing Nasir, the Irish file. I had a visit from Fitzgerald. Iron tough, that guy. They're ready to move."

"I'm meeting Docherty in Malta next week. First shipment set for August."

"Send a team of watchers ahead, two days at least. Make sure your back is clean."

"I'm taking Captain Hassan Ali with me. Our last meeting before the shipment."

"Good. Wrap it all up. Come back and see me tomorrow." He dismissed Nasir with a wave of his hand. Nasir picked up his file and left the room.

Straw Man

CHAPTER 27

The group of men sitting at a long table by the swimming pool at the Hilton Hotel at Valletta must appear unremarkable, Seán thought. On such a polyglot island, the results of millennia of the mixing of bloods, of endless invasions. Phoenician and Carthaginian, Macedonian, Sicilian and Egyptian, Norman, Greek, Arab, Genoese and Venetian. He'd read a guide book. No Irish mentioned.

Nasir and Captain Hassan Ali, dark-haired and dark-skinned, were sitting in the shade of an enormous umbrella, sipping orange juice. Seán was opposite, next to the Skipper, tall and fair-haired, with a nose which looked as if someone had bust it a few times. The two of them were red faced and sweating, tall frothy beer mugs in front of them. Seán wiped his forehead with his forearm and took a gulp of beer.

"Captain, you go aboard with the Skipper." Seán pointed to the other man. "Get an idea of the layout of the hatches and the ease of access. Space for twenty tons, that's for sure."

"A one ton derrick will do the trick." The Skipper said. He had a Dublin accent, soft-spoken for such a hard-looking man. "We'll lash the vessels snug together. If the sea's calm, it won't take a half-hour to transfer the crates."

"We'll be using a large fishing trawler." Captain Hassan Ali spoke slowly, seeming almost reticent. Although his naval training had been in the USSR, his English was fluent. "It'll be out amongst the fishing fleet for several days before the Rendezvous."

"Timing?"

"Night. After midnight. We wait for a high-pressure forecast, calm seas. In summer that's frequent."

Straw Man

"Location? Needs to be easy and empty." Seán asked.

"Lee side of Gozo. If there's no wind we'll RV to the West, close inshore, half a mile, less even, in the shadow of the cliffs. Uninhabited. We'll have a suitable derrick, don't worry." Captain Hassan Ali turned back to the Skipper and continued. "We need to agree signals. Lights. Radio for emergencies only. Any sign of hostiles, we abort. The danger is whilst we're lashed together. We need sharp lookouts during the transfer."

"Skipper, you show the Captain around the vessel, agree transhipment details and signals." Seán said. "I've got administrative matters to go over with Nasir."

"We'll see you back here." The two men got up and walked towards the hotel exit.

It had taken Seán several days before his legs had stopped wobbling as he walked on dry land. His head felt a slight roll. He'd never thought he'd be comfortable lurching around on ocean swells, but it had been a doddle. His first ocean voyage. A landlubber from the mean streets of Belfast.

They'd acquired the *Makaria* from a fishing fleet in Dunmore East near Waterford. Built in 1948 from stout Irish oak, she'd operated as an offshore fishing vessel for over 25 years, based out of Galway and fishing the violent seas off the rugged Kerry coast. She looked like a rusty cork, but the Skipper he'd recruited, Adrian Nolan, insisted she just needed a little tidying up. The bits that mattered were sturdy and well-maintained, he said, and the two old, solid diesel engines were in excellent condition. The asking price was sharp. Seán could see she was workmanlike. Not graceful, too stubby, like a rubber duck, he thought. Top heavy for long sea journeys in rough waters, she'd bob over rather than cut through ocean swells. That was just his impression, he knew nothing of the sea.

Straw Man

He'd had qualms about setting off with Nolan in the middle of a storm in late February and taking her up the East coast of Ireland to the small port of Arklow, where they'd left her at Tyrrell's boatyard for a thorough going over. But Seán had relished life aboard. Once he'd recovered from a serious bout of seasickness. He found himself enjoying the adventure and being away from Belfast. In late April he settled with the shipyard for the works, paying in cash, much to the relief of the owner. The Skipper was well-known for his reticence to reach for his wallet.

On a calm, early summer's day they departed Arklow with a crew of three brawny men and set course due south on a flat sea, having declared their next destination to be Marseilles. After a trouble-free passage through the Mediterranean, they arrived in Malta and moored up amongst the cruising yachts and work boats at the marina on the south side of Manoel Island.

"He's a pro, the Skipper." Seán turned to Nasir. "Greedy bastard, in it for the pillage. No beliefs in any cause. Except his trouser pocket. We used your dollars to prime him good. I've no worries on his account."

"Drug smuggler?"

"So they say. I don't ask questions. Don't care." Seán laughed. "He's smart enough to know he won't mess with the Movement. Knows his way around the coves and bays of the Republic. I'll be with him on board that leaky tub, so that's important. For his safety and mine."

"How many trips this year?"

"We'll get two done, three if we're lucky, before the winter storms."

"And the larger one?" Nasir said. "We'd need to plan carefully for the two last shipments. 100 tons at a go. The ones that count. Next spring?"

Straw Man

"I've one under my eyes. I'm to Hamburg from here with the Skipper. Check the state of it. We'll have it in good time. But we'll be needing money from your side to complete the purchase."

"You see, that must wait until we've seen the first shipment safely through. Those are my orders."

A young couple sat down at the next table, holding hands and murmuring. The girl was wearing a small polka-dot bikini. She looked over at Seán and smiled, then turned away and kissed the man. No, he thought, not followers. But you could never be too careful. Better be paranoid.

"Only a short while and I'll be unloading heavy boxes in the middle of the night." He leaned closer to Nasir. "Another spit in the eye of the Brits."

"Remember to keep your own eyes open while you're at it."

"Think of me on that blessed empty sea. Bugger all to see. Or do."

"We'll meet as soon as you've delivered this lot. Mid-September, Greece. OK for you? One of the islands, where it's easy to spot watchers. Aegina? Usual comms." Seán nodded. "Need to get the second load off back-to-back."

Seán meandered down the lines of boats moored stern to in the marina, precarious wooden gangplanks connecting them to the shore. Peering into the saloon of a blue hulled yacht, his mind went back to Belfast. Glancing into windows of terraced homes on cold winter's evenings, inside lights revealing tableaux of domestic activity. Oddly intimate, theatrical scenes. People frozen in humble acts which challenged you to create their biographies from the clues on offer. He walked on.

Straw Man

He noticed the girl in the polka-dot bikini coming out of the mahogany wheelhouse of a long motorsailer, squeezing a wet towel and hanging it over the rail, attaching clothes pegs. Water was dripping from her hair, her body bronzed. He could make out the head of the man sitting on a deck chair, reading a book. Perhaps they'd eloped, he thought, stolen the boat and sailed off. The man was unsuitable? Probably the family didn't approve. The father would have been angry, the guy too lowly for his beloved daughter. The girl descended the steps into the wheelhouse. He stepped back into the shade of an awning; an estate agent's shop front he saw.

He turned and glanced down at the details of houses for sale. Bright blue swimming pools. Views over rocky bays with limpid water, always sunny. White stuccoed fisherman's cottages, nets splayed out on sandy beaches. Somewhere here was his dream. Like the couple, he'd elope. But alone. He knew no one on this island. A small cove away from the city, near a small fishing village. A clinker-built rowing boat, perhaps a small outboard. He'd catch his lunch. Learn to cook.

He started walking back towards the hotel. He'd know more about catching lunch by the time he'd landed back on Clogga in the middle of the night with Nolan and a bunch of Eastern European weapons. Nolan liked to keep a line out when they were moving. They'd caught and cooked a few grand fish on the voyage down. Tuna and bonito.

A motorbike came racing down the road towards the pier, the driver's hair sweeping out behind him, a red bandana around his head, a thick moustache. With a loud report, the engine backfired. The noise of Belfast. He'd have ducked if he'd been there. Although it would have been too late. Here he'd be able to forget the hatred, rifles pointed in every direction. Stones flying about. God knows if he'd ever get the chance to lay his

Straw Man

hands on Nasir's suitcase of money. For the time being, he could dream. Dreams were safe.

Straw Man

CHAPTER 28

Haydon strode out of his flat and dived down the steep flight of steps that led to the river, heels click-clacking as he descended the ancient stone. Crossing the Tiber on the crowded Ponte Sublicio, he paused in the centre of the bridge, seeming to stare through his thick dark glasses at the dirty river and the island beyond. He enjoyed the zest of counter-surveillance routines, challenging your senses, sharpening your peripheral vision, staying super-alert. The Libyans weren't going to catch them out a second time.

He hurried through the flea market of Porta Portese and entered the maze of narrow streets that made up Trastevere, criss-crossing, doubling back twice and then re-crossing the river by the Ponte Palatino. He thought of it as a sort of Pelmanism with faces and clothing, searching out shapes that stopped too suddenly or hurried on unnaturally fast, above all watching people's gait. You could change your apparel, your looks, your voice, your face, but you could never change the individual way you moved.

Hurrying away from the river, he came to the long, flat expanse that marked the site of the Circus Maximus. He meandered across the deserted area, the spring grass still green underfoot. He stood on a little hummock and turned a slow circle. No one. Closing his eyes, he visualised the death struggles that had taken place there, muscled gladiators with nets and tridents, elephants charging, chariots speeding around the racetrack. And the lakes of bygone blood which had seeped into the earth on which he stood.

Crossing the main road, he turned up the Aventine hill and darted into the Municipal Rose Garden. It was glorious late May; the roses were at their psychedelic best. He wandered along the beds for a while, then sat down on a wooden bench shaded by a tall oak tree. An orchestra of smells

Straw Man

from the massed blooms rose to engulf him. He leaned back and tried to identify individual smells, impossible. A mesmeric low-frequency buzzing of bees crowded his ears. He felt a wave of sensory bombardment.

He'd tasked Peter Etherington with watching Charlie's back. Although he'd warned Charlie about the importance of ensuring his back was clean. But he couldn't trust him to heed the warnings.

"So I keep my eyes open for swarthy men in safari suits and improbably large dark glasses?" Charlie had replied. "Should be easy."

"They've caught us out snoozing in the past," he'd told Charlie," With painful consequences. At this stage we can't take risks, mustn't be seen together."

"Sort of like an extramarital affair?"

"Exactly, and similarly, discovery has painful consequences. Be serious, think of your toenails."

Haydon watched as Charlie wandered towards him. Looking towards the entrance gate, he saw Peter signal with his left arm, then turn away. Haydon took a deep breath. All clear. He waved.

"The smells and colours are spectacular." Haydon pointed. "Temple to Flora, the Goddess of Flowers, just over there. Third Century BC. People have been worshipping flowers right here for millennia."

Charlie was wearing a crumpled beige linen suit, a red rose in his buttonhole.

"Hi." He sat down on the bench and turned to Haydon. "Wouldn't have put you down as a Chelsea Flower Show type."

"I'm a man of mystery. Nick the rose, did you?"

"Funeral. School buddy."

"So young?"

Straw Man

Charlie nodded. "Car crash."

"You watched your back?"

"I'm clean. Did a lengthy laundry run, as you like to call it."

"Pretty poor attempt. We've been watching you."

"Christ! Leave me alone already."

"Your trip? Enjoy holiday time in Tripoli?"

"Nasty, dirty place." Charlie laughed. "But we're galloping ahead. First shipment going off. Delighted our Libyan brethren. I'm going down next month for the delivery and relying on your reassurance. You promise the bits we're sending won't blow up, at least not while I'm handing them over."

"This batch is undefiled." Haydon lit a cigarette and leaned forward. "Not even pork scratchings."

"So we're supplying working parts?" Charlie asked.

"Yes. They can test them to hell and back. You'll be the popular boy."

"Until I'm exposed."

"Stay on your toes and you won't be." Haydon punched him playfully on the shoulder. "Incidentally, well done getting the scientists into play. Khalfari seemed keen?"

"I could read it in his eyes. They conducted an entire *pas de deux* when I proposed it."

"It'll supercharge our plans."

"You can control the South Africans?"

"Put it this way. If the Libyans sign them up for the design and supervision of the centrifuge facility, we can ensure it stays perfectly safe, yes. Completing construction and setting the cascades into service will take at least two years—more like three. Time enough to see our operation away and gone. You'll have retired to Ibiza with an actress."

Straw Man

"I won't be 30. You can't retire 'til you're past 30."

They fell silent whilst two elderly ladies walked past, a stocky terrier growling at them, sniffing aggressively at Haydon's trouser leg. He gave it a surreptitious kick. It sprung back and darted off.

"The Yarpies won't need to take any risks until way down the line. Their designs will be *bona fide*. We only need them to spec a few altered components into the control systems at the last stages. So you need to encourage the Libyans to scrutinize the early designs and work."

"Up to now reaction is positive."

"As I told you."

"Khalfari is supporting us at the Ministry. We've put in proposals for the Great Man-Made-River Project." Charlie ran his hand through his hair. "No whispers about the IRA, nothing like that."

"Patience." Haydon leaned in towards him and touched his hand. "First you need to get accepted as a trusted supplier of illicit materiel."

"I have one thing for you." Charlie frowned and ran his hand through his hair. "Might be relevant."

"Spit is out!"

"I overheard Andrea discussing a payment he'd made for Nasir. At the Minister's request. Three million dollars. They were laughing about the name of the account at the Vatican Bank, which was – this is exact, *'for the widows and orphans of the poor and miserable'*."

"Sickening. Corrupt bastard." Haydon took a notebook from his jacket pocket and starting writing. He showed it to Charlie. "Is this right–?"

"Yes. But be careful with the name, Haydon, mustn't get traced back to me."

"I'll treat it as ultra-sensitive, don't worry." Haydon put his finger in front of his mouth. "Look, I want you to introduce me to Andrea. Square the circle, push out feelers, propose to him we open a backchannel to Nasir and Khalfari. Quiet, useful talks. You can dress it up how you think best."

"I'm not sure you two will like each other."

"Unimportant. Important is we sanitise our relationship in public." Haydon stared at him. "Then your Libyan friends know you and I meet, we allay suspicion. They'll grasp such contacts may lead to useful exchanges."

He sensed that Charlie was reluctant, but eventually he'd agreed to set up a lunch.

"I hear they've fixed a date for Khalfari's official visit?"

"October. Later than expected, there are regional elections in May." Charlie said.

"The PM will meet Craxi and the Minister during the European Council meeting in Milan next month. She's going to raise the matter of Libyan support for the IRA."

"He's unlikely to be helpful, with three million dollars weighing on his mind?"

"PM's handbag will contain bargaining chips, stuff the Italians want. We may get something. Or not."

"Seems improbable."

"She flirts with him; can you believe that? A peculiar thought." Haydon stood up. "She intends to get across how dangerous Italy's support for Libya is becoming for us, she'll ask for increased intelligence cooperation."

After they parted, Haydon jogged up the hill towards his flat. He'd never experienced qualms about launching agents into hostile territory, but he felt a tinge of guilt as he pushed Charlie further over the edge. *Maybe I'm*

Straw Man

getting old? Better harden my heart, he thought, let him earn his bread. Maybe he'll make a fortune and even get to keep it.

"Usable intel. Exactly the sort of stuff we want. Push DAEDALUS to produce more." Haydon was talking on the red secure phone on his desk. The buzzing noise generated by the encryption device distorted Glasson's voice. "The PM will want to be appraised. Pertinent to her forthcoming meeting with the Minister. I lunched with her Private Secretary yesterday and briefed him about this payment. Bribes paid by Libyan Intelligence to senior Italian ministers, not kosher at all."

He leant back in his swivel chair and looked down over the embassy garden. He saw his reflection in the windowpane. Natty in a blue suit with a striped school tie, a red silk handkerchief flowing out of his breast pocket. The gardens were a blaze of colour. He had the telephone receiver tucked under his chin and was lighting a cigarette. He was feeling upbeat. This operation was getting back on track. His operational intuition was rarely wrong. A cloud of starlings rushed past his window, shaping and reshaping every few seconds. Like a magic trick, he thought.

"It's crucial to keep the name of the account tightly controlled Mark. It's single source material and a leak would be catastrophic for our informant. Put him at great risk. You didn't–?"

"–I don't need a lecture on operational security from you." Glasson snapped.

Later, Haydon would remember these words, which he was sure Glasson forgot as soon as he put the phone down. The account name was too memorable, too entertaining. He wouldn't be able to resist making a snide joke about it. About the hypocrisy of Italians, that would delight him. Still, he could rely on the PM's good sense.

"Mark, he's out on a–"

"–if there's more, inform me at once. Time he earned his wages. This operation is costing us a bundle and I want to see payback. Before any Semtex hits the streets of Belfast."

"I'm lunching with the infamous Mr Vispoli. Construction magnate and confidant of Ahmed Khalfari." Haydon puffed on his cigarette, then laid it in the ashtray. "I plan to open a backchannel and feed the Libyans with angel dust to bolster DAEDALUS' hand. I'll let drop we've heard about forthcoming arms shipments, from a highly placed informant in Belfast. Spook them."

"Do that. Stir them up, muddy the waters."

"I'll give them enough so they ask DAEDALUS to dig and find out more? Get them to wonder if they might even turn him, double him back on us."

"Could be just what we need. Work it up. Gotta run."

Running Charlie as a double. That would be something. It might even be possible to go one step further, if he could get the Libyans to convince themselves they had an opportunity to recruit someone inside SIS. Developing and managing doubles was the ultimate challenge for any case officer. More contorted than three-dimensional chess. A long shot, but worth the risk. For him, anyway. After the failure of the aborted break in, it could be perfect pay back.

Straw Man

CHAPTER 29

The Head Waiter led the two men to a corner table of the rooftop restaurant of the Hotel Eden, looking down into the lush private gardens of the Villa Medici. Charlie was agitated. He didn't relish having to talk about Ines with Andrea and was edgy about the prospect of antagonism between Andrea and Haydon. The two of them were opposites in almost every way – personality, politics, morality, sense of humour, or lack of. Underpinning his mood was a subliminal fear of exposure: that somehow the truth about his relationship with Haydon, his duplicity with Andrea, might slip out.

"The wild asparagus is fresh, Dottore, cut this morning. And may I recommend the *fiori di zucca?*"

"Maurizio, bring us two glasses of *prosecco* while we wait." Andrea waved him away with a friendly hand. They sat quietly for a while.

Andrea broke the silence.

"You want to talk about her?"

Charlie examined his friend's face. He didn't detect a trace of sarcasm; he didn't look embarrassed or valedictory.

"I wanted to meet a few minutes early in case you did."

"Who she's with, what she's doing," Charlie's face creased, and he looked away. "I'd rather not know."

"Maybe you'll find a way back together, Kiko? If you care enough."

"No point. We broke up. That's it." The two friends' eyes met. Charlie held the stare. He felt a stab of jealousy. "I was a fool, said unforgivable things. She doesn't want to see me."

Straw Man

"I don't want poison between us, our friendship is valuable–" Andrea paused, then reached out, touching Charlie' hand, "–you two had something serious going. I don't. You know that."

"During my trip to Tripoli, everyone wanted to tell me about how good you two looked together."

"You know me. I'm married, I'm committed. I'm serially irresponsible."

"No poison, friendship undamaged. Can we move on?" Charlie felt himself reddening. "Any blame's on my head, not yours."

"OK, shithead." Andrea sipped his drink. "So your friend Talbot believes quiet talks might lead to improved relations? With a nice English cup of tea?"

"He says. It's worth trying."

"Hard to believe. His government overcoming their rage about last year's events at the People's Bureau in London."

"He's keen to meet you. Knows how connected you are to the Libyan hierarchy. As well as with the powers that be here."

"Can we trust him?" Andrea frowned, taking a sip of his drink.

"It's a risk. If things go wobbly, our friends in Libya won't be happy."

"I suppose anything leading to a reduction in the likelihood of increased sanctions on Libya is helpful to me." Andrea lit a cigarette. "I don't see what's to lose, in any case I'll deny this meeting ever happened."

"That's him over there."

Haydon's eyes took in the body language as he followed the Head Waiter over to the corner table. He sensed tension between the two men, there was something canine, the way they faced each other, somewhere between

Straw Man

cocky and aggressive. They've been talking about Ines, he thought. Tricky. He reached out his hand as the men stood. Charlie made the introductions.

"Haydon, may I introduce Andrea Vispoli, President of Canova. Andrea, this is Haydon Talbot, Counsellor at the British Embassy."

The white-jacketed Head Waiter handed them large, stiff, Menu Cards and hovered, waiting until they gave their orders.

"Haydon, Andrea and I were at school together since we were 10? Neither of us any good, but we had fun. Learned about girls." Haydon noticed beads of sweat on Charlie's forehead. "Not sure I learned the right lessons."

"Too smooth for his own good." Andrea pointed at his nose with his forefinger. "With my enormous hooter, I had to try harder."

"Not true." Charlie smiled. "He'd arrive at school in his brother's red Ferrari, that made up for his ugly snout."

"How did you two meet?" Andrea turned to Haydon.

"Cambridge. I was doing postgraduate stuff. Turkish language. Charlie and I played competitive tennis. He didn't make the University team."

"Haydon was a blue. I partied."

"Kiko tells me we share a common interest in our north African cousins." Andrea said, turning back to Haydon.

"And a mutual friend in Carlo Pollitti."

"A wise owl."

"Mr Vispoli, we have a problematic history with Colonel Qaddafi. Since the break in diplomatic relations last spring, our Italian friends have been pressing us towards dialogue, while our American cousins pull us in the opposite direction."

"Call me Andrea, please. Uncomfortable. Piggy in the hole – isn't that what you call it?"

"I see sense in the Italian approach. A slow process, encouraging trust little by little, keeping lines of communication open. Trying to set up confidence building measures." Haydon smiled. "But they're a pretty bonkers lot?"

"Oh yes. Simple, really, as well as bonkers. Desert Arabs. I like that about them." He stubbed his cigarette out in the ashtray. "I'd be pleased to play a role. Kiko knows my proclivity for peaceful interventions."

"That's how we first met, Haydon." Charlie laughed. "This guy interposed himself in a schoolyard brawl. I was winning, of course, Andrea spoiled it."

"I am a natural born mediator!"

I bet he really believes it, Haydon thought. The Italians consider themselves natural intermediaries. They never want to be forced to take sides. And if they ever are, they always choose the wrong one.

"Andrea, I'm aware how well-connected you are there." Haydon leaned forward and talked in a low tone. "Our particular concern is Northern Ireland. Especially after last October's terrorist bomb. Came within a whisker of killing our Prime Minister."

"Luck was with you." Andrea replied. "But no suggestion of Libyan involvement?"

"None." Haydon opened his hands as if in supplication. "But we've received credible intelligence about plans for arms shipments from Libya to the IRA. Said to include quantities of Semtex. A dangerous escalation. We would like to discuss this with the Libyans, and, in a perfect world, to negotiate it away. I'd appreciate your help."

Straw Man

"I hear you. I can't comment as I know nothing about such things. But I will have words. No doubt I'll learn what they want to put on the negotiating table, they'll have pressing concerns of their own. Sanctions most likely."

"Who will you talk to?"

"I'll have a quiet chat with Nasir el-Maghrebi - you know him?" Haydon nodded. "He'll be interested in talking. It'll be fascinating to see how you two get along, they don't like you English at all."

"What about Charlie then? He gets on with them?"

"He's not really English, Haydon, spent too much time here. He is *viziato*. You know the old proverb? *Un inglese Italianizato, diavolo incarnato*. An Italianised Englishman is the devil incarnate!"

"Would you agree? Is that how you see yourself, Charlie?"

"God only knows what I am. I'm a riddle to myself."

Over lunch, Haydon drank too much wine. As he drove himself back to the Embassy, he hummed *Ode to Joy*, tapping time on the steering wheel. He'd instinctively warmed to the Italian. A rogue, for sure, but oozing charisma. The guy could make a cobra sing. A good man to have onside when things were getting complicated. He wondered what he could propose to ensure the Italian rooted for the right side, however much he pretended to be a neutral in the middle. It would be like conducting a tipsy orchestra, he thought; getting a double agent set up meant herding the disparate actors together to sing from the same merry score.

Straw Man

CHAPTER 30

Rome, July 1985
The Minister hunched forward over a broad antique desk. A neat and compact man, he was friendly, with a quick wit. He was dressed conservatively in a double-breasted navy-blue suit, a white shirt and dark, knitted tie and peered out through over large thick-rimmed glasses, an incipient smile beaming forth. He seemed poised to laugh, to make others laugh. However weighty the topic a sharp witticism was standing ready to be born.

"She was at her barbed best, my dear Carlo." He declared "As subtle as a block of granite. Steel and art deco feathers, side by side, ready to flirt or stab as necessity dictated. I couldn't be sure, I had to stand on tiptoe to gauge her mood. And there we were in the ancient Castello Sforza under ceilings frescoed by Leonardo. The perfect venue for a European Council meeting, the sweet odour of betrayal and backstabbing permeating around every perfumed corner. I felt at home. A Roman republican at home in a Milan palace. Imagine!"

Admiral Carlo Pollitti was leaning back in a deep armchair, sipping from a brandy snifter and smoking a cigar. He waited for the monologue to continue. He sensed the Minister had something gritty and difficult to impart that required a problematical response from him. They sat in amiable silence for a while.

"We were discussing famine in Africa, one of the lesser items on the agenda, not at all controversial – Lomé 3, volumes of cereals for emergency aid, all agreed. We never disagree over gifts to Africa, not even the French bother to make a fuss." He glanced up at the ceiling

Straw Man

then turned back at Pollitti, picking up a shiny green marble egg from his desk, malachite? He passed it back and forth between his two hands, seeming to seek some divine balance.

"And she was charming. Sweet even! Imagine the tremulous clanging of warning bells! That put me on my guard. She walked me down the long corridor, grasping my elbow in her scrawny talons, away from the noisy crowd. All under the benign eye of a vivid Leonardo cabbage. How Bettino was doing such a good thing with his emergency aid programme for Africa. How pleased she was that we had assumed the Presidency. I waited for the flash of steel which I knew must be on its way.

"Widows and orphans, Minister," she announced, her exact words, "in Africa, are they not the ones who suffer?"

"Rhetorically?" I replied

"Yes, and the poor and miserable," she emphasised these words "they deserve our consideration."

"Such a splendid coda. Aha, I understood at once. Graceless threats from a loud hammer. An ugly piece of British blackmail. She was telling me that she knew the details of a recent transfer made by the Libyans at my request to an account that I had specified at the Vatican Bank. An account named *'for the widows and orphans of the poor and miserable'* – a charity account, run by nuns, good women. Ahmed Khalfari's generous contribution to our new era of compromise for peace." He sat back and gazed at Pollitti, pressing his hands together and making a steep arch. "I relaxed. Nothing to worry about after all. I smiled and waited for her to impart her price."

"My dear Prime Minister," I replied "I am touched by your Christian sensitivities. I never imagined this soft core to your well-known iron exterior. We care about these same things. Tell me how I may help you with these miserable widows?"

"And you want me to identify the source of this leak?" Pollitti interjected, staring into his brandy glass and twirling the brown liquid around with a shake of his wrist, leaning down to inhale the dark brown liquid.

"Please inform Khalfari that his people have sprung a leak, a dangerous leak. And if we are to continue working together confidentially, they must plug it, with a hammer if necessary. We can't allow the innermost details of our secret councils to end up in The Times of London, can we?"

"I will bang the table, make it shake." Pollitti replied "Anything else?"

"Yes, she is worried – with good reason – bombs in her bedroom and so forth, about reports the Libyans are about to resume arms shipments to the Provisional IRA. Her back yard. Reliable intelligence, she said. The list includes Semtex, dangerous stuff. Pass the word to Khalfari that we think this a bad idea. She asked for any intelligence that comes our way. I told her we would do this. That you would speak to her people."

"Of course. We know very little, but I'll share what comes our way."

"Whether she thought my offer of collaboration was as the result of her veiled threats or from the goodness of my infamously kind heart, who can tell?" He moved the green marble egg from one hand to the other again and beamed. He looked like the Cheshire Cat, Pollitti thought, and he was just as wise. "But it is in our national interest. Keep the balance right, Carlo. Your phlegmatic personality will win the day."

Straw Man

CHAPTER 31

Abu Salim prison, Tripoli.
Charlie's side was aching from where he'd fallen when they'd thrown him to the floor. They'd tied his hands in front of him, his wrists hurt where the orange plastic rope had chafed. His head itched and ached. He thought he could feel lice crawling through his dirty hair. How long had he been here? He longed to scratch the itch of dried blood on his forehead: he couldn't remember hitting it.

There must be a sandstorm. A continuous red cloud of hot, sandy air blew in through the small barred opening high in the corner of the cell. His mouth tasted of blood and grit. The cell had bloodstains on the dirty white wall, dusty brown scrawls. And what he thought were smears of excrement. There was a concrete slab for a bed, a thin, filthy mattress, a yellow plastic bucket, and a grimy blanket. He hurt everywhere. There was a gagging smell of human waste. He retched.

How had he allowed himself to get involved? Ego. And flattery. How pathetic! An inability to say No. Not some laudable commitment to nation or cause, which Ines would approve of. Not even the sickly lure of money. No, just ego.

They picked him up at Tripoli airport as he was about to check in. Fürrer had taken the previous day's Swissair flight to Zurich, but he'd stayed on to collect an order from the Ministry of Irrigation. He'd paid off his taxi and turned to walk into the terminal building when two men in plain clothes came at him from behind and grabbed his arms, frog-marching him along the kerb a few yards to a closed van. They'd thrown him into the back and jumped in behind him, placing a stinking canvas hood over his head, tying his hands. He bounced around on the ribbed metal floor, trying to wedge himself with his feet against the side of the van. His attempts to talk were met by threats to gag him.

They drove for around half an hour before the van stopped. He felt hands grip his upper arms, pulling him upright and marching him away, his legs following the rhythm of his captors. He could tell they'd entered a building. The noise of their footsteps became muffled. Then he was thrown down onto the floor. He felt hands reaching to remove the hood. As his eyes adjusted to the gloom, he saw the backs of his guards leaving the cell. The door shut with an ominous clang and he was alone.

How was he going to get out of here? He supposed that depended upon how much they knew. And what could they know? If they knew what he'd been doing for Haydon, then it didn't matter what he said, he was doomed. Had something been wrong with the deliveries? Had Haydon lied to him, and the items were sabotaged? Or were they working from supposition?

He needed to keep a clear head, fix his story in his mind before the inevitable interrogation. Whoever was coming to question him, he needed to be plausible. He mustn't let himself get trapped into any admission. He remembered reading a novel about a man waiting to be tortured. How he'd worked to bury the darkest secret far away down, then prepared a series of admissions that he would allow to be extracted from him one by one, always protecting the one thing that mustn't ever be admitted. That he was working for Haydon. For MI6. He lay back on the hard bed and closed his eyes. He tried to sleep. But the questions kept coming.

Straw Man

The sound of heavy boots on the stone floor woke him. He thought it was probably daytime, although the thick cloud of red dust was still blowing in, obscuring the little opening. The door screeched open, tired metal hinges complaining. A scrawny, bearded man with a ragged uniform entered.

"Get up. *Taal!* Come!" The guard barked, aiming a kick at Charlie, who rolled over and managed to hoick himself into a sitting position, then stumbled to his feet. "Move!" The guard prodded him forward along a musty, dark corridor running between rows of cells. Blank, bearded faces stared silently at him from behind small, barred hatches. He was limping badly. They passed through an arch into a dusty courtyard, then walked on towards what seemed to be the entrance to a barracks block. Blowing sand blasted onto his cheeks, stinging where the skin was exposed and raw.

The guard shoved him in through an open steel door. He entered a large, air-conditioned office. Nasir el-Maghrebi was sitting behind a simple metal desk, wearing reading glasses and scanning a thick file. Charlie stood in front of the desk.

The guard barked. "Stand there prisoner, don't move!"

After some minutes, Nasir looked up, an ironic expression on his face. "Mister Charlie, you're not looking your usual arrogant self. You don't like the service here?"

"May I sit down?"

"No, remain standing." He was dressed in a fawn safari suit, which gave him a military look. It was as if Charlie were seeing him for the first time. He could see cruelty on Nasir's face, which he'd never noticed before.

"You have been disloyal, you see, to me, to our friend Andrea. Why? Our relationship was so much in your interest. You stood to gain plenty." He glared at him. "Why did you betray us? My enemies accuse me of letting you in, they claim you've compromised our national security."

"Nasir, there must have been a mix-up. I know nothing about national security. Do I need a lawyer? Can I make a phone call?" Charlie stood up straight and smiled. "Can you get them to untie my hands?"

Charlie held out his hands. Nasir leaned back in his chair, surveying him with a sour expression.

"You don't seem to understand how bad your position is." Nasir waved his arms, gesturing to the windows. "You're in a secret site, you see, no one knows you're here. I doubt anyone would care, even if they did. You have become, tragically for you – a 'non-person'. Time is no longer a factor; you will remain for as long as it takes to convince me you've told me everything I require to know. And I'm not in any hurry."

"I carried out our agreements to the letter." Charlie tried to sound confident but wasn't sure he was succeeding. His throat was dry, he was having difficulty enunciating. "I brought Armin Fürrer down here. We've made our first deliveries; we've put ourselves at risk by helping you."

"My people have special experience in extracting facts, it's useless to resist. There's been no mix up. You'll tell the truth, whether you wish to or whether you don't. It's immaterial to me."

"Nasir. I am a British–"

"–you're nothing." Nasir pointed his finger at Charles. "You can disappear forever. Buried somewhere in the desert, no one would find the largest of your bones. You've broken trust. Confidentiality was central to our dealings."

Straw Man

Nasir nodded to the guard, who grabbed Charlie' head and forced him to his knees, pressing his face down to the floor. "You will lick the floor clean if I tell you to."

"Damn you to–"

"Shut up!" Nasir nodded to the guard, who hit him a stunning blow across the back of his head with his baton. "Answer only when I ask you something. What did you tell Haydon Talbot about a payment to the Vatican Bank? And what else did you tell him about our business?"

Charlie's heart sank. The payment. He mustn't admit it, at all costs. Haydon must have told the Italians, and they'd complained to Nasir about a leak. The circle was too small. That idiot Haydon! Why? But what other explanation could there be? They couldn't have proof, just deduction, speculation? Or else why were they asking? He had to deny, to keep denying.

"What payment? What I told Haydon, as you know, was I was coming to Tripoli to discuss water projects." Charlie could hear his voice was unnaturally high. He made a conscious effort to talk slowly, normally. "I told him I expected to meet you and Ahmed to discuss the matter of quiet talks with him, with the British Government."

"You think I'm some kind of fool?" Nasir stared at him fixedly, twirling his ballpoint pen around in his hand, his face had flushed. "You'll be beaten to pulp if you don't wise up."

"Take him away." He shouted at the guard.

"Get up." The guard reached down and pulled him up by the neck of his shirt. Charlie struggled to his feet.

The phone rang on Nasir's desk. He answered it and spoke in rapid Arabic, swinging his chair around and looking out of the window. Charlie

Straw Man

heard his name a few times. He put down the receiver and turned back to Charlie, scowling.

"I'm going to leave you. I'll be travelling." His voice was calm now. "Use your time wisely, consider the right answer. My people will interrogate you. There will be nothing to distract you. We will not make you comfortable. Your guards will report if you have something you wish to tell me."

"Can I–?"

Nasir nodded to Charlie' escort, who hit him another sharp blow on his neck. He lowered his head and started reading papers on his desk.

Two guards dragged Charlie back to his cell. They were not gentle. He perched himself on the concrete bed and went over the events of the last month, wondering what had gone wrong. His head was throbbing, maybe he had concussion? He supposed that Andrea would have learned of his disappearance. Would he intervene to help him? But then, might he have learned he'd been indiscreet? And Haydon? Somehow, he felt sure no help would come from that quarter. He lay back and tried to sleep.

CHAPTER 32

Clogga Strand, Wicklow.

The sea was calm in the sheltered bay, just a slight swell running, perfect conditions to offload their cumbersome cargo. A half-moon hung low in the sky, casting long shadows on the white fringe of the shore. Seán stood alongside the Skipper, who was leaning out over the rail of the *Makaria*, scanning the horizon through long binoculars for signs of unwelcome company.

Seán tasted the salt in the air and took a deep breath, licking his upper lip, savouring it. He'd miss it, he realised. In his wildest dreams he'd never imagined himself, a stubbornly urban man, seduced by the rough wastes of the oceans. It had been a long couple of months, frequently uncomfortable, but he'd grown to enjoy the lazy rhythm of shipboard life. He'd only had his head stuck out of a porthole, emptying his guts out, for a couple of days. After they'd hit a big storm passing south of Corsica.

"We've done it, Nolan! We've bloody made it!" He clapped the Skipper on the back and danced a little jig. "Long Live the illustrious Leader and his fecking mad fecking eyes! One more in the snout of the bloody Brits. Damn them to hell! The first of many let's hope."

The Skipper lowered his binoculars and looked over at Seán. His dark beard and hair had grown during the voyage; he had a wild look to him. "You can put the blunderbuss away now son, will yer. We're clean. The Garda are sleeping the sleep of the devil."

"Annie, she is. After Annie Oakley." He unslung his Armalite AR-18 from his shoulder and passed it over, butt first. "Annie's not going anywhere. Not 'til we've this lot buried safely under Irish turf."

Straw Man

"Those notches, in the stock." Nolan passed the binoculars to Seán and cradled the weapon, staring along the sight towards the moon. "Are they?"

"–don't ask." Seán pointed the night-vision binoculars towards the shore. "She's my friend, and definitely my enemy's enemy."

He could make out the dark green shapes of three squat lorries parked side by side on the white sand, their tailgates open. He watched as figures ran into the water and lugged heavy boxes up the beach; the shapes seeming to crawl up the thin strip of white towards the lorries.

"When will you be off back to Malta?" Seán asked.

"As soon as I've my fat envelope from you in my pocket." He winked and rubbed his thumb and forefinger together. "Things to pay. The wife needs squaring away. The sooner it's in my itchy palm, the sooner I'll be on my way. Be there mid-September. This fella gets a name change in the meantime. The *Makaria* will become the *Tadiran* before our next jaunt. Keep passing eyes guessing."

The rubber inflatables came bouncing their way back towards the ship, the noise of their engines muffled by the sound of waves breaking on the long beach. A dark face under a balaclava appeared over the side and shouted up. "Just these two fellas to go now?"

The Skipper handed the rifle back to Seán and pointed to two metal ammunition boxes stacked by the rail. "That's the lot there, then we're done."

"I'll head ashore, we've a long drive ahead to get there before dawn." Seán ran his hands through his hair. "It's been a gas being aboard your tub with your ugly mug these long months. Well mainly–"

"–and I'll wait 'til I'm safely moored alongside in Arklow tomorrow morning and smiling peaceably at the world. Then I'll break open a bottle

Straw Man

to celebrate." He turned to face Seán and smiled a slanted smile. "Sure, I'll crack open some large ones. I'll be filthy drunk a couple of days or more, 'til the missus finds me out anyhow."

"We'll be back here again in less than two months."

"Sure I'll be over my hangover by then." He laughed. "Maybe. Let's hope the weather treats us nicely, October can be a right fierce month in the Med. We'd lose a few crates overboard, if we tried loading them onto those small inflatables in rough seas."

"So what–"

"–you'll need to get hold of a couple of solid lighters, for us to drop the boxes down in to. These fellas will be fine to tow them to shore." He pointed at the little ribs, heaving up and down on the swell.

"I'll see to it. 'Til next week, big man." Seán reached out his hand; the Skipper nodded and took it in both of his. "Usual place. Wednesday. At eight. All right?"

They're like giant's paws, Seán thought. He could feel the hair on the back of them. Seems like a gentle giant, but there's a hardness hidden away in there. You can catch it in the edge of his eyes, even when he smiles, a giveaway hint of subliminal brutality.

"Don't be falling in the sea now."

He clambered down the ladder into the bucking rib, hands reached up to steady him. The dinghy bounced away, fishtailing towards the shore. Seán looked back, the tubby *Makaria* silhouetted against the dark horizon. The Skipper had disappeared.

CHAPTER 33

Haydon and Glasson sat on a wooden park bench by the grassy bank of the small lake. They watched as excited children hurled pieces of bread onto the water, arrogant swans sashaying toward them, positioning themselves to seize any gobbets, elbowing ducks and lesser birds out of the way. It was a sunny late August day and St. James' Park was teeming with tourists. Hordes splayed all around the burned brown grass, picnicking, playing, shouting, lying asleep, bare-chested and sunburned, clad in shorts and tee shirts, kicking footballs, licking coloured ice creams which dripped onto the melting pavements. Cameras clicked everywhere.

He would have liked to make his boss squirm and turn the screw until he saw him wince. The ponce had blown the op at a stroke. For what purpose? Showing off. *Stupid cockerel.* But there was no upside in highlighting Glasson's role in leaking the information that led to Charlie's arrest. It was the PM herself who'd dropped the clanger. Which sat noisily unspoken between them. He knows that I know. And I need to keep this forced smile on my face and pretend I'm not seething. Haydon sniffed at the peculiar mix of hay and diesel fumes in the air. It reminded him of candyfloss. Some childhood memory hidden deep in his nerve plexes?

"He's being held in Abu Salim prison. In the south of Tripoli. Not a nice place. We've got someone there who provided confirmation, says he's not looking good." Haydon talked in a low tone, both men staring straight ahead at the lake. "No attempt as yet to contact the British interests section at the Italian Embassy. He's not officially detained. Nothing the Eyeties could do, even if we asked them to. He simply doesn't exist."

Straw Man

"What's our calculation?" Glasson barked, taking two tubes out of his jacket pocket, passing one to Haydon. He started unwrapping a cigar, and then held it under his nose, closing his eyes and breathing deeply. "Is he in danger, mortal or otherwise?"

"Maybe. Certainly uncomfortable. So long as he keeps schtum, they can't be sure. He's too useful for them to burn for no reason."

"Will he? Keep schtum?"

"My instinct is yes, 'tho God knows if they really get to work on him. They've got grisly torturers, according to reports." Haydon said, tucking the aluminium tube into his jacket pocket. He'd smoke it later when he was calm and could enjoy it. "To start with, he'll tell them stories. He's good at that, but he's had no coercive resistance training."

"If he admits, we'll be in a stew."

"He'd be in a worse one. Story over." Haydon made a chopping motion with his hand on his knee. "If they get that first eensy-weensy bit out of him, they'll keep on squeezing the toothpaste tube, and the gloves will come off. Then we kiss goodbye to the whole op. And to him."

"Any way we can spring him?" Glasson bent down and lit his cigar, running the flame back and forth and taking large puffs.

"Yes, but in such a way he comes out smelling like an overripe mango, his relationship with Nasir cemented."

"How do we manage that?"

"We prevail on Pollitti to provide the Libyans an alternative solution."

"Which is?"

"I want to do a black bag job on Vispoli's office. Trawl through it. See if we can find a copy of the transfer instructions." Haydon turned and looked the other man in the eye. "Mark, I'm going to need the Det team for a month or so."

"Have you gone nuts? After February's fiasco at Nasir's flat, Joint would never wear it."

"It's the only way to get DAEDALUS in the clear and TUMBREL back on the rails." A football landed at Haydon's feet. He picked it up and threw it ponderously back to a small boy who caught it and ran off laughing. He wiped his hands clean on his handkerchief. "If the Libyans realise they've burned Charlie on bad intel, they'll want back in for a smooth run for the nuclear stuff. What else–"

–it's your career." Glasson turned and poked Haydon's chest with his forefinger. "You want to chance it, more fool you. I'll sell it as your baby. It goes south, nothing I can do. Have to let the hyenas in."

"I'll take that risk. Otherwise, we do like Nero and watch whilst the IRA distribute Semtex like Smarties to every Paddy on both sides of the Irish sea."

"If you get the document?"

"We doctor it. So it looks like it came straight out of Vatican Bank files. Falsify an NSA intercept sheaf. Make it good enough for Pollitti to buy the lie."

"He'll play?" Glasson asked.

"If it's plausible and we give him enough."

"Give him enough what?"

"More GCHQ transcripts. Wiretapped hotel rooms. Recent calls between Red Brigades leadership hiding out in Paris and their operatives in Bologna. Grade One material about forthcoming ops. I'll promise him more if I have to. He'll play."

Straw Man

"Write it up, make the case. Address it directly to Joint and plaster your name in large letters all over the whole thing." He exhaled a large cloud of smoke. "Your face. Your ass. Nothing to do with me."

"I'll do it."

"You can thank me when you're enjoying the simple life in the private sector."

"Pay and conditions are better." Haydon said. "To add to my headaches, I've got his ex-girlfriend on my case, screaming blue murder. She's an investigative journalist."

"Use that well-known charm." Glasson stood up. He dropped his long cigar and ground it under his shiny black brogues. "I'll get you the Det boys. Get it right this time. Good hunting."

Haydon sat under a large awning by the swimming pool at the Aventine Sports Club, a folio of papers and a large gin and tonic, filled to the brim with ice, on the table in front of him. Ros and Ines were lying face down alongside each other on wooden sun loungers, chatting quietly. Haydon was eavesdropping, his ears extended on stalks. His eyes seemingly focussed on his papers, but behind his dark glasses they were working their way slowly up the two bronzed backs, tanned skin glinting rich with suntan oil, twitching back and forth between the two bodies, comparing the shapes of calves and thighs, taut buttocks, the little fringes of fair, downy hair at the bottom of their spines.

The two women had become close in these last months. Any casual observer would divine the bond between them. More like sisters. His wife looked pretty good, he thought. She was two children and six years ahead

Straw Man

of Ines, but equally alluring. He wondered what Babs would look like lying next to them. Paler, more muscular? His eyes paused as he considered the silken softness of inner thighs.

He felt a strong stirring and turned away; Speedos were not designed for public displays. He watched as a swallow dived into the pool, creating little ripples with its beak as it drank and sped off. The sound of cicadas drowned out the low hum of traffic, only an occasional angry hoot or shouted insult penetrated the high walls surrounding the club. In the background, he could hear the metronomic beat of tennis being played.

It had surprised him when Ros had befriended Ines so soon after the breakup. He wondered whether it reflected something about their own relationship. Taking Ines' side, taking her under her wing. Wounded sparrows bonding in empathy.

"Nobody seems to want to help him." Ines' head was turned to Ros. "Like he's a pariah."

"He'll be all right. He's strong."

"That's what he'd like the world to think."

"He played it too big?" Ros reached over and touched Ines' arm. "Can't Andrea help?"

"I rang him yesterday. Said it'll blow itself out, they'll release Kiko; wiser not to interfere." She screwed up her nose. "Jealousy? I don't like to think it of Andrea."

Ines got up and dived into the pool. She swam a length underwater, her arms distorted and waving along the bottom, then began doing fast lengths of the pool with powerful strokes. Haydon reached down and stroked Ros' hair.

"Still hankers for him?"

Straw Man

"Shush. She'll hear. Talk later."

Ines climbed out of the pool, picked up a towel and pulled it around her, drips spattering from her long hair onto the blue canvas mattress cover. She sat down on the sunbed, shivering a little, hunched up, head down.

"Every choice seems hateful. I feel so much love, here–" she stabbed at her stomach with her forefinger, "–in my belly, in my chest, my whole being, I feel overwhelmed. Overpowering love for both of them, it seems. There, I've said it."

"Well, you've turned your back on one of them, and the other is impossible, unavailable." She turned on her side to face Ines, making a face. "So where does that leave you?"

"I haven't seen Andrea since that weekend, weeks ago, on the boat in Capri. I felt so special." She shivered. "We were so close, well that's how it felt. The two of us. But he has that capacity to make whoever he's with feel special."

"I'll get us a drink. Fizzy water and lemon OK?" Ines nodded. Ros walked up the steps and disappeared into the clubhouse. Ines sat up on the sunbed and turned to Haydon.

"Have you heard anything?"

"Nothing. Since we broke off diplomatic relations last April, our interests there have been represented by Italy." She looks so vulnerable, he thought. Not at all the feisty journalist that liked verbal jousts with the roughest of them. His hand gently stroked his throat. "We've made discrete enquiries. I'd warned him how bad those people–"

"Haydon, wasn't he working for you?" Ines asked. "That's the impression–"

"–you know I can't comment on official matters, Ines." He leaned forward and touched her arm, glancing quickly down to her cleavage, talking confidentially. "Believe me, I'm doing all I can. You have my word."

"Will the Italians help?"

"We're coordinating." Haydon's voice softened. "His situation will resolve soon. Be a little patient. Trust. Andrea's right."

They were silent for a while, neither of them moving. Another swallow made a rush for the pool, its wings a blur of vibration, his eyes automatically following as it sped away. *She doesn't believe me.* But he was as keen as Ines to get Charlie out of his cage, just not for the same motives. Ros reappeared, clutching two frosted glasses. She handed one to Ines, who took it, resting her crossed arms on her knees. Ros sat and faced her.

"Tell me."

"I know I've been greedy. The hurt, the stabbing pains that remind me I've smashed up something good." She brushed a tear from her cheek. "God knows when he'll get back."

"You know you can't have Andrea." Ros smiled. "You can fuck him. If it's worth it, maybe it is. But you're saying goodbye to Charlie."

"I wanted my career, my success. I wasn't giving that up for him." Ines sat up and let the towel drop. "What a mess. I think I need alcohol."

"Haydon? Hear that. We need wine!" He got up and walked off towards the clubhouse.

"You see? Properly trained." Ros pinched Ines' arm, then stroked it.

"Yes, dear." Haydon turned back and stuck out his tongue. The two girls laughed. Ros pulled a copy of *Vogue* out of her bag and started shuffling through the pages.

Straw Man

"That's my two lire's worth. Enough lecturing! Let's get down to proper gossip. I'm tired of serious."

CHAPTER 34

Babs had cropped her hair short. It gave her a boyish aspect; she looked younger than Haydon remembered. Had she dyed it? It seemed lighter. She was leaning back on the sofa, her hand stroking her hair, doing that thing he remembered, curling a strand around a finger. Almost childlike. His eyes moved down. She was wearing a loose jersey, revealing nothing. He couldn't imagine her naked. There was something androgynous about her. He felt a stab of desire. Christ, he had to stay focussed. His career was on the line, this op had to work.

"Good to have you back. Life's been dull–"

"–and there I was, living under the illusion you couldn't wait to see the back of me." She winked, wagging her forefinger at him. "I felt like I had a burning potato up my you-know-what as we raced for the French border on that cold February night. You forgot to say goodbye."

"My butt got singed too."

"Where's that weasel-faced assistant? The one you sent to do your dirty work? He'd best stay out of our way."

"Peter?" He felt his cheeks flushing. "In London. Did the job properly, did he?"

They were sitting in his office at the Embassy. It was late summer and the air conditioning was set too low. He was wearing a jacket, but he still felt cold. He felt a twinge of guilt: he'd sought to steer the blame for the failed op on Nasir's flat in The Det's direction. Crooked of him. Trying to take a leaf out of Glasson's book. Succeeding only in looking like a self-righteous creep.

"I'm not proud of that." He held his hands up in surrender. "Peace offering. Drink at the Hassler bar?"

"Make it dinner and you're on." She turned her head away.

"When?"

"And pink champagne, I have expensive tastes."

"This evening?" A thoughtful look came over his face. He'd tell Ros he'd got an op running. "I underestimated the Libyans."

"We both did. I won't be repeating that." She turned away. "Eight o'clock?"

"I'll book." He stretched his arms above his head, hands entwined, the muscles in his back tightening. He felt himself relax. "Doesn't matter how long this one takes, we need to get it right."

"Thus cometh redemption?"

"Something like that. If we're lucky and get our hands on those bank transfer documents." He laughed. "From zero to everyone will want to slap our backs. If not–"

"Keep those intercepts coming." She took a notebook from her bag. "Useful material. From the last batch of transcripts, it seems he takes his butler and cook with him when he moves to Portofino or to his boat. That socking great apartment stays empty."

"Our informant tells us he lives on his own. No staff living in the palace. Here's a rough schematic." He passed her a sheet of squared paper and pointed with his finger. "His private office is over here. If the documents are there at all, they'll be in that room. No sign of serious security."

"That's what you said last time." She pulled a face and started writing notes.

"Don't rub it in. I've said sorry. Well, sort of."

"We'll sniff the area inch by inch." Babs stood up and packed the papers into her bag. "I'd better get going. Meeting the team to work up the watch plan. We'll aim for a night job, weekend I should think, judging by his past movements. Bags of cover all round the building. I'll flood the area with watchers. Have something for you in a couple of days."

"See you later."

"Maybe. And remember, pink."

Her scent lingered long after she'd left. What was wrong with him? He was happy with Ros, the physical part was good. For him, at least. Why take the risk? It wasn't even springtime, at least spring was a decent excuse. Middle-aged men feeling like young bucks again, the sunshine sending juices and scents coursing through their bodies. Still, it was just dinner. He picked up a file and started to read.

Haydon booked a room in the Pensione Parliamento, a small hotel off the Via del Corso, discrete and little known. The entrance was via a shadowy, tree-lined, cul-de-sac. He came straight from the office, telling his secretary he'd a lunch appointment that would run on and he wouldn't be back. His training was the perfect preparation for illicit affairs. The small deceptions constantly required of him had become second nature and repeated practice ensured a lack of guilt or remorse: a definite bonus.

He shrugged off a shiver of anticipation as he strode the length of the Quirinale Palace, then took the steep steps down two at a time. The usual crowds were milling around the Trevi fountain as he strode past. Before crossing the Via del Corso he paused to check in the reflection of a shop window that his back was clear before hurrying on.

Straw Man

He checked in, paying cash. He felt a twinge of concern as he handed his passport to the elderly lady on Reception. She gave him a bored look and handed him his key.

"I'm expecting a guest, please send her straight up."

"Dial 9 for Room Service, *signore*."

He climbed several flights of stairs to the room, his body tingling with anticipation. There hadn't even been an ironic look from the receptionist at the absence of any luggage. Disappointing that his forbidden pleasures were so evidently banal. He hadn't meant to repeat this, after the evening at the Hassler. Maybe it had been a mistake. Too close to home; and the Office would take a dim view, bang in the middle of a major op. It was different if you were operating alone in a foreign city. The veins in his forehead were throbbing. It had happened as he'd known it would. No way back now.

He opened the minibar and took out a half bottle of champagne. No sense ordering a whole bottle, no way he'd get away with that on expenses. He poured two glasses. Opening the tall windows, he went out onto the balcony and stood looking down towards the entrance to Parliament and the Palazzo Chigi, the Prime Minister's official residence. A dove cooed loudly next to his ear. He turned towards it and caught sight of a paunchy, middle-aged man and a young girl, both naked, kissing behind the net curtains in the next-door room. Well, at least he and Babs would make a better sight.

Staying out of sight behind net curtains, taking pleasure in concealment: just about described his work. Not recommended with a colleague, each had plenty to lose, but they were trained to keep their traps shut. She was so animal, nothing emotional in their relationship, no hint. They weren't interested in the other's private life, didn't ask questions. He looked at himself in the mirror. He attempted to wipe away the dishonest mask that stared back at him.

There was a knock on the door. He opened it, smiled, and handed her a glass. She was dressed in a black and white check silk blouse, cut low, a tight black skirt, her hair was down, her lips highlighted by scarlet lipstick. The tough soldier was nowhere to be seen.

"God you look–"

She raised her finger to her lip. "Shhhh–!" and pushed him backwards into the room, pulling the door closed behind her.

Straw Man

CHAPTER 35

Fear. Daily, stomach-stabbing fear. Charlie recalled that knee-shivering feeling from boarding school when he was five. He thought of the Bible. Forty days in the desert. He'd exceeded that. It had been eight weeks. Time passing so slowly Charlie felt he'd been there forever.

He'd established a meticulous rhythm, resolving to treat his captivity as if it were a long sea passage, segmenting bits of every day into regimented tasks, allowing time to roll over him. A day at a time, an hour at a time. He permitted himself craving thoughts of Ines for ten minutes each day. Minutes he relished, although it seemed a heavy act of self-punishment. Ines and Andrea. He tried not to think of them together. Mainly he tried not to give in to fear.

He exercised punctiliously: press-ups, squats, whatever he could do within his 10 foot by 8 foot cell. Which wasn't much. Not without knocking over the metal bucket that served as a toilet, which he'd done more than once. He'd never been keen on boring gym exercises, now he celebrated each achievement with a little morsel of food that he'd squirrel away for the purpose, typically a handful of bits of dry, unleavened bread. He'd managed 100 press ups in one session. If his jailers didn't damage his body too badly, by the time he got out he'd be stronger than he'd ever been. If he got out.

He kept track of days and weeks by marking the dirty whitewashed wall with his fingernails, alongside ciphers from previous occupants. He'd counted up each of their stays: the longest amounted to 405 days. The lines seemed to get weaker with each successive bundle. How had that ended?

Straw Man

They didn't allow him reading material. His interrogator informed him he needed the time to focus on getting his answers right.

Human contact was limited to a few words of broken English with taciturn prison guards, who brought him his food and escorted him, alone, for one hour a day, to the small asphalt exercise yard. And the interrogations, if you could call that human contact. High concrete walls enclosed the yard. The view was upwards to an endlessly dusty blue sky, now and then broken by white contrails and the silver speck of an airliner glinting high above. He thought about the passengers looking down. Could they see him? Sometimes a raggedy crow flashed past, perhaps hurrying to seek a better life away from this wasteland. Still, he got to move his limbs, counting out loud the sixty-four paces of the perimeter, meditating to the rhythm of his feet, chanting to himself under his breath, hobbling from his injuries.

The food was awful and scarce: cardboard dry flat-bread and a small metal bowl containing a dollop of okra, beans or humus. All of it gritty. He ate with deliberation, focussing on taking pleasure from chewing each horrid scrap. The drinking water was warm, sometimes hot, but in the searing heat of Tripoli's summer every mouthful offered relief. Once a week a silent guard escorted him to the shower block, where he revelled in 10 minutes of sticky bliss under a dripping shower head. When violent sandstorms blew in, he hunkered down, sometimes for several days at a time, sheltering from the cloud of sand under his old grey blanket.

Worst was the night-time wailing from distant sections of the cell block, shouts and cries that echoed back and forth, the only sign of other captives. He scoured his memory for fragments of Papillon's time in his penal colony in French Guyana. He'd read the book twice, years before, and found that

Straw Man

conjuring images of Charrière's hellhole helped him to understand how easy his own incarceration was in comparison.

When they dragged him off for interrogation, he reduced his focus to one minute at a time, counting the dangerous seconds out in his head, breathing in deeply and trying to clear his mind of all thoughts, focussing on images of oceans. Rough seas, calm seas, swells, white horses. Above all, he knew he had to control his fear, or it would overpower and doom him.

His interrogator was Inspector Jadalla, a tall, well spoken, police officer with dark skin, parallel tribal scars on his cheeks and a pronounced limp. A Toureg from the south. Served by a brutal, squat thug - Sergeant Moawia - a monster with a bushy moustache and the slanting smile of an inane sadist. Charlie wondered if he might be suffering from the Stockholm syndrome, as he thought of the Inspector as his protector from this animal. But he knew perfectly well Moawia was Jadalla's attack dog.

The terror of those late-night sessions. Long after lights out they'd wake him with shouts and blows and he'd find himself yanked from his bed by guards, seized under his arms, a stinking hessian bag shoved over his head. He'd feel himself dragged along long corridors, face down, feet trailing in the dust. He could tell by the smell when they passed the ablution blocks, then a changed motion as they angled down a ramp into a dank cellar. He'd feel himself pressed down onto a chair, often accompanied by a blow to his head, the bag removed, his arms and legs pinioned by shackles. Opening his eyes slowly to reduce the shock of the blinding arc lamps trained on him, then shutting them again quickly.

Always the same room, lined floor to ceiling in white hospital tiles. A single plastic armchair in the centre, attached to the floor by taut chains. He'd try not to notice the dried bloodstains on the floor, focussing instead on a single white tile on the wall. They'd leave him like that for what seemed like hours.

He'd try to slow his breathing and chant in silence to himself. Repeating part of a phrase from Corinthians he'd had to learn and recite at assembly one Sunday evening, in front of the entire school. Which he'd forgotten. He'd frozen, terrified he was going to pee in his short trousers, the whole school giggling as he mumbled, then fell silent and stood there and shivered. Since then, the phrase had remained obstinately ingrained in his memory.

"I came to you in weakness and fear, and with much trembling."

Eventually Moawia would enter, a nauseous smell of body odour preceding him, carrying a plastic bucket of iced water. Which he'd pour slowly over Charlie' head. Then he'd point the barbed end of an electric cattle prod at Charlie, waving it back and forth, close to his chest.

"*Maa*, water for you, Engleesh. Better for electrics, you see." He would grunt. "Conduction you see, better with water."

Charlie would close his eyes and clench them shut, forcing his mind to conjure up images of sailing, a regatta off Porto Ercole, hauling hard around the upwind buoy, the great colourful spinnaker bursting out with a huge bang, the dinghy surfing, bucking, out of control, shards of wind across his face, the chill of spray on his chest. He felt exhilarated.

"I came to you in weakness and fear, and with much trembling."

"Good evening Mister Charlie." He opened his eyes. Captain Jadalla was standing in front of him, neat in his grey uniform, a file under his arm. "I do so hope you're finally going to tell me the truth."

Straw Man

CHAPTER 36

"All your vital bits still attached?" Haydon was sitting with Peter, Babs, Rathbone and Skelton, cramped together around the table in The Cage, which was swaying gently. There were steaming mugs of coffee in front of each of them.

"Got a helluva scare when I crept into the hall on tiptoe and was confronted by this tall guy, maybe a foot taller than me, standing right in front of me. Stock still. Nearly had a stroke. Shone my torch in his eyes and realised he was naked, except for a huge fig leaf–" Babs laughed, "– and made of marble."

"Peter and I spent nervous hours waiting for squawks on the radio." Haydon stubbed a cigarette out into an overflowing tin.

"It's more dangerous in this gas-filled death-trap." Rathbone waved smoke away with his hand in front of his face. "We wore balaclavas, no risks from hidden cameras this time."

"Nice and easy, just as we like it." Babs was wearing a black all-in-one, no makeup, hair tousled. They'd come straight from the op and hadn't slept. He smiled over at her, but she turned away, looking at a notebook. "Went in through the fire escape. Took our time. Waited and waited. Then moved in at snail's pace."

"Place is huge, living room's the size of two tennis courts." Skelton said. "No security, alarm wasn't on."

"Flat was empty – intercepts had shown they'd left for Portofino for the weekend." Skelton consulted his notepad. "We entered at 1.15, left just after 4."

"No one could have spotted you?" Peter asked.

"Neighbours stayed asleep. No dogs, no cats even. Lads on watch might as well have stayed in bed, nothing stirred." Rathbone said. "Sitting on comfy velvet sofas sifting through files made a change from roughing it on a filthy floor in Belfast, guns at the ready."

"Much to search in his office?"

"Not at all. First pop, we hit his desk drawers. Standard key. Bingo. Straight off." Babs chuckled. "All the time in the world, sat there for two hours rifling through papers, snapping away at whatever seemed relevant. Got what you wanted, then some."

"What's there?" Haydon asked.

"Bank instructions going back years. The ones you were looking for – $1 million and $3 million to that account at the Vatican Bank, signed, countersigned in Arabic. Bank statements, contracts, file notes."

"Sure?" Peter said. "If so, we're off to the races."

"You'll want to have a goosey at a couple of files, they seem to be personal accounts of Ahmed Khalfari and Nasir el-Maghrebi. Possible kompromat."

Babs pointed to a black velvet pouch on the table. "All there. Nine rolls of film."

"Peter, we'd better get to it. Get them developed right away." Haydon shuffled his way along the bench seat towards the door.

"Make up for the February disaster?" Babs said. "All is forgiven?"

"Let's go through the material before we celebrate. Don't stand down yet." As he brushed past her, he felt her hand linger on his knee.

"There might be follow up required." He smiled.

Straw Man

Haydon and Peter sat across from each other, working their way through the large stack of A4 photographs. Those that looked promising, they laid out in the centre of the long table. Both men were smoking, ashtrays overflowing, dirty ash spilling onto the table. The clock on the wall showed it was past midnight.

"Treasure!" Haydon raised his head and glanced over at the younger man. "Enough to put a noose round the bastard's neck."

"Evidence they've been salting away millions from oil sales for their own benefit. For years. The Leader wouldn't like it, not at all." Peter Etherington passed a photograph across to Haydon and stabbed at it with his finger. "Look at this one from last year. Khalfari instructing Andrea to increase the percentage of income to be diverted to his account. We can fix him good."

"Khalfari might be tricky to pressurise." Haydon scratched his head. "His relationship with Qaddafi might be strong enough to weather the attack, then we'd have exposed our hand for no gain. Not worth the risk."

"So we get even with our nemesis, Nasir?"

"Yes, focus on him, turn the bugger, make him ours." Haydon rubbed his hands together and whistled. "He'd finish up like a burnt lamb kebab if we exposed his corruption."

He leaned back and stretched; his hands entwined behind his neck. This was a turning point. He could see a way out of the maze, Operation TUMBREL would pay dividends. He'd spring Charlie. Hopefully before the poor bastard suffered permanent damage. Tortuous, but he could do it. Spring the trap, throw the noose over Nasir's head, pull it tight. Well done to Babs and her boys!

He felt excitement welling up in his chest. An image of her naked body flashed through his mind, her hair tousled, asleep on his shoulder, his hand cupping her breast, their legs entangled. He shouldn't have done it. That evening they'd drunk too much at dinner and he'd ended up booking a room at the Eden. Indiscreet, unprofessional, and risky. He'd got home far too late for a business dinner, undressing in the bathroom, creeping too carefully into bed. He thought Ros was asleep, facing away from him, but you could never tell. He'd wondered if he'd showered all the smells off him. Women were so damned acute. He had to stop it now, before it all blew up. He shook his head, as if to shut out the thought. Sweeping up several photographs from the table, he passed them over to Peter.

"Peter, these are the actual instructions for the transfers to the Vatican Bank. Look, there's the exact account name the PM blurted out. Make copies. Get them off to London by Queen's Messenger marked Flash Urgent."

"What will you do with them?"

"I want them to doctor up a forged flimsy of a faked NSA to GCHQ intercept, containing these faxed instructions. By yesterday. For me to hand to SISMI. I'm going to ask Pollitti to lie to Ahmed and tell him he's seen the hard evidence, maybe even show him a glimpse."

"The leak wasn't a leak at all?"

"No. A Yankee comms intercept. They'll buy it. They see US satellites everywhere; they think the Americans watch them changing their underpants."

"Which if Allah smiles on us will put DAEDALUS in the clear and pave the way to snare a rabbit."

"Allah will collaborate, believe me."

Straw Man

CHAPTER 37

"We helped ourselves to it around the time of the birth of Christ. Augustus brought it back from Egypt, as one does. God knows how he transported it, it's 35 meters long. Originally in the Circus Maximus, moved it here during the Renaissance." Carlo Pollitti pointed his finger at Haydon. "World class pillagers we were back then. More grasping than even you English! That's saying something, wouldn't you agree?"

They were looking out towards the obelisk that dominated the centre of the Piazza del Popolo. A blue canvas awning stretched out into the street, shading the veranda of the *Ristorante dal Bolognese* from the early autumn sun. The hum of conversation was interspersed with the screeching of tyres on cobblestones, as the perennial Roman road race unfolded in front of their table.

"We were an industrial power. Much easier to cart away heavy marble statues with railway trains and steamships than oxen and wooden runners. So we were able to grab more."

Haydon reached forward and refilled their glasses. Ice-cold *Greco di Tufo*. Light and delicious. No point skimping on Her Majesty's business. This lunch could wear the best wines on the menu; so long as TUMBREL found its way back onto the rails.

"How's the struggle against the forces of evil?" Pollitti said, the corners of his eyes turned down. They had pronounced lines now, Haydon thought. He's tired and worried. Maybe he won't be around for the long run? That would be a blow.

Straw Man

"Endless drama, same as yours. Our bad guys come in slightly different coloured packaging, stories just the same." Haydon turned and fixed him with an encouraging stare. "Carlo, I need your help."

"Your face is more funereal than usual. Can't be that drastic, surely?"

"That leak. Our PM spewed at your Minister in Milan."

"I read you the riot act, remember? You made appropriate penance."

"I did. With a red face."

"What is it now?"

"One of our boys got netted, blamed for the leak. By name Charlie Lomax, you've met him. Being held in Abu Salim prison south of Tripoli. Nasty place." Haydon paused while a waiter leaned down and placed dishes of pasta in front of them. "Our deception op targeting Qaddafi's nuclear weapons programme. You know. My boy is critical to that. I need him out and healthy. In your interest we succeed."

"Not sure what I can do about it." Pollitti smiled, tucking his napkin into his shirt collar, stretching it neatly around his tummy.

"I've got more Paris transcripts for you. BR conversations with PLO and ETA people. Names, places."

"I thought you'd already given me that?"

"Bugged hotel rooms, new stuff. Focussed on the Hyperion School lot. Which your *bons amis* are yet again keeping from you." Haydon tapped on the table. "PLO have confirmed they're planning arms shipments from Beirut to the Red Brigades. You'll have the file, raw intel."

"In return for?" Pollitti replied, stony faced, glancing down at his plate, wrapping spaghetti around his fork. He bent forward and inhaled.

"You inform Nasir el-Maghrebi that the information provided to the PM emanated from an NSA intercept of faxed instructions between a bank

Straw Man

in Geneva and the Vatican Bank. There was no leak. No leak. *Ergo* our guy is clean. I'm hoping they take the electric clamps off and let him go."

He reached into the inner pocket of his blazer and took out a sheet of thin paper, which he handed to Pollitti.

"A flimsy of the intercept. Showing its origin as NSA Fort Meade and copied to GCHQ Cheltenham. Accurate in every detail: names, bank account numbers. You have my word."

"The document itself–?"

"–may not be. But good enough to provide confidence you've seen the evidence." He took a long sip of his wine and looked away. "Maybe you even let friend Nasir have a glimpse?"

They were silent for some time, Pollitti seeming to focus on his pasta, frowning, stirring at little shavings of *bottarga* with his fork. He looked up. "I'll do it."

He exhaled and leaned back. Pollitti could have played it rougher, he'd thought he'd have to give away more. Perhaps he's getting soft? Glasson would be pleased. *What a good boy am I.* He lifted his glass and drained the white wine. He smiled over at Pollitti.

"Can you manage a bottle of *Ornellaia*?"

"If your Government can afford to pay for it, I shall be delighted to consume it." He leaned forward and tapped his forefinger on the table.

"One more thing." His fingers tapped away. "Remember, I'm expecting any intel that comes your way regarding planned Libyan or Palestinian actions on Italian soil. Every morsel."

"I haven't forgotten. Nothing yet. Just the PLO shipments. You'll see the details."

Straw Man

"I wonder sometimes," Pollitti pushed his chair back and fixed Haydon with a hard stare, "if you take our friendship for granted. You think I'm a soft touch?"

"No, to the contrary you always drive a hard bargain. I practically work for you!"

"If things keep going this way, perhaps you will."

"Delighted to. Salary probably better, but you'd quibble about my expenses."

"Our trades are mutually pleasing. That's as it should be."

"You'll let me know when you've met Nasir?"

Pollitti nodded imperceptibly, chewing away.

"I'll send Peter Etherington to your office this afternoon with the Paris transcripts."

Nasir drove his black Mercedes through the narrow archway and into the central courtyard of the Palazzo Vispoli, not slowing down as he passed the uniformed porter who stood up and tried to wave him down from his glass cubicle. It was a late summer's day, a slight breeze pressing at the tops of the tall cypress trees that stood erect in the marble square around the central fountain. He parked his car under the fiery eyes of a large bronze horse's head.

His meeting with Carlo Pollitti had been liberating. All was forgiven. He'd known it: those bastards watched you from above, sucked up your phone and fax signals. Spy in the sky, they were calling it. A new arc of intelligence that changed everything, so they'd probably end up back on camels carrying handwritten messages. That would please the Leader.

Straw Man

He'd always figured Lomax was too obvious, too vain and self-important. The reports he'd received from Inspector Jadalla described a weak man, not able to resist the slightest pain. They'd hardly get started before he'd spill out what he knew, and that wasn't much. The guy hadn't even been subject to extreme treatment. Luckily Nasir had elected to keep the gloves on, resisted powerful pressures from above to increase the severity of the interrogations. He'd left the door open a chink, a way back to the recruitment op.

He bounded up the wide marble steps, turning to make a face at the popes who stared out from their marble niches as he rushed past. Medieval Ayatollahs. No difference between them really, except maybe the popes had better hats. He'd had a narrow escape; his enemies had been lining up to stab him. They hadn't been pleased to see him scampering up the ladder of power. In future he'd make sure he was more subtle. Now he'd be free to get the nuclear purchases back on track, reshape the op, dangle bait to the British. He'd need to be clever with the Englishman, massage him back onside, flatter him. Fill his coffers, seduce him all over again.

He stopped outside the brightly polished mahogany door and pressed the large brass bell, hearing a deep timbre vibrating far away in the bowels of the papal apartment. A butler, impeccable in a white jacket and black tie, opened the door, held it and beckoned Nasir in.

"*Bon giorno, Signore. L'ingegnere* is waiting for you in the drawing room." He gestured towards the long corridor and closed the door behind him. Nasir hurried on, his footsteps echoing off the well-worn flagstones. He pushed the door open and entered a large, bright room. Andrea was reclining on a sofa, reading some papers.

Straw Man

"I'm the bearer of good tidings, my friend." He bowed low and sank into an armchair. "We're off the hook. For that miserable leak."

"How?"

"I've come from Pollitti."

"So, who was the guilty party?"

"There was no leak."

"Sorry?"

"You were right in the first place. The English got the details from an intercepted Fax. NSA job. Snared the incoming transfer transmitted from the bank in Geneva to the Vatican Bank. They must have been listening in on your friend Cardinal Marcinkus. Maybe since the Falklands fiasco."

"That was always the most likely explanation." Andrea sat upright and dropped his papers on the coffee table. "You can't trust anything electronic anymore."

"The Americans handed Pollitti a copy of the transfer." Nasir yawned. "To back up their complaints about corruption in the governing coalition here. And their gripes about the quiet talks with us. He showed it to me."

"I'm relieved." Andrea asked. "When will you release Charlie?"

"Just a few days."

"Why hold on to him?" Andrea lifted his legs back up onto the sofa and lay back, pulling a cushion to him and hugging it. "Come on, Nasir, let the poor guy go."

"I need to move him to house arrest for a few days. Perhaps he could stay at the *Canova* guest house. That be OK?"

"Of course. I'll give instructions. Why?"

Straw Man

"I need to neutralise hardliners around the Leader. Who've been blaming me for the mess, using Lomax as a hammer. I've got to be cautious. I'll look after him, don't worry."

"Khalfari?" Andrea asked.

"Trip's back on. Set for November." Nasir ran his fingers through his hair. "The Farnesina are sending an official invitation."

"Good news, Nasir. Let's drink to it."

"I need a drink. Weight off my shoulder."

"I wonder how much weight our friend has lost?" Andrea stood up and walked over to the drinks cabinet. "He was already skinny."

CHAPTER 38

Charlie was being tormented in the shower one morning by Hassan, one of the more sadistic guards. His hair and body were still soapy when he was yanked out of the shower stall and shoved towards the exit. A tall officer in a well-ironed uniform stood by the door. He shouted harshly at the guard, then ordered Charlie to dress and marched him off to Nasir's office. His clothes were wet and sticky and he was limping badly. The bruises and sores on his arms and legs, where Moawia had thrashed him, were throbbing. Red welts covered his stomach and buttocks stinging from the wet soap, reminders of the electric prongs that had singed his skin and made him scream.

He felt oddly fit, as if he'd mastered a tough obstacle course. *Pride before a fall?* But he felt tired all the time. Tired of the obstacle course. Tired of the emptiness. They marched along in silence, Charlie stumbling to keep up. He refused to allow himself to think about 'the sessions'. He stamped his foot as soon as a memory became a picture in his mind, forcing himself to view the image as if it were just a bad dream, not real at all. He visualised his mother soothing him.

"*It's just a bad dream, darling. Go back to sleep.*"

The oppressive summer heat had faded. For a moment he realized he might start to feel at home in this lousy prison. That was it, he thought. You could get used to anything; it just took you time to acclimatise. He'd lost all idea of time. Day followed day; week followed week. Perhaps he'd become addicted to the rigid routines of daily self-discipline? Was this how hermits raised themselves to a higher spiritual plane?

Straw Man

They arrived in front of Nasir's office. The officer knocked and opened the door for Charlie, then beckoned him forward. To his surprise Ahmed Khalfari was sitting behind the desk, swivelling back and forth in a leather office chair, and smoking a cigarette in a long cigarette holder. He looked up as Charlie came in and waved. Nasir sat on the sofa, dressed in a long white djellaba, picking at his fingers. He smiled at Charlie and winked. Odd. He'd never seen an Arab wink before, maybe he imagined it.

"Sit, Charlie!" Khalfari gestured to an armchair. "Coffee?"

He snapped his fingers at an aide who brought a small cup and filled it from an ornate brass coffee jug. Charlie smelled Turkish coffee and the unmistakable aroma of cardamom. How long since he'd smelled that brilliant scent? What was going on? Some kind of game? Good guy, bad guy? Khalfari turned and beamed at Charlie.

"Good news, my brother! Good news! This morning I signed an order for your release–"

"What–?"

"–after completing their investigations, higher authorities concluded you are not guilty of espionage. You will be free to go. Personally, I was always convinced these were false accusations–"

"–so finally you believe me?" Charlie's voice sounded hollow, his throat dried up, his mind racing. He rubbed at his eyes with his fingers, felt the grit of sand on his fingernail and then the sharp sting from residual soap on his eye. He was momentarily blinded, then a red curtain of black rage descended on him. He was going to get out of this hellhole? Could this be some trick? To get him to confess? No room for a misstep. Play it right, leave this godforsaken country and never come back. *Keep it cool. Let it roll over me.* For a moment he wondered if he was going to burst into tears. No, for Christ-sakes keep it together.

"–never intended offense–" Charlie realised he was mumbling. He shook his head from side to side. "I'm speechless, I must look like a dirty scarecrow." He chuckled nervously and stroked his unshaven chin.

"I regret all you have suffered, you see." Khalfari was saying. "Hard for you to believe, but I was obliged by my position to investigate what were after all serious accusations. I couldn't be seen to be favouring a friend."

Charlie pinched hard at his leg with his thumb and forefinger. He shut his eyes and thought about a calm, flat sea, a small sailing dinghy at anchor. I'm their friend, he thought. They need to know I'm still their friend. No enmity. Smile. He felt the red curtain lifting. He felt light. He was an actor. Opening night flutters in the tummy. Looking up, he beamed at Khalfari.

"God I'm relieved. I need–"

"–have a cigarette, Charlie. Sobranie Balkan, delicious. I buy them in Bond Street." Charlie took one and nodded, Nasir stood up and walked across, holding a lighter out for him. Charlie sucked on the cigarette and felt blood rushing to his head, he felt stoned. "A few days, Charlie. Formalities, you see. I must proceed with caution, brother; manage people who oppose your release."

Khalfari turned his head back and exhaled a column of smoke toward the ceiling. "Andrea has offered for you to stay at the Vispoli Guest House."

"For how long?" He felt the bitter stab of tears behind his eyes again, forced himself to grin. He closed his eyes and saw the little boat cutting through the water, the bright blue spinnaker billowing out in front.

"Soon, my brother. A little patience. I'll work the necessary–"

"–am I free to communicate? Speak to family? Reassure them."

Straw Man

"Of course, of course. Communicate all you wish." Khalfari leaned forward. "Consider yourself my guest. What you want, let me know."

"A long, cold shower. I'm covered in lice and half-dry soap!" What a joke, he thought, now I'm his honoured guest! As if I haven't been his guest for months. I'll smile now, I'll grin. *But I'll fuck you somehow, you lousy worm. I'll skewer you, however long I need to wait.* He breathed in cigarette smoke and beamed at Khalfari. "A large steak."

"You shall have it, brother." Khalfari said. "Now we need to talk a bit, create a legend together. About your unexplained absence. We don't want diplomatic storms. Not good for any of us."

"Lost on a safari in the desert? Like Mrs Thatcher's son a couple of years back. That would be credible." Nasir said. "A long stay in hospital?"

"We presume you'll wish to carry on working with us?" Khalfari brushed ash off his white shirt. "Am I right? No hard feelings?"

"Of course." He grinned and turned to Nasir. An image of Pinocchio's nose growing flashed through his mind. He laughed. "Yes, a long desert trip, that's good, sounds right."

"Meanwhile, you see, your business with us has been thriving." Nasir clapped his hands. "Your colleague Mr. Smith has been busy making money for you."

"Perhaps, ironically, this misunderstanding will even lead to closer relations." Khalfari stubbed out his cigarette and leaned forward. "Work out the details with Nasir."

"Then I can leave?"

"I shall invite you to dinner. Tomorrow, I think. You look too thin." Khalfari squeaked, a high-pitched sound that grated on Charlie's ears. He

Straw Man

pointed towards Nasir. "Nasir will be your escort. He will accompany you whenever you leave the guest house. To ensure your safety."

"Thank you, Ahmed. You can imagine how much I am longing to get home."

"Your friend Mr Smith will arrive tomorrow." Nasir said. "You can catch up with him, attend meetings."

"Nasir will drive you to the guest house." Khalfari stood up and walked around the desk to embrace Charlie. "Your ordeal is over, my friend. Now things will become fruitful."

Charlie took a long swig of bourbon. Neat with big ice cubes. He shivered. The air-conditioning was blowing out delicious blasts of freezing cold air. He felt goose bumps on his arm. His head spun; he rolled it from side to side. He thought he might faint. The liquid burned as it descended his throat, then he felt the painful ball of tension in his stomach melting away. He leaned back in his chair and closed his eyes. He was sitting opposite Fürrer at the dining table in the guest house, a bottle of Jim Beam on the table between them, a bowl of ice next to it.

"How on earth did you get hold of this firewater?"

"Peace offering from our friend Khalfari. *Haraam!* Forbidden!"

"You're exposing me to the risk of flogging? Possession of alcohol is punishable here by 50 strokes of the cane. Not sure I could manage it after my recent hardships. Look at this–" He stood up and pulled up his shirt, exhibiting the mass of red welts on his stomach.

"Ugh! Surely no worse than your famous English public school?"

"True, but I was in training back then."

Straw Man

Fürrer's generous tummy wobbled as he burst into a spasm of laughter, raising his glass high and taking a gulp of whisky. He was wearing a black shirt, salmon red trousers and white lace-up brogues. He looked like a car salesman from Las Vegas.

"You're stick thin Charlie, fading as fast as a Tripoli ice cube. Didn't they feed you?"

"You should try it sometime, you fat bugger. Do you good!" He pointed at Fürrer's belly. "Cheaper than your phony Swiss clinics. We'll finish this bottle in short order, my friend, a celebration, the end of my fast. I deserve it. I feel half cured already."

"You'll be fully cured when I tell you how much money you've made whilst undergoing your slimming cure." Fürrer burst out into another fit of laughter. "We got paid for the first shipments, and this week they awarded us a contract for the water pipe factory. Pleasant surprise when you get home and check your bank statements."

"I'll take an expensive holiday on the proceeds!" Charlie stood up and refilled their glasses. "God, that's good!"

Fürrer paused and pointed towards the ceiling, then lifted his forefinger in front of his mouth.

"We've got a meeting at the Ministry tomorrow to present details of the South African team. They've agreed to take on the project, their terms seem fair." He winked at Charlie and raised his glass. "I'm optimistic this will move ahead."

A servant dressed in a long white *djellaba* entered carrying a large tray. He laid out dishes on the table. A smell of burnt roast lamb assaulted Charlie's starved senses. The waiter placed a platter heaped with chops

Straw Man

and kebabs on the table, followed by bowls of vegetables and a dish containing flat bread.

"The okra and beans are all for you. Help yourself!" He laughed and started piling meat onto his plate. "That's all I've lived on these last months. The lamb's all for me!"

"Cheers!" he picked up a large chop and munched into it, a beatific smile stretching over his gaunt face.

A few days after Charlie' release, Khalfari invited him and Fürrer to dine at an ornate Savoyan-style villa on the edge of the Old City. They sat on a broad veranda surrounded by tall palm trees, looking down on the long expanse of the Mediterranean. A sea breeze wafted over the four men, tickling the fronds of the palms that swished above their heads. To Charlie' surprise they were served excellent Sicilian wine, a strong *Nero d'Avola*. The ban on alcohol imposed by Qaddafi many years before clearly didn't apply to the upper echelons of his regime.

Khalfari was wearing a beige Mao suit. He looked dapper and relaxed and was in a magnanimous mood, playing the role of host as if Charlie were a distinguished visitor. He thought the Libyan looked like a preening King Rat. Fürrer was resplendent in a light green suit, which gave him the look of a fairground tout. His carnival presence guaranteed a jovial evening. Nasir was quiet, restrained in his boss's company, but there seemed something insolent about his demeanour. Not much love lost there, not much respect?

"It's my belief that when misfortunes overtake us, we must strive to give them value, you see, use them to build something positive." Khalfari

Straw Man

turned to Charlie with a ratty smile. "Your tribulations will lead us to closer bonds. We regret these mistaken accusations. My people are too quick to believe the worst of all Westerners, you see."

"An ordeal by fire," Nasir's laugh sounded insincere, "and you came through with flying colours."

"Careful, not too much flattery or he might believe it." Fürrer chortled and raised his glass. His face was redder than usual, Charlie noticed; it looked odd against the green of his suit. "Then he'll become intolerable."

"I offer you my sincere hand of friendship." Khalfari got up from the table and held out his hand. Charlie stood up and took it, Khalfari patting their conjoined hands with his free one. Charlie donned a broad smile; he hoped the mask might just seem real. Jesus! People could convince themselves of anything. Could Khalfari really believe that his arrest and long, painful, incarceration was the basis for a burgeoning friendship? In his mind's eye, he imagined jabbing a rusty knitting needle into the man's scrawny neck. Greasy bastard. He scratched his head, then leaned forward and embraced the other man.

"I'll drink to that." Standing back, Charlie raised his glass and beamed. "Ahmed, my friend. Bygones!"

"Bygones!" Khalfari raised his glass, then sat back down. "I like that word. And a prosperous future, brothers!"

"The South Africans' involvement will be a major accelerant for your programme. You'll have working cascades within two years." Fürrer grinned and slapped the table with his palm, then leaned forward confidentially. "I propose a meeting at our offices in Zurich for the scientists to present their ideas. We'd like your top specialists to be present."

Straw Man

"We prefer the meeting to be here." Khalfari nodded to Nasir. "He will assemble a technical team to consider their proposals."

Charlie drank a lot. He visualised the destruction of the entire Libyan programme. Armageddon. Making a great deal of money whilst he wreaked revenge. Khalfari and Nasir would take the blame when the machinery went up in smoke. Poetic. With luck, they'd end up in the same cell. He was chuckling inside. Don't mess this up. This game is well and truly on.

As the dinner ended and they stood up to leave, Nasir took Charlie's arm and led him off into the garden.

"Charlie, I expect clearance for you to travel next week. I'll confirm this in the next day or so."

"Please, I need to get home. You understand. Every day–"

"–no worries. Next month Ahmed will go to Rome for an official visit." They stopped by a big fountain, lights illuminating the water in a kaleidoscopic display. As Charlie dipped his hand in the water and watched, a small rainbow appeared. "A big moment in the normalisation process. They'll want you home well before then."

He was whispering, holding on to Charlie's arm. "Then my friend, you see, I will rely on you. I'll make this whole thing worthwhile. I promise."

"What do you need?"

"I want you to be my quiet envoy to Talbot. We wish to improve relations with the British. And there are certain things they want from us." He leaned in towards Charlie. "Let him know we can be profitable counterparts. That there are deals to be done. Political deals and commercial ones. Pragmatic mutually beneficial exchanges of intelligence."

Straw Man

"I'll do my best. He's a hard man, stiff, you know, it won't be easy." He laughed to himself as he imagined Haydon's response. "But I'll be pleased to act as your intermediary."

"He's a politician, Charlie. At our level, we all are. In politics everything is possible, everything, even the most unlikely outcomes. All I ask is you carry my messages honestly." They wandered back towards the others. "Deal only with me, brother. Do not speak of this to Andrea or to Ahmed, we keep these things compartmentalised. OK?"

"Understood." He and Charlie walked to their car. The driver held the door open. "Thank you for the dinner, I feel fattened."

"You needed it."

As the two men pulled away in their Mercedes, Charlie saw Khalfari turn to Nasir and pull him aside, arms around his shoulders. "We're back on, Armin. Even stronger than before. You've got my gaunt face and bruised body to thank for that."

Straw Man

CHAPTER 39

Lies, damned lies, and the ones you hope the Divine Judge wasn't watching when you told them. This was one of those, and Haydon smiled and prepared to tell it. He couldn't admit to Charlie he'd burgled his friend Andrea's flat and forged NSA documents, but the guy needed to understand that he, Haydon, had been his Saviour.

They were in the small study at Haydon's flat, Charlie sitting on the black leather sofa, nursing a large glass of red wine. He looks smaller, Haydon thought, like he's been somehow shrunk by his incarceration. Since he'd picked him up the day before from Ciampino airport, his pallor had improved, but he still looked desperately weak. He seemed quieter, more serious. Maybe three months in a Libyan jail would prove to be a Damascene moment.

"Look Charlie, I'm going to answer your question truthfully. I shouldn't, but I owe it to you."

He reached over and touched Charlie's hand, looking him in the eye with a steady stare. "Last month Carlo Pollitti informed me that in July the CIA shared an intercept with him. It seems the Agency has been capturing all electronic traffic in and out of the Vatican Bank. They'd snared a copy of Andrea's faxed bank transfer."

"Why did they show it to Pollitti?"

"The Americans don't like the quiet talks going on between Italy and Libya, they want them to stop, and they don't want Khalfari's official visit going ahead. So they supplied Pollitti with evidence of bribery at the highest level and banged the drum. One presumes there was an implied threat to leak details of the Minister's corruption."

Straw Man

"Why did Pollitti tell you?"

"I went to see him and asked him to help secure your release. I had to come clean about Operation TUMBREL. He agreed. At my request he showed the intercept to Nasir, which is what put you in the clear."

"Christ Haydon, and for three months I've been wishing you dead, and much worse. Leaving me to rot and doing nothing to get me out."

"I gave you my word, I'd never abandon an agent–"

Charlie flushed; Haydon saw a tear forming in his eye.

"I owe you."

"Owe nothing, it's what we stand for. You're on my team."

"Thank you, Haydon."

"Tell me about your ordeal."

Charlie talked for an hour. Haydon kept feeling sharp stabs of guilt. Dispatching him untrained into the clutches of a brutal regime, the blame squarely on his shoulders. Or Glasson's, depending how you looked at it. Charlie seemed removed, dispassionate. He didn't detect any hint of self-pity as he spilled out the litany of horrors.

"Haydon, now for the good bit. The payoff for my suffering." Charlie stood up and started pacing the room. "You're going to like it."

"Couldn't be worse than what you've told me. I'm aghast."

"Nasir tasked me with recruiting you to the Leader's Revolutionary Cause." Charlie laughed and raised his arm in a clenched fist salute. "Recruiting a senior MI6 man is going to send him shooting up in the Colonel's pecking order."

"He's right, it would."

"Told me to tell you there are– *'Deals to be done'*. Hinted at wads of cash."

Straw Man

"I'm in favour of deals. Come to think of it, I'm in favour of wads of cash." Haydon's antennae started vibrating. This was it. Setting up Nasir as a double could be the winning move. Checkmate. "He has my attention."

"I told him you'd be difficult."

"Notoriously hard to get."

"I'm not to mention it to Khalfari." Charlie took a sip of his wine, placing it down on the desk and starting to pace the room again. "Nasir wants to keep it to himself. His ambition was visibly smouldering."

"So now you're recruiting me?" Haydon chuckled. "Irony Charlie, paying me in my own coin?"

Haydon turned his swivel chair to the side, leaning back with his hands behind his neck. Sunlight was pouring in through the window. *But will we get you to go back down there again?* He looked younger, more vulnerable. Had he lost some of that cockiness that was part of his charm?

"I get to share in the bungs?" Charlie laughed. Haydon shook his head and swung his chair back to face him.

"We're going to burn the son of a bitch, and you get to deliver the fatal blow." Haydon made a chopping downward motion with his hand. "Revenge, how do you feel about that?"

"It's said not to be good for the soul."

"All right, you can forgive him, but only after you've burnt him."

"What's the kompromat?" Charlie asked.

Haydon reached into a drawer and brought out a slim folder, which he handed to him.

"Cast your beady. Nasir's Swiss bank account. Authentic statements. In his name. Careless." Haydon jabbed a finger at one document. "National Oil Corporation commission sheets, details of oil trades. Naughty, not his territory. Enough to end his career, then some. Not much forgiveness around Qaddafi. Nasir has enemies who'll jump at the chance of skewering him."

"Wouldn't Khalfari protect him?"

"Sorry?" Haydon chuckled. "That's naïve."

"I might enjoy this."

Haydon reached down and took a cigarette out of a packet, absent mindedly tapping it on the desk. How far they'd come, he thought. He'd signed Charlie up for a bit part. Now he was about to become the star of the show. He'd taken him for a Walter Mitty. You could never tell with people. Challenge them, but you're a fool if you predict the way they'll react.

"We're going to turn him, run him for the long term."

"And in return for our silence?"

"Crown Jewels. The IRA connection, people, shipping plans, dates." Haydon lit his cigarette and handed the packet to Charlie. "But the masterstroke. Turns out you're the real pro!"

"The masterstroke?"

"Is your ploy." Haydon leaned forward and smiled. "We are going to let him recruit me, play to my greed, send his career whizzing upwards. We'll feed him back doses of chickenfeed, I'll create a team to manage it."

"Peace in our time." Charlie whistled. "How many mirrors will you need to run that one?"

"It will dent the IRA badly, for a while at least."

"Knighthood?"

"Someone further up the food chain will arrive in time to seize the laurel garland." Haydon leaned back and blew a smoke ring towards the ceiling. He could imagine Glasson manoeuvring to take the credit. "That's the way it works."

Straw Man

"You'll let that happen?"

"I haven't mastered the arts yet." He laughed. That was the truth, he'd a lot to learn about politics, it wasn't natural to him. "Working on it."

"You'll burst into the bedroom like a jealous husband?"

"No, you're going to drop it on him: we let him stew before reeling him in."

"No danger he goes rogue and unleashes his goons?"

"We watch our backs carefully until he's over the line. I've got the Det team on standby. You'll have round-the-clock babysitting."

"When does he get here? I'm taking Ines to Punta Rossa for the weekend."

"Tuesday. Advance man for Khalfari's official visit, responsible for making the arrangements. Staying at The Eden, guest of the Government. You'll take him to dinner, a celebration. Spend what you like, enjoy yourself. Make a night of it. Then hit him with the snare."

"I can imagine his face–"

Charlie sat down on the sofa. He looks like a child, Haydon thought. So he'd told the lie. But with a good motive. *Which purifies my soul.*

Sunday in the *Centro Storico*. A fine October day. Church bells tolling in all directions. Charlie looked down at Ines. Her face was implacable, almost as if he'd slapped her. She seemed frozen; her shoulders hunched. It appeared like she'd made up her mind and was waiting to endure the final, painful, ending. He placed the little tray on the table, the smell of strong coffee rising to energise him. He sat opposite her at the round table on his roof terrace, their faces shaded from the midday sun by a large umbrella.

Straw Man

A pair of ravens flew fast overhead. He flinched as the birds blazed across the sun, the whoosh of their wings audible as the church bells seemed to fall silent. Wavy shadows passed over them, then a second later a splatter of bird-shit exploded onto the back of Charlie's chair. Some kind of omen? What? Bird-shit on your head was good luck, but two large ravens? They wheeled away and sped off, landing together on the next-door roof, staring at him like a kind of malign jury.

One last chance. I need to get this right. I need to open my soul; so counter-intuitive. No hiding behind humour. Convince her how much I want her. And why I deserve her. He wanted her back more than anything. He noticed red around her eyes, dark bags below them, her makeup was smudged. He cleared his throat.

"I'm not asking you to trust me. I know that's hard."

"I don't. Trust you."

"I had ample time in my rotten cell to reflect on what I got wrong." He poured coffee from a pot and handed it to her. "And to understand how much I need you. I have to go deep inside to find the truth and share it with you."

"Not sure that comes naturally, Kiko. You're a storyteller."

"I wanted to protect you, Ines, to keep you out of the dangerous game we were playing."

"You could have told me? I would have understood."

"It was secret and dangerous and convoluted. I couldn't. I walked into it with my eyes tight shut. When I opened them, it was too late, I was immersed."

"It seemed to me you revelled in it."

"They flattered me, made me feel important."

Straw Man

"Just because you've suffered, and I sympathised, and tried my best to help you, that doesn't mean I've changed my opinion. Of your egotistical–"

"I admit, it's hard to say this, but I must. I was jealous," he paused and took a deep gulp of air, leaned forward and looked into her eyes, "of Andrea, my oldest friend, rich and–"

"–with Andrea, there's nothing there to trust or not. He wants nothing. Ironic! His selfishness is so complete it's a form of purity. No promises, nothing on offer. His greedy orgasm is the history of man. He spreads his seed as a dog pees on a tree stump and moves on. Never looking back." She laughed. "You. You want so much more."

"Christ, that's painful–"

"You need to find out who you are, Kiko. What you really want. You say you want me but–"

"So then–" He stroked her arm gently.

She flinched and withdrew it, reaching up and touching her throat.

"Of course I want you physically. Even just now when you touched me. More than you can imagine. Your smell, your thrusts, your hair, the crack of your voice when you come. But emotionally–"

"–I thought of you every day. Of what I'd say to you, of how I'd hold you. When the lights were blinding me and the electric shocks were like death stabs, I thought of your face." He reached over and stroked her cheek. He could see tears forming, but she remained motionless, closing her eyes as his hands kneaded her hair and moved down to her neck.

"Even though I can't trust myself, I promise to be honest with you. Brutally honest, whatever the cost. What I don't know–"

"–Sssh!" She pulled at him, raising her head, the tip of her tongue flickering through her lips.

Straw Man

CHAPTER 40

Charlie sat at a corner table in the little roof garden of the Eden Hotel, a half-empty bottle of Dom Perignon in an ice bucket perched alongside him. He breathed in the early evening smells from the honeysuckle and jasmine that emerged from tall earthenware pots and chased the latticework of trellises skywards, framing long views out over the Eternal City. He stared up at the mass of flowering creepers that formed the roof of the terrace, pink-faced dog roses smiled back at him.

Nasir was late. Charlie couldn't care less how late he was, he felt on top of the world.

His heart was thumping; it felt like that intoxicating build up to an early evening seduction. He shouldn't feel this way. Too valedictory. *Not clever, tempting fate?* It was just another chapter in a long story, and who knew the ending? Right now it felt electric. He'd gone over and over it in his mind, imagined the look of shock on Nasir's face when he dropped the bombshell. He took a long sip of champagne and closed his eyes. He could almost feel the alcohol dripping down into his veins.

He glanced around the room, looking at the faces and wondering which of the other guests might be Haydon's eyes, keeping a watch over him. For sure he'd have some cover, but he couldn't spot any likely candidate. There was a tall, dark-haired girl sitting alone at the bar. Unusual. She looked away as he smiled at her. Her face was oval, a Modigliani look, Italian maybe? Or Arab? Surely Nasir wouldn't have watchers out ahead of him. He couldn't imagine the puritans at Libyan State Security using female agents. Qaddafi's famous Revolutionary Nuns? The girl was wearing a black trouser suit, a large Chanel handbag perched on the bar next to her, a scarlet crepe scarf around her shoulders.

Nasir stepped through the door and paused, looking around the room. Charlie waved. The Libyan was wearing a double-breasted blue suit with a dark green tie, his hawkish desert face at odds with his formal clothing. Charlie sensed he was in an expansive mood; he beamed, stood up and reached for the bottle.

"DP, my friend. Celebrating something?" Nasir plumped himself down opposite Charlie.

"My freedom warrants the best." Charlie passed him a glass and raised his. "Cheers?"

"Ahmed's visit is the fig on the cake of our relaunched cordial relations with the Italian Government."

"I'll drink to that." They clinked glasses. Nasir leaned back and stretched out his legs, staring over at the girl at the bar. He looks like a cobra, Charlie thought. Agile and dark and ready to strike.

"You see my friend, now we need to build a similar friendship with you difficult British." His face seemed to contort into a slanted smile as he lifted his glass in a mock salute. "Move past the problems of the People's Bureau last year. Into the bigger picture."

"I've news on that front, progress with Talbot." Charlie leaned forward towards the other man and tapped his arm. "He's ready to meet. Deniably, of course. And for me to act as cut-out."

"What does he want?"

"He was specific. Details of IRA contacts. Names, shipment plans, full transparency. He said that this would go a long way towards resolving all issues."

Straw Man

"Unthinkable!" Nasir frowned and rapped his knuckles on the table. "The Leader is adamant about support for liberation movements. Anti-colonialism is his article of faith. Still, it's good to have Talbot's chips on the table. Promising, but impossible. What's his offer? Did he say?"

"Intel on enemies of the regime in London." Charlie leaned forward to refill their glasses, then gestured to the waiter to bring another bottle. "Islamic groups, Muslim Brothers, monarchists, communists."

"Could be a windfall. A new era. Good for him and good for me, our careers."

Charlie sensed a hot stirring of hatred in his chest. He smiled to himself. Payback time. Need for calm. Matter of fact. Friendly. Dishonest. No hint of triumphalism. He relaxed back into his chair, reached into his pocket, and withdrew an envelope.

"Talbot asked me to give you this." Charlie handed the envelope to Nasir. "Told me I didn't need to see the contents. Confidential. He said you would understand."

Charlie watched Nasir as he opened the envelope. He noticed the tremor in his fingers, then he seemed to grip the papers tighter, his dark face flushing pink. He turned away and stared out towards the rooftops, staying silent and frozen for some minutes, before turning back to Charlie with a fierce look on his face. His pupils shrunk to pinpricks, sharp lines forming on his forehead.

"This is an unfriendly act. It's shit! Shit!" He spat, his face angular with rage. "There will be consequences."

"Ahmed, I only know what Haydon told me, which is you would give me a reply."

"You know how dangerous this is for you, Charlie? I can wipe you out, finish you–"

"–why Nasir? What is this?"

Nasir didn't answer. He stood up, folding the documents and slipping them back into the envelope, his hands still shaking, his lower lip quivering. He was red-faced as he bent over Charlie and whispered. "Tell Talbot I don't react well to threats."

He spun around and strode away. At the door he paused, remained motionless for a moment, then turned and sauntered back to Charlie, his face calmer, smiling but intense.

"Tell him to watch out. Driving his children to school. Watching TV at home. Better not sleep too deeply. Things can get rough. Quickly. For you as well."

He turned and dashed towards the elevator.

Charlie rang Haydon from the Hotel lobby phone. The tiny cubicle constrained him, his shoulders were wedged between the walls. He peered cautiously out of the small Perspex window, looking for followers. The operator put him through.

"Charlie?"

"I may have hostiles."

"Description?"

"Tall female, dark hair, black trouser suit, red scarf. Looks Arab."

"Friendly." Talbot chuckled. "Guardian angel."

"Good looking angel."

"Tough as boots. Babs. You'd like her. Covering your back. Report?"

Straw Man

"Message delivered. Quite an impact."

"Finished rather early?"

"Stormed out. No dinner. Nasty threats. About your safety. And mine." He paused, then realised he was breathing too fast. He shut his eyes. "Had to leave half a bottle of perfectly good DP."

"He'll play?"

"Can't tell. I imagine he'll work out what's in his interest."

"Get out now. Babs' people will cover you."

"Next?"

"We wait for him to call. He will."

"If he doesn't?"

"Trust me. Stay low until we wind him in."

Charlie rang off. He felt his pulse still racing. *Fuck you, Nasir! Now it's your turn.*

CHAPTER 41

They set up the meet at Charlie's office in Parioli. Charlie was pacing the room, scratching his head. He was dressed in a dark blue suit and yellow tie, giving him an urbane look.

Perched on a leather sofa, Haydon watched Babs and her technical team laboriously sweeping the room. They found nothing other than the bugs the Libyans installed the year before and a half-empty wrap of white powder concealed behind a bookshelf. Haydon held the little plastic bag up between his thumb and forefinger and stared over at Charlie, his face deadpan.

"Inferior quality, shockingly cut." He grimaced. "Can't you afford Bolivian pure?"

"Nothing to do with me." Charlie flushed and turned to Babs. "Excuse Haydon, he's so embarrassing."

"You've met Sergeant Stoner then?" Haydon chuckled. "You told me you thought she was an Arab?"

"Sorry–"

So easy to read, Haydon thought, relishing Charlie' discomfiture. He had a lot to learn about hiding his feelings, with his Italian upbringing that was improbable. No wonder Ines had seen him off. Surprising the Libyans hadn't broken him, down there in Abu Salim.

"Probably because of how quickly you knocked back the DP." Babs smiled at Charlie. "Don't worry. People often say I've got a Mediterranean look."

Haydon looked over and tried to catch her eye, but she had bent down and was handing a tray of equipment to Skelton. He was lying on his back under the desk, taking photos with a Polaroid camera and fiddling with a small device. She was looking feminine in a flowery patterned dress, her hair held up by a large tortoiseshell clip. Another disguise, that's what we all spend our time doing. A bit like royalty, he thought, swapping uniforms for every outing. Still, she'd make a credible receptionist. No sign of the rugged soldier to be seen. He felt his face flush as his mind went back to that hotel room.

"Disabled. We'll wire the Libyan bugs back afterwards, exactly as they were," Babs said.

"Our mike is here under the desk." Skelton's pulled himself up from the floor. "Voice-activated, ultra-sensitive. Capture a silent fart at fifty yards."

Babs walked over to the mantelpiece and pointed to a tiny hole in the face of a carriage clock. "Video's here, can't see the lens, concealed in the clock face. Looks like the winding mechanism."

"Clever. Your people covering reception?"

"Two, plus me. Toughs. No one will rush us."

"Armed?"

"As ordered. Expecting trouble?"

"Wiser that way."

"Two pairs watching the entrances. Front and rear."

"Escort?"

"Boney's outside to bring him up. Pink FT in right hand, agreed signal. Left hand and target aborts."

"Let's hope he knows his left from his right then."

Shelton started rolling up his tools into a leather pouch. "He will. Arabs use their left to wipe their arses with."

"Better pray there's no shooting or we'll all end up in pokey."

Straw Man

A little too close to the truth, Haydon thought. It hadn't been a problem to get this all approved, but he didn't want to remind anyone of the February fiasco, so he hadn't briefed London about the high risk of the op. Any blame would land on his head, and that would be that. More than the end of his career. A last roll of the dice. What was left to lose? It had to work out. It would.

"We're so far off the books–"

"–still, alive in pokey is better than–"

"–not being certain we aren't baiting our own death trap. He's made nasty threats, this one, he's capable of carrying them out. Let's hope they don't roll up with flamethrowers!"

Haydon turned to Babs and smiled. "Bring back memories, Babs?"

"Don't go there." Babs scrunched her face up. "This time we won't be caught napping."

"Anything I should know?" Charlie sat down at his desk and started clearing it of papers, shovelling them into drawers. He laughed. "This is supposed to be a peaceful meet. Not a replay of the St Valentine's Day massacre. I don't get paid danger money like you lot."

"Joking?" Babs laughed, touching her neck. "I heard your trouser pockets are lined with gold from dirty deals you've done with the devil."

Charlie pulled out his trouser pockets. "Lies, look."

"Nothing to worry you, you're a civvy." Haydon surreptitiously ran his hand up Babs's back. He felt the taut muscles, felt her push back against him. "Although you might end up as collateral damage."

A walky-talky on the table squawked. *"10.17 watcher three target on the move lungotevere heading north OVER."*

Straw Man

"OK. Focus now, guys." Haydon clapped his hands. "15 minutes. If he comes direct." Skelton picked up his toolkit and left the room.

Haydon stood by the door watching Babs as she walked over and sat behind the reception desk. She sat for a while adjusting her makeup, then reached into her large handbag and removed a Browning 9mm Hi-Power, which she laid flat in the open top drawer of the desk.

"Charlie, you make the introductions, then you leave immediately. Walk straight out of the building and keep moving. Don't stop for anything. We'll catch up later."

"We've been over this Haydon. I've got it."

Haydon felt his pulse quicken. What were the chances this would all go bendy? He visualised a hit team bursting into the lobby, gunfire crashing out. No easy exit. He'd been on edge for days, but now an ecstatic rush welled up through his body, followed by a cold calm. Everything to play for. How was Nasir going to react? He lit a cigarette.

"Room's clean. We disabled your devices." Haydon looked over at Nasir. "We can talk openly."

"My superiors are aware of this meeting. We respect your request for deniability."

"We're in unknown territory."

"It's crowded out there in the street! Our people scowling at each other."

"If we're disturbed for any reason, leave by the fire exit; turn right out of the door." Haydon perched on a chair opposite Nasir, hunched forward, his hands pressed together in an arch. "It's covered, our guy is holding the back door for you." Nasir nodded.

Straw Man

"I didn't expect your aggressive move, Mr Talbot." He shifted around in his seat. "Subtle as a Chinese firecracker."

"Call me Haydon." He smiled, then turned away and stared out of the window. "It's the nature of our work. We're each of us obliged to deal dirty cards from the bottom of the same dirty packs."

"I won't ask how you got the documents." Nasir grunted. "When I crashed your bust of my flat last February, you see, I figured you'd lay off for a while."

Straight to the nub, no pretence, no diplomatic fluffing around the truth. Haydon liked it. They wanted the same thing. To recruit the other and announce a victory back home. *Neither of us cares about the issues, we just want a brightly coloured flag to raise high. We can both be winners.*

"Not our interest to burn you. We think you're a voice of moderation in your government. Our natural ally. We'd like to see your influence grow. Help you if we can."

"Kind of you!" Nasir let out a sarcastic groan and shook his head. "And how do you propose to achieve that worthy goal?"

"The same tools we both use. Information and disinformation."

"What are you offering?"

"Intel on your enemies within the regime, people close to the Colonel – those opposed to your policies of moderation, working to dislodge you. And enemies outside: communist cells operating out of London, Muslim Brothers, the business elite linked to the Royalists, some harder line Palestinian groups. Stuff your bosses will drool at. Think about it. A quiet exchange serves both our interests."

"In return?"

Straw Man

"Northern Ireland. Our singular preoccupation. Semtex. Which you intend to send to the Provisional IRA. My recurring nightmare."

"A powerful nightmare."

"Yours is ensuring your homeland avoids getting bombed by the Yankee Air Force, together with further debilitating sanctions. And more personally, avoiding being done in by your enemy Ghereby and ending in a dirty cell in the basement."

"I don't disagree."

"Charlie tells me you propose to recruit me." Haydon walked back from the window and sat down. "That would be a jewel in your *Shashiyah*."

"And you're proposing to double us both?" Nasir laughed. He sounded like a jackal, Haydon thought. *Laugh all you like, just step across the Rubicon.* "You're a devious race, you English, the true masters of distortion."

They fell silent. Haydon could sense the man's mind whirring, calculating. Haydon noticed his foot tap-tapping away on the carpet, his face an immobile mask. He was looking up at the ceiling, avoiding Haydon's eyes. *He's getting there. He's almost there. What he says next will clinch it, or damn it.* Nasir bent his head down and murmured.

"I'd buy the information from you, you see. Buy it. Pay you in cash dollars. With nice photos of you sticking it in your pocket with a fat smile on your face. My bosses will understand that. They believe you'd all sell yourselves for enough dollars."

"Probably true. And what we want?"

"These exchanges, you see. The crucial thing is to protect such valuable intelligence. Always. Shielded by glorious legends. Your Mr Churchill was right when he said, *'Truth is so precious that she should always be attended by a bodyguard of lies.*' Safeguarding the source is the key to our continued good health."

Haydon felt the blood rising to his head. He's in. He's in! This could take them a long way, he thought. *Maybe I just solved the IRA problem.* The veins in his temples were throbbing. He reached out and clasped Nasir's hand.

"How right, Nasir. How true."

"Convince me I'll be safe, Haydon. Free from any risk of leaks. Your enemies and mine. I need a perfect legend, you see, a hermetically sealed box. That's what I need."

Straw Man

CHAPTER 42

Everything was grey. The sky, the trees, the river, even the flocks of screeching seagulls that hovered and circled in the biting wind. Haydon watched them diving and splashing into the dirty wash from the barges that were carrying away mounds of the city's garbage. At least the seagulls seemed to take pleasure from the frigid scene. How he hated winter in London. The damp. The stiff fingers of Jack Frost reached out and stung the tips of his ears and nose as he leaned down.

He thought of Victor Pasmore's melancholy paintings of the winter Thames, indistinct layers of opaque grey and black paint, a touch of brown, murky stains of mist concealing bent, motionless figures. A metaphor for our dark work, carried out in impenetrable shadows? Mist, or was it thick fog, obscuring their grubby world from scrutiny? Exposure to light, that was the omnipresent danger they all feared. His eyes fixed on the rusty buoys bobbing up and down, heaving at their heavy chains against the churning current. What did they presage?

Glasson stood alongside him, arms resting on the Embankment wall. He looked so cocky and impervious, sucking away at a long cigar with evident pleasure. He's such a strutter, Haydon thought. I creep around linoleum corridors in my brothel creepers while he struts the gilded hallways of power, steel heels clack-clacking on the marble floors. A colourful cockerel who knows his prospects are always on the up. Pull me up with you, up the next creaky step on the polished beanpole that leads to the top, where the smiling, self-satisfied, giants live.

"It's a coup Haydon. I had my doubts, believe me. But we're on the verge of pulling it off."

Straw Man

"Not there yet, Mark. Close. Nasir–we've given him the cover name LOMBARD – will have reported back to Qaddafi on our meeting. The prospect of recruiting a senior SIS man will cause a stir. Our fortune is their steadfast belief that we Westerners are all mercenary pigs. Mind you, sometimes I suspect they're not so far off." Haydon shivered and pulled his coat lapels closer around his neck.

"I sense useful money coming our way, which we won't refuse. We'll play it back at them." Glasson laughed; it came out as a cough. "Black funds for the Service are difficult to come by nowadays. A splendid twist!"

"I'll write it up for your approval. I don't want to end up in the dock accused of having my snout in the trough for personal enrichment."

"I've briefed the JIC. Full support. They've agreed to play it long. We need your man LOMBARD to survive and thrive. You'll have a watertight compartment in which to manage him and disguise the product before its dissemination. Back to the old ULTRA days. Absolute discipline! I impressed on our masters how vital it is to protect the source. With Ulster an unholy sieve."

A police car sped along the Embankment behind them, siren blaring, lights flashing. They paused until the sound faded and the lights disappeared into the gloom.

"I'll meet him next week. Reassure him about operational security, give him a file on Abdullah Ghereby – his most dangerous rival – close to Qaddafi, a hardliner. Dirty boy."

"How dirty?"

"Manages relations with Abu Nidal, involved in the recent *Achille Lauro* hijacking."

"We've got stuff on him?"

"Sadistic sod. Whips and chains. Affidavits from damaged tarts. Photos. And I'll feed in chickenfeed about anti-Qaddafi elements in Geneva. Business people. Bits he can use."

"When will he give you the IRA details?"

"He'll drip feed the intel. Tit for tat. Right now he'll give us details of immediate IRA contacts and the coordinates of their next shipment. Imminent. They landed their first load near Arklow in August. You've seen the list. Small arms and ammo. He insists no Semtex until later shipments. Luckily for us. I presume that remains our principal target, together with missiles?"

"Correct. Lean on him, Haydon. No mercy. Squeeze the bastard."

"Obviously we're taping the meets. Each step he takes over the line makes him more vulnerable. More ours. He'll stay ours if we protect him and don't push him too hard. I'm thinking years. With our help, he could end up as Qaddafi's intelligence supremo."

"Now Haydon listen to this." Glasson puffed his cigar. "Our tech boys have developed an ingenious way of inserting tiny transmitters into weapon assemblies so we can track them. They call it 'jarking'. Follow the bastards to their nest, then steer your Det team to the cache. It's a priority."

"I'll work on it. Might take time, it'll be risky. South Armagh seems the most likely destination. We'll need to move with caution around there."

"Are you fucking with me, Haydon? You becoming some kind of pussy?" Glasson glared at him before walking away. "We nearly lost the PM and half the Cabinet in the IRA bombing and you use the word caution? They're soldiers for Chrissakes. They fight, they die, it's what they do."

Straw Man

"I hear you, Mark." Haydon followed him along the Embankment wall. As usual. The guys on the front line were expendable. Par for the course. Orders were orders, Babs would be up for it.

"Good. Let's go to lunch. Celebrate. The PM has asked to see me tomorrow with C, for a private brief."

Straw Man

CHAPTER 43

Nasir did his best thinking on the exercise bike in his office. Berber drumming and chanting played loudly from the cassette player, the thumping vibrations from the deep bass propelling him forward. His place of meditation. Out of the window blowing sand obscured the view of downtown Tripoli.

He thrived on complex challenges, prided himself on his capacity for objective calculation. He increased the pace, his legs pumping away. The more he let himself go, the clearer the visions that popped into his head. The whirring of the pedals and the increase in blood flow to his brain imbued him with an icy calm. The rhythm of the drums sped up, his breathing became laboured.

He was not a timid man. He thought himself inured to the outlandish balancing acts required of him. He was like a desert ice-skater, required to conduct bold diplomatic pirouettes on a thin and melting ice floe. He'd picked up disturbing rumours that Abdullah Ghereby, Qaddafi's brother-in-law, was planning provocative operations in Europe. On his patch. Sabri al-Banna, the leader of the most extreme and bloodthirsty of the Palestinian terror groups, Abu Nidal, had been seen entering Ghereby's offices in Tripoli several times. The Leader and hard-liners around him seemed determined to pursue global chaos, whilst they tasked him with finagling a friendly accommodation with Western powers. If some outrage took place on Italian soil, it would undo everything he'd been working towards. At a stroke.

Still, Khalfari's official visit to Rome had gone well. He'd even met the Pope. Wearing full Arab garb and a dagger in his belt. An offbeat, theatrical,

Straw Man

meeting. Heavy on pomp and of absolutely no substance. The entire trip had been conducted in the same absurd, operatic vein. Except nobody actually sang. The Americans had made an official complaint to Craxi, but Nasir heard from Polliti that behind the scenes they were happy enough for the contacts to go on. It had been a diplomatic success. His success.

On his return to Tripoli he'd been summoned to The Leader's private office at the Bab al-Azizia barracks in Tripoli. Qaddafi had been pleased with the information he'd provided on opposition figures, and the progress with the nuclear purchases. A sign that his stock was on its way up.

His shock about Talbot's possession of the details of his own dark secret had given way to a recognition that this new relationship would be crucial to advancing his career. But he felt a burning sense of bitterness about Andrea's betrayal. The documents could only have come from him. His first and only Western friend. Nasir pedalled faster as a wave of anger burst over him, rage fuelling his pumping legs. Had the leak about the payment to the Minister also come from Andrea? Could Pollitti have conspired with him?

He'd have to change all the accounts. He was authorised to manage black cash to service Haydon and the covert accounts for the nuclear business. He'd mix it all up, wash the evidence, eventually the material would degrade, the documents Haydon held would become stale. And then? New banks, numbered accounts, no names. Tell Andrea the order had come from on high, a reorganisation of State foreign investments. He would suspect something, sure. But he'd dangle carrots and play it nice. New business to come, construction projects. Stroke him a little. Take him down to the Leader, make him feel loved. At the right time he'd take his revenge, make that problem go away. Forever.

Straw Man

And Lomax, could he have conned them all? *Such a vapid man, so avaricious.* Surely he wasn't bright or devious enough to have deceived them through those long months in Abu Salim; the interrogations, the daily observation. He was making too much money from the nuclear deals. No, he was a useful idiot. The culprits were Andrea and Talbot. He would balance up the score, he just couldn't move against them yet. Maybe not for a long while. But he'd have it planned and ready. And meanwhile he'd hold the kompromat on Ghereby tight. Another score to settle.

He slowed his pace, he could feel his heart thumping away; he felt calm. He knew what he had to do. He just needed to be a little patient.

Straw Man

CHAPTER 44

The voyage had nearly ended in catastrophe before it even started. A violent October storm hurtled in, spinning like a drunken dervish, dumping pellets of rain, and blowing like the devil. As the Skipper had warned. They'd sheltered in Valletta harbour for two days, the noise of a thousand halyards clinking out a maddening symphony which threatened to drive Seán insane. He drank too much whisky and lay on his bunk, sweating and sick as a rat. *Seasick in port, imagine!*

On successive nights the two fishing boats rendezvoused close in off the south-western shores of Gozo. Even in the relative calm of the vertical rock bluffs of the Sanap Cliffs, the screaming wind and crazy seas made it impossible to manoeuvre the two craft close together without risk of a catastrophic collision. They inched towards each other, edging in as close as they dared, but monster waves came at them from every direction, colliding with each other in a drunken, carnival barn-dance.

Seán stood next to the Skipper in the wheelhouse, gripping on to the rail for dear life, his eyes almost closed, muttering prayers under his breath. Spume and balls of white water flew through the air, threatening to smash the sailors off their tenuous handholds. The Libyan vessel finally signalled, alternating red and green lights: abort, try again tomorrow.

After midnight on the third night, there was a lull. The Skipper told Seán they were taking a risk; they were in the storm's eye and it would be a brief window before it came back at them with a vengeance. The crews hurried to lash the craft together and worked like deranged soldier ants to transfer the cargo over, the derrick on the Libyan ship whipping back and forth in a berserk jig as sailors struggled to hold guide ropes taut and

Straw Man

keep the heavy, lurching wooden crates under control. Men stood by to haul them down and lash them to struts in the convulsing hold.

As the final crate was being lowered, the wind rose and started to howl. An immense wave crashed into them, causing the two vessels to tilt against each other at a crazy angle. The heavy cargo smashed into the side of the hold like an evil sledgehammer, the crate shattering, spewing a torrent of assault rifles into a clattering spaghetti mound of AK-47s.

On the Libyan boat the derrick swung back, narrowly missing decapitating a sailor who tumbled over and clung perilously to the guardrail until arms reached out to pull him back in. Captain Hassan Ali shouted an order and panic-stricken sailors axed away at the heavy ropes holding the two craft together. Two men fell backwards onto the deck as the ropes snapped, freeing the vessels, which quivered and corkscrewed towards each other, seemingly determined to smash together in a thunderous collision. For a moment Seán watched the other craft swinging and bucking, then clambering high, its sharp bow almost above their heads.

He looked up at the other boat and held his breath. No way they could make it. Next to him the Skipper was leaning right over against the wheel, hauling it to its full extent, but the turbulent water rendered the rudder helpless. Then the two vessels sprang apart as if propelled by some godlike force, and suddenly they were alone. *Jesus, that had been close.* Keep me on dry land, dear God.

It was getting light when he piled into his bunk, soaked and exhausted, sick, but so tired he fell asleep immediately.

Straw Man

He awoke the next afternoon to placid seas and blue skies. Looking through the round porthole, he saw puffy clouds covering the coast of Sicily to the north. He'd been shocked by how frightened he'd been of those rough seas. He considered himself a tough man, a soldier who looked death in the eye and smiled, but he'd felt meek as a child lying moaning on his bunk, so badly seasick he wished himself dead, and filled with terror of those dark depths beneath him.

He made himself a coffee and climbed the companionway to the wheelhouse. The Skipper was standing at the helm chewing the stub of a fat cigar.

"Never seen seas like that before, never want to again." Seán moaned. "I'd face a company of drunken Paras in a foul mood, alone and naked, rather than pass through that misery again."

"I thought you'd died on me. I looked in on you this morning; you were like a ghostly white corpse lying there."

"I'm not so sure myself I'm alive after that rollicking."

"Try that gig enough times outside of summer months, we're going to lose a cargo." He made a chopping sign across his throat with his hand. "Maybe lose me my ship."

"Maybe lose me to a heart attack. I'll need blinkers if ye want me to the finishing post like that again."

"You looked like a drunk leprechaun last night, you did!" The tall man leaned back and let out a deep bass laugh. "You've a bit of colour back."

"Irish green, I'll bet."

"Look, you need to find a better way." The Skipper pointed his finger at him. "Do the transfers on land. I don't want to risk a transhipment at sea again. For all the brass you pay me, more even."

Straw Man

"I'll press for it. We won't be doing another one 'til the spring. If I must be with you, that is. God knows I'd prefer to be anywhere else at all. No offence!" He waved and staggered forward towards the foredeck, gripping the rail in one hand and balancing his coffee in the other.

He sat down at the bow, legs dangling over the side, sheltered from the cool breeze behind the peeling wooden superstructure as the old vessel puttered on towards the afternoon sun. There was a slight swell, it felt like he was being pushed gently in a rocking chair. Sipping his coffee his eyes followed the grey outline of the small island of Pantelleria creeping by. What a change 24 hours made.

Christ, I've to do this ghastly journey one more time, he thought. Then freedom. *Get me through these two trips, Saint Anthony, I beg you.* By springtime I'll have started my new life. Anonymity, peace and blessed solitude. He thought about Geneva. Nasir had told him they'd meet there in January. To hand over the next tranche of funds. He'd tried to convince him to make the meet straight after this trip. He said the Movement needed funds for the down payment on the larger vessel.

"What's the rush, friend?" He'd looked at him quizzically. "We need to get this next shipment tucked away. Then there'll be trust. You've got six clear months to get the larger vessel ready. No, we'll meet in Switzerland in the New Year. Khalfari's orders."

A year on. One million dollars. The figure used to mesmerise him. It seemed like riches. It didn't matter anymore; he just needed enough to create his new persona and build his hide. He'd made his decision long ago. The waiting was just a deep pain in his belly. Every day. He'd suffered a year of living the lie. Watching out to smile at the right times, to laugh at

Straw Man

the right jokes, to sing and drink and be solid with the boys, arm in arm, glass by glass, tear for tear. And wait. And lie.

In his bones he knew this was his moment. He'd mapped his future in his head, visioned his escape. A crystalline image. He felt iron determination, not a hint of fear. Nothing like the fear he felt at facing another bloody storm like that one. Another six weeks and this would be behind him. To live without the burden of a failing cause, to focus on the dull minutiae of daily existence. He wouldn't squander the money; he'd work with his hands; there was always a call for that.

A pod of dolphins appeared and raced each other to ride the bow wave. He could hear their musical squeaks as they swished in and out. With hardly a ripple on the sea he watched fascinated as their sleek, black shapes rushed back and forth at each other just below the surface. Then, from one moment to the next, they disappeared. That's what I have to do, he thought. Disappear as fast and as completely. Dive down and never be seen again.

Straw Man

CHAPTER 45

As Seán was watching the dolphins, high above and to the north of him, visible as a minute silver speck high in the clear blue sky, a Nimrod MR2 reconnaissance aircraft from the RAF's 42 Squadron was monitoring the slow progress of the tubby vessel. Inside the aircraft, a team of 10 operators sat in deep chairs in front of large consoles, managing the reconnaissance using multiple high-tech sensors. The Mission Operator sat at the head of a long table, conversing quietly over headphones with Haydon Talbot, 1,000 miles away in Century House.

LOMBARD had provided Haydon with details of the *Makaria*, now renamed the *Tadiran*, and the dates and parameters for the planned rendezvous offshore Gozo. The two men met at a newly acquired safe house behind the Piazza Navona. Haydon's budget had been rushed through Treasury unopposed, and he was enjoying unused-to freedom of action as the result of the high priority TUMBREL had earned itself.

He'd been prepared for the Libyan to dole out secrets in little teasing slices, seeking to extract something in return for every scrap. But once Nasir started talking he didn't stop, Haydon sat there pretty much mute as the intel spewed out in a long stream, captured by the large tape recorders concealed in the wooden Hi-Fi unit. This was the IRA op in the bag, he thought. They'd interdict it all, sabotage it, roll it up. Story over.

The wild autumn storm had caused them problems. Even at 36,000 feet it was a bumpy ride, the aircraft loitering in a search pattern at the edge of the storm clouds, some hundred miles to the west of Gozo. Its *Searchwater* radar observed the conjoining blip as the Libyan vessel attached itself to the Irish boat to transfer the cargo. As soon as that single green dot broke

Straw Man

into two and separated, the radar operator locked on to the *Tadiran* as she turned westward, keeping a sidewards watch on the Libyan vessel as it steered a southerly course back towards Tripoli.

Over the subsequent eleven days three Nimrods from RAF St Mawgan in Cornwall operated in shifts to maintain uninterrupted 24 hour coverage, monitoring the *Tadiran*'s westward track from Malta to the straits of Gibraltar, then northward through the Atlantic towards Ireland. Haydon spent the long days pacing the Ops room, grabbing occasional naps on a camp bed. A large electronic map dominated one end of the room, a red blip marking the *Tadiran*'s position. Alongside it a TV screen projected blurry black and white images of the ship churning its way northward. Below it a colour display showed infra-red returns from the boat's engine heat, standing out clearly in orange and red against the cold black of the Atlantic.

Haydon had ordered the Det team to deploy forward to the Drumadd Barracks in Armagh, close to the hazardous area controlled by the South Armagh Brigade of the Provisional IRA, a dangerous and well-organised unit. He imagined the team, dressed in civvies, waiting out the days on standby, ready to move out in unmarked cars on command. They knew the area well, over the years they'd spent months hidden up in fields, surveilling the back roads which wiggled in and out of the Republic. They referred to the border area between Crossmaglen and Jonesborough, the principal smuggling route used by the IRA, as 'Bandit Country'.

Passing abeam Rosslare, the Nimrod operators reported the *Tadiran* had edged inshore and was now hugging the Irish coastline, labouring her way north. Unseen and silent, the Royal Navy submarine *HMS Otter* slid westward from Fishguard, taking up position five miles east of the vessel.

Straw Man

The Nimrods flew wide patterns over the Irish Sea, staying clear of Irish airspace, peering down with their sidewards-looking sensors. Haydon paced up and down the room, the long wire to his headphones dragging behind him like a tail, the hum of the air conditioning drowning out his voice.

He checked his watch for the umpteenth time. Another night without sleep. Subordinates sat around the conference table, strewn with different coloured telephones and a spaghetti of black cables. Bored faces, heads down, yawning. A large loudspeaker mounted on the wall provided a live feed from the Nimrod Mission Operator's station. He sat down on the camp bed and thought about trying to sleep, but adrenaline was pumping through his veins and it was no use. He thought back to a night in Belfast, crammed into a rooftop, looking through the night sight on his rifle, waiting for movement in the street below. He woke with a jolt when the speaker crackled into life.

"*OpCom to Zulu, Target slowing stop current position abeam Kilmichael Point Over*"

"*Roger, expand area search box for reception committee Over*"

Haydon sat down at the table. *Game on.* They'd got the bastards, now they just had to watch them across the border to wherever they were going to stash the haul and then set Babs's team onto them. If they were lucky, it would be a remote burial site, unpopulated, that would give the boys time to work their magic.

"*OpCom to Zulu, India Romeo reports three hot signatures on the beach at Clogga Strand one mile north of target stop likely reception, Over*"

"*Roger Zulu Command, re-target sensors and provide live feed.*"

The three screens suddenly went blank and then quickly refreshed. Haydon pointed at the electronic chart where three flashing green dots had appeared slightly north of the red blip that marked the *Tadiran*. A foggy black-and-white image appeared on the video screen. As their eyes acclimatised, the shape of three lorries emerged. On the IR monitor, three separate traces showed the engines of the vehicles were running. The TV monitor switched back to the *Tadiran*. The camera followed as the ship turned in towards the shore opposite the three green lights.

"Look at this." Peter Etherington pointed at little orange trails from engine heat that had left the shore and were moving steadily towards the *Tadiran*. "They're unloading alright. Maybe ribs or lighters, they're slow."

Haydon and Peter watched as the red-flaring heat images and green radar blips shuttled back and forth between the *Tadiran* and the beach. Haydon noticed Peter's feet tapping away on the floor. After an hour the blurry images started to move away as the trucks left the beach and headed north for the coast road.

"Bingo!" Haydon clapped his hands. He picked up the green phone that linked live to Drumadd Barracks. "Babs, three lorries. Leaving Clogga Strand now. Fifty miles south of Dublin. I'm faxing the coordinates through to you as we speak. Fingers crossed the Garda don't roll them up and mess us. No room for errors or bad luck."

"Can't do anything about the luck boss." Babs' voice was fuzzy over the long-distance line. "But we're ready for them."

"Pray to Saint Anthony?"

"Maybe the Paddies have an edge with the saints."

"Is that a nervous laugh? Stay focussed."

"You know us boss. ETA?"

"Can't be at the border before, I estimate," he checked his watch. "zero two hundred at the earliest. Standby. I'll get back to you."

Straw Man

He dropped the phone into the cradle and leaned back. Four hours maybe. He closed his eyes and tried to sleep, but after a few minutes he got back up and started pacing the room again. He and Peter watched, mesmerised by the screens, as the blips moved north, inch by painful inch, bypassing Dublin then taking the coast road past Drogheda toward Newry. At 1.30 he picked up the green phone. Babs answered at once.

"They're passing Dundalk, looks like we've got a hit. They're going to turn west and cross the border by one of those tracks the South Armagh lads control. Can't be far from you now."

"Unit's tooled up and ready to go."

But a few miles before the border, the trucks abruptly turned east and headed out onto the Cooley Peninsula.

"Shit, they're turning away from the border near Jonesborough. What the hell's there?" The orange blips drifted away from the roads superimposed on the electronic map. They watched as the dots came to a stop in a blank area.

"*OpCom to Zulu, we're seeing heat from two more vehicles all five stationary Over.*"

"OK. They're going to change vehicles there, decant the weapons before crossing the border. Unless they're caching them there in the Republic." Haydon leaned back and put his arms behind his neck. "Bets?"

"Why change vehicles?" Peter had produced an Ordnance Survey map and laid it on the table. "Seems to be woodland."

"Looks like farm buildings there." Haydon pointed at the map. "Maybe they're going to cache them there? We'll need aerial footage as soon as it's light."

"Can't be more than half a mile from the border, if that, no marked tracks. Perfect for a hide."

Straw Man

"Perfect for them, not so good for us."

"But our guys, crossing the border—"

"You didn't say that, Peter, and I didn't hear it. Crackling blather is what I heard." Haydon barked. "Get working on what's down there, ownership, details, building plans. Wake people up. We'll presume it's a hide, if the lorries move again we'll revert to the original plan."

"*All stations OpCom time is 05.24 Zulu. Mark your vehicle's position and forward coordinates to my console.*" The voice of the Mission Operator came over the loudspeaker. "*Maximum accuracy, bring the gain right in. We'll triangulate the results.*"

"*Zulu Command, remain on station standby in case vehicles move again Stop see if you can record accurate India Romeo of any dig.*"

"*OpCom to Zulu, confirm Target one sailed north docking now at Arklow harbour Over.*"

Haydon picked up the green phone and started to talk.

Straw Man

CHAPTER 46

A thin line of mist hung low over the flat sea. Seán felt a sudden chill and shook himself as if to fend off the eerie atmosphere. There wasn't a breath of wind as the *Tadiran* motored slowly into Clogga Bay, engine throttled right back, making slow way through the mist. The moon was not yet up. Seán and the Skipper scanned through image-intensifying binoculars for signs of movement. The only sound Seán could make out was a low putt-putting of diesel engines from the two bulky lighters that flashed the recognition signal and then emerged from the gloom and crabbed their way slowly alongside.

The unloading was quick, these larger craft only needed two trips, within an hour they'd stashed the arms in the lorries. He checked his watch, just after midnight. Slipping over the side of the *Tadiran,* he clambered down into one of the lighters with a wave up to the Skipper.

"I'll get my feet on dry land and stay away from you for a while."

"I'll make a sailor out of you if you come back soon."

"Never happen."

He stood in the bow watching the wide beach come into view, his Armalite slung from his shoulder, the squat shapes of the lorries emerging from the gloom. As he waded up the beach, the Quartermaster greeted him with a curt nod. He was a famously suspicious man and looked Seán up and down with an ugly eye.

"You'll travel with me." He had a rasping west Belfast accent. "Jump up onto this fellow here. Hand yer gun to Aiden there, you won't be needing it."

The QMG, as he was referred to, was second in rank only to the Provo's Chief of Staff and served on the Army Council. He had a reputation as

Straw Man

a hard man, some said cruel. Seán clambered up into the lead truck and found himself sandwiched between the QMG and the driver, a silent man with a sharp face.

"I'll be hooding you when we're past Drogheda. Normal precaution. You won't know where you are or where you've been. Better for your health that way."

"Sure, I'll have nicer dreams with your eye shades on."

"You do that." He was shovelling away at his teeth with a pick, Seán could smell a pungent mix of garlic and Guinness. I'll be better off with a bag over my head, he thought. Christ, he'd have to do this all over again within the month. The lorry lurched forward and drove off with no lights, until they were away from the beach and onto the main road.

Once the thick canvas hood had been placed over his head and secured around his neck, he lost sense of time and place. He closed his eyes. His mind went back to the image he'd been building over these last months. The little cottage perched above a sheer rock cliff, the veranda out front, a broad olive tree, maybe a little vegetable garden. It faced down into a narrow bay where the water was crystal clear; he could imagine the underwater rocks sparkling. His clinker built dinghy would be anchored on a buoy just a short swim from the small sandy beach.

He dozed fitfully and woke as the lorry started bouncing badly. It felt like they were driving down a badly rutted track. He reached out and pushed his hand against the windscreen to steady himself. They must have crossed the border by now. He felt the lorry pulling to a halt, and the engine switched off, then he heard the tailgate being lowered and the sound of something like a fork-lift operating. They were obviously carrying the heavy boxes off.

Straw Man

He could hear muted conversation but couldn't make out words. He noticed an acrid farmyard smell. That must be hellish strong to penetrate the hood. That's it, he thought, we're at one of those farms that straddles the border, one half in the Republic, the other in Ulster. Perfect for smuggling. He heard a sudden high-pitched squeal followed by a series of grunts. Pigs, that was it. Clever boys. He chuckled. They'll bury this lot, maybe below one of the sties scattered all around a field. Poor old Brits, with all their electronic gear and their sniffer dogs, they wouldn't have a hope.

"Won't be long now." The hard Belfast voice by his ear was muffled. "Don't move a hair whilst we're stopped, hear me?"

"Difficult to move anything with this hood on." His voice came out muffled.

"Aidan will make sure you don't. He'll be leaving you off at Crossmaglen before dawn." He heard a raucous laugh. "Come back soon and bring some Semtex with you when you do."

Fuck you, he thought, you grizzled bully boy. I'll be a thousand miles away bringing my lunch home, a couple of small rock cod perhaps, warm sun on my face and the little engine on my dinghy purring as I pull into my bay and throw the anchor out. Maybe there'll be a tall village girl waiting for me, long black hair: she'll wave from the house. And you'll still be knee deep in pig shit and pouring rain.

Straw Man

CHAPTER 47

It was what The Det did best. Slow, painstaking reconnaissance. The definition of patience. Advancing yard by painful yard, taking however long it took. Keep changing camouflage like a chameleon. *Grass in our hair and up our noses!* That should be our mantra, Babs thought. Slithering, moving flat on our tummies, elbows, and knees, as slowly as puff adders, immense concentration on each individual movement. Feeling ahead with the palms of your hands. Catch sleep when cover permits, move faster by night than day. And you won't spot us from five yards away, even if you're looking hard. She felt a jolt of exhilaration.

They could do the job in a full day once they got to target. Expose the cache, carefully open the boxes, get going with the jarking. Sabotage maybe five percent, just enough to cause a bit of panic, some blowback, inaccuracy. Insert transmitters into enough items to enable them to follow the cache as it moved around. This was a feel-good op, if it panned out they'd be saving countless lives.

They were operating in two pairs, planning to approach the target from opposite directions. It had taken them a week to set up the recon, but the arms weren't going anywhere in a hurry, she was sure of that. They'd crossed into the Republic below Newry, close to where the frontier line juts south, at the base of the Black Mountain. Well, it was more of a hill, really.

There was no sign when they crossed the border, she didn't care. They didn't have clearance to be on Irish soil. But if they sabotaged a major Provo arms dump and got out unharmed, then she didn't give a hoot what laws she'd broken. And Haydon could take the heat, he was slithery enough for that. An image flashed across her mind. He was on top of her,

Straw Man

his hands pushing her shoulders down, roughly. She shook her head. *Stay focussed now.*

The two teams had fixed an RV time at the target buildings. They had no comms, nothing on their person that could make a sudden noise. Long hours with an expert, an old man with trembling hands, spent practicing bird vocalisation in Recce training had taught them an entire language of birdsong. A change to the RV, or a sign of danger, could be communicated by the bleating of a snipe or the buzzing of a woodcock.

It took them the best part of a day to cover four miles, crawling through bracken, mud and heather, moving cautiously through high woodland, before descending into a narrow valley of farmland carved out of the woods. The aerial shots showed farm buildings to the west of the target coordinates, a few hundred meters. They'd start with the heavy lorry tracks and follow from there straight to the dig. The boyos might have seeded grass, they often did, and after just a week it would have sprouted, but they'd still see signs. Wouldn't be hard.

They spent some hours manoeuvring in close and up-slope of the buildings to a little hump that faced directly towards them, the surrounding fields splayed out below. At first, in the early morning light, she couldn't make out what the little grey boxes were, scattered over the dark-brown fields. Then she noticed the little blobs, like pink ants, in every field. Pigs. And the brown, that was mud. *Christ, surely not!*

"If they buried the cache in those fields, we are truly fucked."

"A detachment of bloodhounds wouldn't help with the stink of pig shit and urine mixed in with mud." Cooper passed the binoculars to Babs. "The smell is disgusting even from this distance."

Straw Man

"Look at it, several feet deep of thick mud, churned up everywhere. Maybe they scattered food all over the place and the pigs would have done the rest. Any sign of a dig will be long gone. They're not fools." Babs scanned her binos over to the buildings. "No smoke. No signs. Let's pray they used the buildings. Maybe I'm being overly pessimistic."

They watched the buildings until midday, no sound of movement, no vehicles, no dog barking, nothing. It was remote enough, you wouldn't ever stumble across it without a tip off. Which she had, Long and Lat, down to the tenth digit. The buildings were the obvious location to sweep first, but their immediate task was to check the area for signs of life, particularly dogs: they often had them chained up near to caches. They'd brought an ultrasonic device they said scared off dogs, and a small bag of meat laced with a powerful sedative. She hoped they didn't need either. Foresight, she thought. We planned for dogs but never imagined our problem would be pigs.

They followed a narrow stone wall down to the farm, crouching low and stopping frequently to scan the buildings. Nothing. The smell was nauseating. The fields looked like bogs of churned up mud and shit. As they arrived at the farm buildings she knelt and made a bird call, Carter and Skelton appeared from behind the little stone house. They were covered in mud and slime. She pulled out a handkerchief and tied it around her face.

"Anything?"

"Nobody within 10 miles."

"You guys don't look so good. Been out on the town?"

"We may not look good, but we got a whiff of you from a long way back. Ugh."

Straw Man

"Let's get started going through these buildings one by one. Carter you get up there and keep watch." Babs pointed up at the flat roof above the cottage.

But there was nothing. Cigarette stubs. Empty beer cans. Evidently the buildings had been unoccupied for a long time. They disturbed a boar sleeping in the living room that ran off, squealing and shitting. They spent two hours scouring every inch for hiding places, but the buildings were derelict and dusty, there were no signs that any furniture had been moved recently.

"Even if we got a warrant from the Garda, we'd need a week with a Caterpillar and then some." Cooper lit a cigarette and sat down on an old rocking chair.

"We'd never get one, and anyway we've got to protect our source. We can't even make a mess of the place."

The fields around the farm buildings looked as if a magician had been at work, creating a great swill of dirty brown mud, often two foot deep, with paw prints perforating every square yard.

"They must've marched the bloody pigs back and forth over this whole place. Not even a vestige of the lorry tracks." Babs slammed her fist into her hand. "Another dead end. I tell you something, this op is jinxed to hell."

Glasson sat at the head of the long table in the Conference Room, glaring at Haydon. There were just the two of them. The large room felt strange and empty. Maybe it was the absence of natural light in the windowless room, the low hum of the air conditioning, or the dullness from the soundproofing which gave their voices a ghostly tenor.

Straw Man

This leaden interview encapsulates my life, Haydon thought, I keep pushing the bloody Sisyphean rock up the bloody hill, only to watch the Fates grab it and throw it back down again. So far, I've managed to dodge it as it bounced past. *I've done my best, but it wasn't good enough.* Now it's out of my hands.

It felt like a malign game where the ending was destined to benefit solely his boss and the IRA. Perhaps it was time to hand over his long-prepared letter of resignation and move on to a life of commercial compromise and relative comfort for him and his family. No gongs, but who cared about gongs, only the puffed up, self-serving types who were inevitably destined to reach the top of the nasty pile. Glasson.

"Thanks to your failure we're immersed in piles of stinking Irish pig shit–" Glasson growled; his face florid. "Or rather, you are. You authorised an op across the border. If they'd been discovered–"

"At all times my team remained within the province Mark." Haydon enunciated clearly, his face deadpan. "My direct orders."

"I hear you. How do you intend to regain the trace?"

"I'm setting up a meet with LOMBARD. He's giving me details of the next shipment, some months off. We'll position our recce team around the farm well in advance. We have one more chance. This was not a disaster; it was a setback. We got close."

"You say. What makes you think they'll use the same hide?"

"Hunch. We'll cover it. Keep trawling intercepts, but we need intel out of Ulster. I'll need to deploy more personnel, flood the shipment from air, sea and land."

Straw Man

"I'm under pressure to hand the file to Special Section. So far, I've resisted, but you'd better make bloody sure no Semtex makes it into IRA hands. Or you're dead meat. This is your last chance."

Haydon picked up his papers from the desk and stood up.

"You'll have my resignation the day that happens."

"I've always supported you, Haydon. But–"

"–you've made it clear. I need your support for this last effort. We've recruited a senior member of the Libyan Mukhabarat, that's a success. I would expect kudos for that. Look, Mark, we have a winning formula, now we need luck."

"Luck we make for ourselves, my friend. Go out and grab it."

As he drove out of the underground garage, he saw a drunk staggering on the sidewalk. *Is that me in a couple of years?* He turned north and crossed the Thames. He felt a migraine coming on. Maybe I deserve this misery. Charlie and Babs, he'd used them both with no concern for their loyalty. His claim to a higher cause was just another form of dishonesty.

Straw Man

CHAPTER 48

They were in Khalfari's office at the Security Headquarters in Tripoli. The windows were closed, and the room was muggy. An overhead fan conducted irregular circuits, clanking noisily as it sent down jerky gusts of warm air. Nasir and Captain Hassan Ali sat on low wicker chairs in front of a metal desk behind which Khalfari was hunched, his head down, scribbling away on a yellow notepad. He wrote with his hand turned almost back on itself, producing an angular child's scrawl.

"Docherty is insistent, Sir." Nasir scratched his head and brushed his fingers through his dark hair.

"Docherty's an ant, a worker bee. He'll do what we tell him." Khalfari looked up and glared. Then he laughed, a rasping, unfriendly sound, his belly vibrating. "We are the milking camel, you see. We do the insisting."

"We came close to losing both vessels, Sir." The navy man wore a smart, white, well-pressed uniform and seemed to be sitting at attention. It amused Nasir to observe his discomfiture, obviously not enjoying reporting tough news to his superior. He had come to loathe his boss. He imagined stamping on his hand as he climbed past him up the next rung on the ladder. "And the cargo. We were lucky, the crews didn't panic."

"That surprises you Captain, does it?" Khalfari looked up, then swivelled his chair to face away from them, peering out of the window towards the dusty parade ground below. Then he turned back to his notepad and continued scribbling. "The crews didn't panic?"

"The shipment got ashore safely in Ireland. I received coded confirmation, Sir." Nasir said. "They're transporting it north. We must plan carefully for the next shipments."

Straw Man

After his betrayal of the shipment to the British, Nasir didn't feel any remorse. The arms had got through. Job done. What happened after that was not his business. He couldn't give a hoot about those Irish lunatics. A mean and sadistic bunch. He hoped suspicion wouldn't land on Seán's head. His friend was different, a gentle soul, not cut out for this dirty stuff. But he'd done his job, he'd shepherded the arms to the Republic. He trusted Haydon's assurances they'd seize the arms in the north, some fortuitous event would lead to their discovery. The IRA would cast around internally for a traitor, a spy in their ranks. There were plenty of those. It was in Haydon's best interests that he survived and thrived.

"What do you propose Captain?" Khalfari barked. "I want solutions, you see, not problems."

"We load their ship at one of our smaller ports - Al Khums or Misrata, carefully camouflaged." The Captain murmured. "We clear out the port of eyes before loading."

"Too exposed from the air, it could never be secure. Bad idea. Nasir?"

"Lease warehouses in Valletta, several of them. Do it through local cut outs, pay them well so there's nothing that could link them back to us. A few locations – the port covers a large area. We load each cargo into a different warehouse, leave it for a few weeks, more even, surveil it, watch them collect."

"How do they take delivery?"

"We give Docherty the location, lock combinations and a range of dates. We give him a week to empty it."

"How would he clear them onward?"

"Makes his own arrangements." Nasir leaned back. "Easy enough. Malta's as crooked as a camel's nose."

Straw Man

"Might be something in it. It would reduce risk." Khalfari swung his chair back to face Nasir. "Getting our stuff into these warehouses, there will be difficulties?"

"No, Sir. We've got good connections in Valletta with the various authorities."

"OK. I'll think about it." Khalfari turned to the naval man. "Captain, you may leave. Nasir, you stay."

After the naval man had left, Khalfari crabbed his way around the desk and pulled up a chair opposite Nasir. He paused for a while, stroking his straggly beard, a cunning shopkeeper's smile spreading across his face. He leaned forward, so close that Nasir could smell the reek of onions and garlic and stared into his eyes. Nasir blinked.

"Do you think I'm some sort of blind man?" He tapped Nasir on the knee. "You've been behind my back to the Leader. Without informing me. I don't like that. The recruitment of the Englishman is my operation. You work for me, you do what I order you, you see. Or perhaps you'd like to be a border guard in the southern desert?"

"The Leader's secretary summoned me Sir. After midnight. I was asleep. Ordered to report immediately, I was in no position to contact you."

"But you didn't report the meeting to me later. I'm not happy. Not at all. More worrying for you, Abdullah Ghereby is not happy. He rang me to tell me all about it, you see." Khalfari frowned and fixed Nasir with a stare. "That's a lot of people with the power to affect your future who aren't happy."

"The operation is shaping into a big success." Nasir felt the eyes boring into him. He turned away. This was not going as he'd expected. He felt the initiative draining away. "Talbot is about to supply raw intel about our enemies in return for cash. I'm going to Rome to meet him next week, hand him ten thousand dollars. His big step, crossing over the line. Then he'll be compromised. His treachery will be on tape, he'll be ours. Our first penetration of MI6. I doubt any other Arab service has managed such a feat."

"That should be excellent news. But it may not be."

"How could it not be?"

"Ghereby is manoeuvring to take over the op. He's working on the Leader." A sharp expression came over Khalfari's face, his eyes narrowed. "His preferred method of problem-solving often involves spades and gravediggers. Which could mean the sudden end of Mister Talbot, and of our promising rainbow. He would see it as revenge for British insults. He doesn't approve of nice, quiet talks going on leading to better relations. He's as subtle as a Red Sea shark with an itchy arse, you see."

"So how am I to play it?"

"Cautiously, so you and I stay healthy. And you keep it close to your chest. You don't report to anyone. To me and to me only."

"If the Leader summons me?"

"Don't play games, Nasir. I'm too old not to sniff out when someone is oversexed with ambition, you see." He stood up and walked back to his desk, waving over his shoulder. "You need my protection, believe me. Get out of my sight and fucking grow up."

Straw Man

CHAPTER 49

Haydon was early. Charlie wasn't due for another fifteen minutes. He sat on a bench in the little arbour, shut his eyes and felt the winter sun warm on his face. It was good to have time alone, tucked up in this haven in the gardens of the Villa Wolkonsky. He'd been suffering from stomach pains. He felt trapped in a chrysalis of impending doom, a sort of end of term sensation. The end of what? The whole Libyan thing? He'd had this heavy, dark feeling ever since the recruitment of Nasir, which promised to be his biggest success.

He watched several blue butterflies perched on purple lilac flowers, slowly opening and closing their wings. Exquisite. A performance that seemed just for his pleasure. A tapestry of mauve and white wisteria framed the wooden structure, almost dazzling Haydon as he stared up. He felt a brief flutter and looked down; a butterfly had landed on his wrist. He looked at the complex design. So delicate, a work of art.

Everything was going well. Life with Ros was harvest home, reborn, revitalised, loving. She seemed to have sensed nothing about his straying with Babs. Odd, women were so damned prescient. Discussions with LOMBARD were going full tilt. The Libyans were getting everything they wanted, Haydon had been feeding him good stuff about opposition figures in London and Geneva. So why this black cloud of worry? He felt the dull throbbing in his tummy again. It had been with him since he'd woken up.

The butterfly flapped its wings and flew off. He looked up. Charlie came jogging into view. He was wearing white shorts and a thick Cambridge sweater, a knitted sports scarf wrapped around his neck.

Straw Man

"I'm late." He panted and slumped down on the bench next to Haydon. "I just saw HE coming up the drive, so we haven't much time."

"Talk to me."

"Good news! They accepted the proposals. $35 million. The South Africans have agreed to build the complete structure for controlling the UF6 gasses in the centrifuge cascades. A massive steel thing. They're going to ship the whole caboodle from South Africa. No problem with the Government there, it's been squared. They need the foreign exchange."

"Fürrer briefed me." Haydon turned to him. "Look, Charlie, the product from TUMBREL has exceeded all our expectations. My masters are pleased. The nuclear and Irish vectors are both nicely poised. You've achieved everything I tasked you with."

"That's worrying Haydon, I'm not used to plaudits from you." Charlie laughed and punched Haydon's arm. "Should I worry?"

"I want you to cool things. Take a holiday, head off somewhere." Haydon lowered his voice. "I meet regularly with Nasir; he comes to Rome. Fürrer, who is Swiss, is out of the firing line, and he gets on well with the Libyans. They like the man. God knows why. There's no need for you to go to Tripoli right now–"

"Are you pushing me out–?"

"You dumb ass, the paranoid act doesn't suit you." Haydon turned to him and looked into his eyes. "There are ominous rumbles out of DC since last month's terror attack at Fiumicino. We've received solid evidence the Libyans shipped the arms in the diplomatic bag, handed them over to Abu Nidal who carried out the attack. The Agency guys are going to want to hit back. It's all going to go bang in due course."

Straw Man

"And the Libyans continue trying to build bridges with the Government here?"

"You know that Peter had a lucky escape? He was checking in for the London flight when it kicked off, he'd got to the front of the queue when the shooting started. Dived under the check-in counter and hid under a metal desk. 16 killed, mainly at El Al, nearly 100 wounded. El Al Security guys shot 3 of the attackers, the fourth is in Italian custody."

"Christ. Is Peter OK?"

"A couple of grenade fragments in his arm. Nothing serious. He's a tough sod, got himself patched up at the airport. He was shocked by how much bloodshed could be spilled in such a small area in a few minutes." He made a cutting gesture with his hand across his throat. "It's a wakeup call, Charlie. We're not playing skittles; these guys don't think twice about spilling blood."

"You think Nasir knew?"

"God knows. But Khalfari's moderate faction is being outflanked by Abdullah Ghereby and the hardliners." Haydon opened his tennis bag and took out a cigar. He rolled it around under his nose.

"Talks come to a screeching halt?"

"It's why it's wise for you stay off the stage. The 6th Fleet is itching to head into the Gulf of Sirte and no one knows what will follow."

"Suits me. Ines will be pleased. She's just back from Ghana."

"You may not believe it, but I'm keen you don't end up back in Abu Salim."

"Me too."

"What's worrying you?" Haydon put his cigar back and turned to face Charlie.

Straw Man

"Can't put my finger on it. Strange dreams. A sense of foreboding."

"Doesn't sound like you. Drink better quality wine?" Haydon stood up and picked up his sports bag. It was odd, Charlie was feeling the same way as him. Maybe he'd failed to spot some subliminal warning.

"I haven't been sleeping well. You may not get my top performance today."

"Better we let him win, good politics. Come on, let's go or HE will be grumpy."

The two men jogged off down the track alongside the aqueduct. They heard the popping sound of tennis balls being hit back and forth across the net.

Nasir strode through the Villa Borghese. A perfect, crystalline February day. Cold and bracing, dark blue cloudless skies, a few contrails way up. Flakes of high cirrus. He shivered and pulled his coat tightly to him. Pausing by the Temple of Aesculapius, he looked over the little lake and caught sight of the tall figure of Haydon Talbot marching along on the other side. The Englishman was wearing a camel-hair overcoat which stressed his military bearing. Nasir increased his pace and followed him across the park and down the hill towards the Piazza di Sienna.

He didn't like Haydon. Not because he'd sprung the trap with the bank documents. No, he admired the way the Englishman had played the blackmail card. It was something else. There was a reptilian quality to him; he was perhaps what they referred to as a 'proper' Englishman. Meaning more dishonest than usual, he thought. His eyes, they bulged a little too much, and there was that crooked half-smile which sang cantos of duplicity.

Straw Man

He'd like to walk up to him right now and stick a stiletto through his ribs. Then smile down at him as he lay there. He rocked his head at the thought. That would have to remain a dream, at least while those documents were dangling and fresh. Maybe Ghereby would do the job for him. Mess up his prize op. No, the best course of action was to extract the maximum from a dangerous situation. Squeeze Haydon whilst Haydon was squeezing him. And wait. *"If you wait by the river long enough, you'll see the body of your enemy floating by."* Sun Tzu knew a thing or two about revenge.

"You're at speed today!" Nasir clapped Haydon on the back and laughed. The taller man started, spun around to face him, then smiled back. "I had to hurry to catch you up."

"Off my guard, need to stay alert. Getting too old."

They sat side by side on a stone bench overlooking the piazza. Several horses were cantering around, jumping impossibly high fences. He saw a tall girl struggling to control her horse, then jump off and shout at it.

"It's my second nature. I don't trust anyone or anywhere or anything. Ever. My eyes see sideways and forwards and backwards. How are you doing?"

"Concerned about the repercussions of your December attacks at Fiumicino and Vienna. I've seen the evidence that the weapons came from your people. Delivered in your diplomatic bag."

"Ghereby's work. I wasn't informed. It's against everything I've been working for. I can't move against him, you see. Not yet. Not even with the material you've provided. He's too well-entrenched, too cosy with the Leader. I have to bide my time. And survive in the meantime. With your help."

Straw Man

"I'll feed you whatever we get on him." Haydon pulled his scarf more tightly around his neck. "But the present risk is the Americans will move against you. There's lots of chatter. Their Sixth Fleet is never far away."

Nasir looked past him to where a man was sitting on a bench, a briefcase alongside him. Good, the photographer was in place. He took a thick envelope from an airline bag and handed it to Haydon. "Ten thousand. Another ten when you supply the file on the London based opposition groups. We're particularly interested in the royalists, the people around Mohammed and Idris al-Senussi. Cousins, claimants to the throne."

"You'll have it next week." Haydon stuffed the envelope into his overcoat pocket. "Our friends in Langley are backing them. They're recruiting mercenaries in Chad, Tuaregs from the Tibesti mountains."

"The prospect of netting them excites my bosses. A lot." Nasir laughed. "They think you're cheap!"

"I am cheap. Well, it's what my friends say."

"I met with Seán Docherty in Larnaca. You're going to owe me."

"Don't tell me!" Haydon chuckled. "You've snatched the bugger, he's all bagged up?"

"Better." Nasir turned to Haydon and grinned. "They came close to losing the last shipment during the rendezvous off Gozo. We've agreed future handovers will be on land, in godowns around the port of Valletta."

"Why is that good news?"

"And you went to Cambridge?" He stared at Talbot, his face deadpan. "We're going to warehouse each shipment, you see, then give the details to Seán. The same day I'll give the details to you. Go figure!"

"So how do they collect?"

"We won't know. We drop the stuff off and watch the place until it's collected. You'll have time to do whatever it is you've got to do."

"The next shipment?"

"March or April. We'll move it to Valletta next month or March. 14 tons."

"Semtex?"

"100 kilos. And two SAM-7s. But please, don't kill the golden goose. It's all set up, so long as you don't get greedy."

"Agreed. You have my word we won't touch the arms before they're in the North. If they get rumbled once they've circulated in the Province, they'll look for internal leaks. Subsequent shipments?"

"They're preparing the bigger ship before the next shipment. No details yet. Something to take 150 tons. There'll be a half a ton of Semtex on the first of these."

"Half a ton? Christ!" Haydon looked shocked. He lit a cigarette and inhaled. "You could blow half of London with that!"

"Well, thanks to me, you'll have warning. So don't drop me in it. We both have a lot to lose."

Haydon sat alone at the moulded plastic table in The Cage, a mug of coffee steaming in front of him. He leant forward and sensed the slight swaying of the room, hanging from the ceiling by its heavy, electronically impermeable, rubber cables. He was elated, LOMBARD had come up trumps. Controlling an enemy operation as if it were your own was a spy's wet dream. How far they'd come from the dark days after the disaster of the failed burglary and Charlie's detention.

Straw Man

Was it a year already since the disaster of the break-in? His career had been crashing, his colleagues eying him with contempt or pity, depending on how much they disliked him. Taking risks which carried a penalty far worse than losing his job. And now? He smiled. His calculated gamble had paid off. They could keep this op going for years if they played it cautiously. He needed to massage his masters' egos and continue to produce golden product. And keep the op in its tightly controlled operational box. His operation, his contacts, his success.

An odd-shaped aluminium telephone rested in a cradle in a metal box on the table in front of him. It emitted a loud humming sound. He reached forward and picked it up, then reached into the box and flicked a tall switch marked 'Scramble'. A red light came on.

"Morning Mark." He heard the buzzing reverberation of his own voice as the cryptographic mechanism began its gyrations. "Read my cable?"

"Got the Paddies on the ropes, have we?" The distorted voice amplified Glasson's 'plum-in-the-mouth' speech. No thanks or congratulations. No, he would have lined up the laurels, planned for his triumph and glory, worked on the honours to come. Haydon wouldn't get a mention. "PM's been appraised."

"We need to play this slow burn." Haydon reached for his cigarettes and tapped one out of the box. "We've a perfect control system in place, eyes on their shipments, no risk of nasty surprises. Belfast and London safe from Libyan Semtex for years. And who knows what intel will follow, for as long as LOMBARD and TUMBREL remain in play and healthy."

"No 10 needs a success, something to shout about. This is it."

"No value in throwing away our advantage for short term political gain."

Straw Man

"You work for the politicians, not the other way round, remember? Not your call to make." Glasson's voice came out like an NCO's bark. "Listen to me. Time to close these terrorists down good and proper. Use a long-delay timer, make it all go bang. They'll see the symmetry – an Eye for an Eye. Old Testament stuff. The press will champion it as an IRA 'own goal', impress the voting public."

"Won't impress the Colonel."

"It will. Impress him that his Irish friends can't be trusted with Semtex. Impress him we're observing him carefully and we'll–"

"–Mark, it is not the right play, surely you see that. We'd be back at square one, scrabbling around for leads." He paused and pulled on his cigarette, inhaling deeply. "In a year or two they'd be back again – new crew, cleanskins, new methods of transport."

"In a year or two maybe I'll be mowing my suburban lawn and you might be working as a gopher for some crappy security company in Salalah."

"We can't risk burning our agents, it's against all–" He heard his distorted voice bounce back at him off the ether.

"–enough lecturing." Glasson's voice was hard. "You need to work out what's in your own interest."

"Can't afford to risk our top agents in country." Haydon held the receiver under his chin and lit another cigarette. Shit, this was going in the wrong direction. He had to head it off. "I must insist on this one, Mark. As operational controller, I'm making the call. We protect our sources above all else."

There was a pause on the line. Haydon could hear the rotating pulse of the machinery.

"Are you still there? You hear me, Mark?"

Straw Man

"I heard you. Your call then. Your operational call. Your memorial?" Glasson's voice echoed back and forth down the line. "Work on the ops plan with Stoner and her team. Keep me posted. Got to go."

The line went dead. Haydon flicked the switch and replaced the handset in the box. He sucked on his cigarette. Jesus. He'd taken a stand. He'd had to. Was that clever? It had better go right now. He sensed he'd just busted his bonds with Glasson. He stubbed his cigarette out violently in the ashtray.

CHAPTER 50

Before her departure for Malta, Haydon told Babs the local Security Service, a small but elite unit reporting directly to the Presidency, were keeping a watch on known Libyan agents operating on the island. Her team would need to stay carefully under the radar. Once again they were right off the books. No diplomatic cover, no protection. Strictly black.

LOMBARD had provided Haydon with the location of the warehouse the same day they moved the arms in. Babs tasked the local SIS Station Chief with renting three apartments in small blocks in Senglea, a small peninsula jutting out from the south into Valletta harbour. Two of the flats had balconies with direct views over the target.

The Det team assembled in dribs and drabs over a two-day period. The ten strong team crowded into the little flats, gear strewn everywhere, the intense atmosphere of a hard operation palpable, the stench of wet clothes hinting at long hours of motionless watching in the torrential winter rain that had greeted them.

"Nasir has operatives keeping the warehouse under surveillance." They were talking over a secure Satphone. "Their orders are to keep watch until after the pickup."

"Thanks a bunch, Haydon." Babs laughed. "You sure know how to make a girl happy."

"You wouldn't like it if I made it too easy."

"Seems a long time ago you dumped me in the shit at Nasir's flat."

"You got over it."

"Fuck you too."

Straw Man

Babs ordered her guys to stay well back, and, after four days of painstaking observation, the watcher teams identified two regular visitors, always operating as a pair, and set about building a record of their routines. No watchers at night, just a couple of cursory inspections every day. For sure they'd be reporting to their bosses they'd kept a 24-hour watch on the site, she thought. Lazy. *Last time you thought they weren't paying attention they outwitted you with embarrassing results.* This op felt pressured. No time to lie up and take it all in. A rushed job was a risky job.

The day before the planned break in, Babs and Cooper observed the watchers at work installing a CCTV camera on a pole opposite the warehouse.

"Odd timing." Cooper was sitting just inside the window, looking through the long binoculars. "Could they have clocked us scoping it?"

"Better assume so. Double sweeps of the area, look out for strange eyes." Babs stood just behind him, holding a small pair of field glasses. "Probably coincidence. They'll want to watch the Paddies taking the stuff out, see how they operate. Makes sense."

"Disable the camera temporarily?"

"Anti-tamper device could blow everything. Better leave it." She put down her field glasses and sat down, running her hands through her hair. "If it's just the one camera, we can manage it; we shadow our entry and exit behind the van."

Just after one thirty in the morning on the fifth night, in driving rain, a beaten-up white Transit van crawled up the access ramp running behind the wharf. Pulling up in front of the warehouse door and obscuring the camera's line of view, the side door opened, and six black-clad figures rushed out. Within sixty seconds they disappeared into the warehouse and the van crept off. At the corner it paused again, and another black shape exited the side of the van. Sheltering behind a wall, the watchman checked his walkie-talkie.

"Red One in position street is clear."

"Mainstay read you five by five standby."

Babs stopped just inside the warehouse door, waiting whilst the team set up portable floodlights, then she slowly circled around the piles of crates, photographing them from every angle, using a Polaroid camera. Skelton and his guys lugged canvas bags, opening them to produce heavy tools and equipment.

For forty minutes Skelton and his team moved cautiously around the crates, searching with powerful torches for any wires or signs of anti-tamper traps and using a broad-spectrum scanner to seek out electronic devices. Finally, Skelton turned to Babs and gave her a thumbs-up sign. The team started prising open the heavy wooden and metal boxes and doctoring the weapons according to a pre-agreed plan, before carefully resealing them with the same painstaking precision.

"Babs, over here." Skelton beckoned to Babs. He pointed. "Thought you'd like to see this stuff before I work on it."

He unscrewed the lid of a heavy khaki wooden box with rope handles, carefully placing the long brass screws into a small plastic tray. Pulling open the lid of the box she could see the tightly packed stacks of plastic wrapped bricks, each labelled *'Explosive Plastic SEMTEX-H'*.

"5 kilos in each packet. Doesn't look like much, eh?"

Babs stared at the orange-coloured packets.

"You're right, looks like nothing." She poked at a packet gingerly with her forefinger. "What could you do with this lot?"

Straw Man

"Blow up the Natwest Tower several times over."

"Our job is to make sure that never happens."

The walkie talked squawked.

"Red One Alert vehicle approaching dark van over Standby"

The team froze. Cooper and another man crept quietly towards the entrance, pulling out automatic pistols from inside their overalls. In the silence they could hear the rumble of engine noise as it approached, then the noise ceased as the vehicle came to a halt.

Just then there was a staccato metallic clatter. All heads turned towards the noise. Skelton held up his hands, then covered his face with his palms.

"Jesus." He whispered. All of them remained stock still, waiting, listening. After a minute, they heard the engine gunning, then slowly fading away.

"Red One confirm Port Security van departed access road heading east seemed to be looking at the camera"

"Chrissakes, what was that Skelton?"

The tall man was scrabbling around on the floor, his head-torch illuminating the wide grating over a deep drain hole. "Shit, shit, shit!" He was holding up a single brass screw.

"As I stood up, I knocked the tray with the screws over. Straight down the drain. We've no replacements. I've only found one."

"Use a magnet?"

"Brass is non-magnetic, won't work."

"What do we do?"

"Use a few from the other box, spread 'em between the two boxes and hope no one looks too carefully. If I put steel replacements, it'll look more obvious. I'll plug the holes.'

"Christ, that would be disastrous."

By four o'clock they signalled they'd completed the work. Babs retraced her footsteps around the crates, carefully checking the positions of each box against the Polaroids. Before four thirty the van crept up to the door, and the team withdrew.

"Job done." Babs reported to Haydon over the secure scrambler phone. "Nothing unusual."

"Well done, Babs. Outstanding." Haydon said. "You activate the trackers remotely?"

"From the sky, even."

"Get any sleep?"

"No. Staying alert. We're monitoring their watchers for signs of activity. Six of my boys will remain to film the pickup and confirm the *Tadiran*'s departure. We've eyes on her, moored stern to in the marina. Three on board as far as we've seen."

"RAF's standing by. Ready to pick her up and track her once you give the word."

"They've got the easy job."

"With luck, they'll use Clogga again, that'll give us a head start."

"Then it'd be back to bloody Armagh for me. Again. That'll be a let-down. More pig shit."

"See you in the office? Celebration drink? Get in today?"

"I've orders to deploy back to Belfast. We'll be tooling up to meet the shipment."

"Pity. I'm going to miss you, Babs." Odd, he thought, orders he'd heard nothing about. He was the Ops commander. *Strange.*

Straw Man

"You'll manage." She paused. "Gotta go, Haydon."

CHAPTER 51

The Skipper stood motionless at the helm, chewing the stub of a cigar between his teeth. His hair was long and wild, he had a buccaneering look to him. Seán stood next to him, an arm rested on his shoulder. The *Tadiran* was heading straight into a strong north-westerly wind, paralleling the Portuguese coastline, heaving up and down over large Atlantic rollers, wide columns of water smashing into the wheelhouse. As soon as they'd passed through the Straits of Gibraltar, turning north for the last stretch of the journey, Neptune had turned the volume up.

Seán felt a wave of relief flooding over him. His last trip. It had been easy and calm, but there'd be no more sea voyages for him. His own little fishing dinghy, that was his future as a seaman, his postage stamp bay, so clear in his mind's eye. No more wild Atlantic storms.

"Ye' look like you've seen a demon Seán?" The Skipper nudged him in the ribs.

"I've been having this dream, feels like a portent."

"Portent of what?"

"That's the point, I don't know."

"Sure you're a steaming pessimist sod." Nolan pointed to the right with his arm. "Look over there, see that grey blob on the horizon. Cape Finisterre. The ancient Romans named it the End of the World. Now that would be a grand place for a depressive bastard like you. Sit in a rocking chair all by yourself, looking out to sea and thinking your miserable thoughts."

Straw Man

"Too cold." The sun had come out but Seán was wrapped against the bitter March wind, a thick coat over working dungarees, a woollen beanie hat drawn low over his ears.

"I'd send you some of my prime Moroccan hash, you'd soon forget the cold."

"I want sun beating down on my rocking chair."

"I'll be sad to part with this old girl." The Skipper hauled the wheel over to starboard as they bobbed over a tall swell, foam breaking as the bow flopped down and they raced down the face of the next wave. "Sunday night we'll make the drop at Clogga, a couple of days and I'll be leaving her in Arklow for sale. She's done us proud these three runs. A poorer vessel would be at the bottom of the ocean."

"I'd rather have my feet on something solid." Seán stamped his foot. "I'm going to ask Fitzgerald to let me off this sea duty. Some young guy can have a go. You and I can drink pints together on dry land. We'll stay pissed and unsteady together without any rollicking waves."

"The new ship we've coming is a biggy. Carry 150 tons. Two trips and the job's done." He turned the helm slightly. The vessel juddered. "Then back to my day job."

"Feeding the Republic with quality dope?"

"Sure, an important public service. Making it a happier place." He laughed. "The whole world should stay stoned and better off we'd all be. Keep me away from clouting the missus."

"I love you, Nolan. Been a pleasure, so it has. Storms excepted." He squeezed Nolan's shoulder. "I'll visit you in your dirty Moroccan gaol, bring you some lice repellent. And a prayer book. Proper Catholic one, leather bound. Might save your soul. If you have one."

Straw Man

"Too late for that. More likely we'll finish sharing the same flea-ridden cell."

He'd miss this, he supposed. Comradeship that sometimes rang true. There was never a whiff of self-righteousness about this man. He knew he was a sinner through and through. Not like those tight-arsed Provo bigots, no better than bloody Prods. Killers who lived for the thrill of killing. Maybe he'd miss the excitement. It was the old story: ninety-nine percent boredom, one percent fear. On his dream island, he'd find a softer form of excitement. He'd learn to scuba dive, that would be something. Catch squid. And a woman? A woman with jet black hair. And dark, fiery eyes. Like his Mam. And a dark, fiery temper to match. His Mam.

"Ye'll make nothing of yerself boy. Yer a waster, but ye've bottle, you do. Better grab yer chances, if ye have any. They won't come often."

He'd take his chances now, so he would. He crabbed his way forward, holding onto the rail, enjoying the bite of wind and spray on his face, the violence as the vessel bucked and rolled.

That recurring dream, it felt so real, like a vision. Of what? Light rushing outwards, a kaleidoscope on acid, bursting out every colour – black, blue, violet all the way to the brightest white, beautiful. The world flashing past, lightning quick. Then he'd awake. He'd struggle to step back into the dream, to grab it back and follow the story, but it was always gone.

He shivered and turned away, edging forward, spray pouring over him, grabbing hold of a rope as the *Tadiran* lurched up and over a large swell. The Skipper was right, he'd seen some malign demon. His stomach was a tense ball. Could there be anything to these dreams? He clattered down the companionway ladder into the small hold. He needed to plan

Straw Man

the offloading, make sure they got the stuff off in double quick time, and in the right order. Off to the beach, onto the trucks and gone, quick.

Metal and wooden crates were lashed tight to struts by taut canvas straps. It didn't look like much, his final gift to the Movement. He leaned down to examine two long metal cases. Stencilled on the side was '*KBM Kolomna 9K32M Strela-2M*'. Shoulder launched anti-aircraft missiles. SAM-7s. Game changers? These would even up the odds, reduce the advantage. Maybe this farewell contribution would change the course of history.

Loading the stuff had been clockwork. Nothing like the craziness of the Gozo storm, a leisure cruise in comparison. On a Sunday afternoon they'd puttered around the harbour to the wharf at Senglea. The lads had worked their magic with thickly stuffed envelopes, any officious eyes working the weekend remained firmly averted. A little crane was waiting on the dock and in less than an hour they'd stowed the cargo in the hold and cast off, steering north past St Elmo's lighthouse towards the distant shape of Sicily.

In two weeks he'd be in Geneva. No more waiting. A farewell supper with Nasir. He'd miss his Arab friend. One of the few he'd miss from this rotten life. He'd grow a beard, a wild one. Dye his hair? Or shave it? Live a hermit life. That would suit him. No more sing songs, red faces, smoke and sweat, no more Felon's Club. He imagined getting on a bus in Chiasso after banking the money. He'd be wearing a hat. *I am Robert James Albert Norton.* That's me now. A trilby, he thought. Head down, hands in pockets, a race for grey anonymity.

The vessel lurched, and he had to grab on to the cargo netting at the side of the hold. His eyes spotted two small wooden crates. '*Omnipol. Explosive Plastic SEMTEX-H*'. He felt a twinge of guilt. How much misery would those two crates cause? The Brighton bomb had been 9 kilos of gelignite.

Straw Man

Here was 100 kilos of Semtex. He'd seen the photos of the devastation, the awful injuries. There'd been raucous celebrations in the club that night, they'd all been drunk and dancing wildly. Like the Battle of Waterloo, one of the boys had said, the grand victory to herald the end the British Empire in Ireland. With these long delay timers and this amount of Semtex, they could bomb their way to kingdom come.

He leaned down and examined one of the khaki-coloured boxes. Odd. A piece of wood had splintered off the side, exposing the wood like a bite. It looked fresh. Almost as if someone had tried to jemmy it? His eyes moved to the screw holes. Brass, but half of them seemed to be missing. He looked over at the other case. The same. He took a screwdriver from his overalls and scratched at the empty screw holes. Someone had plugged them with chippings. He sat down on an ammo crate. He'd like a cigarette, but maybe this wasn't the time. Could someone have interfered with the cargo? Who and when? The SAS boys? The Libyans playing games? Or his own imagination? Had to have been in Malta.

He started unscrewing one of the boxes, heart thumping. Pulling up the wooden top, for a moment he seemed to lose his vision. His focus returned and there it was, a tiny blinking red light, thin black wires emerging from below the plastic packages, disappearing down the sides. Carefully prising up the top one, he glimpsed the timer and cables running below to where he knew a detonator must be pressed right into the explosive. A long delay timer. *Christ Almighty.* Set to when?

They would have programmed it to blow whilst they were still at sea. They were maybe four days out from Clogga. Maybe they had 24 hours, 48 at the outside. Should he alert the Skipper? Demand they abandon ship? He'd never agree. Try to carry the boxes up and heave them overboard?

Straw Man

And what would that brutal QMG do when they met on the beach, his crown jewels missing? Hand him to the Nutting Squad to find out where the explosives had gone.

If there was an anti-tamper device? Motion sensitive? Mercury operated? He'd have to take the bugger apart carefully to find out. His mind went back to the dusty classroom in Bin Ghashir, training in bomb making. So long ago. *'Secure approaches to anti-handling devices'* the lesson had been called. The trainer, a retired sapper from the Egyptian Special Forces. He looked down at the box and traced the wires with his eyes.

Leaning back against the bulkhead, he closed his eyes. He thought of his island. He was helming his dinghy, coming home for lunch, a little wake bubbling out behind him, the outboard purring. He saw his figure standing and waving, holding up a grand rock cod for her to see. She was on the veranda of the cottage, waving back. She was laughing, the scarlet crêpe scarf he'd bought her streaming behind her in the wind. He watched himself throw the anchor out and turn off the engine.

He opened his eyes. He didn't dare to touch the timer, or the wires, not yet. He had to think this out. Slowly. Maybe he could set up a bypass. His hands were trembling. He breathed in deeply. *Calm now, Seán, this is your moment. Total clarity.* He prised up the top package, feeling the weight, turning it ever so slightly on its side and examining the underside. It was then he heard the click. He felt it reverberate through his entire body, the slightest but unmistakable click. Which sounded like a thunderclap. Tripwire. So simple. So deadly. The mercury would have started its short and fatal journey. He dropped the packet and turned his eyes upwards.

"Sure I missed my chances, Mam, but I love you–"

Straw Man

CHAPTER 52

Haydon received orders to remain in Rome, just as air surveillance of the *Tadiran* entered its second, critical, week. Something big was going down, and he wasn't part of it. He was on the outside.

"It's kicking off down your way. Surveillance radars are spinning like greased tops, Sixth Fleet is making smoke." Glasson's voice sounded unusually unctuous. "Colonel's MIGs are buzzing like flies over the Gulf of Sirte, US Navy F14's painting them red. Whole thing will go hot any moment. We need you right where you are."

"I need to be at Ops by the time the *Tadiran* discharges in 48 hours."

"We want you right there in case the Libyan situation bubbles over." Glasson replied. "Stoner's team is on standby at Aldergrove. Routine. We'll patch you in as necessary."

"As the Ops commander I'm required to be there."

"This morning's Exec meeting decided you're to stay and run TUMBREL. Your instructions are to order DAEDALUS to Tripoli. He's to stand by there, ready to deliver an urgent message to LOMBARD."

Haydon picked up a tennis ball off his desk and started squeezing it hard in his right hand. The biggest success of his career, his crowning moment, and Glasson was freezing him out. He could imagine the congratulations pouring in, Glasson showing suitable modesty at his brilliant achievement. *"Your face. Your ass. Nothing to do with me."* Shit!

"I ordered DAEDALUS to stand down whilst the situation in Tripoli is rumbling. It's too risky. I'm getting reports–"

"Exactly which bit of your orders is not clear?" Haydon heard the tough rasp in Glasson's voice. "I'm too busy to argue, Haydon. Get it done

Straw Man

and report to me when you have. The message may need to be delivered imminently; we want him right there in play."

Charlie had a headache. He was sitting in Andrea's study in the Palazzo. He could hear the squeals of children playing in the gardens. The French windows were open. It was a beautiful spring afternoon. A slight breeze floated little tufts of pollen from the garden into the room. He brushed spots of the yellow dust off the sleeve of his cream linen jacket. He couldn't get rid of the suspicion that Nasir had turned against him. He'd heard about meetings from Haydon and Fürrer, Nasir was pushing things ahead at speed. But he felt cut out. Just a feeling. But why? Everything had been going so well until this Abu Nidal outrage at Fiumicino.

"–the Americans are threatening to send the Sixth Fleet into the Gulf of Sirte." Andrea was saying. "They're panting at the chance to have a go at Qaddafi's vaunted 'Line of Death'."

"Since the terror attacks, it's been on the cards." Charlie was lounging on the sofa, reading a magazine. "No one believes the Libyans are innocent."

"The Minister has blamed Iran and Syria in public. But evidence of Qaddafi's involvement is overwhelming. According to Carlo Pollitti, who is tearing his hair out."

"Increased sanctions coming, for sure." Charlie waved his magazine around.

"Nasir had no prior knowledge." Andrea's fingers were tap-tapping on the desk. "Fiumicino bothered him. Everything he'd been – no, what we've all been working for, being tossed away."

"The end of my dreams of boundless wealth swilled from the Libyan trough." Charlie laughed.

"Kiko, your personal enrichment is unimportant in the arc of current events." Andrea stood up and started pacing the room, sucking on the tip of a pencil and scratching his unkempt hair with it. "The Minister has asked me to carry a private message to the Colonel. Last thing he wants is a shooting war that brings his efforts to a screeching halt."

"Qaddafi is spoiling for a fight. But he'll get his face bashed in."

"I'm leaving this evening, Kiko, taking the jet. Come with me?" He turned to Charlie. "Back tomorrow. Khalfari will meet us and take us to the Leader. He's in Tripoli. Pippo Lansa's coming."

"Love to." Charlie stood up and stretched. "I need to see Nasir."

"Ask Ines if she wants to join?" Andrea rubbed his forehead and looked over at his friend. "With all that's going on, it could be the right moment for that interview?"

"I'll get hold of her." Charlie smiled back. Was Andrea out to press his buttons? Press away. He didn't feel the slightest twinge of jealousy. Progress. Not that he thought it was a great idea for Ines to join them. The trip would have its dangers. But with all that had gone before, he had to leave her to make up her own mind, free from his own fears. He smiled as he realised his headache had gone.

"Be at Ciampino by six, if you're not there we'll leave without you. We'll get into Tripoli by nine, bound to be a middle of the night meeting with the Leader, it always is. He never sleeps, at least not at night."

"OK, I'll ring if Ines can join."

Charlie pulled aside the billowing net curtains and trotted down the steps to the garden.

Straw Man

He found Ines at her newspaper's bureau just off the via del Corso. The open-plan offices were buzzing. Phones seemed to be ringing on every desk. Ranks of electric typewriters clack-clacking away, the rhythmic *'ting'* of their bells punctuating the chaos. Ines was in her poky cubicle, frowning and shouting down the phone, her left hand raised as if she were conducting the assonant orchestra. She motioned him towards a low stool encroaching into her neighbour's space, waved him a kiss, smiled, and resumed her frown.

"Ma va fan culo, fesso!" She slammed the receiver down *"Jesu* what clowns! What are you doing here Kiko?"

"Invitation from Andrea. To sunny Tripoli, this evening." He leant down and kissed her on the lips. "Come?"

"In the jet?"

"Yes. Trouble brewing with the Yankees. He's carrying a message for The Colonel. A message of moderation."

"When do I have to decide? I have to file this Sicilian story."

"Be at Ciampino before six latest. Back tomorrow evening." He stroked her cheek and smiled. "We've got dinner with Fiorella and Gianni, we'll be back in good time. I'll pick up some overnight stuff for you at the flat."

"OK, I'll be there, or I won't!" She winked, reaching up to pull his face to hers. "Keep me a seat."

Straw Man

CHAPTER 53

Haydon got back to his office late. He'd met up with his counterpart at the German Embassy for lunch and they'd drunk too much red wine. He felt heavy. He tried to wade through paperwork but kept dozing off. He'd done nothing about his orders. He was too angry, he needed to calm down and think rationally before steeling himself to speak to Charlie and order him down to the lion's den. He heard something and looked up. Peter Etherington was standing by his desk, holding out an envelope. He realised his assistant had been talking to him.

"Repeat Peter, I was lost in thought."

"Urgent incoming." He handed him the envelope. "From Ops, hot from the cypher clerk. Eyes only."

"Leave me."

"Another thing." He handed Haydon a file of typewritten papers. "It's odd."

"What's odd?"

"TUMBREL. Real time transcripts out of GCHQ, copied to London, COMINT recordings from the Vispoli file. DAEDALUS is travelling to Tripoli this evening. Did we know?"

"We did not know. Show me the context."

Peter picked up the pages and leafed through them. "Here." He pointed.

Haydon read the exchange aloud, then leaned back in his chair. *"I need to see Nasir."* Could that bugger Glasson have given orders directly to Charlie, bypassing Rome Station? Impossible, it would breach all protocols. But why on earth was Charlie hurrying off to Tripoli without telling him?

Straw Man

He felt a burst of rage. *That greasy shit Glasson, I bet he bloody did.* He felt the veins in his forehead throbbing.

"OK, Peter, that'll be all. I'll call you if there's follow up."

He took a paper knife and slit open the envelope.

CRASH URGENT EYES ONLY ZZZZZ CRFT1 436VB G44HH 1404851423 LARGE EXPLOSION REPORTED 84 MILES NNW CAPE FINISTERRE 4640035N 1245118W RAF REPORTS NO FURTHER SIGHTING VESSEL TADIRAN PRESUMED SUNK NO SURVIVORS OBSERVED 99SC1 4HJ88 P8UY7 NNNZZ

He held his head in his hands, massaging his temples with his fingers, staring blankly at the terse message. His stomach felt like someone had kicked it with a steel capped boot. *Glasson. Political imperatives.* Nasir was bound to interpret this as a direct attack. And he'd be right. He'd given him his word, to protect him, to protect his source above everything. The only article of faith for any Agent-runner worth his salt. He would read it as a betrayal. All bets off, the end of the pipeline of information about the IRA.

And Charlie? Would Nasir conclude the nuclear sales were a ploy? If Nasir suspected that, Charlie would never make it back from Tripoli. He laid the cable down on his desk and started reading through the transcripts. He scanned them quickly, then looked at his watch. He picked up the telephone and dialled.

Charlie's red Vespa swooped in and out of the heavy traffic along the river, veering across the road to confront the oncoming lanes head on, swerving in at the last moment. He was in a hurry. What a buzz! Horns

Straw Man

bleating all over the place. Olympic traffic-slalom. His left wing-mirror smashed as it met up with a distant cousin head on. Leaning right over, he turned up the hill into Via Garibaldi and as he squeezed the throttle open, he felt the rear wheel squeal and skid on the damp cobblestones. His driving was a bellwether of his mood. He felt invincible.

Adventure! He realised how bored he'd been. Maybe he'd meet the Colonel tonight. That would be a step up the ladder; it would impress Haydon. Pulling the scooter onto its stand, he raced up the five floors to his flat. He picked up the phone and ordered a cab. Taking down a small holdall from the cupboard, he started to pack. He pulled open Ines' drawers, took out a few items and threw them in. Knickers and bra. A blouse. A scarf – she'd need to cover her head in Tripoli. He collected a few bits from the bathroom and added them to his own. He closed the case, walked towards the door. The phone started ringing. He turned back and picked it up.

"Charlie?" He recognised the ponderous tone.

"On my way out the door, flying down to see our friends. Last-minute decision."

"I know." A gong clanged in his head. *'I know.'* What on earth did that mean? "We've got a major flap, I have to see you."

"Not possible, leaving now. Big hurry to get to Ciampino. Back tomorrow evening. Call you then."

"Charlie, have you been having conversations behind my back?"

"I don't even know what that means. Got to run, this will have to wait–"

"Shut the fuck up and listen." Haydon's voice was raised, Charlie had never heard him swear like that. Maybe he was drunk? "I need you–"

Straw Man

"Fuck you too, Haydon. Cab's waiting, gotta go. See you Friday, tennis." He dropped the receiver in its cradle, picked up the case and raced out of the door.

Straw Man

CHAPTER 54

Nasir was enjoying his siesta when the phone rang. It was Khalfari's secretary, summoning him to his office. Immediately. He dressed fast and in no time was driving through the empty streets of downtown Tripoli towards Security headquarters. He felt encloaked in dread; his chest was tight. Ever since the Fiumicino attack, he'd been on edge. What had happened that demanded the urgency?

His boss had seemed suspiciously friendly on the phone, it didn't feel right. His cordial tone reminded Nasir of those scenes in Mafia movies when the guy is about to be garrotted in a car and the obese boss embraces him warmly and pats him on the back before opening the car door for him.

As he entered Khalfari's spacious office, he saw Abdullah Ghereby lounging in the shadows on a leather sofa. He didn't look up. An electric shock ran down his spine.

"Crisis." Khalfari's voice was not so friendly now. He was bent over his desk, staring at something through a magnifying glass. He beckoned to Nasir. "Look at this."

He pointed to a grid of square photographs, the light from a standard lamp reflecting off the glossy black and white sheets.

"Delivered this afternoon by our GRU friends. Soviet satellite images, fresh. Bay of Biscay. That's the north-east corner of Spain there." He pointed with his finger. Nasir bent over and examined them one by one.

"What am I looking for?"

"The Russkies have been doing us a favour, keeping an eye from above on the *Tadiran*, sending us reports whenever their satellite passes overhead. Here, look, she's steaming northwards yesterday morning, then the next pass, this–" He tapped one of the photos. A huge black cloud seemed to obscure the sea over a large part of the photo. "–Bang. Then nothing. Look there, empty sea."

"The ship exploded?"

"What does it look like?"

The veins in Nasir's eardrums were throbbing. He felt sweat bursting out under his armpits. Crooked bastard, Haydon! *You have my word we won't touch them before they're in the North.* He'd allowed himself to be played for a clown. He felt his face flushing. He breathed in deeply and looked directly at Khalfari.

"It sank?"

"Maybe some tiny pieces sank. Not much left to sink. 100 kilos of Semtex and all the rest." Khalfari glared at Nasir. "What's the first thing that comes to your brilliant young brain, Nasir?"

"Sabotage?"

"That was our reaction. Great minds, you see. But who and how?"

"The IRA is riddled with informers, I've warned–"

"Your operational report here," Khalfari tossed some papers on to the desk, "says the IRA collected the arms just under four days after you gave them the address. You state you had a watch on the warehouse throughout. How could someone mount a sabotage op in that short time and not be noticed?"

"Maybe they were experimenting with the Semtex onboard, preparing a bomb?"

"Maybe they fucking played football with it? At sea?" Khalfari grunted. "I've ordered up the CCTV tapes from Malta, we'll see what they reveal. Ideas?"

Straw Man

Nasir felt a dark cloud sinking over him. Sweat was flowing freely; he could feel the wet patches soaking through his shirt. *Was it visible?* They knew something. If he was harshly interrogated, how long would he hold out?

"I reviewed them, nothing–"

"–you see Nasir, Mr Ghereby has been expounding his suspicions to me. He doesn't trust your backchannel talks with MI6, the improbable recruitment of Mister Haydon Talbot."

"Improbable?" Nasir blurted. He looked up at Khalfari, who stared back, expressionless.

"–and Mr Ghereby doesn't trust your Englishman Charlie, or your friend Andrea Vispoli, or Carlo Pollitti. Above all, he doesn't trust you. You see, he's been doing some checking of his own."

"Checking?" Nasir looked over at Ghereby, who scowled back at him. The scowl of a cobra, he thought. A cobra who takes pleasure in his victim's terror, as if he could smell his prey was rendered immobile by fear.

"He thinks they've played you. Or worse–" Khalfari scowled. "He is proposing different, more active measures."

"This is crazy–" Nasir's head was spinning. Could there be a mole in MI6, maybe the Russians had a penetration agent there? Another Philby? How else could Ghereby be so sure? He needed to stay icy calm, but he felt his legs trembling, his bladder felt unnaturally full. "We're on the brink of a major intelligence coup–"

"A shipment of our arms blown up at sea. A traitor in our ranks." Khalfari laughed, then banged his hand hard on the desk and shouted. "A major intelligence coup?"

Straw Man

"I hear that Vispoli and the Englishman are flying in this evening." Ghereby stretched out his hands and stared at Nasir. "They expect to meet the Leader. We'll see–"

"–I cleared this visit with you–" Nasir gestured with his arms to Khalfari.

"–leaving one remaining issue." Ghereby talked over him. "How to resolve matters with Mister Talbot, how forceful our response needs to be."

"I don't follow–"

"I don't care if you follow, or you don't." Khalfari reached down and pressed a bell on his desk. "You work for me; you take my orders. Another failure on your watch."

Nasir looked at Khalfari. He felt rooted to the spot. How had it fallen apart so quickly? How had he been so easily outmanoeuvred?

"Go back over every element of this operation right from the start. Write me a detailed report. By yesterday." He waved him away with his hand. "Get out of my sight."

Khalfari walked over to the sofa and sat down across from Ghereby. As Nasir closed the office door, the two men were leaning in towards each other, murmuring.

For a moment Nasir had thought Khalfari was about to order his arrest. He'd been breathing too fast, and he'd felt the blood throbbing fast in his temples. He shuffled along the dark corridor, his mind racing, his body heavy. Turning the corner, he started down the stairs, then paused on a landing and held onto the handrail. He took out a handkerchief and wiped his forehead. Had the perspiration been visible to Khalfari? Giveaway. He took out a cigarette, but his hands were shaking so badly he had difficulty lighting it. His knees were trembling. *Get a grip.* He sucked in the smoke, felt the burning in his lungs.

He needed to think clearly.

He'd go to the airport to meet Andrea, stay close to him throughout his visit, go with him to the Leader. That would be the sensible move. Get a lift with him back to Rome, that would be his way out. He'd tell Khalfari he was going to confront Talbot, offer him a crazy sum to reveal where the leak had come from. Get him to sanction the payment; he'd see it as worth the cost to smoke out the mole? And once in Rome–

He turned into the lobby, walked past the security desk and out towards the main gate. He was out of that wasp's nest of a building. He felt his body relax. He stopped and stubbed out his cigarette. Looking up at the sky, he saw a crescent moon was rising, Venus was shining brightly just above. He reached into his pocket for his car keys.

He never saw the two guards stepping out from the shadows behind him.

Straw Man

CHAPTER 55

Rain was pelting down. The sky seemed ominous, almost apocalyptic. The taxi sped up the one-way street, raced around the corner and came to a screeching halt right behind a large removals van which was blocking the road. The taxi driver honked his horn and shouted out of the window. Two beefy workers emerged from the back of the van and waved.

"Look mate, we'll be five minutes, finishing the load."

Charlie looked at his watch. 17.00. He had an hour. It was going to be tight. Should he abandon the cab and run on past the truck to find another? He thought about the phone call. What was Haydon on? He'd known about the trip, but how? Unless he'd been bugging Andrea's office. Was that possible? The taxi driver hooted his horn again, a long series of blasts. The workers gesticulated and shouted insults.

That odd question –*'Have you been having conversations behind my back?'* Christ, it was like the last time with the bank account. But this time he hadn't been indiscreet, he'd learned his lesson. He'd told no one about his work for Haydon. Only Ines. Ines. Could she have been careless? He scratched his head.

After an age, the workers raised the tailgate, and the truck pulled slowly away. He checked his watch again. The evening traffic was heavy, but it freed up as soon as they got to the ring road and stayed clear as they turned onto the via Appia and drove fast out past the racecourse. Ten to six. He was going to make it. Just.

He thought about Nasir. Everything changed after the January terrorist attack at Fiumicino. That had brought home the brute darkness of the game he was playing. Maybe it was time to distance himself. Haydon had hinted he wasn't really needed any more. Tonight he'd be extra friendly with Nasir. Mustn't let on anything was changing. He'd make a point of showing how hungry he was for new contracts.

They turned in to Ciampino and took the slip road towards the private aviation terminal. Charlie counted out notes and handed them forward to the driver, adding a lavish tip. The cab pulled up sharply in front of the terminal and Charlie grabbed his overnight bag and clambered out. As he dashed for the entrance, a tall figure emerged from the shadows and blocked his way. He looked up, ready to rush on past.

"Haydon, what the fuck?"

"You're not going anywhere. Not safe. Listen to me, Charlie, you're in imminent danger. Come with me–"

"–but Ines, she'll already–"

"–she's on a train to Florence, my guy watched her board."

"Andrea?"

"I left a message at the VIP lounge. In your name, saying you'd got stuck."

"You'd better have a good explanation."

"I have. Get in the car."

Haydon and Charlie sat side by side on a wooden bench in the little park opposite Haydon's flat. The rain had stopped and clouds of intense evening scent, orange blossom, wafted over the two men as they stared out across the Tiber. The Giardino degli Aranci. Dominated by the overflowing orange trees that thrived in the shade of the creeper-covered walls of the ancient church of Santa Sabina.

Straw Man

He'd resisted answering Charlie's questions on their way back from Ciampino. He was relishing the no doubt temporary warmth of being the good guy. He wasn't used to putting other people's interests, other people's safety, in front of his own. A novel experience. The sun was sinking behind St Peters, seeming to frame the dome in a vast fireball.

"Looks like it's going up in flames." Haydon shaded his eyes with his hand from the setting sun. "*Zeitgeist?*"

"Adds to the *fin de siècle* feeling I've had all week. The same dreams. Not sleeping."

"You're oversensitive, that's your problem." Haydon grinned.

"You've the hide of a sun-dried elephant, that's yours." Charlie reached over and punched his arm. "You don't exactly seem in crisis mode, Haydon. What's the mad flap? You pull me off a private jet, refuse to talk. Now we're sitting on a park bench like a pair of dirty old hobos. What's so sensitive we couldn't talk on your veranda, glasses of cold wine in hand?"

Haydon had never seen him look so petulant. *It's probably just cost me my job to pull him out of the hornet's nest.* He chuckled, then turned and looked into Charlie's eyes. He felt almost paternal, extricating his impetuous protégé from the nasty mess into which he'd lured him in the first place.

"I needed a quiet chat. Away from distractions."

"And I needed to get down to see Nasir. Things are going splendidly; I'm halfway to paradise–"

"–believe me you're not." Haydon's tone was sharp. "You're halfway back to a cell in Abu Salim, hanging by your thumbs, or maybe your balls. Remember Sergeant Moawia?"

"Unlikely to forget him." Charlie winced. "Why?"

Straw Man

"My orders are to dispatch you to Tripoli, where you are to stand by to deliver an urgent and confidential message to Nasir."

"You're not doing a frightfully good job of carrying them out."

"Spot on. I disobeyed direct orders by grabbing you at Ciampino. Look, Charlie, London has blown this op sky high, you'll read about it in the papers. The IRA bit and the nuclear sting, all gone to hell in a cockleshell. Just so preening politicians can achieve short-term political gain. Election coming: democracy in action." He turned to Charlie and tapped his arm. "In a matter of days Nasir will be rumbled, and when that happens, you're blown. It'll be all over."

He scanned Charlie's face. Which seemed to shrink as the words sunk in.

"What do I do?"

"Count your blessings. Count your winnings, move to another table, and don't look back." Haydon laughed, a deep bass noise. "Right now, what you do is report to me that although I ordered you down there, you got delayed and missed the flight, in fact you tell me you've lost your passport."

"OK, I've mislaid my passport. Then?"

"Then you wait, you procrastinate, you fuck around. You're good at that. You tell me any fantastic bullshit story you can invent to avoid going to Libya. And you wait for things to evolve, to see if Nasir survives."

"Andrea thinks the US Cavalry is going to gallop into Libyan waters and save us all from the mad dervishes." Charlie ran his hand through his hair. "The Minister wants to avert a shooting war."

"You can enjoy yourself looking on, waiting for the bugles to blare."

"Haydon, how did you know about my trip? You bugged Andrea's study?" Haydon saw the slight line of a smile behind Charlie's eyes. "Christ, you did, didn't you?"

Straw Man

"Nothing you need to know." He stood up, grinning. "Look, I'm bored with serious, let's move on. My gorgeous wife will be waiting for us. Or rather for me."

They strolled along the path to the main road, then jogged up the stairs to the flat. As they stopped at the front door, Haydon touched Charlie's arm. Peter Pan, he thought. Wounded below the waterline, he still thinks he needs the Libyan success. This will make him nicer, more real. It's true for me too. *At least I hope it is.* The oddest thing about humans, we only do the right thing when we've been well and truly humbled.

"I appreciate it, Haydon. I mean it."

"My soul had been asking uncomfortable questions."

"Get any answers, or it's still comatose?"

"Let's get seriously drunk, we deserve it."

"Good idea. I'll tell you bullshit stories already."

They were tipsy. Three empty wine bottles stood on the bar. Haydon opened another and refilled their glasses, spilling wine on his trousers and brushing it off with his hand. He realised he was experiencing a sense of absolute freedom, divorced from the shackles of ambition that had held him captive for so long. He'd cut the cord of responsibility for TUMBREL, nothing more he could do. Glasson and Babs had blown it; he'd done his best, and that was that. He felt no remorse for Nasir; he hoped the man survived and the pipeline of intelligence continued, but it was out of his hands.

Straw Man

Clinking glasses, Haydon inhaled the perfume of evening jasmine, then took a sip of his drink. They were sitting around a circular metal table on the veranda, the lights of the city splayed out beneath them.

"Where is she?" Ros's voice was soft. He could just make out her face in the shadows. He reached out and took her hand.

"Gone to Florence. Big story." Charlie's face was hidden in shadow.

"I got to know her well these last months." Haydon watched her drawing with her forefinger on the glass table, making little circles in the moisture. "She combines a really combative streak – you need that to survive in the male-dominated journo world – with obvious kindness."

Haydon watched her smile, friendly lines around her eyes. She's so feline, he thought, so full of prescience. *Can she sense my newfound freedom?* He felt the warmth of love welling up inside him.

"Are you kind to her Charlie?" She continued.

"Not always. She can be vicious." He made claws from his fingers and raised them towards Ros. "Since our breakup, we've become gentler with each other. Jailbird time is good for the soul."

"You recommending a stretch in Libyan prisons?" Haydon chuckled.

"I had time to consider my arrogance. And its consequences."

"Awfully grown up." Ros reached out and touched his arm. "Turning your pain into a positive. Maybe you deserve each other at last; your ambitions rubbing away, making you gentler."

"What's she working on?" Haydon leaned back and closed his eyes; his head was spinning. "Which poor sod has she got in her sights?"

"Sicilian story. Motorways, bridges. Sub-standard Mafia cement. Spectacular bribes all round. Greasy politicos." Charlie laughed, ran his fingers through his hair and rapped on the table. "I'm three-quarters cooked. More even. Time to go home."

The phone started ringing inside the flat.

"Phone calls this late mean trouble." Haydon yawned and stretched his back, "Not answering. Off duty. Pissed. They can ring someone else."

It stopped ringing.

After a few moments, it rang again. Haydon waited for a while, then slowly pulled himself up and wobbled his way unsteadily inside. He crossed the living room, picked up the phone and held it to his ear. He turned sharply and looked back, a look of resignation coming over his face.

"You're sure? Keep me updated. I'll ring Pollitti to check what's coming in on his wires. Get back to you shortly."

This is not where the story ends, he thought. Maybe it ends here for Charlie, better it does; he's not cut out for it. *I've just saved his life.* But not for me. He shuffled back onto the veranda, his legs feeling heavy as if there were iron shackles on his ankles, then he stood motionless behind Ros's chair He felt drained. He put his arms around her shoulders.

"Andrea's plane has crashed." He spoke in staccato bursts. "ATC lost contact. About an hour ago. On approach into Tripoli. We're monitoring Libyan radio transmissions. Lots of chatter."

"Christ! Andrea and Pippo–" Charlie stood up.

"They've sent up search and rescue choppers, nothing yet."

"Who was with them?" Ros turned her face up to stare at him.

"Ines and I were supposed to be on board." Her hand went up to her mouth. "Haydon asked me to stay, do some stuff for him here. Ines made a last-minute decision to go to Florence."

They fell silent. Haydon looked up. A jet was passing high overhead, strobe lights flashing. He shivered, a small tube in the heavens. He felt a chill run through him.

"I'd better go round to see Sandra Lansa. Ines' best friend." Charlie hugged Ros. "She may not have heard."

"Ask Ines to ring me." Ros reached out and touched his cheek.

"I need to burn the wires." Haydon noticed Charlie's face was white. Get on top of all that's happened.

He walked with him out to the front door.

"Come back tomorrow morning, I'll have details by then."

"Crazy day Haydon." They embraced. "You saved my life."

Then he was gone.

CHAPTER 56

She was at full gallop, about to jump a wide stream. Her hat had fallen over her eyes and her feet had come out of the stirrups. She grabbed hold of the horse's mane and gripped tightly with her legs. But she knew she was slipping, and the horse was going ever faster. She noticed pointed rocks sticking out of the water ahead. She was falling.

Babs woke with a start. She was bathed in sweat. The phone was ringing by her bed. She was in her sparse single room at the barracks at Aldergrove. Switching on the bedside lamp, she glanced at her watch. 02.05. She pushed her hair back from her eyes and picked up the handset.

"Stoner."

"Did you do it?"

"Haydon, do you know what time this is?"

"Did you do it?"

"How did you get this number? You sound drunk."

"You owe me the truth."

"I owe you nothing. You're being unprofessional."

"You've blown the op. People are going to get hurt. I need to understand why."

"You need to understand chain of command."

"Did Glasson order you to plant the detonator?"

"I'm ending this call."

"So he did?"

She replaced the handset and sat up, running her hands through her hair. Odd, she thought, I thought his strength was his lack of emotion, his *Englishness*. Maybe she'd misjudged him. Perhaps he had a soul after all?

Straw Man

Andrea and Pippo. His oldest friends. Charlie felt the sharp burn of tears forming. He sat down at the kitchen table and poured himself a large Scotch, adding a little water. He took a gulp, refilled the glass. It tasted bitter; he felt the burning descending his throat, followed by a surge of anger. Why? *Those whom the Gods love die young.* The three of them had treated Libya like a game. Fools. Memories flashed through his head. Childhood, sailing, school, always laughter. Andrea's large hooter and deep laugh. He smiled. Loudest when they were doing something bad or dangerous. Preferably both.

That sense of foreboding which had kept throbbing in his tummy these last weeks. They should have been on board, but for Haydon's intervention and Ines' deadline. So random. Or not? Crazy thought. Could it have been Libyan payback? Nasir's revenge? He took another gulp, covering his face with his hands to shut it all out, but as he closed his eyes, the images rushed in. Flying, skiing, spinnaker up and surfing close to the rocks. Two families smashed. He lit a cigarette and leaned back.

The red flashing light on the answering machine caught his eye. He walked over and pressed the playback button. The little tape rotated.

"*Ciao Amore, sono io.* I won't make it. Going to Florence to meet someone about my story. Taking a late train. Back tomorrow afternoon. Haven't forgotten our dinner. Have a fun trip. See you tomorrow. Love you love you Kiko Mmmm."

He sank back into the chair, blood welling to his brain. He felt faint. This was going to change him. Another smack on the head. He closed his eyes and breathed in. Turning on the radio, he listened to commentators speculating that the jet, a Cessna Citation, had been downed by a missile. They were drawing parallels with the Itavia DC9 that had exploded into

Straw Man

the sea north of Sicily several years before. Eyewitnesses then had claimed to have seen a missile streaking upwards just before the fireball appeared high in the sky.

He felt dirty. He took an ice-cold shower to clear his head. He made a pot of strong coffee and drank it hot. Sandra might have heard the news via the radio. He hoped not. He mustn't put it off any longer, however hard it was going to be.

It was nearly midnight when he raced down the stairs and got the Vespa out of the garage.

Sandra answered the door wearing her dressing gown. Her face was mottled, her hair awry. She looked ragged and had been crying. They hugged. She clung on to him; he felt her body shaking.

"Ahmed Khalfari called from Tripoli. Told me the plane had crashed." Sandra emitted a choking sob. "I've been listening to the radio."

"Me too. And praying for a miracle. Praying the reports were a mistake."

"I called the boys. They're driving back from Porto Ercole. I didn't tell them, just asked them to come." She leaned on his shoulder, and they hobbled towards the kitchen. "I'll make coffee."

They stood in silence for a while. Sandra was quivering, leaning against the cooker. Charlie pulled her back and walked her to a stool.

"You sit, Sandra."

He made coffee and carried it to the table. They sat with the cups in their hands, steam rising between them.

Straw Man

"I'm so, so sorry, Sandra. I don't have words. I loved them both. Ines and I were supposed to be with them. Last minute neither of us could make it. Ines went to Florence."

A shiver of guilt ran through his body. And if he'd been the intended target?

"They're saying the plane may have been shot down, but by who? The Libyans? The Americans?" Sandra was leaning forward, cupping her steaming mug in her hands, her eyes red and face contorted in a mask of anguish and pain. "What have you heard?"

"Same radio reports as you. Tension high in the Gulf of Sirte, rumours the Americans might launch a raid. Everyone on high alert." Charlie reached out and touched her hand. "Could have been misidentification, a simple mistake."

But it wasn't. A voice in his head shouted at him, Pippo was collateral damage. And he was indirectly responsible for his death. Those bloody grey men in their bloody grey suits had pulled the trigger. Glasson, Haydon's boss; he'd never met the man. The politicians above him. None of them would miss any sleep.

"You think Andrea had the right clearances?"

"Don't know, perhaps he did. You know him. He thought he was immortal." Charlie felt a stabbing pain in his chest. "Politics is a dirty business, Sandra. Andrea was carrying a message from the Minister to Qaddafi. A message of moderation. Moderation doesn't suit a lot of people. In a lot of places. Not just in Libya, but here and the US and UK."

"You think it might have been deliberate?"

"God knows. Maybe it will come out. More likely not. We were all enmeshed. Big business and politics: identical twins. We liked to play at the top table without paying attention to the rules."

Straw Man

He stared up at the ceiling. Would it be better if she knew the truth? Would it make any difference? Did he even know what the truth was? No. He was just a pawn on a chessboard. Moved around by unknown hands. Grey hands. *Fuck them all.*

"Yesterday when Andrea suggested it, we saw it as just another adventure. Another of the many we've revelled in since childhood."

"I know, Kiko, I know. Pippo loved them." She turned away, her head down, her body shaking with sobs. "Leave me now Kiko."

Charlie stood up. "I'll call you as soon as I get news. Sandra, anything you need, anything, please. Call."

"You were a good friend to him." Her shoulders shook. "You go now. Please. I want to lie down. Be on my own. I'll be all right until the boys get here."

"Ines will come as soon as she's back."

CHAPTER 57

The TV was on in Haydon's study. They sat on the sofa watching the morning news. A US spokesman announced that late last night, US warplanes had launched air strikes against Libya. 100 planes had carried out the attacks, which were *'in retaliation for the Libyan sponsorship of terrorism against American troops and citizens'*. US fighters had destroyed 20 Libyan aircraft and several SAM sites. Libyan air defences had shot down an American F-111 bomber.

"Were you expecting this?" Charlie leaned forward and lifted his coffee cup to his lips. "Why you stopped me going?"

"No, unrelated." That's the truth, Haydon thought, though God knows which of the permutations was the right one. "For which thank your lucky stars."

"RAI is reporting Qaddafi may have been killed. Was that the intention?"

"Possible. The raid targeted his home. There'll be one hell of a purge in Tripoli. It all just got deadly personal." Haydon tapped his finger on the table. "We're upping security at Embassies. The F111s flew from RAF Lakenheath, so Qaddafi will see us as complicit. We're taking precautions. I'll have to move out of this flat."

"This has swiped the story of Andrea's plane off the news. Any explanation?"

"Most likely a Libyan or an American missile." Haydon got up and walked to the window, his hands clasped behind his back. "Both sides will have had their fingers on buttons with tensions running so high. It's easy enough to mistake radar blips. We heard whispers the Italians warned the Libyans that the F111s were on their way."

Straw Man

"The Americans informed the Italians?"

"They'd have to. They used bases on Italian soil for the operation."

"And Operation TUMBREL?"

"Dead in the water, even without the raid." Haydon turned to face Charlie. "We wait for LOMBARD to surface. If he ever does."

"Could Nasir have been behind this?" Charlie leaned forward and touched Haydon's arm. "Payback, perhaps? Maybe I was the target and Andrea collateral? He knew I was coming."

"Andrea's the more likely target. If Nasir believed his old friend had double-crossed him, that he leaked the bank documents we'd pillaged from his office. I doubt we'll ever know."

Haydon looked out of the window onto the veranda. There'd been violent winds in the night. A mimosa tree in a large tub had been blown over, scattering piles of earth and making dirty black stains on the tiles. That's my world, he thought, a dirty world decorated with dirty black stains.

The malign wind would blow Glasson further up the tree; Haydon pictured him wallowing in the glory of his victory over the IRA. He realised he didn't care a damn what this did for his own career. Up, or down or sideways. *Who gives a shit?* The press would have a field day, payback for the Brighton bombing, they'd trumpet. Paddies blowing themselves up made for popular column inches. And the nuclear sting would fade away, a hidden casualty of convenient good news. No one would ever know.

"So the show just goes on?" Charlie's voice cut into his thoughts.

"In our grey world, the show never stops." He turned and smiled. "You survived, Charlie. That's the first rule. Survived to play at another table. Just be grateful."

Looking over towards St Peters he saw the sky had darkened. It had started to rain.

Straw Man

THE END

Straw Man

ACKNOWLEDGEMENTS

My sincere thanks to those wonderful writer friends, long-suffering enough to read and comment on early, and later, drafts, and who offered continuing motivation to a beginner writer. Particularly to Robert Graham, for his erudite and sage advice, and to Maryanne Fitzgerald, who provided practical suggestions, support, and inspiration.

Thanks to my mentor and editor at the Blue Pencil Agency, Oliver James, who held my hand through the process of multiple drafts and revisions, and for his frequent, although unwelcome, exhortations that 'the wastepaper basket is your friend'.

Thanks to Chris Jackson and Dan Whomes and the team at Northside House for their backing, and their faith in the finished product.

Finally, eternal gratitude is due to my long-suffering wife Bella, for sustaining me with good humour on a journey of solitude, strong coffee, raucous curses and key bashing.

Straw Man

Straw Man

Straw Man

Straw Man

ps
Straw Man

Straw Man

Straw Man

Straw Man

Straw Man

Printed in Great Britain
by Amazon